I0590068

THOSE WE SEE IN THE DARK

LEGEND OF TAKANIIM BOOK 1

ROBIN RAKKEBY

Anthornis Press

San Diego, California

Cover illustration and design: Kei-Ella Loewe
Map: Virginia Allyn
Chapter thirty-seven illustration: Seeking Stars Studio
Book Design and Typesetting: Enchanted Ink Publishing

The text type was set in EB Garamond

ISBN: 979-8-9987516-2-2 (E-book)
ISBN: 979-8-9987516-0-8 (Paperback)
ISBN: 979-8-9987516-1-5 (Hardcover)

Library of Congress Control Number: 2025911542

First edition 2025. Printed in the United States of America.

WWW.ROBINRAKKEBY.COM

For battle-hardened girls with weary hearts.

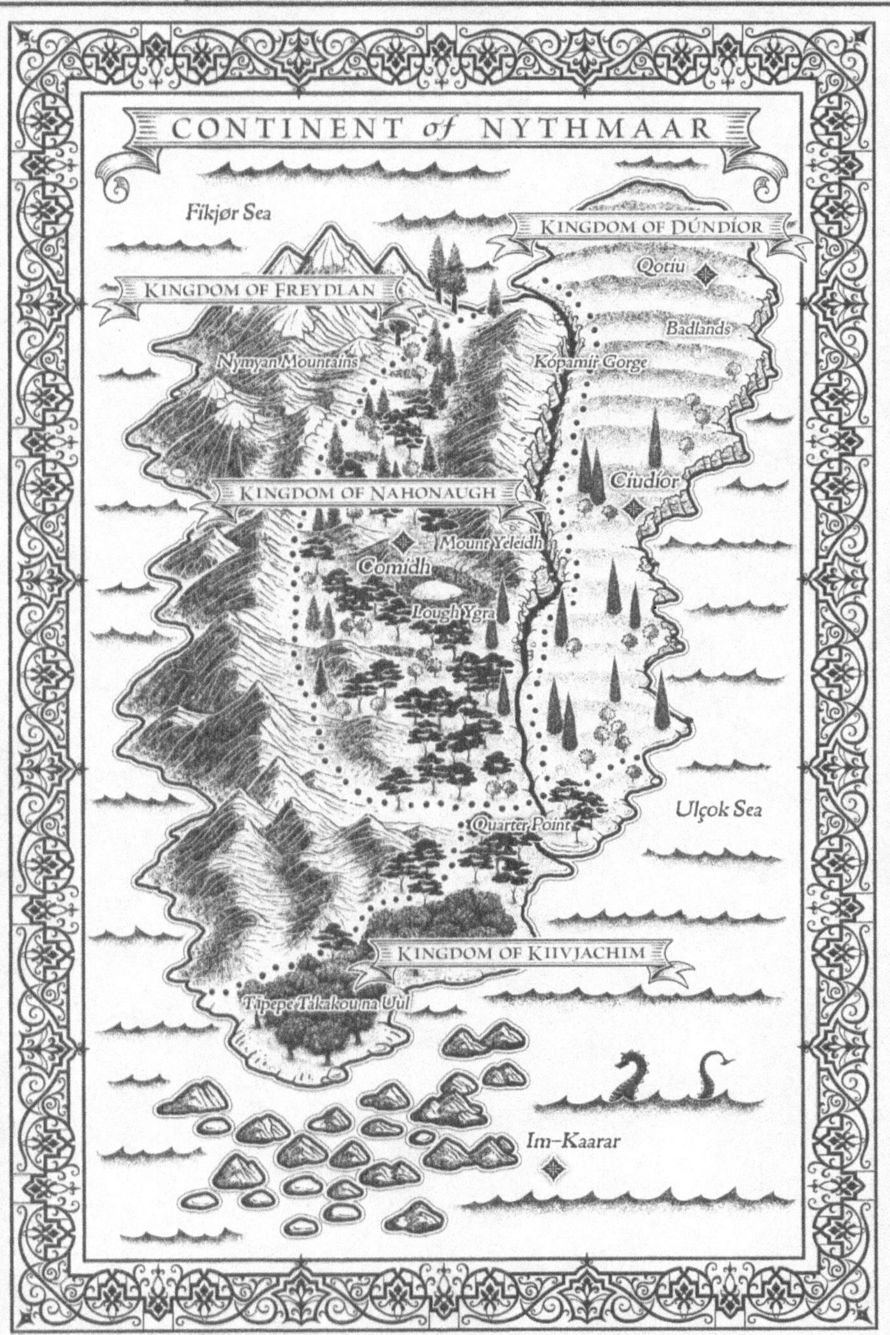

CONTINENT of NYTHMAAR
Fikjør Sea
KINGDOM OF DÚNDÍOR
KINGDOM OF FREYDLAN
Qotíu
Badlands
Nymyan Mountains
Kópamir Gorge
Ciudíor
KINGDOM OF NAHONAUGH
Mount Yeleídh
Comidh
Lough Ygra
Ulçok Sea
Quarter Point
KINGDOM OF KIIVJACHIM
Tīpepe Takakou na Uul
Im–Kaarar

Primary Character Names

Anaís (ann-eye-ees) **Dí Sona** (dee so-na)

Eoghan (o-wen) **Kavanaugh** (ka-vah-na)

Cian (kee-in) **Ó Máille** (oh mahl-yeh)

Simone (si-mohn) **Dí Sona** (dee so-na)

Timun (tee-moon) **Dí Sona** (dee so-na)

Tadeo (ta-day-oh) **Constantin** (con-stan-tahn)

Balendin (bal-in-deen)

Gio (gee-oh) **Toccileu** (toc-chi-loo)

Tadhg (taig) **Ó Máille** (oh mahl-yeh)

Secondary Character Names

Magdalina (mag-da-leen-ah) **Constantin** (con-stan-tahn)

Lochlan (lock-lin) **Kavanaugh** (ka-vah-na)

Katka (cat-ka)

Riona (ree-oh-na)

Trijveson (treej-ves-son)

Ibhar (eeb-har) **Kavanaugh** (ka-vah-na)

Siofra (she-fra) **Kavanaugh** (ka-vah-na)

Toma (toh-ma) **Glaadris** (glad-ris)

Mina (mee-na) **Uí Mháille** (ee vahl-ee-yeh)

Olia (oh-lee-uh)

Daza (da-za)

Tertiary Character Names

Mathúin (ma-hoon)

Tynan (tye-nan)

Fionn (fyun)

Ó Ceannéidigh (oh ken-ni-dee)

Sigraith (sig-rayth)

Ellis (el-lis)

Ruaridh (rur-ree)

Aksel (ack-sel)

Grethe (gre-ta)

Alys (al-lis)

Carys (care-iss)

Macaulay (muh-ka-lee)

Sullivan (sul-uh-vin)

Darach (dar-rah)

Murray (murr-ee)

Bronagh (bro-nah)

Síle (she-la)

Maíréad (muh-raid)

Etrit (eh-trit)

Qamar (kah-mahr)

Liuz (lee-oos)

Paio (pie-yo)

Bazán (bah-san)

Place Names

Nythmaar (nith-mar)

Dúndíor (dune-dee-or)

Ciudíor (see-you-dee-or)

Qotiu (ko-tew)

Ulçok (ul-sock) **Sea**

Kópamir (koh-pa-meer) **Gorge**

Nahonaugh (na-ho-na)

Comidh (com-eve)

Mount Yeleidh (ya-lay)

Maulaidh (mol-ay)

Lough (low) **Ygra** (ee-gra)

Freydlan (frayd-len)
Fikjør (feek-yor) **Sea**
Nymyan (nim-yen) **Mountains**
Kiivjachim (keev-yah-heem)
Tāpepe (taa-pey-pey) **Takakou** (ta-ka-koh) **na Uul** (na oohl)
Im-Kaarar (eem ka-rawr)

Languages Spoken

Dúndían (dune-dee-an)
Nahraeg (na-rye-g)
Freydlensku (frayd-lens-ku)
Kiivjani (keev-yawn-ee)

Miscellaneous Words

Anadali (an-na-dah-lee)
Amadé (am-mah-day)
Ithansfar (ee-thuns-far)
Takaniim (ta-ka-neem)
Fheile (fay-le) **Earrach** (are-rah)
Nanouk'tou (na-nouk-toh)
Kulimaçar (ku-lee-ma-sahr)
Nitróg (neet-rog)
Ælorberry (ay-lore-ber-ry)
Sœndjak (seund-yak)
Hannock (han-nock)
Lé (lay) **da'reagh** (da-ree)
Taebru (tay-brew)
Pachimh (pa-heev)
Nāmi (nah-mee) **Attatikarou** (at-tah-tee-ka-row)

THOSE
WE SEE
IN THE
DARK

CHAPTER ONE
BLADESONG

THE AIR WAS THICK WITH THE SOUR TASTE OF SWEAT and inevitability. Despite the oppressive humidity from the bodies packed into the training arena, Anaís stood tall. Unmoving. Beneath her uniform, a bead of perspiration trailed down her spine and disappeared at her lower back, the fabric wicking it away to join the growing patch that marred her otherwise spotless tunic.

Afternoon sun streamed through the windows and reflected off the polished wood floors, forcing her to squint uncomfortably while she watched the warriors dueling to become Anadali. Normally, the song of metal on metal as swords kissed and broke apart was music to her ears, but the pressure building at the base of her skull turned each strike into a deafening thunderclap. It wasn't long before the rest would follow.

Anaís glanced at the door, then back to the warriors. Thirty had been selected. Few—if any—would advance to join her ranks.

Recruitment only occurred once every three years; it was imperative she remain focused.

Five more minutes. She could hold on for five more minutes.

Pushing off the wall, Anaís walked slowly down the rows of duelists, the steady thump of her boots keeping her grounded in the present despite the mounting pain. Even she had to admit they fought well. Each move was perfectly calculated—a dance of wit and speed as parries redirected strikes and moves transformed into countermoves. Yet there was a ruthlessness simmering beneath their form that made her skin prickle. *This is not the way of the Anadali.*

She turned down another row, stopping when the sharp thwap of steel meeting leather sounded next to her, followed by a muffled thud. She looked toward the noise as the fallen warrior rose to his feet. He was in his mid-twenties, his hair cropped so short he looked nearly bald. Sweat dripped off his brow, which he hastily wiped away before readjusting his grip on his sword. His footsteps were nearly silent as he began to circle his opponent once more, each of them waiting for the other to strike first.

"Scared?" his opponent chided.

The bald one smirked. "Have I reason to be?"

His eyes darted to Anaís as if searching for approval, but his expression wavered when he took in her own—likely a frown, given the concentration it was taking to not sway on her feet. She raised her brow at him, a silent "I'm waiting," before turning on her heel and continuing down the line.

She had made it halfway along the next row when the toll of the midafternoon bell rang out, each strike driving a nail of pain into her skull. Any longer, and she may as well sign her own death warrant.

"That's enough." Her voice cut through the room, an eerie silence following the last ring of the bell. "We will continue tomorrow. Gio will see you to your accommodations."

Murmured voices filled the air, growing ever louder at the anticipation of a break before evening drills. Gio, her unofficial second-in-command, caught her gaze from across the hall and widened his eyes as if asking, "Really? Me?"

Anaís nodded subtly as she strode toward him, the motion sending pinpricks of light bursting across her vision. She squeezed her eyes shut, willing them to leave. She should have been used to them by now, but the sensation disoriented her every time.

"Yes, you," she said quietly when he was close enough to hear, but her tone left no room for negotiation. "Unless you would rather report to King Timun yourself?"

He stiffened, Adam's apple bobbing when he swallowed. "No, Amadé. It's no problem at all."

"Good." She brushed past him and pushed through the double doors that led into the courtyard at the far end of the palace grounds.

Anaís took a steadying breath once the carved mahogany doors shut behind her, dulling the newly revived conversations of the men in the training hall while they gathered their belongings. The air was cooler out here. Drier, too. Spring, it seemed, was aching to make its arrival, but the last breath of winter had yet to leave. She straightened her uniform before striding up the meandering path that connected the training grounds with the main palace. Buds of brightly colored flowers were beginning to uncurl in a plea to welcome warmer weather, while dark-green leaves filled in the desert willow trees that had been stripped barren by the harsh winter.

Everything was being brought back to life except for her. These episodes were becoming longer, more frequent, less predictable. Splitting headaches used to be all that ailed her. Now they were the prelude to a malady that consumed her whole. A shiver ran down her spine that had nothing to do with the lingering chill in the air. Death should not yet seek her at the age of twenty-four.

Anaís took the steps that led to the entrance of the palace two at a time, the additional effort making her heart thump erratically in her chest, but there wasn't time. There was never enough time.

Two guards pushed the doors open for her, saluting as she approached. Anaís dipped her head in acknowledgement and hurried through the foyer. Sheer curtains fluttered in the breeze from the open windows overlooking the gardens below. Anaís walked past one, two, three windows before turning left down the maze of hallways leading to the king's study. The rich wooden floors contrasted with the cream-colored stucco that covered the walls and continued up to the sloping arched ceilings. Vibrant paintings framed in gold hung proudly on the walls, depicting scenes of successful hunts and glorious battles of a time past, but never forgotten.

As a child, her favorite paintings had been the ones depicting her father and grandfather fighting with honor in the Battle of Ithansfar. Now they sent a feeling of unease crawling down her spine whenever she walked past them, as if darkness itself peered at her from behind the shadows painted into the scene. Peace—or rather, the semblance of it—had been King Timun's greatest accomplishment, and he would be damned before he let anyone forget the legacy he had built, the one he worked ruthlessly to uphold.

As Anaís rounded the corner down the final hallway, she instinctively changed her gait, heavy footfalls transforming into soundless steps until she stood in front of the study door. She took a fortifying breath, trying to ease the pain building in her skull. *In through the nose, hold, out through the mouth.* Air rushed past her lips.

Before wariness could deter her, Anaís rapped sharply on the door, the sound sending a new wave of pain through her mind. One minute ticked by, then another. Finally, the silence was broken.

"Enter."

The roaring hearth greeted her with a sweltering embrace, while the draft in her wake agitated the flames and sent light flickering around the study. Condensation beaded on the window pane, splintering the rays of sunlight filtering into the room. The soft woven rug covering the terracotta floor muffled her steps as she walked across the study and stood at attention.

King Timun continued working in silence. Sighing internally, Anaís let her eyes wander across the room. The bookshelf behind the king was filled to the brim with tactical books, charts, and navigational tools, while the large, ornately carved desk where he sat was covered in parchments and maps. A compass here, ink bottles there. Her gaze settled back on her father. The silver of his hair reflected the warm glow of the firelight, softening the frown lines that had found a permanent home on his brow and in the tight draw of his lips.

"The warriors, how are they shaping up?" King Timun asked without looking up from the papers he was sorting through.

"I see potential in five of them. Two, I believe, are fit to become Anadali."

The king glanced up from his parchment, his eyes trailing over her face. The numbness had not crept in yet, but she could feel it pushing at the edges of her consciousness, trying to force its way in. Could he see? Could he tell? If only she could sit for a moment. Maybe close her eyes.

I am Anadali Amadé, she thought. *I will not die.*

"Two?" he asked lowly. "Out of thirty?"

"Yes."

"Captain Tadeo specifically selected them, or are you telling me the captain of the King's Guard is not fit to fulfill the king's best interests?"

Anger flared in Anaís's chest. Fatigue allowed her thoughts to escape before she could tame them. "Your Majesty, let the King's Guard take what the King's Guard needs, but do not let the captain meddle with sacred tradition. I lead the Anadali. He does not know their purpose like I do."

King Timun reclined in his seat, his gaze searing dangerously into her own. "And what is that purpose according to you?"

Trepidation stilled Anaís's tongue, and she swallowed thickly. Nearly a century ago, the king of Dúndíor had formed the Anadali: an elite tactical force of warriors designed to supplement the Dúndían Royal Military. Derived directly from the word "protect," the Anadali served as the hands and feet of the kingdom, protecting the people from threats within and without. Yet for all their might, the utmost sign of prosperity was never having to dull the blade—resolving domestic and international conflicts through diplomacy rather than violence. To hold the position of Anadali was not simply to be an expert warrior. It was a way of life, a code of conduct.

Ten years ago, King Timun had reformed the Anadali and turned them into a living weapon—one he used gratuitously to protect his reign.

Her heart pounded in her chest. She hated how he had twisted and destroyed that what was once honorable. As the years passed, her anger had simmered—though it was cooler now, flickering into shame at herself for not having the courage to fight back. Grief-ridden as she had been in the aftermath of the breach in the treaty ten years ago, perhaps complying had been her only option. But now?

"We were created to serve the people of Dúndíor," Anaís said cautiously. "It is our duty to protect this kingdom in ways the Royal Military cannot."

"And a load of good you did with that before I refined you and your kind." He slammed his hand on the desk, the ink bottle rattling with the impact. Anaís flinched. "This is a new era with new threats on the horizon. War is on our doorstep. We must be prepared. Or have you forgotten *your* purpose?"

An argument rose in Anaís's mind, but she clamped her jaw tightly. No good would come from angering her father more than she already had, and the growing pain in her head was becoming too much to bear. She needed to leave before it got worse.

"No, Your Majesty," she conceded. The words tasted bitter in her mouth.

"You are an indispensable asset to Dúndíor. I did not appoint you as Amadé—as the *leader*—to fail me. Do you understand?"

"Yes, Your Majesty."

"You will teach all of them, and you *will* usher in this new era."

"Yes, Your Majesty."

A satisfied smile curled up on the king's lips. "You see, that wasn't so hard." He leaned forward and began shuffling through the documents on his desk once more. "I am proud of you, my daughter. Your sister may be the future, but you are the one who will secure it for us. Do not let me down."

Anaís bowed, blinking rapidly as a bout of dizziness washed over her. "I won't."

"Very well." He waved his hand at her. "You are dismissed."

She saw herself out of the study, walking as calmly as her body would allow. As soon as the door shut, she ran. Down one hallway, then another, then another—*why are there so many hallways?* Voices caught her attention when she neared the foyer, and she slowed her pace to a determined walk. Head held high, gaze focused directly in front of her, she proceeded with confidence, but her mind was begging, screaming for her to stop. To rest.

She couldn't. Not yet.

Anaís strode past the guards, barely registering the confused salutes they made at the sight of her hasty exit, and hurried down the palace steps. She kept her eyes fixed on the garden entrance.

Almost there.

The rhythmic crunching of her boots on gravel filled her ears.

Almost there.

She imagined the sound of the waves lulling her to sleep. A few miles, and no one would be able to find her—the only one who would have been able to was dead. A few miles and she would be safe. She could walk that far easily, but she couldn't fall apart here. Not now. Not like this.

Almost there.

Her vision blurred, and she rubbed at her eyes. Why couldn't she hold it together? She removed her hands and caught sight of Gio just as he stepped onto the path in front of her. He strode toward the palace, nose buried in the stack of parchment he was reading. Anaís willed her body to step aside, but it was too late. The collision was already set in motion.

Gio grabbed onto her shoulders as she stumbled backward, sheets of parchment fluttering to the ground around them. "Are you okay?"

Anaís blinked. *Why did he have two faces?* "Of course. I'm off to do my rounds."

Gio tilted his head, regarding her with a frown. "Are you sure, you don't look so—"

"I'm fine, Gio," she interrupted. "We have to train all the warriors as Anadali, that's all."

His eyes grew wide as he took the information in. "All of them? But that's—"

"Yes. Later, Gio. We'll talk later." She patted his shoulder and hurried off down the path, ignoring the weight of his confused stare while she made her escape.

CHAPTER TWO
THREADS OF FATE

THE SALTY SPRAY OFF THE ULÇOK SEA COOLED THE early evening air, carried up the cliffs by a breeze that passed through Anaís as if she were a phantom. A familiar, creeping numbness spread through her body, starting at the base of her skull and trailing outward as it consumed everything in its path. An invisible beast that hooked its talons into her and drank until there was nothing left.

Anaís stumbled down the worn path that led to an outcropping of boulders overlooking the ocean. *Almost. There. Almost. There.* Each thought was punctuated by a footfall that rattled her bones.

If she listened carefully, she could almost hear her refuge calling out to her. She was so close to being able to stop, breathe, become undone. She set her sights on the boulder where she so often lay to rest and hurried her pace, ignoring the wave of dizziness that sent a tingling chill down her spine. The need to stop was primal, clawing at every fiber of her being.

She was so close.

Her legs gave out without warning, up becoming down as she tumbled down the hill. Golden reeds of grass buckled under the impact, doing little to cushion her fall as she rolled toward the outcropping. She tried to reach out, to grab onto something, anything to slow her descent, but her arms had already succumbed to the numbness.

Her shoulder slammed into a boulder, air wheezed from her lungs, and the world became still. All she could feel was a deep ache in her side and her pulse thrumming in her ears while she fought to regain her breath. Her mind barely registered the tendrils of warmth radiating from the earth, weaving under her skin and seeping into her body as if trying to return the energy that had been siphoned from her. Anaís took in a labored breath and relaxed into the ground, watching grains of dirt skitter about with each exhale.

There was something ethereal about this place: the peaceful moments before the sun stretched out over the sky and kissed the earth goodnight, the ephemeral transformation of light into color as nature held fast to the lingering touch of day before night enveloped the land. It was a final parting that promised a comforting return, the calm before a new day arose.

This cliff in particular had become one of refuge. It held a quiet stillness that transcended time itself. She couldn't tell if it was simply a figment of her imagination, but something always pulled her back, welcoming her to safety with open arms. It filled her soul and refreshed her weary bones.

Anaís tried moving her head to get a better view of the ocean and sighed when she found it wouldn't budge. The last of her energy had been used to make it here, and she'd barely made it as it was. If she had been caught?

The phantom sensation of blood coating her hands from when she'd watched the previous Amadé die washed over her. It dripped down her arms. Stained her skin. Her heart stuttered in her chest, and in that space between beats she took his place—blade buried in her chest, glassy eyes staring ahead.

His weakness had not been tolerated. Neither would hers.

"No," she whispered aloud, the force of the word pushing the vision away. "That will not be my fate."

Her eyes fluttered closed, the deep rumble of waves breaking against the cliffs below carrying her away from the ache that pressed into her body. Away from the numbing sensation of nothing and everything colliding. The breeze whispered as her mind carried her away—not into sleep, but memory.

"Kulimaçar?" Balendin's question echoed in the training hall, and Anaís couldn't help responding with an eye roll.

Kulimaçar: freestyle combat. Now that she was thirteen, it had evolved to resemble the true meaning of its name: skull breaker. Though it was far from a fight to the death, anything went—fists, improvised weapons from objects around the room, actual weapons. The sole rule was that the fight must start traditionally, with nothing but bare fists, quick wit, and the instinct to win.

But her arms hurt. Sweat dripped down her face and drenched her shirt. Wayward curls of dark hair had escaped from her braid and clung to her neck.

"I need a minute," Anaís huffed.

"The enemy won't give you a minute," Balendin chided. "And rolling your eyes so much will only make you dizzy."

A smile crept up on Anaís's lips as she regarded her master. Balendin was demanding, pushing her past her limits, never going easy on her, all because he believed in her fiercely. Though he was twenty years her senior, she was already just as tall as him. *Men will see you as an insult to their dominance,* he had once told her. *In battle, they will try to cut you down with no mercy. I will train you so they fail.*

Anaís sheathed her practice saber and placed it at the side of the training arena. "Kulimaçar," she said resolutely.

They circled each other slowly, muscles primed in anticipation. Anaís knew he was waiting for her to strike first—she could feel the tension growing between them as she delayed the inevitable—but she wouldn't give him the satisfaction. He would set the pace, but she would dictate what happened next.

Balendin quirked his brow at her, and she could nearly hear him asking, "Afraid, little Nai?"

Anaís tipped her chin up in response. *Make me.*

A smile spread across his lips, crinkling the corners of his eyes. There was a tinge of accomplishment there, Anaís realized. Pride, even. But before she could linger in the moment, he lunged faster than she had ever seen him move before.

Surprise rooted her to the floor.

Balendin barreled into her.

It wasn't until the wall tilted to the ceiling as she flipped backward that her instincts finally came rushing in. Anaís twisted her body and grabbed Balendin's arm as her shoulder hit the floor, rolling with the momentum to send both of them sprawling across the training room. They pushed themselves up with a synchronicity that could only be found between master and apprentice. Anaís's shoulder ached from the impact, but the slight shift of Balendin's stance pushed all thought of pain out of her mind. When he rushed toward her again, she was ready.

Their movements were ferocity disguised as a well-choreographed dance. Anaís blocked Balendin's attacks with practiced ease, but he struck with a precision that unnerved her. Each struggled to overtake the other. How Balendin only had a light sheen of sweat on his brow while she was practically drenched was beyond her.

"You can't beat me if you stay on defense," Balendin huffed.

Frowning, Anaís ducked beneath another punch. He had a fair point, she was absentmindedly shifting to complacency. Competent complacency, but Balendin had seen right through her before she saw it herself. She *had* made the decision to let him set the pace, and she *had* told herself she would dictate what happened next. Was she really going to let him win because she was tired?

"Who said I was on defense?" Anaís blocked another of his strikes and turned to slip his arm through the open space she created. He stumbled forward as she brought her elbow up. Fire burst up her arm when her elbow made contact with his jaw, sending him reeling backward. Surprise flickered across his features as their eyes met, and she had a feeling her expression matched his own. She hadn't expected her stunt to actually work.

Balendin gave her a slight nod. "Not bad." His gaze drifted to his feet. "Next time, watch where you put your enemy."

He used his foot to flick Anaís's discarded saber to his hand, and a flurry of nerves filled her stomach. Unsheathing it, he stalked toward her. Anaís skittered backward, glancing frantically around the room for a weapon while trying to keep Balendin in her peripheral vision. A short staff hanging on the weapons rack caught her eye, and she dove into a roll as Balendin struck where she had been moments before. Her hand wrapped around the staff. She whipped it up to halt the blade with a resounding crack.

The sound echoed across the room. Her chest heaved. Balendin had the decency to look tired. This time, Anaís struck first.

Her vision became a blur of mahogany and silver, sharp snaps punctuating her ragged breaths as metal met hardened wood in a series of blocks and parries. She didn't have time to think, to plan. She acted on instinct alone, trying to trust herself and the training Balendin had put her through.

A low creak echoed through the room as the doors swung open. Anaís startled, dropping her guard only to pull her head back at the last moment as Balendin brought the saber down, slicing her skin from her brow to the top of her cheekbone, the tip of the blade barely missing her eye. Pain flared across her skin, and she staggered back, clapping her hand to her face while trying to ignore the warm blood seeping between her fingers.

Balendin stood frozen before her, a look of horror breaking through his usually calm demeanor.

"Anaís, the king would—" Queen Pedra cut herself off, looking back and forth between the blood slowly running down Anaís's arm and the conflicted look on Balendin's face. "What is the meaning of this?"

"I left an opening."

"We were training."

They spoke simultaneously, each attempting to prevent her mother from angering.

Queen Pedra furrowed her brow, but didn't press any further. "Clean up and come find your father when you're finished. He would like to speak with you." She cast a curious glance at Anaís before turning to leave the room, her dress trailing elegantly behind her.

Anaís's face fell as she stared after her mother. She longed for comfort. She wished she was strong enough not to need it. Embarrassment and shame washed over her, followed by fiery anger at the prickle of tears welling in her eyes. Why couldn't she have stayed focused and blocked the stupid blade? The room felt too crowded standing at Balendin's side. Anaís turned away from him and stalked to the bench tucked in the back corner of the room, kicking her bag out of the way as she slumped down onto the smooth wooden seat. She sniffled and let her hand fall to her lap. Blood pooled in the creases of the palm of her hand, staining her light-brown skin a deep red.

She didn't realize Balendin had followed her until he knelt before her and spoke softly.

"We fight to protect. You have heart; that is why I must push you. So your physical abilities can rise to the occasion. I am proud of you."

"The king and queen are not," she spat bitterly. "I must become stronger, or I will fail Dúndíor."

"You *are* becoming stronger every day, but there is more to strength than physicality. You already have these attributes in spades, however, your parents cannot understand what they are not willing to accept," Balendin said. He took a clean cloth out of a nearby basket and held it out to her. "Lie back," he instructed. "It's not deep, but the face always bleeds more than it ought."

Anaís nodded, not trusting herself to speak, and scooted herself down so that she lay across the bench, her feet dangling off the end. She closed her eyes and pressed the cloth against the cut.

"Remember what I have taught you," Balendin continued gently. "Intellect will always best brute force. Truth ensnares even the smallest lie. Compassion is more deadly than malice."

She let out a shuddering breath. "And what if those aren't enough?"

Balendin placed a gentle hand on her shoulder. "Look at me, Anaís."

A tear rolled down the side of her face as she met his gaze.

"A warrior's greatest strength is not in their ability to kill and destroy. We are called to uphold all that is good, all that is love. We are protectors. This is the very word we live by. *This* is the honor woven into the lifeblood of Anadali. Fight for Simone, fight for your people. And I will fight for you. Do you understand what I mean by this?"

She nodded again, her dark hair frizzing as it rubbed against the bench with the movement.

"Good." Balendin gave her a small smile. "Now, let's check this cut."

Anaís removed her hand from her face to allow him to lift the cloth.

"Ah, right as rain. Stay there." He discarded the bloodied cloth and retrieved a new one from the basket, pouring disinfecting solution onto it until it became saturated. "This will sting," he warned.

Silence hung between them while he dabbed the blood from her brow and cleaned the wound. Once satisfied, he tossed the cloth to the side and pulled a healing ointment out of his own bag, followed by a bandage.

"There. You might have a scar, but you will match me now," Balendin teased.

"Do you think I look fearsome?" She sniffed, but a tentative smile grew on her lips.

"The most fearsome warrior in all the land." He grinned, giving her his hand to help her up. "Come, you have a meeting to attend."

Those were the greatest gifts he could have given her: the humility to flow through all she could not control, and the strength to stand firm in the face of despair. Yet, while he had a confidence in her that could move mountains, he allowed her to be a child. He never said as much, but Anaís had the distinct impression that when Balendin looked into her eyes it was like peering through a looking glass into his past. It was his duty to train her as Anadali. It was his responsibility, he seemed to have decided, to care for her as a younger sister. Consequences be hanged.

The next day, a solid metal eye mask encrusted in gems of various shapes and sizes was left on her bed. When Anaís picked it up and inspected it more closely, she was surprised that there were no slits for her eyes. For all intents and purposes, it was absolutely useless.

Curious, Anaís turned it in her hands and lifted it to her face, securing it into place. It should have been heavy, but the mask was light as a feather as it settled against her forehead and rested atop the bridge of her nose, the contours of the metal molding perfectly to her features. What was more fascinating was the light filtering through her closed eyelids. She should have been shrouded in darkness, but when she opened her eyes, a brilliantly clear image of her room met her vision. A note fluttered to her feet, and she bent to pick it up. On it was a message scribbled in Balendin's rushed writing.

Wear during knife fights.
Sorry about your face. - B

That had been what felt like a lifetime ago. The sliver of a scar was the only thing she had left of him.

* * *

ANAÍS OPENED HER EYES AND watched as the last rays of the sun dipped below the horizon, light and shadow rippling across the surface of the ocean before sinking beneath the waves.

She believed his words, at the time. But now Balendin was dead, and the version of Anadali he'd fought to instill in her had died with him ten years ago. The king had made sure of that when he ordered her first kill.

Now, the heart of the Anadali was corrupted, their purpose twisted as the king succumbed to his own desire for absolute control. Absolute power. There was no revoking the oath that bound the Anadali to loyalty. As Anadali Amadé—their leader, and as Anaís Dí Sona—the king's daughter, there was no escape. Rapid response. Reconnaissance. Assassination. Desolation. That was the new code of conduct of the Anadali.

There was nothing she could have done to stop it.

Would Balendin still be proud of the person she had become? What would he say about what was happening to her? Would he still think her worthy of the title "Anadali Amadé" in spite of it? She knew in her heart the answer would be yes, yet she couldn't stop the sinking sensation that her weakness would bring the same fate upon her as it had him. Weakness was not tolerated, and the king would not have loose ends. She would be snipped from the tapestry of the kingdom quickly if he were to discover the condition plaguing her body. But nothing could be done—her research had proven fruitless, and she did not trust the confidentiality of the palace healers.

When lots had been drawn following her younger sister's birth, perhaps it was fate that Anaís had been selected as Anadali while Simone was declared heir to the throne.

Anaís shifted her weight and watched a fragment of stone skitter down the hill before coming to a rest in a clump of golden grass.

I am not weak. I will not die. But I hope I will be as lucky, to have someone catch me when I fall.

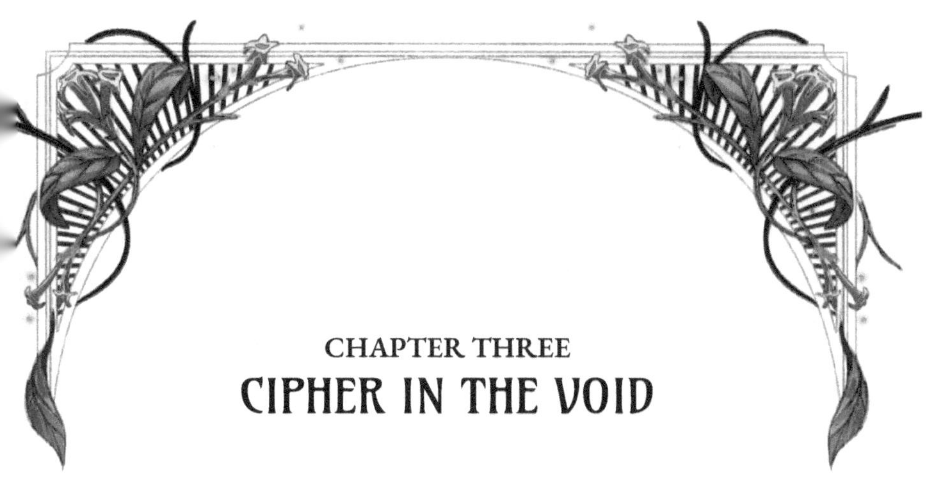

CHAPTER THREE
CIPHER IN THE VOID

Darkness had long fallen by the time Anaís found the strength to push herself off the ground and make the journey back to the palace. The evening's chill settled deeper into the night, her breath leaving her mouth in cloudy puffs as she crested the hill that overlooked the ocean below. The night was clear, creating an inky backdrop for the stars to burn brightly against. A smile formed on her lips as she mapped out the different constellations Balendin had taught her to find as a child—the Gem Box cluster near the South Star, Ankaa's rich golden hues shimmering in the Firebird Nebula, the milky-blue halo engulfing Toutahi in the Ni'ika constellation. Rather than getting lost in infinity, the night sky was the gateway to the galactic center of the universe.

Look to the stars, they will show you the way. Balendin's words flowed through her like a soothing balm to her soul.

A gust of wind blew the hood of her cloak off her head and sent a chill rippling through her, but it was nothing like the dry cold that plagued her home during the winter, when katabatic winds rushed over the land to tumble into the sea, flattening the golden grass that covered the hillsides and forcing even the sturdiest trees to bow in their presence. The wind was ruthless and unforgiving, but it was also familiar—an echo of the same deadly force that had forged her long ago.

And yet, the swift approach of spring brought her an odd sense of hope. The winds drifted off into a peaceful slumber, making way for a brief rainy season and new growth before the scorching heat of summer stripped the land barren again. Each season was an ephemeral state of dangerous beauty. Such was the way of nature—an ever-changing constant.

She reached up and began unbraiding the plait that tamed her long, dark curls, letting her hair fall down her back only to be swept away by the wind. This was a cold she could welcome with open arms.

By the time she made it back, her nose had gone numb and she couldn't feel her hands. Anaís drew her cloak tighter around her shoulders and pulled her hood back over her hair. Maybe she *couldn't* quite welcome this cold with open arms.

The needles of the cypress trees rustled as she followed a path that would lead her past the sand gardens toward the residential wing of the palace. While warriors were granted certain freedoms under King Timun's iron reign, getting caught outside the grounds without express permission of leave would only create more questions than she was willing to answer. The king had a habit of wanting to know what those closest to him were doing at all times. So long as anyone she crossed paths with thought she was finishing her rounds, she would be fine. Hopefully.

Never mind that she had missed evening training for the new recruits.

Rounding the corner, Anaís picked her way across the stepping stones meandering through the meticulously kept sand garden. Little clusters of cacti and aloe plants topped with fiery winter blooms had been planted in harmonious patches, while geometric designs had been raked into the sand. Today, the artisan had drawn a great winged serpent with jagged scales and wicked fangs.

The sound of crunching sand drew her attention toward two guards walking by the end of the path. They slowed at her approach. Anaís's heart thundered in her chest, but she forced herself to hold her head high. Everything was fine. She outranked them. The guards saluted smartly, and she greeted them with a curt nod. Stepping off the final paving stone, Anaís continued on her way. They continued on theirs.

She released a quiet breath through her nose. *So far, so good.*

Hurrying her pace to a purposeful stride, Anaís exited the sand garden and turned left, only to stumble to a halt. A familiar black cloak with gold embroidery snapped around the corner of the western turret as an Anadali followed the path leading to the courtyard where her and Simone's rooms were. A wing that was off limits save for select members of the Royal Guard.

There was only one reason one of her men would break that order.

Anger and indignation rose in her chest. The Anadali were *hers*; the king had no reason to interfere more than he already had. Anaís leaned against the garden wall and pressed the heel of her palms against her eyes. No, the king had *every* right, and he was probably looking for her. This was the longest her condition had ever kept her from the palace.

Missing family dinner for the second time this month was a risk. She'd thought it would be worth it to keep prying eyes off her failing body. Instead, it had only garnered interest. The king had made his move in sending one of her own as a spy. Though she could not retaliate, she *could* make a move of her own.

Where are you off to, Anadali?

Anaís pushed off the wall and turned in the opposite direction of her chambers, melting into the shadows as she made her way toward the palace. She glanced around before running through the tussock grass and deftly climbing the lattice that guided the growth of bougainvillea along the stone walls. Nearing the top, she wedged her hand into the junction between the sun-lightened stones and picked her way up the face of the palace before pulling herself around the ledge of the roof. Anaís scanned the grounds for signs of the Anadali from the pathway, but all she could see was a pair of the Guard patrolling along the far end of the garden. They walked next to the bubbling stream that meandered through the grounds, body language alert while they monitored their surroundings.

When they crossed over the footbridge that connected the gardens to the front of the palace, Anaís crouched low and hurried across the narrow ledge, rising slightly as she neared the edge of the rooftop to gain speed before silently leaping across the gap between palace wings. Anaís rolled her landing on the lower level of the tiered roof, using the slope and the momentum to propel herself forward and launch over the garden where the guards had crossed moments before. She caught hold of the edge of the parapet and pulled herself up, ducking into the shadows between the stone railing and a palace turret.

Closing her eyes, she paused to listen, but her ears were met with the rustling of leaves and the rhythmic chirp of crickets. It did little to reassure her. Never before had she felt such pride for the competency of her Anadali and frustration at herself for training them so well.

Stepping out of the shadows, Anaís walked along the merlons of the parapet before climbing onto the adjacent roof and looking out over the courtyard. A breeze brushed past her, the fluttering of her cloak mirroring the anticipation that buzzed through her body. She had discovered this route when she went free-running at dawn earlier that week. It wasn't the easiest path, but it was exhilarating and nearly impossible to see from the ground when executed correctly.

Besides, if she wasn't going to catch the Anadali out here, she might as well wait for them to find her and ensure Simone was safe in the meantime.

Filling her lungs with the night air, Anaís exhaled slowly to release the tension from her muscles. She took a few steps back, bounced on the balls of her feet, and ran forward to leap off the roof. She jumped three times across the buttresses and sprinted down the sloping archway before swinging around the side of the palace and alighting on the window frame that led to her sister's room. Anaís pushed the windowpane open and climbed through, landing softly on the rug that covered the hardwood floor.

"You know we have doors for a reason," Simone said without looking up from her book.

Anaís shut the window and drew the curtains closed, then padded across the room and plopped herself on the armchair next to the fire with a shrug. "Only if you want to get caught."

Simone looked up from her book, a smile playing on her lips. "And what were you doing that warranted not getting caught, hmm?"

"Oh, stop it," Anaís swatted her sister away. "It's nothing like that, I just..." She trailed off and sighed.

"It's happening more frequently again."

It wasn't a question. Anaís knew she couldn't hide from her sister, but she also couldn't risk burdening her with the truth. The day Balendin died ten years ago was the day Anaís had been born in blood, and it was in the kingdom's thirst for blood that she was drowning. She weighed the options in her mind before choosing the one she willed herself to believe was true.

"I'm fine."

Simone nodded but didn't look convinced. Instead, she lay her book face down on her bed and walked across the room to where a covered platter sat on the mantle of the fireplace. She lifted the lid and ducked her face away as steam billowed into the air.

"I had it brought up for you," Simone said, handing the bowl of mutton stew to Anaís.

"Thank you?" Anaís looked questioningly at her sister. "I'm right here, though. I could have gotten that myself."

"I know. You looked comfortable."

A look that Anaís couldn't quite place flickered across her sister's face, so she said the only thing she could think of to say. "Oh."

She accepted the bowl and felt herself melt farther into the soft fabric of the armchair as she took the first bite. The stew was warm and perfectly seasoned with herbs and spices. She tucked into her meal while her sister returned to her book. The fire popped and crackled rhythmically in the hearth, the sound of her metal spoon clinking against the ceramic bowl punctuating the silence. Anaís glanced at her sister when she realized the sound of pages turning no longer accompanied the ambient melody of the room. She pushed the last of the vegetables around the bottom of the bowl with her spoon and tried to figure out what she could say to ease some of the burden off Simone's shoulders. Maybe if she gave her sister a partial truth?

"Normally, training the recruits wouldn't be a problem, but with negotiations on the horizon, growing tensions, the threat of war, it's..."

"A lot?" Simone supplied for her as she slipped a bookmark between the pages of her book and set it on the bedside table.

Anaís nodded.

"And the nightmares?" Simone asked. "Are they back?"

Anaís shrugged noncommittally. "No, they're all right."

That was true too. Mostly. For a time, her dreams had consisted of memories that made wakeful exhaustion seem much more appealing than risking rest. It had been a problem since she was a child, even more so after Balendin's death. Until one night, when everything had changed—an oddity her grieving heart had clung to like a lifeline, a secret she never dared utter aloud, lest it disappear as quickly as it came. How else could she rationalize the comforting presence that drew her into safety when the horrors struck? It was a warmth that kept the familiar sensation of ice from flooding her veins when terror tried to creep in. A shield that dared the nightmares to even think about trying to haunt her in the darkness.

No, sleep was not the problem it used to be. Her problem had somehow seeped into the land of the waking, and she wasn't sure what to do about it. She'd thought she could keep going. Maybe another day or two, then she would rest. What a load of lies that was.

"I didn't mean to worry you," Anaís continued.

Simone smiled, but it slowly faded as she picked at a loose thread on her quilt. "I don't know what's going on, but this is the second time this month you've disappeared. You look like death. I don't want to see you get hurt."

"I know, and I won't."

Simone regarded her in earnest, but the determination Anaís forced herself to project left no room for doubt. She had no intentions of anyone discovering the full extent of her ailment, if at all. Should the swift hand of death come, she would go down fighting—for herself, for her promise to keep her sister safe. No, she had been death's accomplice far too often for it to try to snuff her out so easily.

That seemed to satisfy Simone's worry for the moment. A familiar mischievous glint filled her eyes and Anaís felt relief settle over her as her sister's humor returned. "You'll never guess what I discovered today."

Anaís leaned forward, reciprocating her sister's excitement. "Do tell."

Simone opened her mouth to speak, but shut it quickly when she caught a glimpse of the clock on her nightstand. Lifting her finger in silent anticipation, Simone tiptoed to the door and pressed her ear against the polished wood, waiting for the guard to pass.

They may have royal blood, but they were just as trapped as everyone else, if not more so. It would be foolish to be lulled into a false sense of security.

Muffled footsteps trailed down the hallway, then disappeared. No checks tonight. Simone slumped against the door. Anaís relaxed into her chair. A deep creak emanated from the courtyard, sending both women jumping out of their skins.

Anaís looked to the window, a futile instinct since she had drawn the curtains.

Simone waved her hand to catch her attention. *Followed?* she signed, raising her eyebrows in question.

Likely, Anaís signed in return.

Slowly, she crept toward the window, Simone's uneven breaths the only sound in the room. Anaís drew the curtain back just enough to peer outside. Under the shadow of the roof on the opposite side of the courtyard, Gio was attempting to shimmy his way up the rain pipe by her rooms. A black cloak with gold embroidery on the hem billowed around his body.

I'll be back, Anaís signed, letting the curtain settle back into place.

Anaís slipped out the door and down the hallway, avoiding the moonlight spilling onto the floor through the uncovered windows every few meters. She stopped at the window at the end, closest to where Gio was still struggling to find a grip to pull himself over the overhang and onto the roof. She pushed the window open and leaned lazily against the frame, smiling as a slight jump ran through Gio's body at the sound of the window latch unhooking.

His perception is improving, Anaís thought. Then he subtly shook his head and continued trying to hoist himself up. She sighed internally. *Never mind.*

Gio had shown immense promise during the trials six years ago, and she had taken him on as her first apprentice. He was strong, eager to learn, and immensely loyal—all traits Anaís tried to develop and refine as she passed on the knowledge Balendin instilled in her. At the time, it was her own small act of rebellion against the king's vision of a reformed Anadali.

Unfortunately, Gio was also eager to please, which the king had no doubt picked up on. He was more willing than others to jump on certain tasks with unreflecting haste. Now he was a full-fledged member of the Anadali, and it filled Anaís with a strange mixture of pride at Gio's accomplishment and sadness as the last of her efforts to keep the heart of the Anadali alive slipped through her grasp.

She should have known the king would leverage her own apprentice against her. Gio was most likely acting out of concern for his missing master, but whatever he reported to the king would be interpreted how the king wished. Therein lay the danger.

"Enjoying the evening, Gio?" Anaís asked with an air of disinterest.

Gio froze like a nuknuk caught in a field before a hannok swept down to enjoy its meal.

"I suggest you answer me."

He shifted his body, the rain pipe creaking under his weight. "The king was inquiring of your whereabouts. He...wants to meet with you."

Well, that was an unfortunate turn of events. "Now you know whereabouts I am." Her voice drifted across the courtyard, cool as the night air. It did little to freeze the fear his words brought. "Did he wish to meet tonight?"

"No. Um. Tomorrow would suit him better." Gio swallowed nervously. "But he wanted to know why no one could find you earlier."

"If you could find me, I wouldn't be Anadali Amadé, would I?"

He shifted again, a metallic groan emanating from the protesting rain pipe. "No. No, of course." His voice sounded as strained as the pipe he clung to.

Anaís let out a quiet breath through her nose. *Gio, you loyal idiot.* "I was doing my rounds, as you should be doing yours."

"I am—"

"Not by accosting a rain pipe and waking half the palace."

He wrapped his arm around the pipe and wiped the palm of his hand on his uniform before reaching back up to get a better grip.

Anaís sighed. "Get back to your chambers, Gio. And try not to hurt yourself on the way down." She shut the window before he could reply.

All clear? Simone signed when Anaís reappeared in her room.

Anaís nodded, finding her place in the armchair again as a new weariness settled into her bones. "It was Gio. The king wanted him to find out where I was."

"What did you tell him?"

"That I was doing my rounds, as he should have been doing."

"Your rounds?"

Personal rounds, Anaís signed, before saying, "So, your discovery?"

Simone sat back on her heels and brought her hands together in a silent clap as excitement overtook her once more. "Well today I had a meeting with Father's Royal Advisor about the diplomatic talks in Nahonaugh that I'll be attending next week. Our conversation got me thinking. Obviously, these talks are long overdue, given that the breach of the Treaty of Ithansfar happened ten years ago."

The taste of smoke and ash filled Anaís's mouth, and she swallowed, trying to wet her suddenly parched throat. Trying to rid herself of the flavor of death and the flood of memories that came with it. She focused on Simone's words, letting them ground her from her mounting panic despite them being the source.

"But why did that breach occur so shortly after the Battle of Ithansfar?" Simone continued, unaware of the turmoil swirling in Anaís's mind. "It was only twenty-one years after the truce was declared and the treaty signed—a blink of an eye in the span of history. What changed?" She paused as if remembering something important. "Do you remember what Llúcia taught us in our history lessons about the lead up to the Battle of Ithansfar?"

Anaís shook her head, intrigued.

Simone smiled conspiratorially. "That's because she didn't teach us anything. Even the texts I've read during my independent studies have been impossibly vague. The breach of the Treaty of Ithansfar is a blemish on our history—*recent* history. Everyone knows it happened. Everyone knows of the consequences of the fallout—we're living in them today. Restricted trade routes, safe passage to key cities and ports eliminated on both sides... I could go on. But no one talks about the *why*. Why did the breach happen? More importantly, why did the Battle of Ithansfar happen? This wasn't a territorial battle like the ones of our ancestors. Our kingdoms were established; there was at least the semblance of peace between Dúndíor and Nahonaugh. It's...suspicious.

"And now, thirty-one years after the battle and ten years after the breach, we're to have diplomatic peace talks between two kingdoms whose rulers seem to be content with peace in their own lands and animosity at their doorstep. Why the change of heart?

"I went to the library. I knew I wouldn't find anything new about the Battle of Ithansfar itself, so I looked at the aftermath in our present and searched for connections to the past instead." Simone looked at her with wide eyes. "Anaís, this was the fallout of a century of strategic sabotage from both sides. Both sides working together to bring about one another's downfall. This spans *generations* of rulers. How does that make sense? It doesn't!"

Anaís slumped back in the armchair, turning Simone's words over in her mind.

"I think there's a cipher in the void. A message in all that is unwritten," Simone whispered. "I need to find out what that message is. Who or what is behind this? If we know the why, we can stop this pattern from continuing. We need these diplomatic talks, we need true peace in these lands, but there's something someone *isn't* saying."

Shaking her head, Anaís leaned forward. "And you're going to try to figure this out in Nahonaugh? During the talks that could change the course of our history? It's fragile enough as it is."

"This is more than simply our history. This is our reality. Our *future*. I can't help but think something is amiss here. I need to get to the bottom of it."

"You're sure this isn't a fantasy you've construed from reading too many mystery novels?" Anaís tilted her head toward the book lying inconspicuously on Simone's nightstand. "I know that's not a book on international policy." She knew Simone wasn't joking about this either, but Anaís had to be certain. Her sister was proposing a conspiracy that implied a complete reconstruction of their government, that could only solidify the military state their father had created. But *why*?

Their father's iron rule following the breach in the treaty was supposed to be temporary. No one allowed in, no one allowed out. Curfews. Restricted trade. A strict measure of protection for the people following the breach...unless he was biding his time. Delaying the retaliatory strike to bypass the armor and pierce the soft underbelly of an unsuspecting opponent. All at the expense of his people, not for them.

You will usher in this new era. Anaís swallowed.

"How did you know?" Simone's question and nod at the bedside table dragged her back to the present.

"You painted the cover to hide the title. Lovely design, by the way. Petyor is the—" Her words cut off as a pillow hurtled into her face.

"Don't. You. Spoil. The. Book."

Anaís hugged the pillow to her chest and laughed, trying to dampen the nerves swirling in her stomach. "I was only joking. But you're ignoring my question."

"You better be joking," Simone grumbled, but a small smile tugged at the corner of her lips all the same. "And it's not a fantasy. I want you to come with me to the negotiations. I would feel better knowing someone I trust with my life *and* with this information was there."

That gave her pause. She was loyal to her sister—would go so far as to die for her—but she had sworn an oath to the king. If she found incriminating information on either kingdom, she was sworn to report it to her father. And any information in his hands could be twisted as he pleased. Experience had proven that. If she found evidence and took matters into her own hands, she would have to go against him and risk sending the kingdom she was sworn to protect into civil war. Could she risk the weight of that choice on a hunch?

Anaís swallowed. *What if it's not a hunch?* She was a warrior, trained to face any trial with calm calculation. So why did the thought of going against the father she had grown to both love and loathe terrify her?

"Don't you normally take someone from the Guard on these little excursions? You don't trust Tadeo?" Anaís asked instead, trying to find some levity despite the sinking feeling in her stomach. Though she had a suspicion that trust was only a small aspect that prompted Simone to request her company. Anaís also knew that despite her own apprehensions, she would do whatever Simone asked of her.

"Of course I trust him," Simone laughed.

"So you don't want to be distracted, then?" Anaís tilted her head at her sister, waiting for her to take the bait.

If the furtive looks between Simone and a certain Tadeo Constantin, Captain of the King's Guard, were anything to go by, they were smitten with each other. While Anaís did *not* appreciate his involvement in the selection of Anadali recruits, she *did* trust him about as far as she could throw him. Which was a surprising distance, as proven during their altercation last week when she had confronted him about his intentions with Simone. He seemed honorable enough. Although Simone had never confirmed her feelings for the captain, the blush creeping up her cheeks told Anaís everything she needed to know.

"I'll come with you," Anaís blurted, trying to distract Simone from whatever was going on in that head of hers. "Really though, why do you need Anadali for diplomatic talks?"

"You're a real piece of work, you know?" Simone tried to glare at Anaís, but the remnants of the dreamy look on her face only managed to turn into a disgruntled stare. She shook her head and straightened her posture, an air of seriousness replacing the playfulness that was there moments ago. "I don't need Anadali," she clarified. "I need my sister."

CHAPTER FOUR
A LIFE FOR A LIFE

NAÍS WOKE WITH A START, GRUMBLING AS SHE rolled over and rubbed the sleep out of her eyes. It was just after sunrise, and while she was looking forward to getting out of the palace and into nature during the week-long trip to Nahonaugh, all she *wanted* to do was retreat into the security of her dreams. She closed her eyes against the soft glow of the morning light filtering through her curtains, trying to settle back into the cocoon of warmth that had enveloped her moments ago. A bird squawked outside her window, and the last tendrils of sleep drifted away with the sound.

She sighed. *I could punch that bird.*

Pushing off the covers, Anaís dragged herself out of bed and padded over to her wardrobe to don her traveling clothes and pack for the trip. Simone had insisted she prepare the night before, but Anaís lived by the principle that if she forgot it in her haste, it wasn't a necessary item to begin with. Besides, they would only be gone for just over two weeks, including the journey there and back. How much preparation could she really need?

Anaís dressed quickly, putting on black trousers and a soft tunic before choosing a cloak and tossing it on her bed to put on later. She wasn't as enamored with appearances as Simone, but there was something lovely and powerful about the way the right set of clothes made her feel. Her fingers ran along the fabric of her court uniforms before she decided upon a few different options. A pair of loose black cotton trousers and a fitted shirt in the same color—perfect for snooping around at night—joined her uniforms in the trunk. The fabric was light, yet warm enough for the mild evenings of central Nahonaugh, with enough give that she could comfortably move about without hindrance. She pulled a few different gowns for dinner, mostly because she knew Simone would start a riot if she only brought one option. Finally, she gathered her sleeping robe that had been unceremoniously thrown on the floor and folded it next to her uniforms, shutting her trunk with a satisfied snap.

She reached her foot out to nudge the wardrobe door closed, but a glint on the top shelf caught her eye and she froze, foot stalling midair as she stared dumbly at the mask—the one Balendin had given her all those years ago. Her foot fell to the floor, and she took a step forward, her fingers absentmindedly trailing along the thin scar stretching from her left brow to her cheekbone, just missing her eye.

At the time, Balendin had told her the solution was simple—don't get hit—and she had practiced until that was the case. But close quarter combat was synonymous with fighting dirty, and she had seen more eyes gouged out than she cared to count. That, and the comforting weight of the mask helped keep her grounded.

Shaking her head to clear her thoughts, Anaís toed the wardrobe door with her foot. She hadn't worn it since his death; there was no need to start now. The latch of the door clicked shut.

Anaís didn't move, couldn't move, as the memory that captured her the evening prior came back in full force.

I will fight for you, he had promised. And he had kept that promise until his last breath. She didn't deserve to wear it, not after she had failed him despite all he had taught her. But she also didn't want to face the kingdom responsible for her mother's death without him.

With trembling hands, Anaís opened the wardrobe door. *To wear during knife fights.* His scrawled handwriting filled her mind's eye, disappearing again in a blink. In the arena of diplomacy, the tongue was the sword. An unfitting metaphor for arguing the necessity of a mask, though perhaps in this roundabout way, it was enough. She wanted it to be enough.

Before Anaís could second-guess herself, she lifted the mask off the shelf, turning it over in her hands and watching as the gemstones reflected the early morning light, sending spheres of color dancing around her room. It felt different from the last time she had worn it. The curves of the metal followed a form that was familiar yet new. A curious sensation prickled at the back of her mind.

Would it still fit?

Before she could test her theory, a sharp knock sounded at the door, sending Anaís jumping out of her skin. The mask slipped from her hands and landed with a thud on her sock-clad foot, inciting an un-royal string of curses. Anaís knelt, putting pressure on her offending toe to ease the pain, when a softer knock sounded.

"Your Highness? Are you all right in there?"

Anaís let out a breath, then shook her head with a wry laugh. "Yes!" she called, pushing herself up and shaking out the ache in her foot. "You may enter, Katka."

Her lady's maid appeared in the doorway with a knapsack in hand. Katka's crimson tea-length dress swished around her legs as she came to an abrupt stop. "Your Highness, you are already dressed?"

"Yes, I was just heading down," Anaís replied, taking the proffered knapsack from Katka. Rearranging a few of the items, she carefully placed the mask inside. It would be foolish to wear it, but having a piece of Balendin nearby was comfort enough.

Katka's blue eyes widened when she looked at the trunk. "And you are packed?"

"Is that so surprising?"

"When you were younger, yes," Katka laughed. "Though perhaps not anymore. It's been so long since you've gone on an extended trip."

Anaís frowned. "Since *I've* gone. Are you not coming?"

"No, Your Highness. I was told it's too dangerous, with you going as Anadali." Katka wrung her hands nervously before clasping them behind her back. "Captain Tadeo said the king would like to speak with you before you left."

Anaís's stomach plummeted as she recalled her encounter with Gio last night. This had to be about her absence. Gio's report. Or had the king somehow caught wind of Simone's suspicions? She would fight anyone who tried to lay a hand on Simone, but if the king ordered *her* to punish Simone... Anaís felt sick.

"Your Highness." Katka laid a gentle hand on her shoulder, quieting her swirling thoughts. "The captain did not seem worried."

Anaís nodded once, composing herself. "Thank you, Katka.

Fetch a porter for my things, please. I'd like to leave as soon as the meeting is finished."

"Of course." Katka dipped into a curtsy and hurried out of the room.

Anaís inhaled, releasing her breath slowly as she tried to calm her nerves. Then she slid on her boots and strode toward the inevitable.

❋ ❋ ❋

THE MAPS THAT HAD LITTERED her father's desk the last time she was in here were organized neatly on a shelf. Instead, a book was propped open in front of him. Anaís stood at attention while subtly tilting her eyes downward to try and make out the writing on the page. Her father always made her wait, and today the silence grated against her with vehemence. She needed some distraction to prevent herself from breaking prematurely in his game.

The clock on the mantle ticked away the seconds. A pop from the fireplace sent a burst of light flickering across the room.

King Timun cleared his throat and shut the book with a snap. "At ease."

Anaís shifted her stance, folding her hands in front of her.

"Simone asked you to accompany her during the diplomatic negotiations, did she not?"

"Yes, we are prepared to leave shortly. But if you have other duties for me, I'm sure she would be happy to have Captain Tadeo accompany her."

"No, no." He absentmindedly twisted the emerald cufflink of his shirt. "This is very good—what I wanted to discuss, in fact. I have a request."

She had not expected such a benign start to the meeting. "Your Majesty?"

"It will be simple." The king waved his hand. "There is some information from their library I need you to extract. Anything you can find on the waters of Takaniim, record it. Bring it to me."

Anaís frowned, but quickly smoothed her expression as she thought.

Takaniim—"lifestream," in the Old Language—was a sacred lake that had mysteriously disappeared centuries ago, moving from history to legend as time and memory reformed its story. Balendin had told her the tales when she was a girl, ones passed along from generation to generation by the storytellers of his family. Never before had she seen a written account. But if the king wanted it, find it she must.

"It will be done," she said.

"Ah!" He held up his finger, a comical gesture that drew Anaís's attention to the darkness hidden in his expression. She straightened her spine, as if *that* would help her stand against it. "Not quite. One more thing. This year, as per the tradition of House Kavanaugh, King Ibhar's son Eoghan will ascend to the throne on his twenty-eighth birthday."

"I am aware." Though where her father was going with this, she hadn't the slightest idea. As the illegitimate son of King Ibhar, Eoghan's path to kinghood had been nonexistent. Then his half-brother Mathúin—the only legitimate son of the king and queen—had died of pneumonia two years ago. While she did not know much about Crown Prince Eoghan, he was rumored to be even-tempered and respectably intelligent, if his studies in literature and philosophy at the university were anything to go by.

King Timun cleared his throat. "I want him dead."

"At the diplomatic talks?" Anaís gaped at him. Did her father wish to start a war or end one?

"Oh no! Stars no," he laughed. "During Fheile Earrach—Nahonaugh's spring festival. It begins in a month, so you have plenty of time to prepare. This is simply an opportune occasion to gather information on the palace's infrastructure, the abilities of the guards, your new target..." He trailed off, leaning forward in his chair. "You haven't met him yet, have you? During one of your other excursions?"

"No," she answered simply.

"I see. Yes, very well." He clapped his hands together. A nostalgic smile formed on his lips, but quickly faded as his eyes brightened with mirth. "This will make things right again, won't it?"

Was that all? Information on a mythical lake and preparations to assassinate a crown prince. What of Gio coming after her? Part of Anaís begged her to count her blessings and leave. If he didn't bring it up, why should she? But her father always knew. Even if no one told him, somehow he always did.

"I'm afraid I don't understand," Anaís said slowly.

"You will see, in time. Now, off you go. Long journey ahead." He rose from his seat to putter about the study, picking various books off the shelves and organizing them into neat stacks on his desk.

Anaís stared at him while he worked, unable to bring herself to move toward the door. Something was not adding up, but she couldn't place her finger on it.

"I know Mother's passing was hard on you," she prodded, waiting to see how he struck.

He paused mid-reach and turned to look at her. "I have the fiercest warrior in the four realms and my best diplomat entering enemy territory, I am on the cusp of a discovery that will change *everything*, and Pedra's death"—he nodded at Anaís—"will be avenged." Her father gently slid the book in his hand back onto the shelf and approached her.

"A life for a life will not avenge mother's death," she said carefully. "It will only carry the cycle of war back to Dúndíor."

The king stopped in front of his desk and leaned against it, considering her. Finally, he said, "This is diplomacy, not war. They broke the treaty and it ended in my wife's death. I had *every* right to retaliate with war, but I did not. Why?"

Anaís swallowed. Ten years ago, the borders had closed. Then martial law had been enacted, the military expanded, the Anadali reformed. Dúndíor had stood on the precipice of war for *ten years*—a time that had consumed her. How had she not noticed that war had never come? "I do not know," she whispered.

"Because war alone would not present the opportunity before me. This is a tipping point." He sighed as if weighing his next words. "As fate should have it, this tipping point requires the removal of the crown prince and you, my daughter, are excellent at removing unwanted things. After all, it is what must be done to keep our people safe. As Anadali Amadé, you of all people should want that." He leveled her with a stare that chilled her to the bone. "If you are able to complete your duties according to the oath you swore. If you *truly are* the best this kingdom has to offer, only you should be able to neutralize a threat such as him without"—he looked up and tapped his chin as if thinking—"ah yes, bringing the cycle of war back to Dúndíor." He considered her another moment before adding lowly, "You notice I do not care where you disappear to, because you always return. You always excel. Do *not* make me start questioning you."

Anaís released a quiet, steady breath. At least Simone's theories remained hidden. Given her father's insinuations, Anaís had a sinking suspicion her sister was right.

Unfortunately, her father's words carried with them a tangible threat. Anaís tensed as her skin began to burn in memory of the pain that would await her should she fail. Her death at the end would be a kindness.

"And the diplomatic talks?" she asked, squeezing her hands together to dull the phantom pain.

"They are a necessary step toward cooperation—building trust, diplomacy." He paused, his deep brown eyes pinning her in place. "It is vital they see you mean their prince no harm. His assassination *cannot* be linked to this throne."

Anaís nodded. "I will not fail." It would take a miracle to succeed.

"That's not good enough," King Timun snapped. "You *must* accomplish this task. Do you understand?"

"Yes."

"Will you do it?"

She sucked in a deep breath and pushed uncertainty aside. "Yes."

King Timun nodded, satisfied. "I've sent word ahead. King Ibhar demanded a smaller retinue to avoid undue tensions, given the political climate. I've assured him only our best would be in attendance." He leveled Anaís with a meaningful look that said they did *not* know an Anadali was coming. "Captain Béhar will be joining you, as will a lady of Simone's choosing. King Ibhar assured me you all would be graciously taken care of."

"Understood, Your Majesty."

Her father nodded, then paused to pluck a stray thread off his coat, twirling it between his fingers before letting it fall to the floor. A chill ran down Anaís's spine when his eyes met hers again. "Simone cannot know of your task. Wouldn't want to cause her undue worry."

"Of course, Your Majesty." Her words were steady, though she felt anything but. "That would not be wise."

"Good. Off to it, then." He waved his hand dismissively. "It's a long journey. Wouldn't want to be late."

DARKNESS STILL CLUNG TO THE sky when Anaís, Simone, Béhar, and Magdalina set out on their seventh and last day of traveling. To-day, Béhar drove the horses while Anaís took up position inside the carriage with Simone and Magdalina, one of Simone's ladies-in-wait-ing who happened to be Tadeo's younger sister. The journey had gone by more quickly than Anaís anticipated.

She glanced over at her sister before resting her head against the plush carriage seat to watch the world outside go by. Simone had handled the journey better than Anaís imagined she would as well.

When they were children, they'd spent their summers running away from duties by playing in the canyons near the palace. They made camp under wild shrubs, branches arching and twisting to their own whims, creating a canopy under which the two young princesses found refuge from the blazing summer sun. A long dip in the gently flowing waters of a brook that branched away from the river gorge replaced bath time. Fresh ælorberries with their sweetly tangy golden juices running down sticky fingers became a dinner as succulent as any the palace chef could create. The sisters ran as wild and free as the nature that surrounded them, but unlike the wilder-ness, they would have to be tamed.

Now, the woman sitting next to Anaís looked every part the young queen she was meant to become. Anaís was immensely proud of this version of Simone. If anything, the last few days had taught her that the little girl she'd once known never truly left. She had simply been refined into regality, just as Anaís had been forged into the woman she was today.

Though she knew Simone wanted her here for support, she couldn't help but feel a swell of gratitude for how much innate trust her sister had placed in her. She would not let Simone down, even if their father's plans did add an unforeseen twist.

"What are you thinking about?" Simone asked, whispering as to not wake Magdalina across from them.

Anaís tilted her head toward her sister, the pastel colors of dawn breaking through the dark of night and adding a wash of color to Simone's tawny-brown skin.

"Our old brush forts and ælorberry suppers. And I think we should stop for a rest soon," Anaís said. "We've been riding for hours; you must be hungry."

Simone shot her a questioning look. "You're worried about *me* being hungry?"

"*I'm* hungry," Anaís deadpanned, "and I don't think it would be in anyone's best interest for me to show up to Nahonaugh absolutely famished."

A surprised laugh burst from Simone, and she clapped a hand over her mouth, relaxing when Magdalina's head lolled to the side and she remained fast asleep. "No, those diplomatic talks would become decidedly undiplomatic."

Anaís nudged Simone's shoulder with her own, but the bright smile on her lips softened the gesture. "We'll carry on until we reach the base of the mountains; then, I'll signal Béhar to stop. There's nowhere safe to pull over once we enter the pass. We can rest and have breakfast there before heading on."

The rhythmic clopping of hooves crunched along the dirt path, and the sound of birds chirping flittered through the breeze as nature began to wake up. The sky clothed itself in pale shades of pink and orange as the first rays of light burst forth in a grand entrance. The rainy climate of Nahonaugh created a lush landscape that admittedly made Anaís little envious. The craggy gorges and hearty foliage of her desert home gave way to flowering valleys and dense forests that covered the mountainside. Even the air felt more welcoming as it filled her lungs, no longer dry and grating. Shadows pooled under trees and between the delicate folds of flower petals as the morning light grew stronger, as if the remnants of night were playing hide-and-seek with the day. By the time they reached the base of Mount Yeleidh, the entire valley was bathed in a soft, golden glow.

Anaís tipped her head toward the open window. "Béhar! Find us a spot for breakfast."

"Aye, Amadé!" his muffled shout returned.

Magdalina startled, blinking wearily at Anaís and Simone. "Have we arrived?" she asked, her light brown ringlets slightly squashed from napping.

"Not yet," Simone smiled gently. "We're stopping for breakfast first, then it's a quick trip through the pass."

"Lovely," Magdalina said, stretching her arms above her head as much as the carriage would allow.

A short fifteen minutes later, the carriage trundled to a stop beside a small meadow. Béhar tied the horses to a tree, allowing them to chomp merrily at the grass while the women laid out a picnic of bread, hard cheeses, dried meats, and the fresh fruit they'd purchased at a village market the day before. Béhar started a small fire to boil some water for tea.

"We need to set some ground rules," Anaís said, sorting through the tea to decide which one to brew. "Particularly surrounding my position as Anadali. A diplomatic meeting after a decade of thinly-veiled animosity is bound to go off script, and King Timun has a few...errands for me to see to."

"Of course he does." Simone sat back on her heels. "Are we allowed to know?"

"The less you know right now, the better."

Simone gave her a pointed look. "We are all we have in Nahonaugh. I trust each of you with my life, but we must work together."

"And we are," Anaís assured her. "But we cannot risk unintentional slip-ups. My work relies on stealth. That is all I can tell you."

Simone sighed. "Right, well, you stick to your stealth work and make sure nothing funny goes on behind the scenes. Magdalina and I will take care of diplomacy."

"And me?" Béhar asked, lowering himself to sit at the edge of the picnic blanket.

"You will serve as Royal Guard to Her Highness and Lady Magdalina," Anaís told him. "We will only be in Nahonaugh for three days during these initial negotiations. Do not let them out of your sight."

"Save for feminine matters, of course," Simone quipped. "Bathing and the like."

A fierce blush crept up Béhar's neck as he looked everywhere but them. Magdalina stifled a laugh behind her hand.

Anaís tipped her head back toward the sky. "What do you think I'm here for?"

"Sorry," Simone giggled, taking the tea box resting before Anaís and selecting an herbal blend of ginger, lemongrass, and rosehip. She placed it into the teapot and removed the now-boiling water from the fire, then poured it over the mixture and closed the lid to let the tea steep. "What else do you have on the agenda to discuss?"

Anaís worried her lip, thinking. "They will recognize me as Anadali," she finally said. "In fact, I want them to. The problem lies within my position as Amadé and the fact that they *know* it is Anaís Dí Sona, firstborn of House Dí Sona, who holds that position. They cannot know that is who I am."

Magdalina looked at her with wide brown eyes. "Why not?"

"Because of what occurred on the day of the breach, among other things. And we may be in a cold war of sorts, but information still crosses borders. They know what the Anadali are capable of. Sending the Amadé herself has...implications. That threat alone might be enough to start a true war."

"Well, they're about to know." Béhar gestured between Anaís and Simone. "Anyone with eyes can see that the two of you are related."

"Yes, thank you for that, Captain," Anaís huffed.

Simone was short where Anaís was tall, curvy where Anaís had lean muscle from a lifetime of training. Their faces, however, held an uncanny similarity. The only differences were the scar that ran from Anaís's brow to cheekbone and the color of her eyes. She hadn't intended to wear the mask, but concealing her identity would be a small inconvenience to pay if it protected their lives. At least it only covered the upper half of her face, so she would not have to remove it during mealtimes.

"Never mind." She looked at Béhar. "You've given me an idea. I apologize."

He waved his hand good-naturedly. "Pass me the jerky and all is forgiven."

Anaís tossed a strip across the picnic blanket, and he caught it in his mouth, accompanied by Magdalina's enthusiastic applause and Simone's joyous giggles.

Jovial conversation filled the morning as they continued munching on their breakfast, though Anaís found it difficult to fully relax. She had a role to play, and she had to play it to perfection. She *would* be questioned. But she would also be expected to behave a certain way. She needed to figure out what that was and play into it—feed them what they anticipated while adding a flavor of her own to hide the taste of their self-made poison.

Anaís glanced at her sister. That, and she had to let Simone think she was merely ensuring nothing suspicious was happening behind the scenes. Especially after the thinly veiled threat their father had made.

Popping a berry into her mouth, Anaís closed her eyes as the sweetness from the juice pulled her back into the present. All she could do was plan for what she could control and prepare for what she could not.

Yes, she would have to be on alert at all hours, but she would also be away from the palace in Dúndíor. Away from the memories trapped in its walls. She was still doing as the king commanded, she was still a weapon, but in her own way, she was free. Besides, she wouldn't be killing anyone.

Not yet, anyway.

Anaís brushed the crumbs off her trousers and stood. "I should probably finish getting ready so we can go."

Simone nodded. She was already dressed in a blush-pink gown. Gold embroidery embellished the bodice, adding structure to compliment the ethereal elegance of the layers of chiffon that formed the skirt. How she managed to travel comfortably in that, Anaís would never understand, though she did admire her sister's dedication to regal perfection.

Anaís made her way to the carriage and unclasped her trunk to find her uniform jacket: a smooth black cotton with intricate beading of pearls and diamonds, and gold chain covering the shoulders in place of spaulders. The gold-embossed insignia of the Anadali glinted proudly against the black-stained leather cuirass that fit over the jacket. Such finery would be a waste of craftsmanship in battle, but she supposed in a way she was walking into a battle of wits. In the arena of diplomacy, first impressions mattered. She fastened up the clasps and secured the belt around her waist, ensuring her daggers were properly in place.

Opening her knapsack, Anaís pulled out her worn leather bracers and fastened them around her wrists before tucking her throwing knives into the slits. Then she removed the mask. Before she could overthink her decision, she walked back to the picnic area and held it out to Simone.

"Could you..." Anaís trailed off.

Simone's expression softened. "Of course." She pat the blanket in front of her. "You truly thought of everything, didn't you? Are you always this meticulous on a job?"

She lowered herself where Simone had indicated, closing her eyes as Simone untied the ribbon holding her hair back and gently ran her fingers along her scalp to divide it into sections.

"Proper planning prevents piss-poor performance," Anaís replied with mock seriousness, given she hadn't planned this at all.

Simone snorted a laugh. "And what is that supposed to mean?"

Anaís cracked an eye open to see Simone peering over her shoulder. "Plan well, don't die."

"Charming." Simone flicked Anaís's cheek, then set to work intricately braiding her hair, weaving the mask's ribbons into the plait to hold it in place.

A firm hand pressed against the back of Anaís's head, and her eyes fluttered open.

"I need you to tilt your head forward. You keep leaning into me."

"Sorry. Feels nice," Anaís mumbled, but she obeyed all the same.

Stray dark curls brushed her cheeks while the rest of her hair cascaded down her back in a rope of intertwined braids and twists. The mask covered the top half of her face completely, leaving the lower half exposed. Much to her amazement, but not to her surprise, the mask molded against the planes of her face perfectly. She wasn't sure how, she wasn't sure why, but Balendin's design—whatever he'd done—was unmatched.

Simone squeezed her shoulder and stood, walking around Anaís to assess her handiwork.

"Well?" Anaís stood and straightened her uniform. "Is it all right? Too much?"

A mischievous smile brightened Simone's face. "No, this is perfect. In fact, I can't decide if they're going to be in awe of you or terrified out of their minds."

"Both," Magdalina said, her eyes dancing across the mask, Anaís's uniform, the weapons strapped to her person. "Definitely both."

Anaís rolled her eyes, though her companions couldn't see the gesture, and settled her gaze on Béhar, who regarded her with a contemplative frown. "Do you have anything to add, Captain?"

"Get in the carriage." He looked at each woman in turn, his serious demeanor sabotaged by the grin that he couldn't quite suppress. "We have history to make."

As the carriage rolled back onto the path toward their final destination, Anaís sent a quick glance out the window to ensure they hadn't left anything behind. Brief movement in the shadows of the trees caught her attention. Squinting, Anaís tried to stare deeper into the darkness. Heaviness lingered in the air, snuffing out the birdsong as if the forest itself struggled to inhale. Anticipation hummed under her skin, while a distinct warning tugged at the back of her mind.

Something was staring back.

In a heartbeat, air rushed into the lungs of the forest and the morning filled with birdsong as if nothing had happened. But it had, hadn't it?

Anaís shook her head and turned her attention toward the countryside around her, but she couldn't help the prickle of anxiety that ran through her. Something *was* there. But what?

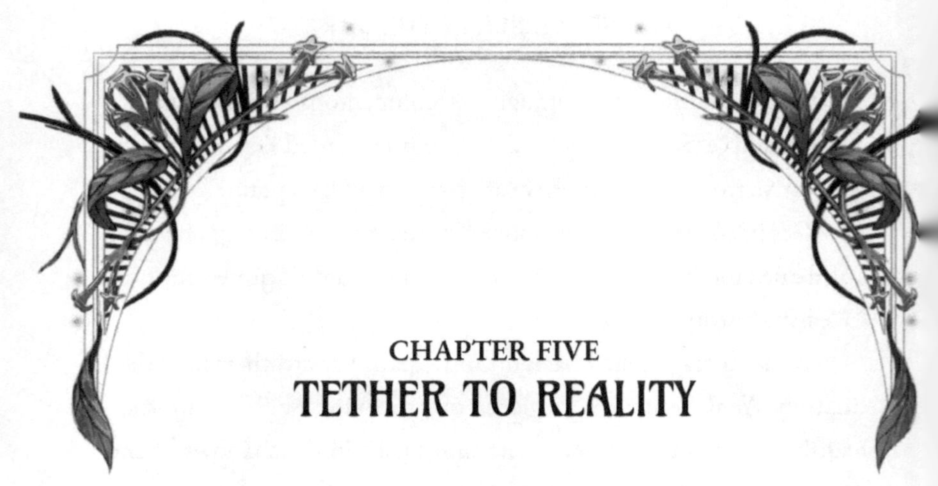

CHAPTER FIVE
TETHER TO REALITY

Eoghan Kavanaugh pushed a rasher of bacon around on his plate, cutting it into smaller and smaller pieces every few moments to keep up the proper appearance of breakfasting. He had risen early, as always, with the intention of spending a quiet morning in the palace gardens before attending to the day. Unfortunately, the queen had also risen early, as she *rarely* did, with the intention of trapping him in an endless monologue of lectures lest he forget his duties as Crown Prince. How could he, when it was the morning of what was, perhaps, the most important span of negotiations Nahonaugh had seen in recent history?

"It keeps the peace, it upholds the image, and people are happy." Queen Siofra leaned back in her chair and sipped her tea. "The Kingdom is *happy*."

"Of course, Your Majesty," Eoghan said absentmindedly, giving her a brief smile of encouragement to carry on, which she did. With gusto. All for the better, really—he had checked out of her tirade half an hour ago and had no desire to bring attention to his lack thereof.

Instead, he contented himself to nodding at appropriate intervals and discreetly watching the servants bustling about the formal dining room. Windows were polished until spotless, the curtains steamed to perfection, and the room adorned with tastefully overstated floral arrangements. The sweet yet earthy aroma perfuming the air had almost reached the point where Eoghan could pretend that he was, in fact, outside in the gardens. Fheile Earrach—the week-long festival celebrating the beginning of spring—was three weeks away, and the palace staff had gone above and beyond to ensure every room was staged to mesmerize Dúndíor's visiting diplomats. Though his presence, and that of the queen, did not interrupt their work, he could tell that it added an undercurrent of pressure to an already high-strung environment.

"More tea, Your Highness?"

Eoghan startled, looking from his neglected cup of unsweetened black tea to a new member of the service staff. The steward of the palace had hired as many helping hands as he could in preparation for the negotiations and the festival—all of whom needed to fit the steward's stringent standards. Eoghan could only guess that spurning his breakfast was not taken as a sign of a lack of appetite, but a lack of satisfaction with the meal before him.

"No, thank you." He took a sip of his tea and raised the cup in a subtle "cheers" before returning it to the saucer. "This is perfect."

Queen Siofra cleared her throat, dragging his attention back where it belonged. "These ideals of far-off lands, you've seen them demonstrated in war. Witnessed how they destroy. They're displayed plainly in the tainted minds of those you fight." She tapped a heavily jeweled finger to her temple before folding her hands in her lap once more. "These foreign writers you're so interested in—they don't know the tribulations of real life. Of blood. Of honor. All of what we do—what you *will* do—is for the happiness of Nahonaugh, so our citizens can live in peace."

"As your rule has always made it so," Eoghan acquiesced, "so then shall I."

And he did want peace between kingdoms. He did want his people to live in a world where their needs were met and their voices heard. Unfortunately, his concept of peace and that of the king and queen were not one and the same.

When he was a child, it hadn't taken Eoghan long to realize that with the right perspective, even a palace was nothing more than a gilded cage.

He did not remember his mother. The king had desperately needed an heir, then found himself with two—one legitimate, one not—and a dead mistress. According to rumor, she had passed months after Eoghan's birth. Complications, they'd said.

Eoghan glanced at the woman across from him. Somehow he didn't think so.

While his father had kept Eoghan in his favor—insisting he be raised in court and treated as a royal son—the queen ensured Eoghan remained far from the heir, far from political import, yet held tightly under her thumb. He'd once felt a sense of pride when he reflected on his adolescent years and of the countless times he'd tried to rebel and keep his mind, his only place of solace, as his own. His time studying at the university had been a breath of fresh air.

Then Mathúin died, and everything changed.

Rarely did Eoghan speak his mind now; it had been drilled into him time and time again not to, and as his attempts at autonomy tightened the already short leash of his freedom, he learned how to comply. *Speak how you ought, not how you want. Your people demand it of you. The future demands it of you. We demand it of you.*

Regardless of how he spoke—or not—he wasn't so sure it mattered anymore. In fact, his change of tune might have only made things worse, delaying the inevitable until the inevitable demanded to be heard. The only problem was that the inevitable, as he once believed, was not the queen. Or his father. No, the inevitable presented itself in the form of premonitions that stalked him in the light of day. Today, it plagued him in the form of an unfamiliar pressure that he couldn't quite explain.

The ambient clatter of the servants was a little too loud. The false sweetness in the queen's voice was a little too grating. A moment alone in the gardens would have helped. But now he was trapped. He could smile and nod and pretend to care, but he was only human. Whatever hunted him was decidedly *not*. Eoghan would break first, and he could not afford such a display here.

A cold caress brushed against his shoulder, then drew away. The breeze smelled of fresh morning air and dew-kissed grass. If it didn't break propriety, he would've hugged whoever had opened the window. Or give them a raise. Eoghan looked over his shoulder, only to find all the windows remained shut. Odd.

Turning to face the queen again, a strange movement caught his eye. Mist—or fog, he couldn't quite tell—swirled on invisible currents, blooming and growing the more intently he stared, as if it thrived on his attention. Could no one else see this?

The servants continued their work as if nothing was the matter, though they did so behind a veil of haze. Queen Siofra was still talking. Eoghan was still paying attention. But he wasn't paying attention. He was here. Where was here? Why was she acting like nothing was happening? Couldn't anyone—

Something cold billowed around his ankles and tore his gaze downward. Fog pooled around his feet before slowly twining up his legs. He shook his foot. *Stop.*

It swirled in the wake of his movement, coalesced, and continued upward. Breath caught in his lungs. *Stop.*

The fog hesitated before gently wrapping around his chest. The coolness of its presence seeped through his jacket. Seeped through his shirt. Sank into his skin. A shiver raced down his spine. His heart couldn't decide if it wanted to pound out of his chest or cease beating altogether.

"Stop." The word came out of his mouth in a terrified whisper.

The fog stilled. Then it dispersed, retreating to the corner of the room and taking the unfamiliar pressure with it. He tilted his head at the fog. It tilted its head back—if fog could have a head—regarding him as if *he* were the anomaly. He was, in a way. This was...not his realm.

Eoghan pressed a hand to his chest, breathing deeply until the thrum of his heart calmed to a reasonable pace. The chill of his skin where the fog had wrapped around him felt all the colder.

"Where am I?"

Silence stretched between them. He wasn't sure why he expected anything else.

"How do I get back?"

The fog seemed to bristle at that.

"Why am I here?"

The fog expanded, stretching across the wall into a swirling abyss that beckoned him to enter. To leave the palace behind, the queen's tirade behind, his *questions* behind. Because it had something to show him. It had *answers*.

Is this why I've been paranoid for months? he wanted to ask. *Have I finally gone mad?*

Eoghan didn't say any of that. Instead, he strode toward the fog, stopping as he toed the line between realms. Then he dipped his head. Closed his eyes. And let the fog consume him.

WHEN EOGHAN CAME TO, THE air tasted of fresh dirt and damp rock. A flame-blue glow licked at the darkness blanketing his surroundings, caressing the silhouette of jagged rock formations with unearthly light. He glanced about, his breath swirling around him as it condensed in the cool air. Lumps of gravel pressed into his side, and he braced his hands against the cave floor as he pushed himself to sitting.

There were no torches, yet he could see. Everything about this place felt heavy but not dark, like it was resting and he'd caught it having a good dream. *It's not real*, he told himself. A tickle brushed his skin as the fog wrapped around his hands, up his arms, taunting—no, *daring* him to recognize that this was real.

Eoghan clenched his fists, disturbing the fog with the movement, then stood. Speckles of light flickered across his vision and he blinked rapidly, trying to clear the lightheadedness that clouded his sight. Only he wasn't dizzy, and the lights didn't clear. He shook his head, feeling foolish, and tried to peer deeper into the cavern. Starlight appeared to dance along the walls in the distance, forming lazy ripples as it kissed the peaks and valleys of the stone. It was mesmerizing. Ethereal. Where he needed to go.

He took a step forward, then froze. No, that was decidedly *not* where he needed to go. He needed to return to the palace for the negotiations that were about to change everything.

Eoghan whirled on the fog, nearly slipping on the damp stone beneath his feet. "Take me back."

It looked at him smugly, then turned tail and drifted deeper into the cavern. The soft light in the distance bloomed like a tea flower in hot water as the fog drifted through it. Then the fog rounded a corner, the light settled back against the walls, and Eoghan was alone.

He took in a steadying breath. Released it in a stream of grumblings the queen would *not* have been pleased to hear. Then followed the light himself.

Strangely, the deeper Eoghan wound through the cave, the less his apprehension became, transforming into something akin to excitement. Like moth to flame he followed the light, gingerly stepping around rock formations and ducking under low-hanging stalactites. Eoghan pulled himself up a ledge before shuffling sideways through a crack, venturing farther into the belly of the earth. Time slipped away from him as he continued onward until finally, blessedly, the light bid him welcome.

An antechamber opened before Eoghan. A celestial glow illuminating the space and washing the cavern in a lilac hue, like soap bubbles before they popped. He turned in a slow circle, admiring the way the light rippled along every surface of the cavern. It was the most beautiful thing he had ever—

Eoghan sucked in a breath and stumbled forward, his feet carrying him of their own volition. That...*that* was the most beautiful thing he had ever seen.

A lake stretched out before him, its surface a placid mirror that diffused a glowing light emanating from its center. No, not any light—stars. Thousands and thousands of stars glittering and swirling within the depths of the waters, scattering shards of silver, amaranthine, and rose light about the space. The water itself was clear, gradually transforming into a rich navy blue as it plumbed the depths of the earth.

He wanted to run to it, dip his hands into it, but something kept him tethered in place. He was not afraid, he was...he was awestruck. Unworthy of being in the presence of something so magnificent. Yet he had a feeling this was only a small sliver of grandeur—a promise of what was to come. There was more he needed to learn first.

The fog returned to his side, inviting him into its midst. Eoghan stepped in readily.

He wished he hadn't.

Pain lanced his mind. It cut into his skin, his bones, his very soul. He wanted out. He wanted it to end. Death would have been a kinder fate, but death was not an option, and the fog had more to show.

A scream clawed its way out of his throat. Eoghan ground his teeth to stop the noise, and blood bloomed in its stead, filling his mouth with the tang of copper, a silent scream in its own right. He swallowed. Breathed in through his nose. And nearly gagged on the scent of decomposed flesh.

It's not real, he told himself. But there was no getting out. No going back. Only going through.

He would see what the fog wished him to see.

Eoghan pried his eyes open, and a blinding darkness greeted him—one that showed him nothing, yet filled his mind with tormented howls and gnashing teeth and eyes, unblinking eyes that watched. Waited. Ready to consume. He had never felt so empty. So alone. So hopeless in his pitiable twenty-seven years of existence.

They couldn't touch him—that one truth gnawed through the terror that gripped his mind and paralyzed him in place.

It's not real.

He couldn't feel the fog that nudged his skin to tell him otherwise. But it was there, in his mind, along with everything else.

This is real. This is real. This is real.

The ground shook beneath his feet, agitating the death and decay into a churning stench. He stumbled backward, tripping over unseen rocks. The earth groaned as fissures split the ground around him. A roar echoed from the depths as smoke darker than that of his guide rose from the bowels of the earth. There was no doubt in Eoghan's mind that if he inhaled it, he would die. He tried to gain his bearings to escape, but there was too much chaos, too much pain.

Light burst across his vision, burning everything in its wake. Burning through the darkness, the horrors. Burning *him*. His blood boiled, his skin melted, yet while everything was consumed and riddled to ash, he was...

Alive.

The clink of a teacup pulled him back to reality as the last wisps of fog disappeared into thin air. Eoghan took in a shuddering breath and wiped his clammy hands along his trousers before looking to the queen, who met his gaze as if nothing happened. She had merely returned the cup to its place on the meticulously painted porcelain saucer. He blinked. She carried on.

Eoghan nodded absentmindedly, but stopped when bile burned a trail up his throat. If he couldn't pay attention earlier, he certainly wouldn't be able to now. Whatever that had been, he never, *never* wanted to see it again. He was the crown prince, set to rise as king at the end of the harvest season, and here he was absolutely losing it.

During the day, he was plagued by a sense of foreboding. Now, apparently, it was turning into visions. It wasn't until sleep took him that he was able to truly escape. Find freedom.

The fact that his dreams were starting to take shape—were no longer mere impressions—he kept to himself. Eoghan wasn't sure what to make of it, and it felt too personal. No, *sacred*, to utter aloud. No one would have believed him anyway. Connections such as this only occurred in Tales of Old.

And so he was alone, yet not, for in dreams he could see the bond that connected him to his kindred soul. A finely woven thread of gold and emerald and brown. It was the one thing he could take into the land of the waking, a kaleidoscope of colors that brought him comfort whenever he saw them. The rich brown of soil after a rainstorm, the golden glow of a sunrise, emerald hues that breathed life into the forest. Each glimpse was a reminder that he had the power to choose. To fight. Even when it seemed as if all hope was lost. It was his tether to reality when reality seemed like a dream.

Eoghan squeezed his eyes shut. With premonitions chasing him and fog sending him into strange visions, one would think the magic that had disappeared long ago had reawakened just for him. Now more than ever, he needed that tether. Even if it came from the same source that plagued him.

"Eoghan?"

"Hmm?" His attention went to the queen across the breakfast table. Crumbs from her finished scone sat daintily on her plate. His breakfast, on the other hand, had barely been touched—mangled piece of bacon notwithstanding—and his tea had long gone cold. Eoghan took a sip anyway. If anything, he could use the caffeine.

"Have you been paying attention to anything I just said?"

Eoghan leaned forward, folding his hands on the table. "I—"

The rest of his sentence caught in his throat. A splotch of soot was smudged across his dark-brown skin. He quickly tucked his hands onto his lap instead. It was real. The lake. The beauty. The darkness. The pain. He rubbed his thumb against the back of his hand, watching in equal parts horror and fascination as the soot smudged farther.

"Eoghan!" Queen Siofra snapped.

He swallowed. Negotiations began today, and fog had just pulled him into another realm. He no longer had the luxury of behaving as he ought. He didn't *want* that luxury anymore. Above all, he didn't want to make policies founded upon sly machinations as the queen did or rule with complacency as his father did.

The iridescent flash of a hummingbird outside the bay window momentarily caught his attention, its feathers shifting from emerald green to metallic gold. Today would one day mark the start of a new chapter in the history books; his words, inked on the pages.

He had a voice. It was about time he used it.

Eoghan gave the queen a warm smile. "Of course. You were just mentioning the merits of mental manipulation to placate an entire kingdom in order to create a false sense of control while convincing the citizens to do your bidding as necessary."

Queen Siofra gaped at him.

Eoghan drank the last of his cold tea in one go. "If you'll excuse me, Your Majesty," he said as he lightly pushed his chair back and stood. Nausea from the remnants of the vision swirled in his stomach, but his mind seemed to clear when he stepped away from the table. "I have matters to attend to."

The hummingbird flew away as Eoghan left. His world was crumbling around him, but if he didn't think too hard about it, he could pretend the pieces were simply falling into place.

THE FRESH AIR OF THE gardens washed away the last of Eoghan's troubles, making room for the excited tension mounting in him at the prospect of negotiations. He was a bastard prince thrown into a role he was never meant to have. While he may not have been conditioned to be the perfect king since birth, he was no fool either. Nahonaugh and Dúndíor would find a middle ground, he was sure of it.

Sunlight crowned Mount Yeleidh to the east, painting the clouds over the lake with streaks of gold. The princess and her entourage wouldn't arrive for a while yet. In the meantime, he knew who he needed to find.

Cian was perched on a bench in the back gardens, nose buried in a stack of parchment. Eoghan and his childhood best friend turned royal advisor had been nearly inseparable since quite literally running into each other at Fheile Earrach as boys. Eoghan may have had a half-brother by blood, but Cian was the brother who mattered.

The sound of Eoghan's steps drew Cian's attention out of the documents, tension leaving his face when he saw who approached.

Standing, Cian dipped into a bow coated in mock formality. "Your Highness."

Eoghan copied the movement. "Royal Advisor."

"Someone's in a good mood," Cian laughed.

Eoghan shrugged. It was his favorite time of day, the initiation of a new beginning. With the imminent arrival of Princess Simone from Dúndíor, this day would herald many new beginnings. It was the first time in ten years a diplomat from either kingdom had entered the other's borders with the intent to actually *fix* anything. Eoghan expected tension; welcomed it, even. Tension was simply the growing pains that preluded change. In this case, he hoped it would usher in an era of peace between both kingdoms.

"It's a beautiful day filled with endless possibilities," Eoghan finally said. "And the negotiations start today."

Cian shook his head with an unamused huff. "Only you would be excited for negotiations with an enemy. At least they're only here for a handful of days. Not enough time for them to sink their claws in, but still."

"How could I not be excited? We have the chance to change the course of history. Don't give up on hope just because you don't see any."

"It's not that I don't see any, there is none. The people of Dúndíor are..." Cian trailed off, searching for the right word. "Barbaric. They take pleasure in slaughtering."

Eoghan tilted his head at his friend. "Have you ever been there?"

"You *know* very few have since the Battle of Ithansfar, and none have since the breach in the treaty." He shot Eoghan a pointed look. "But we won—"

"I believe that war ended in a mutual truce."

"It was a bloodbath, and we made it out with nothing but honor," Cian snapped. "They're the ones who breached the treaty, and now they have the gall to crawl back for peace?"

Eoghan frowned. The Battle of Ithansfar and the treaty that followed had happened before either of them were born, but they'd grown up with the stories. Relations hadn't become truly hostile until after the breach in the treaty ten years ago.

"Do you know what they call their special forces? *Anadali*. Protectors," Cian continued. "As if such an honorable word could atone for the violence they're capable of."

That piqued Eoghan's curiosity. He knew of Dúndíor's elite division of warriors. He had never stopped to think about what the word *anadali* meant—not as a title, but how it was derived from the culture of Dúndíor during the Anadali's founding long ago. Dúndíans had always been a warrior people, but their society was woven together by an indomitable spirit rooted in integrity. While he knew the Anadali were a force to be reckoned with, they weren't known for their brutality. Were they?

"I'm sorry, I didn't mean to upset you." Eoghan squeezed his friend's shoulder. "Today there will be no foreign special forces. No talk of bloodshed. It's time for a new era."

Cian gave a noncommittal grunt.

Eoghan wanted to give his friend a good shake, but refrained. Sometimes Cian needed to brood before seeing reason. Still, it didn't stop Eoghan from saying, "Not everything is so one-dimensional. We can use the lessons of the past to guide our steps toward the future, but we should never walk that path in fear. The sacrifice of those who fought can be honored while we bring forth a new day for those who still hope for tomorrow."

"You and your philosophizing," Cian grumbled, giving Eoghan's shoulder a shove. Though a smile threatened to brighten his stony countenance. "Sometimes I really hate you, you know."

Eoghan laughed. "Yet somehow I'm always right."

"Perhaps you should factor that into your consideration when you remember you're the one who asked me to be your royal advisor." Cian grinned, though it slipped from his face when he released a resigned sigh. "I just don't want you losing sight of what's important during these negotiations."

"What would be important, then?" Eoghan prodded.

"Forging a way toward peace—by *any* means necessary—that will benefit Nahonaugh. We don't know what awaits us."

"Cian, trust me. I know to not let my hope blind me. The threat of war on the horizon should these negotiations turn awry?" He sighed. "It's very real. Our people *need* the borders to open again. We have no ports to the north. Navigating the mountain passes to ship bulk cargo through Freydlan has caused more casualties than profit. We have many natural resources to offer, but Dúndíor has the keys to the sea. Nahonaugh has only thrived because of the resilience of her people, and yet her people suffer. I will not allow that to continue."

"I know. Just...making sure." Cian looked at the sky and frowned at the position of the sun. "I should get going. I'll be greeting the princess and her entourage."

"Right, well. I'll see you at the meetings then. I need to finish preparing."

Cian's frown deepened as he took in Eoghan's appearance. "Yeah, what did you do? You've got..." Cian rubbed the side of his own jaw.

Eoghan mimicked the movement, huffing a sigh through his nose when more soot appeared on his fingertips. "How terrible is it?"

"You look like you've taken on an apprenticeship as a chimney sweep," Cian deadpanned.

"Who's to say I didn't?" Eoghan retorted, waving his hand dismissively at Cian's rude gesture as they parted ways.

The queen hadn't seemed to notice the soot, so hopefully it wasn't quite *that* bad. Though the reminder of his vision left an uncomfortable feeling in the pit of his stomach. Maybe he could slip away in the evening to take his emotions out in the training arena, so long as the negotiations didn't fall apart first. If only one thing worked in his favor today, he hoped beyond hope that the negotiations would be it.

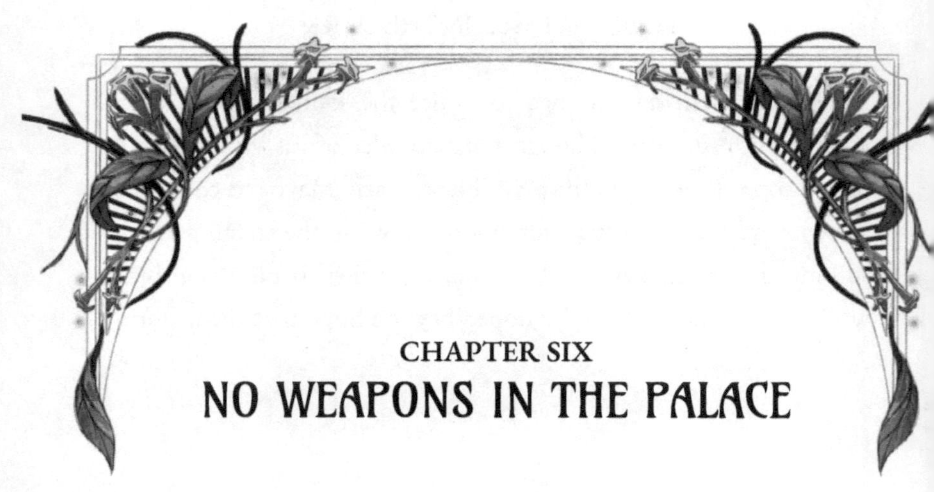

CHAPTER SIX

NO WEAPONS IN THE PALACE

ANAÍS DIDN'T THINK SHE EVER HAD, OR EVER WOULD again, see something as magical as the palace before her. For one, it was on an island, in the middle of a lake, surrounded by densely forested mountains as far as the eye could see. She had never seen so many different shades of green and blue together in one place—from the muted hues of the cloud-speckled sky to the rich, inky lake shimmering in the sunlight. Even the forest seemed to meld into itself to create a jeweled shade of green she never imagined possible.

The carriage jostled as it rolled onto the elegantly curved bridge that stretched from the mainland to the island. That was, she noted with a tinge of disappointment, the only way into and out of the palace grounds, something she would have to take into consideration when the time came to end the prince's life. Peeking her head out the window, she glanced over the railing and caught sight of the bridge's trussed design and the steep drop-off of the cliff. It would take some exploring now and improvisation later, but it didn't seem too difficult to scale across the beams without getting caught. She righted herself in her seat, startling as Simone cleared her throat next to her.

"Yes?"

"Care to share your observations with the class?" Simone asked.

"We're high up," Anaís said, then laughed at Simone's unamused expression. A bit of an engineering lesson wouldn't hurt, she supposed. "The bridge is over-engineered to make it look more impressive than it actually is."

Magdalina leaned forward. "How can you tell?"

"See those trusses?" Anaís pointed to the slanted beams that connected to the base of the overhang. "They're unnecessary. The force distribution carries across those ones there, and spreads evenly down the beam spanning the length of the bridge. They could have been left out completely, and the structural integrity of the bridge would have been exactly the same."

"Oh." Simone and Magdalina said in tandem.

Anaís could see Simone mulling over her words in her mind, trying to piece the bits of information together. She didn't know whether she should be relieved or afraid for her life when—Simone's eyes widened a fraction—there it was.

"You're analyzing the bridge to climb it, aren't you?" Simone hissed.

"I can neither confirm nor deny that accusation."

"Have you seen the drop?" she shrieked quietly.

Anaís gave a small shrug. "I've seen bigger."

That seemed to give Simone pause. She glanced out the window again before looking back at her sister as if she were seeing her for the first time. "Have you?"

Anaís turned her head forward, but she couldn't help the smirk that tugged at her lips.

"Stars above! You have, haven't you?"

"I'm Anadali Amadé, I've done many things." She glanced at her sister out of the corner of her eye. "You realize you're staring, right?"

Simone whipped her head forward and sat ramrod straight. "No I'm not! I guess..." she sighed, slumping down ever so slightly, "I never fully understood what it is that you do. I still don't pretend to but"—she glanced outside again—"I'm glad we're on the same side."

Magdalina nodded in assent, eyes wide as she looked between Anaís and the open window.

"If it makes you feel any better," Anaís said, "I have no idea how you two survive these diplomatic functions. Schmoozing is a skillset I've never managed to master."

Magdalina shrugged. "It's only conversation."

Anaís looked between the two women. "It's schmoozing."

Simone leveled Anaís with a smug grin. "Whatever you say, oh great Anadali, doer of many mysterious things."

"I'm going to regret saying that, aren't I," Anaís mumbled.

The carriage rattled as it rolled from the bridge onto the island, crunching along the compacted gravel path as they approached the palace. Rather than the warm stucco and artfully stained wood that made up her home, the palace of Nahonaugh towered above them in brilliant white, accents of pale blue and gold decorating the turrets that reached to the sky. The architectural display mirrored the surrounding mountains, though the palace did so with a refined elegance.

Expansive gardens surrounded the palace, stretching beyond Anaís's sight. To her desert-accustomed eyes, the water required to upkeep the gardens was a sumptuous display of wealth in and of itself. Though she supposed it was much easier to accomplish in Na-honaugh's wet climate. Their plants were quite dainty, too—she had the impression that if the sun shone too brightly, they would simply wither and die. Hopefully Nahonan royalty weren't as soft as the flowers they seemed to pride themselves in.

The carriage rolled to a stop. Anaís startled as Simone caught her hand, curiosity piquing when she reached across to take Magdalina's hand as well. Simone looked between the two of them, a fierce determination in her eyes, before giving their hands a reassuring squeeze and settling back into her seat once more. It wasn't quite the same as a fierce battle cry, but it garnered a similar effect. Anaís found herself sitting up straighter. The nerves that had unwittingly filled her stomach dispersed, replaced by the same calm focus she felt in the moments before a fight.

Gravel crunched as Béhar descended from the box and rounded the carriage. Then, without preamble, sunlight flooded the interior as he opened the door. Simone swept elegantly from the carriage, taking his proffered hand as she descended the steps. How she managed to execute such a movement without tripping over layers of tulle Anaís didn't know, but she was impressed nonetheless. Magdalina followed, her pale-blue silk gown shimmering in the sun.

Anaís left the carriage, and the ambient clatter of the courtyard plunged into silence. The approaching footmen stuttered to a halt. The guards shifted, clutching their weapons more tightly. Simone raised her chin at the silence before ascending the palace stairs, Magdalina following swiftly behind. Anaís and Béhar exchanged a glance before striding up the steps and falling into place behind the two women.

Strangely, the royal family was not present. Instead, two guards stood dutifully at attention on either side of the palace entrance while a third man waited for them in the center, looking almost bored. Freckles dotted his pale skin, which would no doubt darken his complexion as spring melted into summer. His vibrant, neatly coiffed ginger hair contrasted with the deep blue of his eyes, while the calculating sharpness of his face sat at odds with the relaxed slope of his lithe body. He was a man of opposites, yet it created a harmonious intensity that even Anaís had to admit was intimidating.

The only thing that broke the illusion of stately assuredness was his outfit—a dark-grey ensemble, complete with a gold-buttoned justacorps, which would have been incredibly boring if it weren't for the pleated white silk cravat around his neck. Anaís couldn't decide if she found it amusing or frightfully hideous.

Perhaps Nahonan men simply had poor taste in fashion.

His weight shifted evenly over both feet when they drew nearer, alertness and a tinge of respect coloring his otherwise indifferent posture. Simone stopped before him.

The redhead bowed deeply. "I am Lord Cian Ó Máille, Royal Advisor to His Highness Prince Eoghan Kavanaugh. I will be escorting you today. It is an honor to host you and your entourage, Your Highness." Cian spoke in Dúndían, his Nahraeg accent lilting through. "I must make you aware that King Ibhar has issued a decree that no unverified weapons are allowed on the grounds during these negotiations. I hope that doesn't pose a problem for you."

Simone dipped her head in acquiescence. "None at all, Lord Ó Máille. I come unarmed. Anadali, if you will?"

Cian stiffened as he faced Anaís, his eyes lingering on the mask-covered portion of her face. Though he composed himself quickly, the tension held in his jaw remained a permanent feature. It was clear he was not a fearful man, but a man to be feared. He would be one to watch.

Anaís stepped forward, unsheathing the two daggers secured in her belt in a swift motion and flipping them in her hand so the hilts faced Cian. He took them carefully and placed them on the silver tray carried by a member of the waitstaff who had appeared out of the palace not moments before. She pushed up her sleeves and removed the bracers hidden underneath, ensuring the throwing knives were tucked securely within before passing them to Cian. They joined the daggers on the tray. Her wrists felt oddly empty without the familiar caress of leather. She tugged her sleeves down and moved to step back, but a suspicious tilt of Cian's head kept her in place.

"Is that really all?"

At least they couldn't take her hands from her. "Weapons are not the only way to kill a man."

"Naturally." His voice was smooth yet cold. The rehearsed cordiality of his earlier greeting transformed into a biting threat. "Unfortunately, we can't have *any* unverified weapons in the palace." Though he stood still as stone, his eyes drank her in. "You are Anadali, are you not?"

Ah. She was the weapon, and he knew the weight of that title.

"She will be allowed inside." Simone chimed in, tilting her chin up at Cian.

"Of course," he replied. "We simply need to take some additional precautions in the meantime. We were unaware you would be bringing such heightened security."

"As you said, additional precautions. I can assure you she won't be a problem, Milord."

"I'm counting on it." He inclined his head toward Simone before returning his attention to Anaís. "Before we part ways, I must insist you wear this."

Cian retrieved a gem-encrusted bracelet from the waitstaff who, Anaís noticed, had taken the weapons tray inside and returned with the bracelet in its stead. She tilted her head at Cian as he came to a stop in front of her. He was a hair shorter, and it brought her immense satisfaction when she realized the slight tick of his jaw was due to the fact that he now had to look up at her.

"What is it?"

"A welcome gift. Your wrist, please." His sharp blue eyes stared defiantly into where her own would have been, had she not been wearing the mask.

Anaís held out her left hand, watching as Cian locked the bracelet around her wrist. A large gemstone slid over the mechanism, creating a seamless pattern around the cuff. It almost looked as if it were a part of her.

"How thoughtful." The words flowed sweetly out of her mouth, but they were delivered with venom. "I wouldn't like to ruin it when I bathe. How can I remove it?"

"There is no need. And I wouldn't try. You might not like the results." He dropped her wrist and looked at Simone, his expression softening into one of schooled neutrality. "We'd best be going, Your Highness"—Cian looked to Magdalina—"my lady..." He trailed off.

Magdalina executed a perfectly shallow curtsy. "Lady Magdalina."

"Charmed," Cian replied smoothly. "If you would follow me, I will show you to the reception room so you can relax before the meetings begin."

"Milord." Béhar rested his hand casually on the pommel of his sword. "I must guard Her Highness at all times. If I am to respect the wishes of your king, I must comply with his decree before we can follow you anywhere."

Cian waved his hand good-naturedly. "We were informed well in advance by King Timun that you would be joining us. Your position and the weapon you carry have already been verified. Unfortunately," he continued, his voice taking on a harsh edge as he faced Anaís, "you have yet to be processed. You will wait here."

His ability to change demeanor so quickly was going to give Anaís whiplash. "It's not a problem," she said simply. Better to comply now and find leverage elsewhere.

Cian responded with a terse nod, then turned to the others and gestured toward the entrance of the palace. "Shall we?"

Simone took Cian's proffered arm and he guided her inside, Magdalina and Béhar following closely behind.

"Can she really see with that mask on?" Cian asked as they disappeared into the foyer.

"So full of questions," Simone tittered, before she composed herself and whispered loudly enough for Anaís to overhear, "You would be surprised of a lot of things she can do."

It was said in jest, but the threat was palpable. A strange mixture of gratitude and pride swelled in Anaís. While she hated watching her sister enter enemy territory without her, this was well and truly Simone's arena. How she managed to remain remotely civilized with that condescending toad, Anaís could never understand. Thankfully, she didn't need to. There were other matters to attend to.

Clearing her throat, Anaís schooled her expression and redirected her attention toward the guards. She and Simone had agreed to mask her identity, but she hadn't planned on being barred entry to the palace. Anaís glanced around, checking the shadows for prying eyes. Or, in this case, ears—following the Battle of Ithansfar, few bothered learning the language of their neighboring kingdom fluently. Though perhaps as Anadali, any eavesdroppers would assume her fluency was a given.

The fluttering of a curtain and flash of shadow on the second story drew her attention upward, but the lack of movement that followed eased her concerns.

She gave a slight nod to each of the guards before saying in Nahraeg, "I'm going to perform my job and verify the safety of Princess Simone's room. Are you going to make this complicated, or will you let me through?"

They looked blankly ahead.

"Right. I'm just going to..." She took a step toward the entrance, but halted mid-stride when the guards swiftly crossed their staffs to block her path.

"No weapons are allowed in the palace."

Technically no weapons were allowed on the grounds either, yet here she stood. Her fingers twitched at her sides, and she clasped her hands behind her back to quell her rising temper. Fighting a palace guard within minutes of arriving wouldn't be the best for diplomacy. But what else was she supposed to do? Stand there like a fool and stare them down in a passive-aggressive game of "don't blink?" Not that they could even *see* her eyes through the mask. She doubted they would take kindly to her leaving to roam the grounds alone.

The faint crunching of footsteps sounded behind her, slowly growing louder as the mysterious intruder approached. Anaís took in a breath, letting it out for a count of five before glancing over her shoulder. A woman in uniform strode down the pathway toward the palace, the severe expression she wore at odds with her otherwise youthful countenance.

"Fionn, Tynan, she's with me," the woman called.

The guards immediately stood down, bowing their heads and bringing a fist to their chest in a respectful salute. The woman dipped her chin in acknowledgement before looking at Anaís. A strange mixture of curiosity and hatred swirled across her features, but it disappeared as soon as she spoke.

"I am Captain Riona of the Queen's Guard," she said in Dúndían. "It is an honor to meet a member of the Anadali." She bowed.

Anaís's eyes widened at the fact that the captain of the Queen's Guard could speak her mother tongue. Perhaps Dúndíor was the only kingdom foolish enough to cut itself so completely off from the rest of the continent. "Thank you, Captain. The honor is mine."

"Follow me, if you please."

Anaís looked at the open doors Riona had disappeared through, then at the guards who looked as if they had just eaten a handful of sour ælorberries.

"Gentlemen." She nodded at them when she walked past. This time, unhindered.

IF THE PALACE'S EXTERIOR WAS extravagant, Anaís wasn't sure how to appropriately describe the interior. She had a mind to call it gaudy and overdone and leave it at that, yet as she followed Riona through the halls of the palace, those words would have been a horrible reduction of the craftsmanship infused into each detail.

Intricately crafted crystal chandeliers at least twice her height in diameter hung at intervals down the corridor—high enough to illuminate both the ground floor and the open-air corridors on the upper levels, and low enough to be lit with minimal peril to the servants tasked with their upkeep. They were currently unlit, but with the way the late-morning sun streamed into the palace, they wouldn't likely be used until evening came and the heavy velvet curtains were drawn for privacy.

Delicate bas-relief sculptures of native flora adorned the cream walls, which rose so high that Anaís needed to crane her head back to fully take in the ceiling. She refrained, wanting to maintain some semblance of dignity, but her quick glances upward revealed the attention to detail didn't stop when it was inconvenient for the onlooker.

Anaís lowered her gaze to the imperial staircase at the end of the hallway. It too was ornately decorated, with gilded columns flanking the entrance and supporting the upper levels, while a sweeping balustrade that looked to be carved from a singular piece of wood followed the curve of the staircase to create an organically airy railing. Even the intricate inlay of the wooden floor was replicated on a smaller scale on each of the treads.

Anaís itched to get a closer look as they approached, but rather than going up the staircase Riona turned to lead them down a maze of hallways, through an arched door, and up a winding set of well-used stairs. It wasn't any less ornate, but the smaller space and Riona's voice pulled her out of her silent reverie.

"If you are cleared, you will be given a tour and allowed to use the main staircase."

"Thank you."

A stilted silence hung between them as Anaís mulled over the unsaid implications of Riona's statement, and of the reception she had received upon entering the palace grounds. Anaís knew herself, and she knew who they thought she was. They were right to be afraid, but she didn't want that to hinder any progress Simone might make.

"Will my presence pose a problem for the negotiations?"

Riona's lack of response was answer enough.

"I understand I am not allowed inside the palace for the time being," Anaís continued, "but I cannot reasonably be asked to leave the grounds while Her Highness remains."

"Excuse my forwardness, but you do realize you are a security threat. Do you not?"

"I did not realize *one* Anadali would cause such worry to those in a palace filled with guards. I am relieved it is only I who came and not Her Highness's standard entourage. This should save you much time on your...security clearance."

Riona abruptly stopped and looked over her shoulder, lips pressed together in a thin line. "While waiting for entry, you may walk the palace grounds. However, you may not go to the southern sector, the western sector, or the—"

"Perhaps it would be more prudent," Anaís interrupted, "if you told me where I *can* go."

"You may stay in the northeast sector. Do not bother anyone. Report back to the main entrance at sundown."

"Am I to be supervised?"

Riona glanced at Anaís's wrist. "You are not allowed inside—this being the sole exception—until you are cleared. Supervision will be reassessed at such a time."

"Understood." Anaís did not understand. In fact, she found the policy overkill and, frankly, asinine. But, when in Nahonaugh... Or so the saying went.

CHAPTER SEVEN

THE TREECARVER

Sending an Anadali without properly notifying an enemy kingdom was perhaps the dumbest decision Anaís's father had made in recent history. Clearly, he had not taken Nahonan bureaucracy into account when planning for her to gather information regarding the legends of Takaniim or the man she was meant to assassinate. After five hours of infinite iterations of the same question—"Why are you here?"—in almost every language on the continent, Anaís was released from captivity. As per the conversation she and Riona had in the stairwell, she was begrudgingly sent to the back gardens to wait until a final decision was made. Not an ideal location to accomplish either of her tasks. Given the pace with which her case was being processed, she doubted she would be cleared until it was time to return to Dúndíor.

Regardless, her current predicament was too great an opportunity to squander. She was outside. *Alone.*

Anaís frowned at the cuff around her wrist. It was as beautiful as it was annoying. The polished silver shone brightly against her warm brown skin, and the multitude of tourmalines and diamonds encrusted on the bracelet sent shards of colored light dancing across her face as she rotated her wrist in the late afternoon sun. The location of the clasp had completely disappeared into the jeweled motif; the only indication it could come apart at all was the marquise-cut tourmaline at the center of the design that covered the locking mechanism. She vaguely remembered her tutor teaching her about the electromechanical properties of various gems and minerals. Something about piezoelectricity and diamond-based resonators.

Welcome gift. Sure. If you consider tracking to be a gesture of goodwill and trust.

Still, she would have done the same in their place. Anaís had no doubt they were able to tell where she was, but she also had no doubt they were expecting certain behaviors from her. If she sat still, it would draw suspicion. What foreign enemy wouldn't do some reconnaissance when handed the opportunity? Dropping her hand to her side, Anaís looked around the gardens and selected a meandering path that disappeared into the trees, leading north.

Moss cushioned her feet as she walked beneath the canopy of trees. She almost felt bad for treading on the delicate plant with her sturdy leather boots, but when she turned around to look at the moss she had walked upon, the imprint of her footstep was gone. She frowned, her attention dropping to her boots and the moss on which she stood. Cautiously, she lifted a foot and glanced at the plant beneath. The small leaves immediately began uncurling, stretching skyward as if filling their lungs with air now that the weight of her boot had been released. Her eyes grew wide in wonder at the sight. Gently, she placed her foot down a pace ahead and lifted her other boot, turning her head so she could watch the moss stretch its fronds once again.

She continued down the path, slower this time, taking in the beauty of the lush nature around her. Small white flowers grew amongst the moss, reminding her of spring's version of snow—fresh, pure, and beautiful. Light filtered through the leaves overhead, softening the early evening sun into a dappled glow. Somewhere far off to her right she heard muffled, rhythmic tapping—similar to the sound a treecarver made as it tapped at the bark of trees with its beak. Maybe they had a similar bird in Nahonaugh?

Anaís paused. The rational part of her mind urged her to continue scouting the property, her feet itching with the need to move forward so she could account for all possible scenarios—both good and bad—that could arise the night of the assassination.

Yet her curiosity, the part of her awakened by unfurling moss, whispered to her through the breeze that drifted amongst the canopy of knotted branches above her head. She looked down the light-dappled path, then into the welcoming safety of the forest.

Technically, this *was* scouting...

Cool darkness surrounded her as she disappeared into the trees. While the mossy path acted as her guide toward a predetermined fate, it felt as if some innate compass carried Anaís over roots and boulders, past dainty bluebells and curling ferns, and beneath swaying branches of aspen and beech as she wound her way through the forest.

Her fingertips skimmed along the bark of a sturdy pine as she rounded its trunk and hoisted herself onto one of the lower branches to catch her bearings. The wood was rough and slightly damp against her skin, as if the morning dew had retreated into its woodland home before the warmth of the sun could chase it away.

Closing her eyes, the song of the forest faded away as her ears attuned to the rhythmic *pap-pap-pap* of the treecarver. Her lips quirked up. The bird must be very persistent. Anaís jumped off the branch and readjusted her course to head northwest toward the back of the island.

Rounding a boulder embedded in the slope of the hill, she emerged on the other side to find a pathway much like the one she had left moments ago. This time, instead of a mossy trail covered by a canopy of trees, the forest parted to make room for a stone pathway that led to an ornately carved arch before wrapping around the cliff and disappearing into the unknown. Glittering flashes of the sun dancing across the lake peeked through the foliage, beckoning her forward.

Anaís stepped through the stone archway and made her way lightly down the steps on the other side. The sound became louder and more distinct as she went. It almost sounded like...training day when she taught the Anadali new forms, fists pounding against sandbags before she allowed them to practice on each other. Anaís furrowed her brow and crept down the flagstone pathway. She rounded the corner, and the sight before her froze her in place.

Another short set of steps lead to a grassy training field overlooking the lake and mountains that surrounded it, and in the middle of the training field was her target.

Prince Eoghan.

His brow was drawn in concentration as he moved with the bag hanging before him. Each step was artfully placed, each strike met its target with deadly precision. He was about a handsbreadth taller than her—unusually tall by Nahonan standards—and filled his space with a subtle, assured confidence that drew her in. His rich mahogany skin glowed under a sheen of sweat, muscles rippling as he moved through the ebb and flow of his forms. While she had seen countless warriors go through countless forms, never before had she seen someone filled with so much raw power move with such refined grace. It was mesmerizing.

Anaís shook her head, snapping herself out of the thoughts she'd momentarily lost herself in. She had seen plenty of other men fight; he was no different. Though she couldn't deny there was something familiar about his presence. Anaís briefly considered going back the way she came and exploring the other path farther. Despite her tracker, it would not be wise to be caught wandering such a private sector of the grounds alone, least of all by—

"Enjoying the view?" Prince Eoghan asked in Dúndían.

Eyes wide with horror, Anaís looked in the direction of the prince, who had stopped training and now regarded her with a curious tilt of his head. Thank the stars she had elected to wear her mask. Staring like an idiot wasn't the best look for a trained warrior.

Anaís composed herself and took the last few steps down to the training field, stopping near the edge of the cliff. "The palace is situated at a rather nice vantage point over the lake."

She knew it wasn't what he meant, but she needed to deflect, and she had to admit—the scenery was stunning. Fog rolled down the mountains and pooled over the lake, softening the rich blue water into a hazy lilac grey. Lush green trees lined the mountains as far as the eye could see. If she lived in a place such as this, she would never be stressed another day in her life. She loved Dúndíor, but the desert climate could never compare to a place as vibrant as this.

Eoghan tugged a navy-blue tunic over his head and crossed the arena toward Anaís, stopping a few paces away. She eyed him carefully. They had never met, but she knew very well who he was. She wasn't sure if she wanted him to know that or not.

"I apologize if this is forward but, who are you?" Anaís asked, deciding to play ignorant to see how he would react.

"Eoghan Kavanaugh, at your service," he replied with a slight bow.

Anaís replied with a bow of her own. "My apologies, Your Highness. I did not know."

"Quite all right. I have a 'no formalities during training' rule. Though, I must apologize for my forwardness as well. I heard news of your arrival but don't remember seeing you with Princess Simone during the meetings today. Is all well?" Unlike everyone she had interacted with thus far, his question was not posed as a pleasantry laced with malicious intent. Instead, his words held a gentle concern, his true question hiding within his gaze. *Who are you truly?*

He could never know. Instead, Anaís lifted her wrist with the bracelet attached. "Your king has a 'no foreign weapons in the palace' policy."

His brows rose in surprise. She couldn't tell if it was because of his father's decree, or because she had actually obeyed. "And so you left Her Highness?"

"Under the protection of a Dúndían Royal Guard," Anaís retorted. "Her Highness is neither a damsel nor is she in distress. Unless you intend for these peace talks to be less than peaceful." She tilted her head at him in challenge.

Eoghan looked to the sky and sighed. "They're giving you a room to sleep in at least, are they not?"

"I thought camping sounded rather nice," Anaís said, gesturing to the forest at the edge of the training field.

He mumbled a curse under his breath. "I'll see that your accommodations are sorted, then. I do apologize for the reception you've received." He opened his mouth as if to say something more, then closed it. Dipping his head in another small bow he said, "It was lovely meeting you."

Turning, Eoghan made his way back to the training bag and raised his arms to strike. It was a clear dismissal, though a kind one. Stars knew she savored the peace that accompanied training alone; she could not deny him that. Yet her feet remained planted on the field as if captivated by the melody his fists beat against the bag.

Eoghan glanced at her and paused, the hint of a smirk playing on his lips. "Would you like to train together?"

Anaís looked down to hide the heat flooding her cheeks, only to realize her feet were already in a fighting stance. She hadn't even felt herself mimic him. Traitorous body.

"I assume your journey has left you a bit restless," Eoghan said, drawing her attention back to him.

Fine then. Two could play at this game. "And reveal my secrets to you? Not a chance."

"Yet you took secrets from me not moments ago."

"I took nothing that wasn't given to me first," Anaís shrugged.

He leaned against the training bag with far too much confidence. "What's your least favorite skill?"

Anaís crossed her arms while she considered his question. The breeze off the lake tickled her skin. There weren't many weapons or forms of combat that she wasn't well versed in, and yet...

"I can't say I enjoy archery," she admitted.

"Then you're in good company. We can improve a derelict skill and be mutually miserable in the process."

"Sounds splendid." Why did curiosity have to take her this way?

"Unless you have somewhere more exciting to be?"

At the end of the day, did it really matter? In three weeks' time he would be dead by her hand. That thought struck her harder now that they were face to face.

"It'll be fun." He held out a bow to her.

Anaís sighed. Before she knew the thought had formed, the words had already left her lips. "Sure, why not?"

Eoghan tossed up his hands as yet another one of her arrows pierced the center of the target. "I thought you said you were terrible at this!"

Anaís quirked her brow at him, which she belatedly realized he couldn't see when he carried on.

"Positively rubbish!" Eoghan cried dramatically. "Outlandishly untalented!"

"I believe the term was 'do not enjoy.'"

"Well, your humor should improve when you see how atrocious I am at this," he muttered as he nocked the arrow.

He inhaled and pulled back, slowly releasing a stream of breath. Anaís could almost feel the moment of stillness relax into the atmosphere when his body became one with the bow. The hollow *twang* of the bowstring reverberated through the air as the arrow flew across the field and sank into the target a few inches away from her own arrow.

She gave him a sidelong glance. "Hideous. I need to wash my eyes out with soap."

Footsteps drew their attention to a familiar man walking down the flagstone path behind them. Eoghan waved, but Anaís felt her stomach plummet to her boots—any ounce of levity she had felt was swept away at the sight of the *toad* walking toward them.

The easy smile on Cian's face fell into one of forced pleasantry as Anaís strode to Eoghan's side. The lord was a nuisance, but that didn't mean she was going to stand down. Besides, if she was going to assassinate the prince, she needed to know who might try to get in her way.

"Fraternizing with the enemy?" Cian didn't shout, but his voice carried across the field nonetheless.

Eoghan huffed out a sigh. Cian's prickly behavior must have been a common occurrence. In fact, if she had to hazard a guess, Cian was the staunch traditionalist to Eoghan's less-than-traditional diplomatic methods.

"We're not trying to make enemies this week, Cian. This is part of the negotiations. Diplomacy. Exchanging tactics, as it were."

"He's fraternizing," Anaís deadpanned. She couldn't help herself. There was something about this place, about Eoghan, that made her want to rewrite the future. It was a treacherous thought—one she could die for—but in this time between the king's orders and the night her blade fell, could she not enjoy her first taste of freedom in over a decade?

What if Eoghan wasn't the enemy?

The question came unbidden to her mind, but what could Anaís truly do? If she went against her king, she would die. History had proven it.

Guilt gnawed at her when Eoghan laughed at something Cian said. Sighing, she shook her head and made her way to the side of the training field to put the bow away, but not without glancing over her shoulder and catching the subtle shift in Cian's demeanor now that she was farther away. He seemed softer, more human. Perhaps his prickly personality was only for those he didn't know. That, she could understand.

Cian glanced around Eoghan's shoulder and frowned. "Where are you going?"

"To put the bow away?"

His eyes narrowed as he stared at her a beat too long, but he seemed to come to some sort of decision as he turned his attention to Eoghan. "Dinner preparations are nearly finished. You should return to the palace."

Anaís turned, trying to see whatever Cian had seen while keeping an ear on their conversation.

"I suspected you didn't come down here to join us," Eoghan replied.

The fast-waning sunlight cast shadows from the upper part of the island across the training arena, deepening at the edge where the field met the forest.

"An astute observation," Cian retorted.

There wasn't anything unusual she could see, and she didn't have the feeling she was being watched. Excluding the attention lingering at her back.

"I'll see you at dinner, then?" Eoghan called to her.

Anaís looked over her shoulder and inclined her head politely. "If you so wish, Your Highness."

"I do."

"Then it is done."

Cian huffed a sigh and gestured to the bow in her hand. "It's not going to put itself away."

"An astute observation, Milord," she said as she turned and made her way to the weapons storage, Eoghan's rich laugh lightening her heart while sending regret stabbing into her chest.

There was a reason she avoided meeting her targets before killing them.

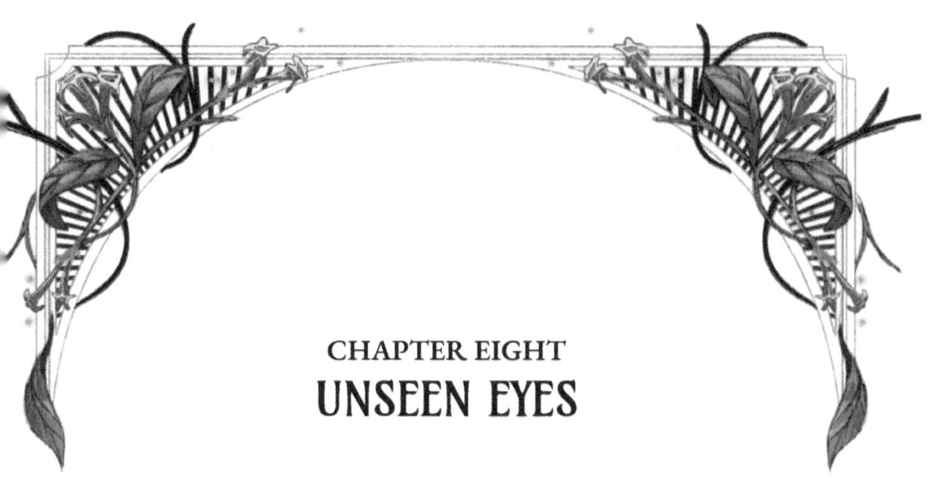

CHAPTER EIGHT
UNSEEN EYES

Eoghan cast a quick glance at Cian as they turned down another corridor toward the residential wing, the echo of their footsteps breaking the eerie silence. Long shadows crept down the hallway, darkening alcoves and seeping the day's heat from the walls. The final rays of the setting sun reflected off the polished wooden floors and transformed the once-invisible dust into drifting embers.

Cian had been on edge all day—more than usual, anyway—and even with the unexpected arrival of the Anadali, Eoghan had a suspicion there was something more. Cian had a tendency to approach life with a certain intensity Eoghan understood deeply, having more or less grown up with him. He also knew that Cian never told him the full story of what had made him study politics at the university rather than take a merchant apprenticeship near home—something Cian's father had dearly hoped for.

Sometimes Eoghan thought he saw glimpses of Cian's past, the quick glances thrown over his shoulder as if he was looking out for a ghost, the rigid front he put on for everyone regardless of which duties he performed. Even when the two of them were alone, the tension Cian held in his jaw and the way his eyes flitted to the shadows remained a permanent feature, as if he existed in two places at once.

Whether it was paranoia, habit, or something deeper, Eoghan couldn't be sure, but these talks were doing more than forging an alliance of peace.

They were digging up something Cian wanted to leave buried.

As much as Eoghan wished he could take away that burden, Cian did *not* like to be coddled. Neither did Eoghan. They'd decided a long time ago that in a royal court filled with pleasantries and dancing between the lines of all that was said and all that was not, blunt honesty between them was an unbreakable rule.

"I don't like her." Cian's voice echoed in the empty hallway, startling Eoghan out of his thoughts.

He cast another glance at his friend. Hopefully blunt honesty would serve him well today. "You kicked her out of the palace and threw a tracker on her. You don't like her because she doesn't like you."

"When I met her this morning, she threatened to kill a man," Cian snapped.

"Were those her exact words?"

"No, but—"

"Cian." Eoghan strode in front of his friend and walked backward, forcing Cian to stop and make eye contact with him. "No one is dying. No one is plotting anything. Why are you making enemies of potential allies?"

Cian glanced at something behind Eoghan's shoulder before meeting his gaze with defiance. "Why are you making allies of our enemies?"

"What is this really about?"

The look on Cian's face softened slightly, but the tension coiled in his posture only seemed to wind tighter. "I'm worried about you."

Eoghan opened his mouth to make a retort but it died as Cian raised a hand to silence him.

"As your royal advisor, it's my job. As your friend, it's my duty." He glanced at something behind Eoghan again before speaking lowly in Freydlensku. "And something within the shadows seems to be moving."

Eoghan would have laughed at his friend if he himself hadn't been sucked into another realm less than twelve hours ago. Cian raised a brow at Eoghan's silence.

"I don't see it wise to turn and gawk when shadows have eyes that think themselves unseen. I trust your judgment," Eoghan clarified in the same tongue.

Though the language native to Freydlan wasn't widely known in Nahonaugh, Eoghan wasn't sure how effective it would be at dissuading shadows from eavesdropping. Turning his head slightly, Eoghan used the reflection of the window to catch a glimpse of whatever hid behind him. Murky darkness that swallowed everything in its vicinity stared back, mocking him. He didn't put it past Cian to be able to see things he couldn't, and he *hated* the feeling. Never before had he felt so thoroughly exposed.

A shiver crawled down his spine. Being sucked into a vision would be preferable to this.

Eoghan tilted his chin toward a door leading to a parlor. Cian raised his brow and Eoghan tipped his chin again, this time with more force. Cian glanced into the shadows, his frown deepening as he saw—or failed to see—whatever was there before turning on his heel and stalking into the room.

The lock clicked shut. Eoghan took in a breath. Cian cut him off with a sharp look and an entirely unhelpful "Not yet."

It wasn't like Eoghan would *speak* before the room was secured, but he had to smile at his friend's caution. He settled onto the arm of an overstuffed chair, watching while Cian made his way methodologically through the space, checking shadowed corners, drawers, cabinets, shelves, and furniture with equal intensity. By the time he finished, Eoghan almost felt bad for the harsh fluffing the seat cushions had been subjected to.

Cian stepped in front of him, arms crossed as he gave Eoghan one of the most uncomfortable stare-downs he'd ever had the displeasure of receiving.

"Why did you get so close to her?" Cian pressed, though he kept his voice barely above a whisper.

"I haven't been getting any closer to her than anyone else." Eoghan shifted in his seat. "You may call it fraternizing with the enemy, I call it digging for ulterior motives. We're having negotiations with Princess Simone, yes?"

Cian raised his brow as if he was following Eoghan's train of thought but couldn't see where he was going. When he offered no comment, Eoghan continued, "There are always two sides to a coin. This Anadali is the side the princess wants to keep hidden. Why did they send her instead of more members of the Guard? What does it mean to be Anadali? Our borders have been closed for so long that we're missing key aspects about their culture, their people, their military tactics. Spies can only tell us so much, but this Anadali is *here*.

I can't understand these nuances if I push her away. It would be wise for you to follow my example."

Cian nodded, but a skeptical frown hampered his assent. Eoghan could almost see Cian's mind meticulously weighing his rationale in search for a flaw in his logic. It was times like these that the way they could read each other like open books frustrated Eoghan to no end.

Cian finally spoke. "So you're keeping a close eye on her?"

"In a manner of speaking."

"Through thinly veiled hospitality."

"Genuine hospitality," Eoghan huffed. "We need a treaty that lays the groundwork for real, lasting peace. I can't achieve that by hard-lining negotiations. We have to understand who they are as a people—in *all* aspects—so we can strike a fair balance that will prevent anyone from getting desperate enough to break the treaty *again*."

"Logical," Cian mumbled, more to himself than to any argument Eoghan had made. His gaze drifted to a painting on the far wall as if weighing whatever he wanted to say next. Finally, he asked, "Are you sure that's all?"

A memory of the fog billowed in Eoghan's mind, chilling him from the inside out. With a day's worth of time acting as a buffer, he could finally recognize that it was a beautifully horrifying experience. One that had irrevocably changed him. *No, it's not all,* Eoghan thought. But how could he explain it? He owed it to Cian to at least try.

"I had a...vision of sorts," Eoghan admitted.

An unreadable look flashed across Cian's face and he took a step back, slowly lowering himself to sit on the sofa behind him. Silence stretched between them. Eoghan itched to break it.

But then in a whisper, Cian spoke. "I told you that something within the shadows was moving. It has been happening for weeks now, but today the shadows stilled. They were watching you and the Anadali, as if waiting for something to happen. Was that"—Cian swallowed thickly—"was that the vision? Was it connected? She's the only thing that's changed..."

A strangled laugh escaped Eoghan. Mysterious fog dragging him into new realms *and* shadow creatures watching him in this one. All in one day. Lovely. Just what he needed.

"No—" Eoghan's voice caught and he cleared his throat. "No, I don't think so. During the day I feel these...premonitions. I thought they were nothing noteworthy, brushed them off as paranoia. But this morning, I..." He ran a hand through his hair and slid into the seat of the armchair. This was the part of the story where Cian would think him insane. "I had a glimpse. A darkness is coming, awakening from the deep. Perhaps it was never asleep at all."

He let out a breath and met his friend's eyes. Rather than the judgment he feared, Cian's features had settled into something akin to understanding. Perhaps they were all mad here.

Tension melted away from Cian's posture, replaced by a resignation Eoghan hadn't seen since they were boys. "There *is* something happening. And it's spreading, I fear," Cian finally said. "You're right, about the treaty. We cannot risk a conflict on two fronts. I apologize for the way my behavior has hindered progress." He scrubbed a weary hand down his face. "This vision, does anyone else know?"

"No." Eoghan shook his head.

Cian looked toward the door as if he could see through it. "I might have an idea," he muttered, before shaking his head and smacking his legs to stand up. "Right, we don't want to be late for dinner. And you take ages to prepare, so—" Cian made a shooing motion toward the door.

Eoghan fixed his friend with a glare. "Right, and you can't leave me with that statement and nothing to follow it up with."

Cian's silence was louder than any response he could have given. Eoghan sighed. "I'm not going to like this idea, am I?"

"I'm afraid neither of us will."

Eoghan shook his head and stood. "All right, I trust you. Just let me know, yeah?"

"Always do," Cian said before unlocking the door and stepping into the hallway, Eoghan following behind. Though the chandeliers above now lit their way, the palace felt darker than ever before.

CHAPTER NINE
THE TEA INCIDENT

SILVERWARE TINKLED AGAINST PORCELAIN DISHES, A joyous sound that almost succeeded in covering the stilted murmur of conversation that filled the formal dining room. It would no doubt take longer than an afternoon to smooth over relations that had been cold for a decade, but—Eoghan noted with hopeful satisfaction—this was progress. Or at least the semblance of it.

Princess Simone laughed at something that Lochlan, Eoghan's cousin, said from across the table. Cian stiffened at the burst of sound, then relaxed. The Anadali sat passively through it all, her half-mask glinting dangerously in the candlelight as she took dainty bites of roast venison. She had not yet touched her goblet of wine, and the server hovering in the back corner shifted nervously on his feet as he stared at it, an indecisive dance between wanting to remedy her beverage situation and fear of losing a limb if he did so.

Eoghan caught the server's eye, then subtly tapped his teacup and tilted his chin toward the Anadali. "Fetch her some, please," he wanted to say. The server blanched, nodded once, and scurried away.

Queen Siofra's hand brushed Eoghan's arm, and he turned toward her. Displeasure radiated from the queen, souring the air and stifling his lungs.

"Just because you're a bastard doesn't mean you ought to give the wench preferential treatment." The queen's gaze flicked from the Anadali to Eoghan, then she smiled sweetly and returned to her meal.

Eoghan's heart stuttered, a violent wave of frustration flowing through his veins. He'd had an abundance of patience to spare this morning, but after all that had transpired today, it was decidedly empty. He took in a calming breath regardless.

"Did you know she was coming?" Eoghan asked softly. "You have been in contact with King Timun; you should have known who was in the princess's retinue. Or have we simply descended from courtly pleasantries into barbarism? Not granting access to—"

"Enough, Eoghan," King Ibhar snapped quietly, meeting his son's gaze over the top of Queen Siofra's head before looking forward so as to not draw attention. "King Timun was abundantly clear that he was only sending his best, with a retinue small enough to not add undue tension. You know how the mixing of courtiers can be. What we did not know was that he would be sending an *Anadali* with them." He spat the title like a curse. "We adapted as we saw fit. They are lucky we are even continuing with the negotiations at all with an affront like this."

Eoghan nodded slowly. It was not what he would have done, but it did not seem wise to press the issue. Not with so many present. Not with the king and queen's current mood.

"And Eoghan," his father continued. "Once the princess and her entourage leave, there is something I must speak with you about."

Cold fear seized Eoghan. He forced himself to take a slow breath, then another. Stern though his father may be, King Ibhar was not an unkind man. With all the changes happening, however, it very well could be that was no longer the case. Not trusting his voice, Eoghan gave a sharp nod, gritted his teeth, and let the conversation die. For the sake of appearances, perhaps their temporary truce would last.

"Did Lord Ó Ceannéidigh tell you of the new brew Glenwyn Distillery is preparing for Fheile Earrach?" Aengus, Eoghan's uncle, asked King Ibhar from across the table. "I hear the infusion they used to bring out the floral notes was a great success."

A quiet breath of relief escaped Eoghan when his father and—surprisingly—the queen became engrossed in the conversation. He took another bite of his meal, finding solace in the relative calm as he allowed his gaze to wander aimlessly. It drifted past his aunt, a smattering of visiting nobility, Counselor Trijveson of Freydlan, Lady Magdalina, the captain, and Princess Simone, before finally coming to rest on the Anadali as if content to make its home there.

Her mask glinted as she turned her head. Though the covering over her eyes prevented her gaze from meeting his own, he had the distinct impression that she was watching him with equal contentment. It was in the way her posture seemed to relax. The way her lips tilted into the ghost of a smile that softened her features just so. Something tugged gently at his heart. What he would give to feel the full effect of her stare.

Behind the Anadali, the server Eoghan had ordered to bring tea entered the room with cautious steps, lingering at the outskirts. Even from this distance, the trepidation in his expression and the tremor of his hands was evident.

It's poisoned. The words drifted through Eoghan's mind, curling around his conscience like a vine and squeezing until it suffocated all rational thought. Or perhaps it was perfectly rational, what with the blatant disdain that seemed to follow the Anadali wherever she went. But surely no one would *act* on it. That would be—

His chest tightened as the image of her lifeless body slumped against the table flashed through his mind. The server looked up from the trembling teacup. Before Eoghan could second-guess himself, he beckoned him over with the flick of a finger.

"Your Highness?" The server's voice warbled softly as he stopped beside Eoghan's seat.

Eoghan held his hand out to accept the tea. "May I?"

The server balked.

Eoghan cleared his throat.

Carefully, the server passed him the cup. Eoghan raised it to his lips, breathing in the warming aroma of cinnamon, cardamom, and black pepper before taking a small sip. The tea tasted divine and comfortingly familiar, breaking through his haze of panic to make room for delayed embarrassment—an odorless, tasteless, or slow acting poison could have been used.

Or nothing at all, and he was merely a paranoid fool.

Eoghan glanced at the Anadali, who tilted her head curiously. The motion drew a small smile from him. He would rather be a fool than see someone dead. Especially when that someone was becoming something of a friend.

Eoghan passed the cup back to the server. "What is your name?"

"Ellis." The server straightened respectfully, though he regarded Eoghan with a cautious mixture of awe and confusion. Not a murderer. Simply a boy new to the job—one who was most likely terrified of foreign warriors and baffled by a prince's odd behavior.

"The tea is perfectly steeped. This will do." Eoghan tipped his chin toward the Anadali.

Ellis bowed, then hurried around the table to present her the tea. She accepted it with a nod and a quiet comment that seemed to ease the tension in Ellis's shoulders. Then—inexplicably—she returned her attention to Eoghan, brought the cup to her lips, and savored it as he had. Eoghan dropped his gaze to his plate as his face burned with embarrassment, a smidge of satisfaction, and an affection that he did not care to examine beyond the fact that it was, undoubtedly, present. By the time he composed himself and glanced up from his meal, she had been drawn into conversation with his aunt, the moment long forgotten.

THE REST OF DINNER PASSED uneventfully, at least when compared to the tea incident. Dessert left something to be desired. Post-dinner mingling left him empty.

Eoghan leaned against the doorway as he looked out over the sitting room, the shadows darkening the corners drawing his attention away from the company socializing around him. A mere week ago, his greatest sources of concern were his upcoming coronation and how he would navigate the king and queen holding predominant seats on his advisory cabinet when his policies differed so greatly from theirs.

How fickle those worries seemed now.

It was like they were waiting for something to happen. Eoghan kneaded the back of his hand where soot had once marred his skin. Were these incidents related? He shuddered at the thought. Whatever was happening, he could not face this alone.

Eoghan glanced to where Cian, Princess Simone, and her Anadali were sitting by the fireplace, their posture far more relaxed than it had been during dinner. If he was going to be king, he was glad to have Cian as an advisor he *could* trust. Still, what could two people do against visions and creatures hidden within the shadows?

Heaving a sigh, Eoghan pushed away from the doorframe to join Riona and Lochlan in the sitting nook by the far window, giving wide berth to the boisterous conversation his uncle and Captain Béhar were engaged in.

"She doesn't seem so terrible. The Anadali," Lochlan said to Riona as Eoghan sat beside the former.

Riona gave the Anadali a sidelong glance. "If you don't mind cunning ruthlessness, sure."

"I thought you respected the Anadali?" Lochlan gave his cousin a nod of acknowledgement as Eoghan settled into his seat.

"I do," Riona shot back. "That's the key word—*respect*."

"Why? What's different about them from other guards?"

"They're not guards. They're a specialized combat force...a different breed of warriors altogether. Their skill, strength, and intelligence are unmatched, and they're sworn to protect their kingdom by any means necessary." She lowered her voice conspiratorially. "Do you remember stories of the skirmish at the border?"

"The one that broke the treaty?" Lochlan furrowed his brow as he thought. "My father had to process the paperwork in the aftermath, but he didn't tell me much about it. Why?"

"Rumor says that one Anadali, a child, took down three of our soldiers. Alone."

Lochlan's mouth dropped open. Eoghan leaned forward. He hadn't heard about this.

Riona nodded. "It took another two soldiers just to take them down. Now imagine what an adult Anadali could do." She cast a glance at the woman sitting by the fire. "Letting one into Na-honaugh, let alone into the palace, is a disaster waiting to happen."

"Do you really think she would risk anything during negotiations? Ones for peace?"

"No." Eoghan spoke up, surprising himself. "No, I don't think she would. There are ways to protect a kingdom other than fighting. I think both she and Princess Simone understand this. We are trying to end a conflict, not start a war."

Riona breathed out a sigh. "I fear you are too trusting, Your Highness."

"Sometimes trust is the first step to change. Stars knows we need it. We can't go on this way. Why do you think they're here?"

Riona frowned but didn't argue. "I still don't like it."

"Nor I, but what other choice do we have?"

A contemplative silence lingered between the three, broken as quickly as it had come as Lochlan guided the conversation to a lighter topic. The shift only served to sweep Eoghan back into his own thoughts—ones he was trying to avoid.

Riona had a point. What statement was the princess trying to make by bringing an Anadali with her? Did she truly feel so distrustful of him and his people, or was it out of respect? She sought to bring the best of her people, a sign of trust and honor for his kingdom. Maybe it really was nothing at all.

Eoghan fought the instinct to rub his temples, but he could feel a headache forming behind his eyes. All of this thinking was taking him in circles and it infuriated him, but he couldn't seem to stop.

His gaze settled on the Anadali, as if observing her from afar would give him a clue to at least one of his many questions. She wasn't sitting as upright as she had been earlier. Her weight was shifted onto her left hip, forcing her to lean against the arm of the chair. Though he couldn't see exactly where her attention was directed because of her mask, she was only partially paying attention to the conversation—a quirk of the lip when Simone or Cian laughed, a brief comment thrown in every so often. At a passing glance, she seemed to be enjoying herself. Yet as he observed her, he realized she was following just enough social cues to make it look like she was invested. Either she felt more comfortable after eating and spending time with people in the palace to *lower* her guard, or she was absolutely exhausted and fighting against showing it.

She made a comment to Princess Simone, who nodded in response, although a flicker of uncertainty crossed her features.

Interesting.

The Anadali rose gracefully, albeit slowly. Cian tried to clamber out of his chair to rise with her, but she urged him to sit back down with an elegant wave of her hand. She gave a slight bow to the guards as she passed them on her way out, then she was gone.

"If you'll excuse me," Eoghan muttered, his eyes on the empty doorway where the Anadali had disappeared through not moments before.

Standing, he forced his attention away from the doorframe and made his way to the fireplace where Simone and Cian talked animatedly. Where Cian had been cold and calculating not but a few hours ago, that had been replaced with a cautious trust Eoghan had not seen in a while. Perhaps peace would be good for all of them.

"May I join you?" Eoghan asked.

"Of course!"

"Absolutely not."

Simone and Cian spoke simultaneously. Eoghan gave Simone a gracious nod before rounding the chair and lightly shoving Cian's shoulder as he took the seat next to him.

"Is everything all right with your Anadali?" Eoghan asked.

"Of course. She was tired from the journey today and wanted to retire," Princess Simone said with an air of nonchalance. "Why do you ask?"

"They've become friends," Cian interjected before Eoghan could speak.

"Oh?" Simone leaned forward in her seat, surprise written clearly in the lift of her brows.

Eoghan suppressed a frown. He wasn't familiar with Dúndían customs, but if he'd overstepped by making the Anadali's acquaintance, he didn't want her to suffer the consequences because of his ignorance.

"We simply trained together before dinner. I thought it would be wise to do so as part of fostering peace between our two kingdoms."

Cian gave him a cheeky grin. "The Anadali called it *fraternizing*, I believe."

"Huh." Simone sat back in her chair, rearranging her already meticulously placed skirts as she thought.

"I apologize if I overstepped—"

"No, no. It's fine." Simone waved her hand as if to bat his worries away. "Thank you, by the way."

"Whatever for?" Eoghan asked.

"For allowing her to stay in the room next to my own. And for granting her a tour of the palace and a place at dinner. I do not appreciate how she was treated upon arrival, nor do I appreciate the delays in seeing to her accommodations, but I understand these are not normal circumstances. Your willingness to overcome animosity despite your reservations did not go unnoticed to me."

Eoghan shrugged lightly. "It's the least I could do."

Simone nodded, a smile Eoghan wasn't sure how to categorize curving her lips. "She really let you train with her?"

"It was His Highness's training grounds," Cian defended. "He let her train with him."

"It wasn't *letting*," Eoghan corrected. "I asked politely."

Simone shook her head as if she were amused by something they couldn't understand. "If there is one thing you must know as the relationship between Dúndíor and Nahonaugh progresses, it is this—the Anadali do not *fraternize*, they do not share tactics, they rarely interact with any other than their own, this one least of all." Her dark eyes held Eoghan's own in a piercing stare he did not dare look away from. "One does not *let* her do anything. She simply does, or does not, and she doesn't do anything without very, very good reason."

"Is that a threat?" Cian asked.

"No. It is a step in the right direction."

Eoghan tilted his head. "Meaning?"

"It means"—Simone leaned back in her seat—"she does not see you as her enemy."

"I don't intend to be."

"From her point of view, that is not for you to decide."

Cian looked like he wanted to say something more, but remained silent when Eoghan gave him a subtle shake of his head. Instead, he changed the subject to the state of trade routes while Eoghan mulled

Simone's words and the events of the day in his mind. It only made his headache grow worse.

Perhaps the Anadali had the right idea in retiring early for the night after all. If he wasn't Crown Prince, he would try to get away with it too.

CHAPTER TEN

WRAITHS IN THE NIGHT

JUST AS THE MOON PULLED THE EBB AND FLOW OF THE tide, so too did it seem to guide Anaís's rest—she had been drifting in and out of sleep ever since she left the sitting room and curled up under her blankets. Now, as pale moonlight streamed through her window, she knew her nap had officially ended. Sighing, she pushed her covers back and sat up.

The archery session with Eoghan had done her a world of good, though she would never admit that to anyone. It surprised her how tightly wound she had become after a week of traveling with company. She was used to her own rhythm of long days and didn't realize that adding others into the mix, even a sister she loved dearly, would throw everything off-kilter. Now it seemed her thoughts were clearer, her mind more focused for the task at hand. Namely, breaking into the library without anyone noticing, finding what she could about the sacred waters of Takaniim, and leaving without a trace.

Simple.

If only she could get this cursed bracelet off.

She perched at the edge of her bed, studying the arrangement of tourmalines and diamonds around the center stone that hid the locking mechanism. Cian's word of warning niggled at the back of her mind, but she had to try. There was no way she would make it to the library, let alone get the information she needed, with this attached to her arm.

Anaís wiggled the central gem, brows furrowing as it rotated slightly before settling back into place. Perhaps it didn't need a key at all...maybe the stone *was* the key. She rotated the stone in the opposite direction, but immediately let go when heat seared her skin. A stream of air hissed between her teeth as she squeezed her forearm to distract her nerves from the pain. It was definitely a directional lock, and that was very much the wrong direction. Cian hadn't been joking when he said she wouldn't like the results. Lesson learned: solve the puzzle correctly the first time.

The stones glistened innocently in the moonlight. Bringing her stinging wrist to eye level, Anaís scrutinized the various shapes of the gems organized around the central stone—some were baguette-shaped, some almond, some spherical. It almost looked like...

Her eyes widened. Lowering her wrist, Anaís strode to the window and leaned against the sill to take in the star-freckled night. The Gem Box Cluster glinted like a treasure trove in the dark. *Look to the stars*, Balendin had said, *they will show you the way*. She smiled at the night. The cluster in the sky and the cluster adorning her wrist matched perfectly.

There were still three weeks until the first day of spring, which coincided with the first day of Fheile Earrach. Perhaps the central gem represented their planet.

She sucked in a breath and braced herself for the searing pain to come should her suspicions be wrong. Slowly, carefully, she turned the central gem to follow the position of their planet relative to the constellation each day, starting on the day of her arrival to the palace and ending on the first day of Fheile Earrach.

A soft click punctuated the silence and she flinched, releasing the gem as it rose up to expose the clasp beneath. She unhooked it and slid the bracelet off her wrist. The cool evening air stung her burned skin. If anyone asked, she had jostled the bracelet in her sleep, and it injured her then. Tucking the bracelet beneath a pillow, she slipped into the night. For now, she was free.

The parts of the palace Anaís had seen when Riona finally gave her an official tour took her breath away. Every detail, down to the way the crystal chandeliers reflected the sunlight during the day and sparkled under the candlelight at night, was exquisitely executed. It only served to make the contrast of how the palace appeared in the dead of night all the more shocking. The façade peeled away to bear the true nature of the palace.

Darkness. Secrets. Mysteries hidden behind every turn, every door.

Sticking to the shadows, Anaís crept down the imperial staircase, her feet not making a sound on the polished steps. The library took up residence just off the main hallway, which Riona had pointed out during the tour. Anaís paused before the library doors. Tall and ornately carved, they stood as regal sentinels guarding the secrets of the books lying within. Soon, they would guard her own secrets too.

She removed the two long pins holding her hair back, then knelt before the lock and inserted them. Anaís worked the pins in tandem down the length of the lock until the bolt gave way and a satisfying click emanated from inside the door. Sucking in a breath, she turned the knob and pushed it open. A muted pop echoed into the library when the wooden doors separated. Anaís pulled her hairpins out of the lock and ducked into the library, shutting the doors behind her lest anyone who heard the sound came looking.

Moonlight flooded the library through the windows along the far back wall, bathing the center of the room in a milky-blue glow while casting shadows between the rows of bookshelves lined up like sleeping soldiers. The outer walls of the library were also covered in books, as if they themselves were made of the stories contained between ink and parchment. Armchairs in the back of the room nestled next to a dark fireplace while a spiral staircase led to the upper levels of the library, which was at least three stories tall.

Twisting her hair into a knot, Anaís secured it with the hairpins and redirected her attention to the expanse of books before her. *If I contained information about a sacred lake that had been reduced to legend and long forgotten, where would I hide?*

Her shoulders sagged with a sigh. *Probably not conveniently in a library.* Regardless, orders were orders.

Silent as a wraith, Anaís wove between rows of bookshelves, cataloging the bronze plates announcing the genres of each section. While this floor held an exorbitant amount of books, it also seemed to only house nonfiction tomes: International Policy, Agriculture...

Her gaze drifted to the vast expanse of the back wall where the history section stood. If all else failed, the upper levels of the library most likely held mythology and folklore, but this seemed as good a place as any to start. Shrugging, Anaís began her search.

The bottom shelves housed nothing of interest. Even at eye level, the titles were the likes of *The Mysterious Disappearance of Twansley*

Park—Simone would appreciate that one—or *The Swarfmaster's Cousin*. Perhaps fiction and nonfiction were mixed? Anaís let out a frustrated huff. Walking backward, she tipped her head up, scanning row upon row of books. The tomes seemed to grow taller and thicker as their place rose on the shelf. Another bronze plate glinted in the moonlight far above her head. Squinting, Anaís could just make out the inscription scrawled in Nahraeg: Ancient History.

Plopping her knapsack on the ground to mark her spot, Anaís walked the length of the shelf to retrieve a rolling ladder. The well-used wood of the rungs creaked as she climbed to the top for a better view—though books still towered beyond her reach. Sure enough, a bronze plate reading "Ancient History" was nailed into the bookshelf. Anaís skimmed the titles and was reaching up to retrieve *Encyclopædia of Time* when another plate far above caught her eye. "Restricted Access."

Anaís grinned and gave the spine of *Encyclopædia of Time* a pat. "I'll be back," she whispered.

Balancing on the top rung of the ladder, Anaís gripped the lip of the shelf above her and gave it a wiggle. It didn't budge. She pulled herself up, carefully wedging her feet against the bookshelf to avoid disturbing the books before repeating the process until she balanced eye to eye with the Restricted Access plate. Anaís glanced longingly at her knapsack on the floor below—a small bundle of fabric now that she was up so high—though it wouldn't have fit more than one of the large books anyway.

Skimming the titles, Anaís selected *Pre-Nythmaarian Geography* and *An Anthology of Protohistoric Life*, balancing them in the crook of her arm as she slowly climbed back to the ladder. She plucked *Encyclopædia of Time* from the shelf with her free hand before sliding the rest of the way down the ladder.

Anaís arranged the three books in front of her on the floor before sitting back on her heels and tucking herself against the shelves at her back, making sure she wouldn't be visible from the library entrance should someone decide to enter.

They were thick tomes, the leather binding softened with time and wear—surprising, considering they were now trapped in a section destined to be forgotten. Which one to begin with, she wasn't entirely certain. *An Anthology of Protohistoric Life* seemed reasonable enough. Shrugging, she pulled a roll of parchment and a quill from her pack and scooted the book closer to her. She had to start somewhere.

Sketches interspersed with text shuffled past as she leafed through the pages, skimming the words as she went. Maps of the continent long before it contained its current borders, the flowing script of Ancient Kiivjani, and genealogical trees dating back hundreds of years fluttered by. She furrowed her brow as a whisper of a memory surfaced. A crackling fire. Balendin's warm voice. Fantastical stories. These stories, she realized, woven together to fit the imagination of a child. She'd always thought these tales were make believe, spun to bring wonder to herself and Simone.

Yet here they were in their brutal glory, staring at her through the window of time as if to dare her to deny the truth of their existence. Balendin had certainly altered some of the tales and left others out altogether. But the fact remained: he knew, and he desired to pass on even a smidgen of truth to her and Simone. It was almost as if their past—rather, their origin—was set on a destiny to be forgotten. The threads of time bridging two different eras snipped away as the story refused to be passed along to the present.

Her heart thrummed with excitement as she flipped through the pages with haste. If the book contained these stories, there was a chance Takaniim was nearby. Anaís was about to give up and move on to the next book when her hand slipped, and the pages flipped to a sketch of fjordland surrounding a massive lake. The fjordland, she recognized. It stretched from the outskirts of Dúndíor to the borders of Nahonaugh and meandered down to meet the jungles of Kiivjachim in the south. Although time and climate had softened some of the landscape's features while sharpening others, it remained largely unchanged. What was *not* the same was the large body of water that flooded the valley floor and engulfed her beloved craggy gorges. This body, at least as it was depicted in the sketch, was massive. Placid. A mirror reflecting the secrets of the heavens above. She began reading the text, and what she saw made her heart stop.

Takaniim. "Lifestream" in Ancient Kiivjani.

Anaís's hand lingered on the page as excitement gave way to caution. How did her father know—or even suspect—that this information would be here, in the library, in a kingdom no one from Dúndíor had been to in a decade? And if he knew, why hadn't the one who told him given him this information already?

Her job was to do as she was told—no questions—but this... Anaís closed her eyes, rubbing her temples as she thought. If only she had the foresight to ask Balendin about these stories when he was still alive. Maybe then she could have deciphered her father's motives.

Shaking her head with a sigh, Anaís dipped her quill in ink and began to transcribe the text before her.

> *Two and a half thousand years have passed, and the*
> *disappearance of Takaniim remains a mystery. While*
> *the majority of historians believe the supernatural nature*

of the lake's disappearance to be a myth, a handful of written accounts uncovered by archeologists indicate the possibility of a strange event:

"There was a loud sound, like the roar of thunder as the sky ripped in two. But the night was clear and the stars looked sadly upon me. When dawn broke, the sun sat alone in the sky, its reflected counterpart gone forever." — Excerpt from a shepherd's record, clay tablet.

"The wind raged, the ground trembled, and the roof I spent three days fixing caved in. Pa sent me to fetch water to clean up, but the damn lake was gone." —Author unknown, rock carving.

Regardless of the manner in which it left, the absence of such a large body of water reshaped the landscape of the continent of Nythmaar. It disrupted migratory patterns, the lack of a central source of water forcing even non-migratory mammals to seek new homes. Samples from curated bone collections suggest a rapid period of extinction and adaptation in the century following this event, likely spurred on by the subsequent dramatic changes in weather patterns on the eastern and western coasts of modern day Dúndíor and Freydlan, respectively.

Anaís kneaded her hand to ease the forming cramp. Setting the parchment to the side she skimmed the rest of the page, which recounted various geological investigations. Jotting down a few notes, she carried on.

Less researched are the inexplicable phenomena in the centuries before and the years shortly after the lake's disappearance. Notable archeologists have categorized these accounts as regional folktales, though that does not diminish the cultural or religious significance these stories played during this forgotten era:

"Simmer for five minutes, then mix the resin with—

Anaís blinked, then carefully lifted the page. The entire section had been torn out—the section she wanted, no, *needed* to read. These were the continuations of stories Balendin had told her as a child. Stories entire civilizations were built upon, even if no one else cared to remember. Her heart sank when she turned the page, only to find the text rendered illegible by spilled ink.

Balendin had told her of the great battle and the inception of Takaniim—how it was a gift from the Creator to bless the lands and the people who thrived there. He had told her of the sœndjak—the scheming, treacherous creatures of the deep—who were defeated but not destroyed.

She wanted to know more, read more. What other mysteries of the past had been lost to the present?

Anaís rolled the quill between her fingers. Should she document the story Balendin had passed on to her? It seemed strange to pen oral tradition. Was this even what her father cared to know? Hesitantly, Anaís began writing again.

The creak of a door echoing in the empty library froze her in place, quill stalling mid-word. Ink from the tip bled into the parchment as she strained to listen. All was quiet, save for a soft "huh" that entered the library behind the ghost of the creak.

Anaís shoved her supplies into her knapsack, keeping her eyes glued to where the door would have been had the bookshelf not blocked her view. She needed to hide. Now.

Slowly, quietly, she slung her knapsack onto her shoulder and peered around the shelf. The door was open just a crack, but it was enough for the dim glow of the moonlit hallway to lighten the shadows shrouding the library entrance.

A muffled voice drifted through the silence. "What is it?" The words were uttered in Nahraeg.

As quietly as she could, Anaís closed the book, gathering the rest of them in her arms before clambering to place them back on the shelf. *Encyclopædia of Time* slid into its rightful place in Ancient History, and with a quick glance to the door Anaís scaled the bookshelf to replace the two restricted tomes.

"Nothing, I...never mind. I'll see you tomorrow." Another voice responded in the same language.

A tendril of warmth tickled her mind as she tucked the last book securely on the shelf. She scrunched her nose at the sensation, chasing it away before it could grow. The timbre was familiar, but she couldn't place the voice. It was unnerving how simply speaking a different language could mask an identity.

"Sure you don't want help?" the first voice asked.

Anaís hurried down the bookshelf, half sliding, half freefalling, before landing nimbly on the ground with a roll. She needed to do something with the ladder, or else whoever was about to enter would know someone had moved it. As quietly as she could, Anaís gripped the ladder and walked it back down the aisle of bookshelves. She was moving away from the door, but at least this corner of the library was darker, more hidden. Hopefully it would give her a better chance for escape when whoever was out there came in here.

"It's all right."

Her heart fluttered at the voice, and she gripped the straps of her knapsack to steel her nerves. She crouched into the shadows of a bookshelf to ready herself. The door swung fully open, then clicked shut.

Silence followed in its wake, and hidden within the quiet she felt it. A soft, familiar tug.

Pressing a hand to her chest, Anaís willed the sensation away. This was no time for fear. No time to make a mistake. Besides, who-ever entered wasn't moving. Why would they suspect anything to be out of the ordinary? Why would they—

Because she hadn't locked the door behind her. Anaís mentally kicked herself. She hadn't expected anyone to enter the library when the moon had only just begun its descent from its zenith. It was a novice mistake. One she shouldn't have made. One that would get her killed should she be caught.

Assured steps echoed through the silent room, the pull around her heart growing stronger as he approached. Whoever it had been was no longer looking for a book; they were looking for her.

"Who's there?" His voice rang through the emptiness of the library, and electricity shot through her veins as warmth enveloped her very being. She was floating, falling, being pulled apart and put together again. His presence drew her forward, as if she was lost and he was her lifeline.

Her feet stuttered to a halt, fear gripping her chest. The lifeline. The familiar tug. He was here—the protector in her dreams—and tonight, he was anything but safe.

His footsteps stopped somewhere in the middle of the room, but the room was spinning. Why couldn't she focus?

"You can show yourself now, and you will only be lightly pun-ished for crimes against the crown."

She needed to breathe, but the air was too heavy, too thick—a weighted blanket settled atop her, promising the comfort of serenity if only she would stop fighting. What was she fighting again? She wanted to go out and meet him. Be enveloped in his presence. Safe.

No.

This was not a dream; there was no way he could be here.

His footsteps echoed through the library again, softer this time, as he paced forward. "Or you can wait until I find you and be executed for treason."

Warmth tingled up her spine, and she pressed the heel of her palm to her ears, the rapid beat of her heart whooshing through her mind and thundering against her ribs as she curled in on herself. *Stop talking, go away please please please go away.* Her body shook as she took in a breath. She pulled her tunic over her nose and mouth to muffle the sound as she took another breath, then another, the warm air fanning across her chest as she tried to calm down.

"Have it your way."

Her breath hitched.

"I will find you."

Footsteps followed in the wake of his promise, but he remained silent. It took every ounce of control to get herself to stop shaking, but after a few moments in the blissful quiet of the library she finally pulled her tunic away from her mouth. Her raging emotions soon calmed to a spring rain, every feeling neatly tucking itself away into the recesses of her mind as she let her instincts take control and muscle memory guide her actions.

When he moved, she moved. When he stopped, she stopped. Their footsteps and silence blurred together in tandem, a deadly dance of the hunter and the hunted. Another beat of silence evaporated into the air when the cadence of his footsteps changed. The back of her neck prickled as she listened. Each step became a little louder, more distinct, as he crept across the library.

He was close. Too close.

Anaís ducked along one of the shelves, his silhouette flickering between the books when he crossed the other side. She peered around the shelf toward the middle of the room and scooted around the corner, pressing her back against the cool wood. Not a moment later, two more footsteps sounded before he stopped and a heavy silence filled the library. Even the books themselves held their breath in anticipation while he seemed to consider his next move.

In the blink of an eye, his silhouette turned down the side of the bookshelf where Anaís had been not moments before. She crouched low and crawled to the opposite side, moving synchronously with him around the shelf like wraiths in the night.

Pain lanced through her chest, as if the thread around her heart pulling them together had snapped. He sucked in a sharp breath. Time froze, watching.

Slowly, tentatively, his footsteps carried on as he walked across the middle of the library toward the far end where the armchairs and fireplace were. She relaxed against the bookshelf. No, the hunter would not keep his promise after all.

Turning in the opposite direction, Anaís continued to make her way down the corridor of bookshelves toward the front of the library. There was only one way in or out, or so it seemed. Regardless, there was no sense in trying another way when there was no guarantee of escape. She had taken enough risks for today. Crouching behind the last bookshelf, she listened for an indication of his position, but all was quiet.

Something wasn't right.

An eerie darkness blanketed the library, followed closely by a wave of uncertainty. She could barely see her hand in front of her face; no one would be able to see her if she departed from the safety of the bookshelf, yet fear slowed her movements as if she were wading through mud. Finally, she maneuvered around the shelf and peered into the center of the room.

Heavy curtains draped across what had once been the expanse of windows at the far end of the library, veiling the moon. Only a sliver of ghostly light slipped through the junction of the drapes. The soft cadence of boots directed her attention to where the spiral staircase would have been. The silhouette of a man momentarily appeared in her vision before sinking into darkness, reappearing briefly every four heartbeats when the sliver of light skittered across his body as he wound his way up to the second level.

She leaned against the bookshelf and looked toward the door. If she were anywhere else in the library, she would have been trapped. Not even instinct could guide her through an unfamiliar pitch-black room. This side of the room, however, was not entirely unfamiliar.

Anaís closed her eyes, envisioning the space between her and the door. She had thoroughly scouted the library when she entered, and she would have to trust herself to make it out. If she ran, she could make it in about forty paces. She didn't recall hearing the door lock when he entered, but she could have missed something. It was a risk she would have to take. Rising to a low crouch, she took a steadying breath in, exhaled, and ran, counting each step as she went.

On the thirtieth stride she slowed down. On the fortieth stride she came to a full stop, then crept toward the door until her hand pressed against the carved wooden panel. The motif dipped beneath her fingertips as she trailed her hand across the door, pausing when she met the cool metal of the doorknob. She glanced over her shoulder toward the spiral staircase and listened for his footsteps.

A hush captured the library as she waited. He was waiting too, she realized.

Holding her breath with anticipation, Anaís turned the doorknob, begging the pin to slide free from the adjacent door. It did. She positioned herself to the side so moonlight from the hallway would not shine on her like a beacon. Then she pulled.

Light streamed into the library. A sharp "Hey!" echoed through the room. The faint outline of a man launched over the second story railing. Anaís darted through the opening. He landed deftly on top of a bookshelf before jumping to the ground and rolling with the momentum. She slammed the door shut before he could stand.

Anaís's heart hammered behind her ribcage as she dashed up the imperial staircase. There was no place to hide—the moonlight was too bright, the palace too open for her to keep going up the stairs without being seen. She was running out of time.

A column with an ornate top caught her eye, and she raced toward it. Her fingers grabbed onto one of the arrises as she swung herself to the opposite side of the column and clambered up it, tucking herself within the shadows of the intricate carving of the capital.

The library door opened and slammed shut. Heavy breaths filled the hallway. She pushed herself farther into the shadows, not risking looking around the column. Her thundering heartbeat filled the silence while she waited, still as stone, for him to continue his search. After a beat, his footsteps echoed down the hallway, carrying him away from the staircase.

Anaís leaned her forehead against the column, the cool marble offering little reprieve from her mounting headache as she strained to listen for anyone else who might come. Her fingers trembled as she dug them deeper into the carvings, her chest ached from trying to stifle her rapid breathing, but she would not descend. Not until she was certain he wouldn't be coming back this way.

By the time she eased her way down the column, her fingers had gone numb and her legs were cramped. The moon rested much lower in the sky, casting sharp shadows throughout the hallway that had once been bathed in its light. Anaís shook out the aches before alighting the rest of the stairs and hurrying back to her room.

The door clicked shut behind her, and she leaned against the smooth wood. Once steady, she pushed off the door and shoved the knapsack into the deep recesses of her trunk. She pulled a silk robe free from a tangled bundle of clothes, sending them sprawling across the floor. Anaís didn't care. All she wanted was to get out of her stealth clothes. It didn't matter that they were made from soft, finely woven cotton. They were suffocating, heavy, weighed down with memories of the library. She wanted them off. Now.

Her hands shook as she shucked off her shirt and pants, adding them to the pile of clothes on her floor. *Pull it together Anaís. It. Wasn't. Real.*

It felt so real.

Her fingers fumbled with the robe when she tried to turn it right-side-out, but the silken fabric slipped to the floor. She wanted to scream. Instead, she snatched it up, tugged it on inside out, and slid into the safety of her bed. Sharp pressure dug into the back of her skull as soon as her head hit the pillow. Gritting her teeth, she reached back and yanked the hairpins out, throwing them across the room into the trunk before slumping back against the pillow. Simone would have scolded her for not braiding her hair before bed. Not that it mattered. She wouldn't go to sleep, not if her dreams were becoming reality.

Anaís absentmindedly reached for the bracelet she had hidden under the pillow next to her. The metal was cool against her skin as it settled around her wrist and locked into place. She ran a finger across the raised edges of the gemstones, letting the familiar pattern of the constellation rub raw into the pad of her finger as the ornate motif decorating the ceiling burned into her vision. She couldn't shut her eyes. Wouldn't shut her eyes.

The one comfort she'd found in sleep had turned into a waking nightmare.

CHAPTER ELEVEN
NOT A PLEASURE

EOGHAN LEANED AGAINST A VINE-COVERED PILLAR overlooking the rose gardens. After the interruption to his routine, the stress of negotiations, and an all-too-eventful evening, he needed tranquility now more than ever. Unfortunately, someone else had commandeered his favorite spot for herself.

The roses in bloom tilted toward the rising sun, mimicking the posture of the Anadali standing in their midst. She rested against the stone railing in a patch of sunlight, her face tipped toward the sky. Eoghan imagined her eyes would be closed as she soaked in the first warmth of the day. Riona and Lochlan had hypothesized about the reasoning behind the mask last night, but he still didn't understand why she had to wear it while she was here. He had never heard of an Anadali wearing one before, and it felt secretive. Shouldn't both sides be trying to build trust?

He glanced at the bracelet around her wrist. Maybe they hadn't been entirely trusting of her either.

Her tracker would need to be analyzed—especially after the night he had in the library. He wasn't sure what had compelled him to go so late, especially not with the threat of fog lurking and shadows creeping. It had felt like a tether drawing him home. But then, as quickly as the connection had come it had frayed and snapped. The aftermath had left him shaken and hollow, though he was starting to feel better now.

Regardless, it had all been for naught. Whoever was in the library had escaped; it had been like chasing a ghost. All he had to show for it was a sore ankle from jumping to the first floor.

He shook his head to clear his thoughts. The Anadali's behavior thus far had done nothing to incriminate her, but he could not dismiss the possibility. Perhaps trust only went so far.

Do I trust her?

No. But he wanted to. She intrigued him, drew him in in a way that was oddly satisfying. He didn't understand it yet. He did not know her face, did not know her name, yet, over the few conversations they'd had together, it felt as if he knew her beyond the words they had spoken. It was...unnerving.

She was unnerving.

Maybe she didn't have to be.

A gust of wind rose off the lake, the flowers surrounding the Anadali swaying to its song. Errant curls escaped her plait as the wind enticed them to join the dance. She reached up to tuck them behind her ears, but rather than fix the problem, more strands of hair twisted free, brushing against her neck as they, too, were carried away by the wind. It was as if part of her refused to be tamed.

Eoghan inhaled deeply, the lingering tension from last night's events seeping away as his lungs filled with the fresh morning air. He was exhausted, but he cherished the morning peace too much to waste it on a lie-in. Breakfast wouldn't be ready for another thirty minutes, and no one expected anything of him until then. He wanted to keep it that way. Besides, there was something else he would rather be doing.

Dew kissed the hem of his trousers as he walked through the grass toward the rose garden.

"You're awake early." The Anadali jumped at the sound of his voice behind her. "Sorry, I didn't mean to startle you."

She turned to face him and bowed. "Forgive me, Your Highness. I should have been paying more attention."

"It's quite all right." He chuckled at the apprehension in her posture. "My 'no formalities' rule extends to the hours before breakfast. You may call me Eoghan."

Her lips quirked into a small smile as she relaxed against the column. "What brings you to the gardens this early, *Your Highness*?"

He mimicked her stance. "I enjoy the solitude."

"And yet here you are." Her tone was dry, though the way she gestured at the lack of distance between them indicated a warmth he had yet to see from her—a warmth he clung to like a flower blooming toward the sun after a long, harsh winter.

"I'll begrudgingly admit I do enjoy your company as well." Eoghan added.

"So I'm a last resort?"

"No, that's not—never mind. What brings you to the gardens so early?" He mentally slapped himself. *This* was why he usually avoided talking to people before breakfast. He should have known he wouldn't have been able to carry a conversation.

She bit the inside of her cheek as she considered his question. Eoghan watched her movements carefully. Not being able to see her eyes may have put him at a disadvantage, but he understood people well enough to know that eyes only told part of the story. Her head tilted ever so slightly as she looked just beyond him, lost in thought. Finally, she directed her attention back to him, but it seemed distant. As if she were remembering something she would rather forget.

"Couldn't sleep," was all she said.

Silence stretched between them, and Eoghan's thoughts hummed all the more. Couldn't sleep because her accommodations were uncomfortable? Couldn't sleep because her thoughts kept her awake?

None of those questions were appropriate for him to ask, and it wasn't his business to pry, but the longer the silence stretched the more insistent the humming became. He realized the sound wasn't in his mind but next to him—the hummingbird from yesterday morning was back, watching him curiously while he suffered under a flood of thoughts. Just as he opened his mouth to break the silence, she spoke.

"It's peaceful here." It was a whisper, more a wistful admission to herself than a confession to him.

"It is," he replied anyway.

She glanced at him, as if surprised to hear his acknowledgement. The sun had risen high enough in the sky that it glinted off her mask right into his eyes.

It was childish, not entirely diplomatic, and certainly not what the future king should concern himself with, but he wanted to lift her spirits. Take away the weight that burdened her, even if he already carried too many weights of his own. He wanted to behold the fiery woman he caught glimpses of beneath the stoicism.

Eoghan squinted and looked at the ground. "Is that why you wear that thing? To blind your enemies?"

"It's one of the perks, but no. It's more practical than that."

"What could be more practical than incapacitating your enemies?" He lifted his hand to try and block the flare of light, but it did little good. "Sorry, do you mind if I..." Eoghan awkwardly sidestepped so the sun didn't glint off her mask when she turned to face him.

There it was—an amused smirk. The fiery woman was back.

"I'm not a soldier. It's not often I line up in a field to stare down the adversary. The work I do is more...specialized." The Anadali tilted her head as she regarded him. "Have you ever had your eyes gouged out, Your Highness?"

He frowned to suppress his smile. "No, I cannot say that I have."

"Nor I, but the process is quite gruesome to witness." She tapped the edge of her mask. "This helps me avoid that experience."

"A worthy shield, though the act of eye removal seems a bit uncivilized for a trained fighter," Eoghan mused. "Don't you think?"

"I appreciate an honorable kill as much as the next warrior, but those I face aren't always concerned with civility."

His smile broke free at the playful lilt in her voice. "And so you incapacitate them before the battle even begins."

"I suppose I do." She inclined her head in a slight bow, as if to hide the smile growing on her lips. "If you'll excuse me."

He watched as she turned and ascended the stairs toward the palace. Her movement was mesmerizing, water flowing smoothly down a river. Graceful, steady, powerful, completely unfazed by anything in her path. He imagined that even in the face of the most stubborn obstacle, she would carve right through it without hesitation. And when the storm came and the waters raged? He would gladly be caught in her currents.

❋ ❋ ❋

Anaís strode toward Captain Béhar, who stood guard outside of Simone's room. "Report," she said quietly.

He gestured to the room across from Simone's. "Lady Magdalina entered Her Highness's chambers about an hour ago to prepare for the day. A lady's maid is currently assisting with hair and dressing matters. As for last night, there is nothing abnormal to report." Béhar glanced down the hallway, then back at Anaís, brows raised in question. "Were you successful?" his look asked.

She had briefed him on the need-to-know details of her outing, as he would see both her comings and goings from his post in front of Simone's door.

Anaís nodded once in reply.

The tension seemed to bleed from his body. He nodded back.

"Thank you, Captain, you are dismissed. Take the next few hours to rest. I will have food sent to your room."

Béhar gave a sharp salute before making his way to his own room. He yawned loudly, the sound echoing down the hallway until it was cut off by the shutting of his door.

Now that Anaís thought of it, she was exhausted too. A dull pain pulsed at the base of her skull, bringing with it a spike of worry. *It's just a normal headache from a poor night's sleep*, she thought. *Nothing will come of it.* She massaged the back of her head, loosening her braid as if that would reduce the tension. It did not.

Resigned, Anaís rapped on the door twice and called, "Your Highness, I'm entering." She paused for her sister's call of admittance before slipping in and closing the door behind her.

Simone sat at a vanity at the far side of the sitting room, morning light glinting off the collection of hair jewels arranged before her. Several hairpins bobbed between her lips, curving with her smile as she silently greeted Anaís.

"I told Her Highness I would finish pinning the plaits myself," a lady's maid said while she expertly twined Magdalina's hair together, though the style wasn't nearly as intricate as Simone's. "However, she insisted I attend to Lady Magdalina."

The two were situated at the opposite side of the room, Magdalina perched atop a plush velvet settee turned makeshift hair station. To the left was a beautifully carved fireplace and a sofa that matched the settee. To the right was an arched opening that led to an airy study.

"It is only because the art of hair should never be rushed, Miss Ní Thormadha," Simone replied sincerely. "If we are to be on time, I must attend to the ordeal of choosing ornamentations myself."

Magdalina smiled at her friend. "Stars knows it takes you an eternity to decide."

"Says you," Simone laughed.

Stepping farther into the room, Anaís ran her hand across the back of one of the chairs situated before a bay window near Simone's vanity. A light breeze played with the sage-green curtains, a perfect color to compliment the beauty of the palace grounds and the rose gardens in the distance. She put her back to the window. Hopefully Simone hadn't spotted her with the prince earlier.

Contrary to her word, Simone quickly affixed the last of her hair ornamentations in place, then turned to face Anaís.

I see you made Prince Eoghan's acquaintance, Simone signed, keeping their conversation private despite the seemingly distracted chatter between Magdalina and Miss Ní Thormadha.

Anaís suppressed a wince. So she *had* seen them. *Playing the spy, are we?* she signed back.

You would know, Simone replied with a wry smile, though the gleam in her eyes sent Anaís's heart into a staccato rhythm—it was the same look she got when she tried to solve a mystery in one of her books before the protagonist did. *That's not the first conversation you've had with him, is it?*

Anaís folded her arms in front of her chest. As much as she wished to confide in Simone, this was not a plot for her to solve. She was not allowed to know. King Timun had ordered as such.

Does Eoghan have information? Simone raised her brows in question, then waved her hands as if dismissing the thought. *Of course he has information, he's the crown prince. But what does he know that Father wants?*

Anaís pressed her lips into a firm line and shook her head once.

Wrinkling her nose, Simone set to the task of applying her makeup while she schemed. She alternated between an assortment of creams and pigments that were foreign to Anaís. Simone dabbed a rose color on her lips, then froze, an unreadable expression on her face.

Father doesn't need information, does he? Simone signed tentatively. Then, with movements so small it looked like a whisper, she added, *Father wants you to kill him.*

Anaís's throat bobbed as she tried to swallow. She did not know what their father would do if Simone found out, only that his threat was palpable.

Her chest constricted. Her throat closed. Anaís finally sucked in a sip of air only to realize that her arms were numb, and a new panic flooded her veins. *It's merely a lack of sleep, it's not your condition. It's not your—*

A gentle touch on her shoulder pulled her back to the present. Simone guided Anaís to one of the chairs by the window, lightly pushing on her shoulders to get Anaís to sit before lowering herself into the chair opposite.

"Shall I prepare your documents?" Magdalina asked from across the room. Anaís jumped at the noise.

"Yes, thank you, take your time," Simone called.

Anaís took a deep breath, then another. The numbness in her arms turned into pins and needles as it receded—she had crossed her arms too tightly and cut off circulation. Kneading the palm of her hand, Anaís contemplated what to say. Simone knew she was correct; anything Anaís said to the contrary would only be an insult to her sister's intelligence.

She settled on the truth.

Yes, she signed weakly.

Simone worried her lip. *How much time do we have?*

Until Fheile Earrach. I don't want to do this, but I must. You remember what happened to Balen— Anaís cut off the sign of his name as her hands shook. She squeezed her hands into fists and instead signed, *When Father tells you of his plans—and he will—you must feign surprise. He cannot know that you know.*

I will, Simone promised, then looked over her shoulder.

The lady's maid had left the room. Magdalina had returned to the settee and was now contemplating a row of shoes aligned neatly like soldiers.

Simone rose and squeezed Anaís's shoulder. *Rest here,* she signed. *We'll be ready in thirty minutes.* She glided across the room. "Magdalina, have you chosen your shoes yet? Oh! Those are marvelous! Come, you must help me pick out a pair."

Magdalina trailed after Simone, the two women venturing to the wardrobe to accomplish their quest. Moments later, quiet chatter punctuated by giggles drifted into the sitting room. It only served to make Anaís's thoughts louder as the weight of her memories pulled her into the past.

Intellect will always best brute force. Balendin's voice floated through her mind. *Truth ensnares even the smallest lie. Compassion is more deadly than malice.*

Her father's voice echoed back. *And a load of good you did with that before I refined your kind.*

She had thought time would heal the hole Balendin had left in her heart, the one she had carved out with her father's knife. Somehow, it had only made it worse.

Balendin had raised her to bend but never break, while the king carved her into the rock that stood against the raging sea. What happened when the lightning struck? When the ground shook? When her own force of nature was destroyed by none other than nature itself? Had she met her equal or her opposite last night in the library? And why, oh why was her time in Nahonaugh resurrecting the hope and curiosity that once made up the fabric of her being?

None of it mattered. Regardless of who she was or how she came to be, there was nothing she could do to change her path now.

Eoghan would die by her hand. How she wished he did not have to.

CHAPTER TWELVE
ILLICIT AFFAIRS

BREAKFAST WAS UNPLEASANT, TO SAY THE LEAST. Anaís's favorite meal of the day turned into a cacophony of over-exuberant conversation, woven with Simone's inconspicuous glances between Anaís and Eoghan. Anaís knew it was an unconscious reaction, but it was giving her eyes whiplash—if such a thing could exist—and worsening her headache. Eoghan, thank the stars, hadn't seemed to notice, though Cian had caught Simone's eye on more than one occasion. Anaís simply hoped he would suspect an illicit romance between herself and the prince, as horrifying as that would be.

After the waiters had served a second round of coffee and tea and Anaís's untouched cup had grown cold, Simone discreetly shooed her away before heading to the meetings, this time with Eoghan, Cian, and Magdalina. Béhar had appeared just in time to trail sleepily behind.

Anaís sighed as she looked over the bridge that spanned the straight between the island and the mainland. The water churned despite the stillness of the late morning, as if it knew what she was plotting and had more than a few choice words to say about it. She toed a rock—her halfhearted response to the waters raging below—and it rolled off the cliff edge and tumbled through the air before the lake swallowed it. What else was she supposed to do?

She had already gotten information from the library and received a tour of the palace from Riona. Eoghan must have done something to get her into the suite next to Simone and convince the guards she wasn't a threat. As much as she wanted to go back to read more about Takaniim, the memories of her encounter kept her well away from the library. She had yet to figure out which wing held Eoghan's rooms. Thankfully, her question as to how she would cross the bridge unseen had answered itself.

It was simple, really, with the tangle of trusses and deliciously wide beams making up the base of the bridge. That was the problem—it was *too* simple. Now all she had left was the task that would make her upcoming mission a reality. Yet no matter how hard she tried, she couldn't convince herself to move away from her current position.

She shifted on her feet, swaying slightly. Numbness licked against the back of her mind, but her stubbornness shoved the sensation back down. This was not a time for weakness or rest. It didn't matter that nothing made sense—the lifeline, Takaniim, her condition. She had to see this through, her own thoughts on the matter be hanged.

Wind whipped across her face, carrying with it the sound of footsteps and the smell of spring fighting to break through the last of winter.

Anaís kept her gaze focused over the bridge as she broke the silence between herself and the man standing next to her. "I thought you had meetings?"

"I thought I'd come check on you," Cian replied.

"Did I wander too far?"

"No."

"I know what this is, Lord Ó Máille," Anaís retorted, lifting her wrist shackled by the bracelet. "You don't have to lie to me."

Cian shifted next to her but remained silent, confirming her initial appraisal of the bracelet.

"Why don't you trust us?" she asked instead.

"Princess Simone has given me no reason to distrust her. But while you have managed to fall into Prince Eoghan's good graces, you have yet to do so with me. I'm out here doing my job." Cian's eyes bored holes into the side of her head. "What are you doing over here?"

Anaís forced a demure smile to grace lips. "I thought we had a fine time after dinner last night."

"There were maybe three words spoken between us," he bit back. "I hardly consider that notable."

"And this conversation right now?"

"Less than friendly. Stop changing the subject."

"All right." She turned to face him. "You want to know what I'm doing? What I *normally* do when tasked to protect someone. I understand that your best have secured the grounds, but I am obligated to verify."

"This island is impenetrable."

"Is it?" she retorted. Cian opened his mouth to argue, but she cut him off. "And to shed light upon your apparent confusion, I have not managed to fall into *anyone's* good graces. I am understanding those Her Highness is working with. Princess Simone assured me of your goodwill. She also knows that should anyone attempt anything, they would be dead before their hand reached their weapon."

"And you think you could protect her from that, all the way out here?" he scoffed.

"Would you like to test your doubts?"

Cian's nostrils flared, but he clenched his jaw and remained silent.

"If you want to give me a lecture on trust, give me a lecture," Anaís continued, the jeweled bracelet glinting in the sun as she raised her wrist to make her point. "Don't count on me to listen."

"So you trust the princess's word, yet you still don't trust us." He had the audacity to sound offended.

"Prince Eoghan has given me no reason to distrust him," Anaís countered. Her headache flared and she squeezed her eyes shut against the pain, thankful her mask allowed her this one mercy. She sucked in a breath, then released it slowly. Relax. She needed to relax. Calmly, she added, "While you've managed to fall into Princess Simone's good graces, you've yet to do so with me."

"That's the second time you've parroted some semblance of my words back to me. Not very original in the arena of comebacks."

Anaís shrugged. "Sometimes you have to feed people their own stupidity to help them understand."

Cian gaped. Properly gaped. And it was all Anaís could do to not laugh. "I do hope we have a chance to reconcile trust," she continued. "Based on what Her Highness has indicated, we will be seeing more of each other in the future."

"I don't see why," he huffed. "You're not her advisor."

"Yet here I am."

A hostile silence prickled between them, but neither dared fill it. Much to her dismay, he did not return to the palace. Instead, he joined her, looking into the distance as if trying to see what she could see, which was—she begrudgingly admitted to herself—not much. She already had everything she needed. Only her stubbornness kept her rooted there, staring dumbly at the waves crashing against the cliff face of the mainland. He was simply the fool standing next to her. While that thought alone somewhat tampered her frustration, it wasn't enough to quell her skepticism of Cian.

She would spare him for Eoghan, who had, for better or for worse, weaseled his way into her good graces. What he found in Cian she would never understand. Though perhaps, if Cian felt the same level of loyalty to him as she did to Simone, his barbed demeanor would be reasonable. Stars knew she was being less than cordial in a diplomatic arena. Perhaps they were more alike than she cared to admit.

Cian shifted, then turned to make his way back toward the palace. *About time.*

"Your presence is required in the meeting room," he called without looking back at her.

Anaís furrowed her brow. He could have led with that. What was the point of that entire conversation then?

"Why?" she shouted back to him.

"Does it matter?"

No, she supposed it didn't. Anaís sighed, then fell in step with Cian as he led them across the grounds.

❋ ❋ ❋

A STRANGELY PLEASANT COMBINATION OF fresh air and the smooth musk of the cigar held between King Ibhar's fingers filled Anaís's senses when she entered the meeting room after Cian. The tip glowed ember as the king drew on the cigar, wisps of smoke curling around his face. He gave Cian, then Anaís a courteous nod before slowly releasing the smoke from his mouth.

Queen Siofra sat to his right, her posture the antithesis to her husband's. A prickle of discomfort washed over Anaís's skin as the queen's eyes narrowed and trailed down her body.

"Thank you for joining us. Please, sit." Eoghan sat at the head of the table. He looked tense, especially when the queen changed the subject of her scrutiny from Anaís to him.

Wordlessly, Anaís dipped her head into a bow before making her way past occupied chairs and lowering herself into the open one next to Magdalina.

"By Nahonan law, there must be at least four witnesses from each kingdom to form a fair consensus regarding the acceptance, reform, or overturn of the proposed terms for this treaty," Eoghan spoke again, his attention focused solely on Anaís. "Counselor Trijveson will then have a month to draft the treaty, whereupon we will reconvene these meetings to further refine and, ultimately, finalize the treaty. Are you willing and able to fulfill this duty as one of the four for Dúndíor?"

She met his gaze. Though her mask prevented him from seeing her eyes, it felt as if he were looking into her. Mentally shaking the thought away, she confirmed his request with a "Yes, Your Highness."

"Excellent. You have already met His and Her Majesties, as well as Lord Ó Máille. Have you been introduced to Captain Lochlan yet?" Eoghan asked, gesturing to a man she had seen at dinner the night before but hadn't paid much mind to. Now that she had a closer look, she could see similarities between the two men in the slant of their nose and cut of their jaw. Though where Eoghan's presence captivated attention with the welcoming grace of a cool breeze on a warm summer's day, the debonair slope of Lochlan's posture reminded her of a sated lion walking amongst prey.

"Not formally, no," she said, turning her attention to the man in question. "I am Princess Simone's Anadali. It is a pleasure to make your acquaintance." Anaís extended her hand to shake his.

He glanced from her mask to her hand, a disarming smile gracing his lips.

"Lochlan Kavanaugh of the Royal Guard." He took her hand in his and pressed a featherlight kiss to her knuckles. "The pleasure is mine, My Lady."

Either she had slept through one too many etiquette lessons as a child, or the lion had an appetite after all. Too much of an appetite.

She had it in her right mind to cuff him over the head, but with the way Simone directed a subtle keep-your-mouth-shut glare in her direction, she resigned herself to leaving the thought in her mind. When she glanced back at Eoghan, he seemed about ready to box Lochlan about the ears himself. As quickly as it had come, his expression settled back into princely calm.

"And I'm sure you have yet to meet Counselor Trijveson," Eoghan continued, gesturing to the elderly man sitting across the table from her. He almost looked *too* friendly to be in politics, what with the fluffy white hair atop his head and the wrinkles about his eyes hinting at a lifetime of smiles.

"It is a pleasure to meet you," he began. "I'm from Freydlan. King Ibhar and King Timun recruited me a few months ago to act as a neutral party in the recording of these meetings and drafting of this treaty."

Anaís nodded. "The pleasure is mine."

The meeting began with details of border crossing—merchants and diplomats gaining access to cross first, followed by a tiered scheme for citizens so neither kingdom became too overwhelmed during the transition period. Parchment shuffled around the table, quills scratching as details were refined, locations where citizens could obtain travel documents determined, and border crossing checkpoints solidified.

It wasn't until they moved on to the beginnings of trade negotiation that Anaís found her attention wandering. When that attention latched onto something, or rather, someone, even her fiercest efforts couldn't pry her eyes away from the man in question—and with good reason.

By the glint in Cian's eye, something was wrong.

Horribly wrong.

Anaís followed his line of sight to a stack of papers by King Ibhar's arm. From what she could read, it was a document outlining the paperwork necessary for merchants to trade between kingdoms, and regulations for establishing brick-and-mortar shops should they decide to move their base of operations from one kingdom to another. Merchant licenses, tax details, a register of wares sold or services provided and the location of conduct, and specialized stamps under a new Cross-Kingdom Sector of the guilds.

She squinted at the designs, trying to make out the intricate details of each stamp. They appeared to be dependent on the profession of the tradesman, which was to be created by a committee of headmasters of each trade and selected advisors from Nahonaugh and Dúndíor. A stamp bearing the Cross-Kingdom Sector's insignia sat proudly at the footer of the document, guarding the signatures next to it.

It was clean, simple, perfectly logical, and provided no viable indicators for Cian's sourness. Unless—

"No." The word slid sweetly through Queen Siofra's lips, silencing the room. "I believe that is a mistake. Three days in either kingdom is more than enough time."

"This is a treaty, and concessions must be made." Gone was the prince who held himself with an elegant assuredness. Eoghan's demeanor had turned cold as stone. "Those terms were revisited earlier this afternoon. Your presence was sorely missed; however, this was the agreed-upon solution."

Cian tore his gaze away from the document. Simone's brow rose slightly, but did nothing to otherwise betray her surprise. King Ibhar relaxed into his chair as he blew out a contented puff of smoke. Had Anaís's lips been covered and not her eyes, she would have smiled. She had hoped Eoghan had a backbone. Now she knew.

The queen let out a noncommittal hum, but her stare cut deeper than any dagger could. "Very well. Carry on."

Anaís looked back to Cian, but the interruption seemed to have pulled him out of his trance. Suppressing a sigh, she paid attention to the meeting once more.

The hum of chatter filled the room like the buzz of flies over a dead carcass. As soon as Simone and Eoghan entered the reception room to celebrate the end of the first stage of the peace treaty, courtiers, council members, and nobles alike swarmed them. The surge of bodies separated Anaís from her sister and forced her to the edge of the fray. She didn't mind; Captain Béhar had remained glued to Simone's side, and it was easier for Anaís to observe the crowd for threats when she wasn't a part of it. The large, hexagonal reception room was architecturally beautiful with whitewashed walls, sloping alcoves, and towering pillars, but the design also meant there were more nooks in which illicit affairs could occur.

A waiter passed in front of her and Anaís plucked a glass of water off his tray, idly lifting it to her lips as she scanned the room. Magdalina was chatting shyly with a nobleman who looked to be her age. Simone held audience with Counselor Trijveson and another lord whom Anaís vaguely recognized. Béhar stood nearby, Simone's ever-present shadow. Anaís's gaze drifted to where she had last seen Eoghan as she took a sip of her drink.

Her search cut off with a choke—this was definitely *not* water—catching the attention of a stately looking woman nearby. She eyed Anaís's mask with interest, extricated herself from the man accompanying her, and made her way past the few people separating them.

"Are you all right, miss?" she asked in stilted Dúndían. "You are from Dúndíor, no? I don't believe I've seen you before."

"Yes. And I'm fine, thank you." Anaís subtly poured the liquor into the potted plant next to her. If it was going to be useless for hydration, the empty glass could at least act as a scapegoat to get out of this conversation.

Time to play the schmoozing game.

"It has been so long since I've met anyone from there. I'm Countess Sigraith." The woman beamed, extending her hand toward Anaís.

She wasn't expected to kiss it as Lochlan had done for her, was she? Opting for the safer route, Anaís briefly clasped the woman's hand in what she hoped was a ladylike shake.

"Anadali," she replied, giving a quick smile before looking over the countess's shoulder to resume her scan of the crowd. During her moment of distraction, Simone had disappeared into the masses. Anaís knew her sister would be fine handling a room full of eager socialites, especially with Béhar by her side. It was herself she was worried about. Celebrating a successful mission by sparring with fellow Anadali was enjoyable. Participating in social revelries infused with more rules than she could count? Not so much. Though this Countess seemed amenable.

"I've never seen this style before—how exciting!" the Countess exclaimed, gesturing at Anaís's mask. "Oh, it will be lovely once the border is fully opened, don't you agree? The opportunities for innovation in fashion and textile design will be limitless."

Anaís smiled weakly. "I would love to continue this riveting conversation, but I'd like to get a drink to ease the tickle in my throat."

"I'll come with you!"

"You're too kind; that won't be necessary."

When Anaís moved to brush past, a gloved hand gripped her arm. It took all the propriety she had left to not rip the countess off of her.

"Please?" the woman whispered, her dark hair cascading over her shoulder as she leaned forward. "I've been trying to find an excuse to leave Gearóid's conversation for the past half hour. I'd rather not go back."

Anaís stiffened. "Did he hurt you? Threaten you?" Her gaze darted around the room, looking for the man in question, but he was nowhere to be seen. She needed to find him, find Simone. Make sure she was okay.

"Goodness, no," she laughed. "Gearóid couldn't harm a fly. He's just so terribly *boring*. Going on and on about trade routes and taxes and Kópamir Gorge, wherever that is."

The tension building in Anaís's chest deflated, then re-inflated with curiosity as she registered what the countess said.

"Kópamir Gorge?" Anaís asked. Kópamir Gorge was where Takaniim had blessed the lands with its waters before it disappeared. Though Gearóid was more likely lamenting over the difficulties the gorge might pose for potential trade routes.

"Oh yes. Somewhere east of here? I'm not sure. Terribly boring." The countess heaved a dramatic sigh, then perked up. "Your throat!"

"My what?" Anaís barely refrained from jumping out of her skin.

"I've been prattling on for far too long. Come come, let's get you another drink."

Anaís resisted the urge to rub her temples. The fatigue from scouting the bridge pressed against the recesses of her mind, and trying to navigate social niceties only seemed to expedite its progress. What she needed was sleep. Maybe she could convince Simone to retire early, if she could even find her.

The countess pressed a fine-stemmed glass into Anaís's hand, the liquid within bubbling and golden. Did no one drink water at these events? She took a tentative sip, if only because it would be rude not to, and stifled a wince as the honey-flavored alcohol burned her throat on the way down.

"Your Highness!" the countess gasped.

Hope filled Anaís's heart as she turned to see her sister, only it wasn't Simone at all.

"Countess Sigraith," Eoghan returned the countess's enthusiastic greeting with a smile. "It is a pleasure to see you, as always."

"You must meet my new friend Anadali! She's traveled all the way from Dúndíor for this momentous occasion."

"Yes, we've been acquainted. I was actually hoping to steal her away, if you don't mind. We have some business to discuss."

"Of course, of course! Oh look, there's Lady Caoimhe! Lovely seeing you, Your Highness. And you, Anadali! I hope we meet again soon!"

The countess puttered away with renewed purpose, the silence filling her absence both disarming and peaceful. If ever Anaís needed to create a distraction while working undercover, she would be sure to emulate the countess's lively demeanor. Perhaps schmoozing wasn't useless after all.

"Are you all right?" Eoghan asked, pulling her out of her thoughts.

"Yes? Why would I not be?"

"The countess is lovely, but she can be a bit much. You looked like you needed some backup."

A smile lifted her lips before she could stop it. "So, business?"

"In a manner of speaking. I'd like to talk with you." He gestured to one of the many arched alcoves. "Perhaps we can go somewhere more quiet?"

Her smile fell. What if someone accused *them* of illicit affairs? She glanced at the alcove, then at Eoghan. Surely he did not have any ill intentions. "Lead the way," Anaís conceded.

Eoghan held his arm out to escort her. When she didn't take it, he cleared his throat. "Are you coming?"

"In the absence of Princess Simone, my duty is to protect those of diplomatic importance to Dúndíor. I need both arms to guard you, Your Highness."

"Understood. Please, this way." He schooled his features into the same princely calm he wore during the meeting, but as he brushed past her, he whispered in her ear, "It's Eoghan."

The timbre of his voice sent a pleasant tingle down her spine. Anaís blinked, mentally shook herself, and followed him through an archway into the hexagonal room's smaller cousin. Rather than the stately grandeur of the reception room, a cozy atmosphere filled this one. Clusters of wingback chairs and velvet-clad settees created an intimate yet inviting setting, their occupants talking amicably in lowered voices. The crackling fire in the hearth across the room punctuated the conversations as it kept the pre-spring chill at bay.

A familiar voice rose above the murmured haze, and Anaís turned toward the sound to see Lochlan and Cian talking with Simone, Béhar, and Magdalina. So that was where her sister had sneaked off to. Simone caught her eye and shot her a look that screamed "What are you doing?" Cian raised his brow at Eoghan in a way that asked him the same question, most likely for a different reason. She doubted the prince had plans to kill her.

Rounding their seating area, Eoghan moved to the back of the room where two wingback chairs faced the hearth. "Please, have a seat." He gestured to one of the chairs, separated from the other by a small side table.

Anaís obediently lowered herself into her seat as Eoghan relaxed into his own. The fire popped contentedly.

"This isn't an interrogation," Eoghan said. "You can relax."

"Of course." She shifted until her back brushed the soft cushion of the chair.

"How long have you been Anadali?"

Anaís stiffened. "I thought this wasn't an interrogation."

"It's not." He shrugged. "I'm simply curious."

While she had grown to expect his openness "off duty," as he so aptly put it, it was difficult to reconcile that with the diplomatic prince she had recently come to know. If he introduced this conversation as business, was this diplomacy? His request to call him Eoghan said otherwise. He was just as disarming as the countess, but in a decidedly different way.

She liked it. She hated it. She wanted to see where this conversation led.

"How long have you been a prince?" Anaís inquired.

Eoghan tilted his head at her. "Are you implying I've asked a stupid question?"

"Should I be?" she asked, matching his posture. This banter, she could handle.

"Shall we simply converse through questions then?"

"That wouldn't make for much of a conversation."

"No, it wouldn't." The curve of a smile softened his features. "I told you this morning, I enjoy your company. I've gotten to know Princess Simone's policies through the talks and her personality in between. I would like to get to know you better too."

Anaís blinked. Of all the things she had expected, it was not this. "Why?"

He shrugged. "I need to know if I can trust you."

She regarded him for a long moment. His expression was earnest; how she wished he would look upon her with skepticism instead. How she wished she *could* be worthy of his trust.

"You can trust what I say is honest," Anaís began carefully. "You can also trust that whatever I do, it is because I'm bound by duty to protect my kingdom."

"I would not ask anything less of you."

Anaís nodded. "Thank you."

Silence lulled between them, this one more comfortable than the last, as if the cocoon of warmth created by the fire had time to wrap itself around them and create a safe pocket to exist in. Anaís sank a little deeper into her chair and tilted her head toward Eoghan.

He was watching her, but rather than the princely grace she had grown used to seeing since she met him—even when his actions ran contrary to what royal etiquette dictated during their moments of privacy—he wore a peaceful softness. As if, for this small moment in time, he didn't have the weight and expectations of an entire kingdom resting on his shoulders. He gave her a small smile before asking, "What led you to join the Anadali?"

He really didn't know, did he? *I was born into it. It was my destiny.* She settled on a partial truth. "An Anadali helped raise me. I wanted to follow in his footsteps."

If Anaís had a choice in the matter, if she could pretend for a moment that the course of her life was directed by her actions alone, she would have become Anadali because of Balendin. Because of his honor.

"How old were you?" he asked.

"I was three." Eoghan's eyes widened almost comically, and Anaís fought to stifle a laugh at his bewildered expression. "The way of the Anadali is different from that of guards."

"That it is," Eoghan laughed. "What does it mean to be Anadali? I know you can't tell me your secrets, but I feel as if all I know are legends. What does it mean to *you*?"

She frowned.

"I'm sorry. That was too forward of me."

"No...it's fine. We are warriors called to protect, but it is more than that. Our duty, our purpose is rooted in integrity. Occasionally I gather information, as you're doing now." She tilted her head in what she hoped conveyed a pointed yet amused look. "Sometimes justice must come through unsavory means. But I do what I can to carry this out with respect."

"And the Anadali who raised you taught you this?"

Anaís nodded.

"He sounds like a good man."

"He was."

Eoghan's expression softened and he looked back to the fire. When he finally spoke, his voice was quiet. "Thank you. For sharing a part of yourself, and his memory, with me."

Anaís only nodded. She didn't trust her voice, or the intimate silence that seemed to pull them together. Tilting her head away from Eoghan, she looked into the fire. The roaring flames had settled into a warm glow as the evening slipped by. Despite the ache, it was the first time she had spoken freely about Balendin to anyone. Even briefly. Though Eoghan didn't know nearly all that transpired, she felt as if he understood, in a strange way. A peaceful way. He and Balendin could have been friends in another life.

Eoghan sucked in a breath as if he was about to say something, then released it slowly.

Anaís turned to look at him. "What?"

"Hmm?" He stirred in his seat.

"What were you going to say?"

"Oh. I...nothing."

She tilted her head at him, understanding dawning. "You fell asleep, didn't you?"

"Yes?" Eoghan ducked his chin, hiding his expression as he ran a hand through his hair.

After her sleepless night, early morning, time spent scouting the island and bridge, and the tension of the meeting, the reprieve of sitting by the fire had relaxed Anaís to the point that she almost didn't feel the exhaustion anymore. Now that she was aware of it, tiredness overcame her like a tidal wave. And to think Eoghan had to be alert the entire day with negotiations? No wonder he had fallen asleep.

"Don't worry, you didn't snore," Anaís teased. "We should call it a night anyway."

"Ah, good. I'm glad you weren't subjected to that." He stood. "You have a long journey tomorrow. I shouldn't have kept you so long."

"It's all right." She rose from her chair and instantly regretted it. Numb dizziness rushed through her body, and she swayed on her feet. Not this. Not here. It was bad enough when it almost happened in front of her father, but in front of the future ruler of an opposing kingdom? She blinked rapidly, trying to chase away the darkness filling her vision. There was no way this was staying a secret.

Eoghan's lips moved but no sound came out.

"I'm fine," she wanted to reassure him, but her tongue felt heavy in her mouth. Her legs gave out and she was falling, falling...

Steady hands gripped her arms and lowered her gently to the floor, her head coming to rest atop a pillow. Her eyes drifted closed, and she forced air into her lungs to keep herself conscious. In, out. Her chest rose and fell with labored breaths. The smell of cedarwood and black tea enveloped her in a comforting hug, easing the panic from her bones until feeling fluttered back in.

A muffled voice spoke somewhere above her. The butterfly touch of a hand brushing away an errant strand of hair trailed across her skin, curved around her jaw, and alighted on the edge of her mask. Her hand shot up and grabbed Eoghan's wrist before he could move it.

"Anadali?" Her title cut through the haze.

"I'm okay." Her voice sounded weaker than when she had last spoken.

"Let me take you to a healer."

"No, I..." She opened her eyes and Eoghan's concerned face slowly came into focus. "I didn't realize how tired I was. I apologize, Your Highness. That was unprofessional of me."

"It's all right." He took a breath as if to steady himself. "It's been a trying few days."

"It's nothing I can't handle," she mumbled.

"I didn't mean..." Her pillow shifted. "I've found it trying, at any rate," Eoghan confessed quietly.

Anaís turned her head to the side. Perhaps it *had* been a trying few days. More than she wanted to admit. Though that was the least of her worries—her fingers were still curved loosely around Eoghan's wrist, which was settled by her head.

"I'm sorry." She released her grasp, curling her hand into a fist as the phantom warmth of his skin sank into her own.

Her pillow shifted again as he put his hand down and settled his weight on it. "It's all right, take your time."

She laid there a moment longer to gather her bearings, but when understanding dawned on her, she wished she hadn't. There was no pillow under her head. No, her head was resting on Eoghan's thigh.

She shot up, embarrassment heating her cheeks as she tried to ignore the steady hand hovering by her shoulder.

"Easy now. How do you feel?"

"I'm okay," Anaís repeated, glad her voice sounded a little more normal.

She stood slowly, Eoghan staying near but not touching her. Finding her feet, Anaís gave Eoghan a slight bow. "I apologize again, Your Highness. And thank you."

He shook his head. "No need. Let me escort you to your chambers."

"I wouldn't want to keep you any later." She straightened the wrinkles out of her uniform. "Besides, I should be escorting you. Not the other way around."

"Then we're both off duty. Please? I would feel better knowing you made it safely." Anaís opened her mouth to argue, but Eoghan hurried on, "And it's not out of the way. I stay in the wing adjacent to yours."

Just like that, reality came crashing in. She knew where to find his room. The last task of her mission was complete.

Unbidden tears prickled the corners of her eyes. This wasn't the future ruler of an enemy kingdom. This wasn't some threat her father saw. This was a friend. Maybe they were on opposite sides, but who was drawing the dividing line? She wished she could turn back time and decline his offer to talk. Instead, she took his proffered arm, ignored the way her fingertips tingled from the brush of his sleeve against her skin or the way his strength seemed to bolster her own, and let him lead her back to her room in silence.

CHAPTER THIRTEEN
THE ROCK

The morning chill wrapped around Eoghan like a blanket—a sorry comfort for his confused heart and enraptured soul. He had seen the Anadali, the princess, and her entourage off as he would any other diplomat, but as he stood atop the front steps of the palace watching their carriage become nothing more than a speck in the distance, there was no denying it. The Anadali had left, and Eoghan felt as if she had taken a part of him with her.

When he had asked to speak with her last night, he hadn't expected her to agree. Hadn't expected her candor, the warmth of her company, or the inexplicable feeling of peace that enveloped him while they talked together. For the first time in a long time, life had felt *right*.

The sound of the palace door closing caught Eoghan's attention and he turned, dipping his head in greeting as Cian crossed the distance between them.

"You saw them off?" Cian asked.

"Yes, they left a while ago." Eoghan looked back toward the mountain pass. They were long gone by now, yet it still felt as if he could see her.

"That went well. Better than I anticipated, at least..." Cian trailed off, then heaved a weary sigh. "I suppose you were right. They weren't...horrific."

Eoghan beamed. "What was that?"

"They weren't horrific?"

"No, the other thing."

"That went well?" Cian raised his brow, but a mischievous smirk betrayed him.

Eoghan laughed. "Close enough."

"There is something, though." Cian adjusted his cufflinks, then tugged his sleeves and stood up straight. "Do you know where Counselor Trijveson is?"

"At breakfast, I think. Why?"

Cian shook his head. "Just something about the trade routes. I think they're fine, but there's something I'd like to double check."

"Thank you for negotiating them. I wouldn't trust anyone else with those details."

"You forget I was a merchant's son before you dragged me into this mess."

"Oh I dragged you, did I?" Eoghan scoffed.

"Kicking and screaming."

"You do have leave to visit your mother, you know that right? You've earned it."

Cian toed the ground with his boot. "I was planning to visit her for Fheile Earrach, actually."

"For the whole week?" He didn't bother hiding the surprise in his voice. Eoghan knew Cian's childhood home held memories he would rather forget, though he would suffer them for her. Despite Cian's closed-off demeanor, he had nothing but the purest love for his mother. "Bring me one of her pies when you come back, will you?"

"She'll probably send me back with a half dozen and a request for you to come along next time," Cian grumbled.

"I could come along this time." The front door of the palace opened, and Eoghan dropped his voice as the king stepped out. "Stars knows it would do me some good to step away for a day or two."

"And risk sending the kingdom into shambles?" Cian chided. "Not a chance."

Eoghan held back a snort of laughter. "Bring me two pies, then. And tell her I'm coming for Midsummer. I want to help plant the fall harvest."

"Done." Cian's eyes darted to where the king stood. "Good luck."

"Likewise."

Cian left, bowing to the king before making his way into the palace. Eoghan turned his attention back to the mountains. If this was the meeting his father had forewarned him of two nights ago, he was going to need all the luck he could get.

King Ibhar put his hand on Eoghan's shoulder. Eoghan dipped his head into a bow, though it was difficult to execute it properly with his father's hand holding him in place. "Your Majesty."

"My son."

Eoghan looked up, confused. "Father?" He meant it as a statement, but with the way his voice lilted upward at the end it sounded more like a question.

King Ibhar squeezed his shoulder and released him. "Come. There are some things we must discuss."

Eoghan swallowed past the lump in his throat. "Of course."
Nothing good ever came of a request such as this.

IT WAS PROBABLY WISE HIS father had not outright said he wanted to show Eoghan a rock. Especially not a rock hidden in a velvet-lined cigar box stowed away in his father's private smoking room. No, incredulous laughter was not something the king would take kindly to, especially when his demeanor was as serious as it was at present. Even so, every iota of disbelief struggled to stay concealed within Eoghan. So it was that he found himself sitting across from his father in said smoking room, gaping like a fish.

The rock—or was it a stone?—settled in the palm of his father's hand was entirely unremarkable. The dark, smoothly polished surface looked to be worn down by time rather than the planned craftsmanship of an artisan. Still, nothing could have smoothed over the pinholes that traversed the entirety of the stone.

Looking up at his father, Eoghan finally said, "That's a rock."

King Ibhar nodded without a trace of humor. "Correct you are, son." He sat back in his seat, running his thumb over the object in his hand. "This relic was entrusted to the High Chief of Clan Kavanaugh when Takaniim still provided for the lands, and was passed from chieftain to chieftain, generation to generation. It is part of our history, our culture."

"It's not..." Eoghan didn't want to offend his father, but he was also completely baffled. Might as well spit it out. "It's not *just* a rock?"

His father smiled. "You're doing a better job at feigning understanding than I did when my father showed this to me."

"What?"

"I'm not mocking you, Eoghan. It's called a nitróg. A combination of *ni'itrat* from the Old Language and *maróg* from Nahraeg, as it was known centuries ago."

Eoghan wracked his brain from his linguistics classes as a child. "Guide pebble," he guessed, then frowned. "Guiding stone," he corrected himself. That sounded better.

"In name alone, as far as I'm aware." King Ibhar looked Eoghan in the eyes, completely serious. "The queen does not know of this relic. And though I love Siofra with all my heart, she cannot discover it."

Eoghan raised his brow, and his father's expression softened.

"Its true purpose and power may be forgotten"—he turned the stone over once in his hand—"but that does not make it any less real. Any less important. Any less *dangerous*. You may think me soft, Eoghan, but I am aware that I allow her voice to have more weight in the governing of this kingdom than she lawfully has a right to. She is cunning, and her ideas are valid. I didn't marry a fool." He looked Eoghan in the eyes. "I also didn't sire a fool. You are *my son*, Eoghan. This is a gift of kings, and you are to be king. *You* are what this kingdom needs. These last few days have proven that to me."

Eoghan blinked, stunned. Never in his life did he think he would hear his father imply he was worthy. As a son. As a king. "Even after I disobeyed you?"

His father raised his brows. "Did you?"

"I know I did not lead the meetings in a way you or Queen Siofra desired."

"No, you did not. But your actions were not taken out of spite—that much was obvious to me. You made your decision, negotiated an agreement with a kingdom we have not seen peace with in ten years, and did not waver when challenged."

"And the queen?" Eoghan questioned.

King Ibhar chuckled. "Do not expect a pleasant meeting with her."

"You support her?"

"She wants the best for her kingdom; how could I not? But you're a grown man now—have been for a while. I can make suggestions to you, but I cannot control you."

His father's words carried with them hope and reassurance shackled by the weight of dread. The past, and the hurt Queen Siofra had inflicted, was not something Eoghan could simply undo. He knew who he was—what he was. He also knew who he wished to become in spite of all that had transpired.

But now that Eoghan held the future in his own hands, how did he move forward?

It would not likely be in the direction the king and queen wished, though his father did not seem disappointed by this fact. Eoghan couldn't tell if it was understanding or a peculiar sense of foreboding that hummed in the air between them. Regardless, it was a feeling entirely foreign to him.

Eoghan willed it away, focusing instead on the rock perched teasingly on the table between their two chairs. It was so small. So plain. Yet strangely beautiful.

"Go ahead." His father nodded at the rock.

Eoghan reached out, but hesitated. His father had said its purpose had been buried with time, but what if...no. His father had held the rock and nothing had happened. Feeling foolish, Eoghan picked up the nitróg.

As if recognizing his touch, a strange warmth spread up his arm, like a warm spring breeze in liquid form. Curious, he rotated the stone between his fingers. Flecks of silver, lilac, and blue glowed from within. It reminded him of the constellation of stars he'd seen in...the vision.

Eoghan dropped the nitróg with a start, curling his hand into a loose fist. The stone clattered to the floor, then rolled to a stop by King Ibhar's feet.

"It is a shocking sensation, isn't it," King Ibhar laughed as he retrieved the rock. "Frightfully cold for such a little stone."

"Oh. Yes. Frightfully...cold..." Eoghan looked from the rock to his father.

Fog floated by a bouquet of flowers in the corner of the smoking room, regarding Eoghan from behind the veil separating realms. From the corner of his eye, King Ibhar turned to place the stone safely away in its cigar box as if nothing was the matter.

Go away, Eoghan mouthed. The fog made no move to cross over, though it seemed content to settle into the flowers just to spite him. Shaking his head, Eoghan returned his attention to his father.

"When it is time for the stone to be passed on to you, you will know," King Ibhar said.

Eoghan glanced at the box, then back to the fog. It was gone. He wasn't sure if he should be relieved or terrified. "When I am king?" he asked.

"Perhaps." His father shrugged. "This gift was not made for man, nor was man made for it. But you will know."

"How?"

"Eoghan," his father chided. A certain sadness hid in his expression, but there was also a pride Eoghan had never seen before. "Trust me."

CHAPTER FOURTEEN
THE ART OF ASSASSINATION

I WILL RIDE OUT, CAMP, ASSASSINATE, AND IMMEDIATELY return home," Anaís said, trying to contain her exasperation. "Why are we having this meeting?" She clenched her jaw as the words slipped out.

A messenger had intercepted the carriage as soon as they entered the capital, bidding Simone and Anaís to come to the king's study at once. After both women had given their reports, King Timun had revealed his assassination plans to Simone. Though her sister had received the news with perfect nonchalance, Anaís's heart had yet to settle back to a normal rhythm. All she wanted to do was take a bath, take a nap, and sneak a snack from the palace chef. Instead, she had to sit through this nonsense.

Simone furrowed her brow. "Why not stay in Nahonaugh to avoid unnecessary travel? It's only five days until the festival begins."

"The new Anadali aren't going to train themselves," King

Timun said before Anaís could speak. "As Amadé, she must see to all her duties. This is how Anaís operates."

It really wasn't. It was how *he* operated. Anaís simply listened. Though at this point she was tempted to not listen at all.

King Timun glanced at Anaís with a disapproving frown, and she stiffened, then sat up straight in her chair, adopting a posture that was both regal and reverent. A posture fit for Anadali Amadé. When had she dared to become so lax?

After spending a mere three days in the company of a certain crown prince, it seemed. Both too long and not long enough.

Simone looked between the two of them. Though she hid her expression well, Anaís could tell she was upset with their father's stringent plans. Whether it was concern for Anaís's condition—which was ridiculous—or genuine disbelief that Anaís could pull off this mission, Anaís wasn't sure. Nonetheless, Simone drew herself up and leveled a respectfully commanding look at the king.

Now *that* was certainly a move only her younger sister could get away with. It filled Anaís with pride. At least one of them could carry on the benefits of time away from Dúndíor.

"As the diplomat who negotiated peace with Nahonaugh while observing their court, I would like my suggestions on this matter to be heard," Simone declared.

King Timun leaned forward, folding his hands on the desk in front of him. He directed a challenging stare tinged with a hint of respect at Simone. "Let's hear it."

Simone nodded as if that was the only acceptable response to her demand. "Anaís shall arrive the day before Fheile Earrach, posing as a foreign visitor. This will give her a political opportunity to learn more about the people of Nahonaugh. Though we spent time with the royal family and their entourage, we need to know where their citizens stand on these new policies. She can do this by attending the festivities on the opening day. No one knows her face or who she is."

"How so?" King Timun interrupted.

"I did not show my face during the talks," Anaís said carefully. The king loathed anything that hinted at Balendin's existence. "I wore a mask."

He frowned thoughtfully, then nodded. "Resourceful thinking." An inkling of pride colored his voice; Anaís cursed herself for wishing to be the recipient of that praise again. Their father looked at Simone and prompted, "Carry on."

Simone smoothed her skirts before saying, "The first day of the festival should be for gathering intelligence only. Guards will be rested and alert for any attacks. Therefore, the assassination should occur on an unremarkable day, not correlating with anything."

"Which is why Anaís was going to attack on the second day," King Timun drawled, though not unkindly. "She is well-versed in her art; details such as these were untangled years ago. However, I do like the thought of gathering additional information. Yes. I will need to... No, that won't be a problem," he muttered to himself. "See to it that it is done. I trust you can build a cover."

Anaís wanted nothing more than to reach across the desk and slap some sense into her father. Simone had never been a part of her assignments. Had never asked or seemed even remotely interested so long as Anaís arrived home safe and sound. But today Simone was trying, and her ideas, despite her lack of tactical training, were *good*.

She glanced at Simone to find her sister practically beaming.

"I already have some ideas for this," Simone said, standing without being dismissed. "I will work on them right away."

With those final words, she swept gracefully from the room.

King Timun pressed his lips together contemplatively, ignoring Anaís in favor of rearranging her notes on Takaniim. She tracked his movements in silence. Opening a locked drawer, he removed another stack of documents and shuffled through them, tucking her notes between the pages at various intervals. A scrap of paper fluttered out of the pile, gliding across the desk to land in front of her. Her father snatched it up, but not before she caught a glimpse that made her blood run cold.

It was the missing page from *An Anthology of Protohistoric Life*.

"Anaís?" King Timun's eyes grew sharp as he studied her, expression morphing from thoughtful to cold. Fear and indignation froze her in her seat.

With only four words, she could confront him. *What are you planning?* The question stayed locked away behind closed lips. She was ten years too late.

Anaís would have given anything for Balendin to come back and make things right again, but he was dead, and the memories of him were buried by brutal days and cold nights and the painful re-indoctrination of how she was meant to serve the crown as Anadali Amadé.

She should have been a protector, but she was a coward—afraid of what she could do, but more afraid of what would happen to her if she did not do it.

Fear, it turned out, was not a fickle thing. The king counted on it. And so she would do what she must.

"Your Majesty?" Anaís said.

"Bring us the future."

Obedience settled over her shoulders like a well-loved blanket—too tattered for its own good, but too sentimental to dispose of. "It will be done."

* * *

ANAÍS POPPED ANOTHER BITE OF honeyed cornmeal cake into her mouth. If she couldn't take a nap or a bath anytime soon, at least she could have a snack. Her usual chair by Simone's fireplace cradled her like an overstuffed hammock, one arm of the chair supporting her feet while the other served as a pillow for her head. Simone, on the other hand, was currently pacing a hole into the rug.

"You'll need a profession you can slip into comfortably without it screaming 'hello, I'm an assassin'," Simone said. "Though it must still be suitable for a Freydlanian woman."

Anaís swallowed her bite of cake. "Silversmith?"

"Can you hold a rudimentary conversation about silversmithing?" Simone asked. When Anaís shook her head, she sighed. "It's for the best; metalworking is considered a masculine profession there. How about a seamstress?"

"Is sewing fabric together different from stitching a person back up?"

"Of course it is!" Simone glared at her. "A nanny, then?"

Anaís snorted a laugh.

"Florist?"

"Allergic."

"Pastry chef?"

"You don't need to do this," Anaís huffed.

Whirling, Simone jabbed her finger at Anaís. "Yes. I do."

She shook her head. "I could have done it the way I normally do."

"I know you would have! That's the problem," Simone snapped, then spun on her heel to continue pacing. "What state would you have been in if you rode hard for twenty-odd hours, waited in a forest for who knows *how* long, broke into the palace unseen, killed the prince unseen, escaped the palace *unseen*, then rode back home. Without breaks. Assuming nothing went wrong."

Anaís bit the inside of her lip but remained silent. The reality was, Simone was right. She wouldn't have been able to adhere to her father's proposed timeline, even on a good day. Nahonaugh was too far, the mission too crucial, her condition too...

Anaís didn't want to think about it, but she had to. Her life depended on keeping it at bay for as long as possible. Maybe she *would* be able to assassinate the crown prince without incident, but what of the trip back to Dúndíor? What if something did go wrong at the palace and she had to fight?

"This way, you can rest," Simone said gently, interrupting Anaís's thoughts. "Without having to hide. You can enjoy life, if only for a day. This isn't a holiday, but please. Please let me help you with this burden."

"This isn't a burden you need to bear," Anaís argued, though there was no weight behind it. She was too tired to properly debate with Simone, and...she wanted a break. Even a small one. Still, it didn't stop her from saying, "What of the threat of war that will fall on your shoulders in the aftermath of the prince's death? What of whatever else is brewing in the shadows?"

"That's just it though," Simone began. "Whatever is brewing—we're in it together. And I think this might be part of it."

"How so?" Anaís frowned.

"Talk to the people. Uncover the secrets of their city. I think you might be able to find something. This will put us in a position to be ready."

Anaís shook her head. "Nahonaugh will be weakened for whatever is coming—she won't have an heir, won't be a strong ally."

"But if you fail Father, I won't have *you*."

Their gazes locked. Simone didn't know what had happened that fateful night. All she knew was one day Balendin was there, and the next day he was dead. It wasn't difficult to interpolate the reasoning for his...demotion. Under King Timun's rule, an Amadé who failed a mission was awarded the title of traitor. The title of traitor carried with it an unpardonable death sentence, circumstances be hanged.

Simone knew enough. In that moment, that was enough.

"I will pose as a textile shop owner," Anaís said as the idea formed in her mind, carefully capturing and inspecting each thought before breathing life into it. "From a small town in Freydlan. The need for trade from various regions will explain why I'm proficient in Nahraeg. And despite my relative disinterest in fashion, I *can* hold rudimentary conversations on fabric."

A slow smile curved Simone's lips. "What's the difference between linen and cotton, then?"

"There are many, though the ones I find most notable are the climates the crops are grown in and the textures the fabrics can produce." Anaís rose and plucked a pillow off the chair before continuing. "Dúndían cotton is most renowned for its long fibers"—she squinted studiously at the fabric and gave it an approving nod—"which creates a finer weave and produces a softer, more luxurious fabric. Flax grows most readily in the warm, humid region of Northern Nahonaugh and is a sturdier, more breathable option. Unfortunately, while it is ideal for Nahonan summers, it's a heat-leaking death trap in the face of Freydlanian winters. Hence why the reopening of trade along the Nahonaugh-Dúndíor border will be advantageous for craftswomen such as myself." She tossed the pillow to Simone. "You may observe."

Simone caught the pillow, blinked, then laughed. "You made that up."

"Maybe I did. Maybe I didn't." She hadn't—Anaís had wondered why the blankets in Nahonaugh felt different, and a quick mosey through an agricultural book she'd found at a shop on the road back to Dúndíor had told her why. "Either way, it's convincing enough. Now, if you don't mind us breaking for a while, I really could use a bath."

CHAPTER FIFTEEN
MEMORIES OF FLESH

DAYS SLIPPED BY AND CIAN STILL COULDN'T GET THE Cross-Kingdom Sector's insignia out of his head. Hard stone pressed against his slippered feet, followed by the soft cushion of the woolen rug. He pivoted and retraced his steps—seven paces on the rug, fifteen on stone. Usually, his study was a safe haven for the untangling of troublesome thoughts. Tonight was no different, with the exception that he couldn't quite grasp the thought he sought to untangle. He had a sinking feeling it would need to be dug up first.

Counselor Trijveson had made no fuss when Cian asked to see the trade documents following the departure of Princess Simone and her Anadali, and he readily answered Cian's questions about the merchant seals. But no matter how deep Cian dug, no matter how hard he pried, all of the documentation was pristine. Dates matched, signatures verified, maps accurate, ledgers unforged. Everything was fine.

So why had seeing that seal been akin to laying eyes on a forbidden secret ripped from the dark recesses of his mind?

Perhaps it was him—*he* was not fine.

Cian's head slumped into his hands, and he dug his fingers into his hair for what must have been the twentieth time that evening. He was coming undone at the seams, his memories loose threads pulled from the fabric of his past with nothing but his own fear to stop them from unraveling. He squeezed his eyes shut, willing himself to think. This was the one time he needed to remember everything he'd worked so hard to lock away.

Air hissed through his lips as his lungs expanded from the lack of oxygen. *Breathe, remember to breathe.* It did nothing to stop his chest from constricting, nothing to stop the lightheadedness that sent tingles down his spine and left him wanting to crawl out of his own skin. He was verifying the origins of the seal for Eoghan, for Nahonaugh, for himself. He sucked in another breath of air, then pulled on the thread as hard as he could.

The fabric ripped.

Memories fluttered by.

His mother's smile, the flicker of firelight on a cold winter night, the smell of warming spices wafting through the house, the tinkling sound of cutlery against ceramic growing louder, louder, transforming into glass breaking, loved ones fighting, "I'm proud of you, son," fists pounding, "Get out of my sight, son," hands that held, hands that hurt, both the same, both different.

He couldn't keep searching; he *had* to keep searching. For Eoghan.

Memories continued to fly by until he caught a glimpse of hazy afternoon light filtering through a window, and time froze. Dust danced slowly through the leather and pine scented air of his father's study. A young redheaded boy not more than eleven years old sat at the chair behind the desk, feet dangling inches above the floor. A smattering of freckles dusted across his nose and cheeks, continuing along his arms exposed by rolled up sleeves—just how his da used to wear his shirts in the late springtime.

It's too hot for sleeves, but too cold for none, Da used to say.

The boy opened a drawer in the desk and rifled through it before pulling out a copper stamp. It had seemed so harmless, so innocent at the time. With intricate patterns carved into the face of the metal, how could any boy have resisted such a foreign curiosity?

Cian's heart ached as he watched the memory play out before him, but he had to know, had to see.

The door swung open, sending the lazy dust into a swirling frenzy as a man entered the room.

"Look what I found, Da!"

Compassion on the man's face at the sight of his son morphed into rage when he laid eyes on what was in the boy's hand, on what was stamped on the paper before him. The man stalked forward, anger bubbling to the surface ready to be unleashed when consequences met flesh.

Cian's eyes shot open before the rest of the memory had a chance to play out, but he could still feel the phantom pain of the belt against his skin. His fingers tapped a haphazard melody against his desk as he tried to ground himself. It was the same stamp; he was sure of it.

When his father left on a trip the next day, Cian had sneaked into the study after his mother had gone to sleep and stamped the design onto one of the pages in his journal. Retribution, his past self had thought. A secret trophy of rebellion. His father made the last strike, but Cian wanted, needed, to make the last move.

Looking back now, he knew the action was foolish, despite the fact that his father was long gone.

Cian pulled a tattered leather-bound journal from the recesses of his desk and ran his thumb over the soft string that kept the pages from fluttering out. He hadn't laid eyes on it since he'd haphazardly shoved it into this very spot, after Eoghan had convinced him to move to the palace and study politics at university. Cian had thought that time, a new chance at life, and the reassurance that he could support his mother with the finances he would gain in court—and later as a royal advisor—would bury the hurt of his past.

Instead, time had left him with a burning numbness of repressed pain shackled by a child's nostalgia for all that could have been. But his body remembered the source of his scars, an account of the truth only it could read. Now his past was coming back to haunt him.

Holding his breath, he opened the journal and turned to the last page.

The insignias matched.

His chair clattered backward. Cian strode across the room, pulling more papers off the shelf—trading accounts, maps, official documents, business records. He shuffled through them, looking to see if there were more secrets hidden within. A trail. A pattern. He must be missing something.

A sharp pain dug into his side, and he realized he had walked into his desk. He shifted his hip and sat on the edge, parchment crinkling under his weight. His eyes burned as they skimmed document after document, various piles growing next to him in an order that made sense to some part of his consciousness. A tingling sensation spread through his leg as blood flow slowed from the awkward angle of the desk against his thigh. He ignored it, focusing on the papers before him—on the new thread he was finding. This one connected his past to his present, slowly weaving a new pattern into the memory he had torn open not moments ago. He stood to move back to his chair, but a spell of dizziness and the absence of feeling in his leg sent him plummeting toward the ground.

A resounding *thunk* echoed through the study as his hands slammed against the desk to steady himself. The room swayed. Darkness danced across his vision. The sensation subsided, and he looked up, squeezing his eyes shut and blinking rapidly to clear them. The shadows were too long, he realized. The flame flickering too fast. An illusion. That must have been what it was.

He pulled out another candle and touched the wick to the flame, waiting for its light to burn strongly before removing it and blowing out the other one. Then, carefully, he stood back and observed the fruit of his labor.

Papers were scattered across his desk. To any onlooker, it would have resembled the epitome of chaos. To him, it was a map. One document pointing to the next, secrets buried in secrets. Slowly, carefully, he had peeled back the layers, and now it was laid out before him as plain as day. His father had been—*was now*—up to something. What, he didn't know. But the paper trail didn't bode well for anyone.

Cian needed to get to the bottom of it before someone else caught wind. Despite his volatile nature, his father had always said he worked for the good of their family, for the good of the kingdom. Cian's conflicting emotions waged war against one another in his mind, and he shook his head to rid himself of the feeling. Nothing his father was doing could be nefarious. Could it? Not against his mother. Not against the kingdom.

He leaned against the wall and wrapped his arms around himself. Could he bear seeing his father again after all that had transpired?

The memories he had exhumed would not return to their graves easily, yet he didn't *want* to see his father hurt. Firm resolve settled in his core, and he pushed off the wall.

For Eoghan. For Nahonaugh. For himself.

Cian needed to know.

CHAPTER SIXTEEN
THE TRAITOR

An acidic blanket of smoke smothered Anaís's lungs and mouth. She spat, trying to rid her tongue of the putrid flavor, but the smoke had already embedded itself into her. A wave of nausea slammed against her as she rolled to her side and sat up. Matted, blood-soaked strands of hair stuck to her forehead, though she couldn't tell if it was her blood or someone else's. At this point she didn't care; she had to move before it was too late.

Too late for what?

Anaís lifted her head toward the palace, squinting against the red haze of the sun that filtered through the smoke-filled air. A memory flickered to life in the recesses of her mind, fading as quickly as it came, but she grabbed on to what she saw like a lifeline.

Balendin.

A cry ripped from her throat. Pushing herself up, she ran toward the palace. She knew where she would find him. Where she found him every time. Her footsteps pounded against the ground, but the loose gravel kept slipping like the shifting sands of an hourglass.

"Balendin!" she tried to scream, but the wind forced the sound back into her mouth. She sprinted the rest of the way toward him. Grit bit into her skin as she skidded across the ground and dropped to his side. Blood pooled under his body, saturating the gravel he lay on.

His right arm was gone.

"No, no, no! Balendin can you hear me!"

He didn't stir, but she knew he could hear her. This was not the end.

It never was.

The world tilted, and Anaís found herself standing before King Timun. He sat on the throne, his spine ramrod straight, shoulders drawn back and down. Tension wound his muscles, reminding her of a feral animal waiting to pounce. Anaís swallowed and shifted on her feet under the weight of Balendin leaning against her, under the weight of her mother's body at the foot of King Timun's throne, her lifeless stare looking past Anaís into eternity.

The king's eyes bore into Anaís's own, his face twisted into a calm rage. "What. Happened."

Anaís tightened her hands into fists and pressed them against the small of her back to try and stop the trembling. *Be brave, my child*. It was the last thing her mother had told her before Anaís left to complete her rounds that morning. Now all she heard was the numb ticking of the gilded clock as the reality of the past twelve hours pressed against her, pulling her under into the depths of an endless abyss. It meant nothing. The sound meant nothing. But she couldn't help but feel, *know*, that the clock was ticking down the time she had left. The time until—

"Explain yourself!" The king's voice echoed off the walls of the throne room. He was standing now, but Anaís's mind didn't register any of it. What was there to explain? Her mother was dead. Balendin had almost died...

Balendin nudged her side—the movement slumping him farther against the chair—but Anaís couldn't keep her eyes off the tourniquet wrapped around the stump of his upper arm. She had failed him.

"Go ahead, Anaís," Balendin's voice broke her out of her trance and she wiped her palms against her uniform, standing at attention.

"A small patrol of warriors from the Dúndían Army was holding off Nahonan rebels at the border. The Nahonans were in violation of the Treaty. Five fighters slipped through the ranks and made for the palace." Anaís's voice felt distant, detached, as if she were listening to herself speak underwater. "I cut them off and held ground. Three were eliminated." She nodded absentmindedly, trying to remind herself there was redemption for her yet. "As we were fighting, one of them set fire to the hillside. It spread quickly. In the chaos, they got the upper hand." Her breath caught as shame gripped her heart, and she had to force herself to keep speaking. "I was not able to perform my duties." Her voice cracked. "I do not know the rest, as my mind was not awake." She glanced briefly at Balendin before drawing her attention back to the floor, frozen in place.

The king's gaze trailed over her and settled on the blood that ran down her temple, carving a trail in the soot that covered her from head to toe. He nodded, weighing her words in his mind. A darkened shadow fell over his expression while he studied Balendin. "State your duty."

"I was to protect the queen," Balendin rasped.

"And you have failed." King Timun's voice cracked. "Your oath as Anadali Amadé is broken."

Anaís could feel the king's gaze searing into her skin as his attention returned to her, but the fear that consumed her kept her eyes locked on the ground.

"What happens to traitors?" King Timun growled.

"They perish," she whispered.

"I will not repeat myself."

Anaís stood straighter and lifted her eyes to meet his own. "They perish, Sir."

King Timun drew his dagger and gestured lazily at her. "Step forward."

Ice crawled down her spine. She was going to die. For not fighting until her last breath, for letting the rebels get past her, for failing to get to Balendin on time, for failing to help him stop the murder of her mother, for failing as Anadali.

"Papa?" she choked out.

"I am your king!" His shout echoed through the chamber. The command in his voice drew her body forward against her own volition. He flipped the dagger around and held it out to her. "We have need for a new Amadé," the king said, his voice eerily calm. "I need you to relieve this traitor of his duties."

Anaís's fingers curled around the hilt of the dagger as she took it from her father's grasp. "I do not understand."

King Timun placed his hands on her shoulders and turned her around to face Balendin. His breath tickled her ear when he spoke. "You fought until you could fight no more, yet somehow you managed to save the one who had more to give. This is the quality I seek in my Amadé."

"He was dying," Anaís whispered. "He had nothing left."

"And yet here he is." The king shoved her toward Balendin. Anaís stumbled, catching herself before she ran into her mentor. Her friend. Her brother.

"It's okay," Balendin murmured. "Do it how I taught you."

"I can't."

He reached up and tucked a wayward strand of hair behind her ear before settling his hand on her cheek. A sad smile tugged at his lips. He wiped the trail of blood from her temple with his thumb. "Please."

Tears blurred her vision as she looked at him. How could she? How could she end the life of the one who raised her? Who cared for her?

How could she not? There would be no mercy if the hand of death came from her father.

"Balendin of Qotiu." The king's voice echoed in the throne room. "You have been found guilty as a traitor to the crown and to the people of Dúndíor. You are hereby relieved of your duties." A *crack* echoed in the room, the king's staff striking the floor. Anaís flinched. "Your life forfeit." Another crack. "Your honor removed from the pages of history." *Crack*. "Your name shall never be uttered in this kingdom again, under penalty of death."

An eerie silence enveloped the room, waiting for the judge to pass his duties to the executioner.

"Anaís?"

She glanced back at her father.

"With dignity." He gestured toward the dagger hanging loosely between her fingers.

She drew her shoulders back and stood tall, fingers curling

tightly around the hilt of the dagger, but when she returned her focus on Balendin she could not hide the anguish that ripped through her heart.

"A'ti mok tae," she whispered in his native dialect. *I love you.* Then, without hesitation, she struck.

Blood painted her hands red as the dagger sank into his flesh and tore through his body. Yet it was pain that burned through *her* chest as if the dagger was ripping through her own skin and bone. The agony built, mounting inside her until every thought, every movement, every fiber of her being was consumed by it. She was burning, suffocating, an inferno blazing without oxygen. It wasn't until she pulled the dagger free that she realized she had been screaming, and all at once the pain let go and time held its breath.

Balendin swayed, a look of calm washing over his face when his gaze met Anaís's own. "I love you too, little Nai."

He slumped, Anaís falling with him, and as life left his body, it felt as if a part of her died with him. The tiled floor pressed against her still living flesh, sending tendrils of ice weaving through her skin. She shouldn't have been allowed to feel anything—neither hot nor cold, rough nor smooth—for as long as Balendin could not feel it too. She reached out to touch her mentor one last time, but the world tilted again and everything went black.

A peaceful darkness descended, wrapping around Anaís in a comforting embrace. In the quiet, she could hear water lapping against a shore. A soft breeze caressed her skin, fresh forest air filling her lungs and clearing away the last of her ashen nightmare. She had never been here before, yet this place *knew* her.

All was calm. All was as it was meant to be.

Like a flower unfurling to greet the morning, lights began to bloom within the lake—blush and lilac and silver hues that kissed the fog resting atop the water. Grass tickled her calves as she made her way down the shore, stopping at the water's edge. Fog swirled around her ankles. A familiar tug around her heart grounded her, beckoning her neither here nor there. Her lifeline had brought her to safety.

Anaís closed her eyes, resting in the presence of her comforter. She hadn't felt the connection this strongly since the night in the library. At the time, it had terrified her. It still did. But this time she did not want to run; she wanted to drown in the peace he brought.

This time, she stayed.

A BIRD SQUAWKED AND ANAÍS jolted awake, blinking against the sun streaming through her window. She rubbed her eyes, trying to rid herself of sleep. How could she truly wake up if her nightmares were simply memories relived?

But the second dream? She had never been by that lake before. And the presence—the one that had protected her since she was a child. It *was* stronger this time; more tangible. She wasn't sure how to feel about that. It was one thing to accept their connection when everything was but a dream. But when it seeped into reality?

The thought sent a jolt of fear down her spine. Anaís rolled away from the window and pulled the blankets over her head. Her excursion to the library in Nahonaugh had followed on the heels of an already tiring day. A *long* day. What she had felt was most likely a figment of her imagination, for dreams could not become reality unless they were reality first. If her nightmares were any proof of that.

Letting out a sigh, Anaís closed her eyes. For now, she did not need to worry about any of that. Five more minutes. She would let herself soak in the serenity between dreams for five minutes. Then she would get up, face the day, and—

Incessant pounding on her door jolted her upright.

"Anaís?" Simone shouted softly through the door. "Anaís are you there?"

A blessed pause stilled the air while Simone listened for life, then the pounding began again. Anaís slumped back down with a grumble. There would be no sleeping after all. She took in a breath and glared at the door as the pounding continued, followed by another brief pause when her name once again floated through the door.

Time to face the day. And the menace that had woken her.

"There's no need to whisper, Sim!" Anaís shouted, kicking off her blankets and padding across the room. "You've already woken half the palace with your incessant"—she yanked the door open, revealing a wide-eyed Simone with her fist raised—"pounding."

Her sister's hand dropped to her side. "You're late."

"For what?"

"You leave today."

"I know."

Simone tried to peek around her. "What were you doing in there?"

"Sleeping."

"It's half seven. You usually wake up with the sun."

Anaís rubbed her hands across her face with a groan. She hadn't realized she had slept in. "The sun said I could have a lie-in," she grumbled.

She wasn't *too* far behind schedule, but that was still time she could not get back. Inns always had a stringent late policy during festival seasons, and the one Katka had arranged for her was no different. If she rode hard, she could make up for lost time, so long as she didn't run into any other delays on her way out of the palace.

"Right," Simone scoffed, and she pushed past Anaís to settle in the plush armchair by the unlit fireplace. "Well, your lie-in is officially over, and you still need to pack."

Anaís let the door swing shut and flopped across her bed. If she couldn't sleep on it, she could at least enjoy the soft plushness before she spent all day on horseback.

"I've already packed," Anaís countered. "One dress for Fheile Earrach to blend in with the crowd, one all-black ensemble for sticking to the shadows and hiding bloodstains, and one extra pair of traveling clothes. For traveling."

"Okay...that's a start." Simone nodded before pulling a face somewhere between a grimace and a laugh. "Please don't get blood on your clothes."

"It's not my blood. Besides"—she shrugged—"sometimes it can't be helped."

"Can't you just...do it cleanly?"

"The heart is a pump. Blood is under a certain amount of pressure so it moves through the body, as it's supposed to. I cut, it squirts—"

"Okay!" Simone plugged her ears. "Okay! I get it. Too much detail. Moving on."

Anaís shrugged. "I thought squirting was quite a mild way to put it."

"It's disgusting, is what it is." Simone shuddered, then adopted her royal posture once more. "Right, well, you might have started to pack, but I've added a few more things. A few simple dresses for your cover. A different option for the festival. Some shoes—"

"I'll only be there for four days! How many clothes do I need?

"You're a textile maker going on holiday, Nai. Trust me on this."

Anaís blew out a breath. "All right, but if I'm late because my horse was carrying too much, it's your doing."

CHAPTER SEVENTEEN
TOPPLED SERENDIPITY

A SHEEN OF SWEAT COVERED ANAÍS'S BROW, WHILE errant curls and a halo of frizz adorned her once tightly plaited hair. The straps of her knapsack dug into her shoulders, numbing the ache that had settled deep within her bones after a hard ride, but it was of no importance. She could deal with the loss of sensation tingling the tips of her fingers later. For now, she had to make it to the inn before it was too late. She hadn't counted on needing a permit—and being denied one—to ride her horse through the city center directly to the inn.

Anaís looked from the map gripped tightly in her hands to the street and back again, trying to orient herself as masses of people flowed around her, their footsteps tapping a cacophonous harmony against the cobbled street as they rushed about their business. Some darted in and out of shops that lined the streets, others formed queues to purchase fresh fruit and vegetables at the market stalls. Others, much like herself, were travelers coming to the capital city for Fheile Earrach, trying to make their way through the jubilant anticipation that pulsed through the streets—the heartbeat of the city.

The anticipation only managed to encourage her heart to beat a little faster, her anxiety to rise a little higher. She was going to be late. She *loathed* being late.

With unfeeling fingers, Anaís stuffed the map into her cloak pocket and began the laborious journey of gracefully shoving her way through the masses, dodging carts and skirting around couples with linked arms as she went. She stopped short for a child to dart in front of her, only to be barreled into by a man in a stuffy three-piece suit. He gestured wildly at her, but she only had eyes for the inn that was now mere steps away.

Warm candlelight filtered through the linen curtains and pooled into the street, illuminating the cobblestones while the night sky swallowed the last vestiges of sunset. The door swung open on well-oiled hinges, and the soothing scent of cedar and pine enveloped her as she stepped into the inn, washing over her in a wave of calm. The hustle and bustle of the city faded into a distant lull as soon as the door clicked shut.

Anaís brushed some hair off her face, which stuck to her skin from the combination of humidity and sweat, and made her way toward the reception desk. A middle-aged man with dark-brown hair much too unkempt for his neatly tailored suit stood hunched over the desk, helping an elderly couple. Spectacles sat low on his nose as he read through his bookkeeping list; likely they'd kept slipping down throughout the day, and he had finally given in to their will rather than push them up for the umpteenth time.

It seemed like his day was going much the same as hers.

The wooden floor squeaked when she queued behind the couple the receptionist was currently helping. He glanced up at her, keeping his finger pressed against the page of the book so as to not lose his place.

"I'll be with ye in a moment."

Anaís gave him a warm smile. "No rush," she reassured, a carefully manufactured Freydlensku accent lilting through her Nahraeg.

He returned his attention to his task at hand and Anaís took the time to finally set her knapsack down, flexing her fingers when pins and needles came rushing down her arms. She looked around the inn. Katka had chosen well. Richly colored rugs adorned the dark wooden floor, topped with furniture like islands in a forest sea. Anaís wished she had chosen to curl up in one of the chairs rather than stand—the leather looked buttery soft.

The receptionist gave her a strained smile when she turned her attention back to the front desk. She gave him a friendly smile in return—no need to stress the poor man—and perused the art adorning the back wall. A blueprint of the original inn hung in a rustic wooden frame, while a painted landscape of Nahonan countryside hung beside it in burnished gold. A sign with delicately curving letters written in Nahraeg sat in a frame on the front desk. Anaís stared at it, willing the calligraphy to transform into words. What she saw made her heart skip a beat.

Dear guests,

Due to the influx of travelers during festival season, there is a two-hour tardiness policy. If you are unavailable for check-in during this period, your room will be given to the next waiting guest. Thank you for your understanding in facilitating a smooth season.

Kind regards,

The Staff of Tirn ni Canaiught

She couldn't be more than two hours late, could she? Anaís pulled out her pocket watch with shaking hands and pried it open. She was supposed to be checked in three hours ago.

Lovely.

"Ah, found ye!"

Anaís's head shot up at the sound, but it was simply the receptionist talking to the couple. He ran his hand through his hair and turned around to fetch the keys to their room. She clicked her pocket watch closed and tucked it back into her cloak, keeping her eyes trained on him. He was definitely stressed, but he seemed nice enough. Surely her slight tardiness would be okay. With the price she paid for the room, it had better be okay.

The couple took their key and picked up their bags before making their way toward the winding staircase on the far side of the lobby.

"I can help who's next!"

Anaís stepped up to the counter, setting her knapsack back on the ground with a plop. "I have a booking for Toma Glaadris."

"All right." He turned his attention back to the book, flipping straight to the G's on the first try. His fingers grazed over the lines of reservations inked onto the paper, her name mumbled under his breath as he went. Then, as quickly as he started, he stopped. And stood there. Unmoving. The beginning of a frown appeared in the space between his brows.

Anaís leaned against the counter and peered over the edge to look at the book. "Is something the matter?"

He looked up at her, then back down at the paper, the frown blooming into an expression that clearly said *I have unfortunate news for you.* "Yer not Toma, are yeh?"

"The one and only." She tried to sound optimistic, but she knew what was coming before the words left his lips.

"I'm sorry, lass." His shoulders deflated as he met her gaze. "We have a strict two-hour policy during festival season. Your booking was canceled and given to someone on the waiting list."

"But I—"

"I know." He sighed and ran a hand through his hair again. "I cannae change the rules. Believe me, I would if I could."

He did not know, and she had it in her right mind to not believe him either. But he was run thin, as was she. Really all she wanted was a bath and sleep, and he was currently preventing her from achieving both of those things. Still, there would be no sense in shouting at the poor man.

Anaís opened her mouth to tell him it was all right, but quickly snapped her mouth shut at his expression. She must have had murder written on her face, as the more he studied her in her silent—albeit abated—frustration, the faster the blood seemed to drain from his own. She tried to school her features into something more pleasant, but the damage was already done.

"Ye might have some luck at the inn down the lane." His Adam's apple bobbed as he swallowed. "Tell them Ruaridh set yeh. That might help."

"Can't you just—"

"No, I can't." Ruaridh pushed his glasses up the bridge of his nose for what must have been the first time in hours. "Next!"

Sighing, Anaís grabbed her bag and weaved her way through the crowd of guests who had gathered in the foyer, waiting to check in. She tucked her hands into her cloak while she walked, lightly touching the throwing knife hidden under her sleeve. The feeling of the familiar cold metal pressing against her skin helped ground her as she prepared to face whatever was to come next. What was Balendin's favorite phrase again?

Look to the stars, they will show you the way.

She pushed through the doors and squinted as her eyes adjusted to the dark. *Look to the stars.* She tilted her head toward the night sky, filling her lungs with air and holding it for a heartbeat before releasing it slowly. As the air left her body, so too did the last of her frustrations. All that was left was the diamond-speckled sky that stretched above her, and the endless possibilities that lay before her. *They will show you the way.*

Anaís turned to try and find whatever inn Ruaridh had gone on about. Instead of meeting open road, she was met with a human-shaped wall, an explosion of fruits, and a very surprised *oof* as said human toppled to the ground.

The dull *thunk* of plump, ripe produce bruising on the cobblestones broke Anaís out of her stupor and had her scrambling to the ground to help the fallen woman...and the very sad fruit.

"I'm so sorry!"

"Oh hush, nothing an old lady can't handle," the woman chided as she righted herself. Her long strawberry-blonde hair was swept back into a loose braid that fell over her shoulder, soft wisps of hair framing her face. It had probably been a striking shade of auburn in her youth, although the burden of time had stripped it of its richness. A lace-trimmed cream apron that now had a light smudging of dirt across the front was tied neatly around her waist, adding volume to her otherwise thin frame.

Though Anaís was certain they had never crossed paths before, there was something familiar about this woman that tugged at the back of her mind. It wasn't unpleasant per se, but the sensation that she was looking through a boarded-over window of her past left her feeling slightly unsettled.

"Are you lost, dearie?"

Anaís blinked, heat flushing her cheeks when she realized she had been staring at the woman while trying to place the memories that teased the back of her mind.

"Oh, umm, I'm looking for the inn down the lane? An Com—" she paused, trying to remember the name of one of the other inns she had passed. Never in her life had she been so utterly unfocused, or so utterly out of her element. If she didn't get her act together now, *she* would be the one meeting her end. Not Eoghan.

Though perhaps being a slightly foolish but respectful foreigner would do her some good in a pinch. No one would suspect an assassin out of *this*.

"An Comidh?" the woman supplied hopefully. She stood and hoisted the basket of fruit onto her hip.

"Yes! That's the one."

"It's right down that way." She gestured in the direction opposite to where Anaís had headed before glancing at the inn she came out of moments ago. "If you didn't have luck there, I'm afraid your odds won't be much better at An Comidh. They're usually the first to book up."

"I'll give it a try anyway, thank you."

"If your luck runs out, I run a small inn near Lough Ygra. It's about a thirty minute walk from the edge of town. There's still a room left, if it's not too far from your final destination. It's got beautiful views of the palace too. I'll make sure it stays unbooked for tonight." The woman nodded resolutely, then turned on her heel and toddled off back the way she came.

"Thank you!" Anaís called after her. "I'll keep that in mind."

* * *

AN COMIDH WAS, IN FACT, booked up. Ruaridh's name hadn't done anything to help, though it did get Anaís a pitiful yet understanding look and a less-than-helpful "Why don't you try Tírn O'Lochaigh?"

By that point, she was too tired to argue. It was all one big, minor inconvenience she had brought upon herself. This problem wouldn't exist if she hadn't bothered to stay at an inn, but Simone was right—traveling for a day and camping in the forest before assassinating the crown prince was a disaster waiting to happen. That didn't mean she wasn't going to feel sorry for herself as she made her way down the dirt path toward the inn at Lough Ygra.

Her horse, unsurprisingly, shared the sentiment. He wasn't content at all to be moved from the stable Anaís had originally boarded him in to one on the other side of town—riding the long way round due to permit restrictions. Though the expansive meadow and extra carrot Anaís gave him before taking her leave did improve his mood.

If only the same could be said for her. Each crunch of her footsteps as she made her way down the gravel path the stable hand had helpfully pointed her along served only to bolster her worries that were all too happy to make themselves known, now that she was too tired to stop them.

This is the worst idea I've ever had.

It's a great idea; it's secluded, away from prying eyes, an elusive getaway.

I've never met these people before.

I've never met the other innkeepers before either.

Yes, but this is different.

How is this different?

It's a strange lady who...

Like an itch, the memory moved every time she came close to re-membering who the woman was. The more she chased it, the more desperately she needed to know. She stopped walking and closed her eyes, allowing herself to wander through her memories instead. Golden fields sprawling until they kissed the horizon filled her mind, sticky orange juice tickled her skin as it dripped down her chin, and the taste of vanilla biscuits melted on her tongue while the smell of roses lining the walkway of the palace dusted the night air surrounding her. Certainly those memories were her own, but now there was no Simone, no Balendin. Not even her mother.

There was simply a lonely hole begging not to be filled.

Anaís looked up to the sky and sighed, watching the stars wink at her through the clouds swirling above. They watched in return as she turned her head back to earth and pressed onward into the unknown.

Where had time gone? What happened to the fruit-sweetened days with wind in her hair and river water splashing beneath her feet? When training was intertwined with wisdom, and even her darkest days in the palace were brightened by childlike innocence?

The lingering impression of her dream wasn't helping. The bitter ache and the warm comfort intertwined into a gnarled ball of yarn with neither start nor end. She thought she was doing better, but there were still days—especially like today—where it seemed as if everything was split between life with Balendin and life without him. The longer he was gone, the harder it was to hold on to who he raised her to be.

He was her lighthouse, and she was a lone sailor making her way through a storm without end. Without his light, her memories had been darkened by the shadows he'd kept at bay during her youth.

She thought back to her musings that morning. Round and round she seemed to go. Maybe Simone was right. Just this once, as Toma Glaadris, she would allow herself to simply exist.

Before she knew it, she was standing in front of the door, her fist poised to knock.

With a resigned sigh, she brought her fist down against the smooth wood three times in quick succession, took a step back, and waited to see where the stars had led her.

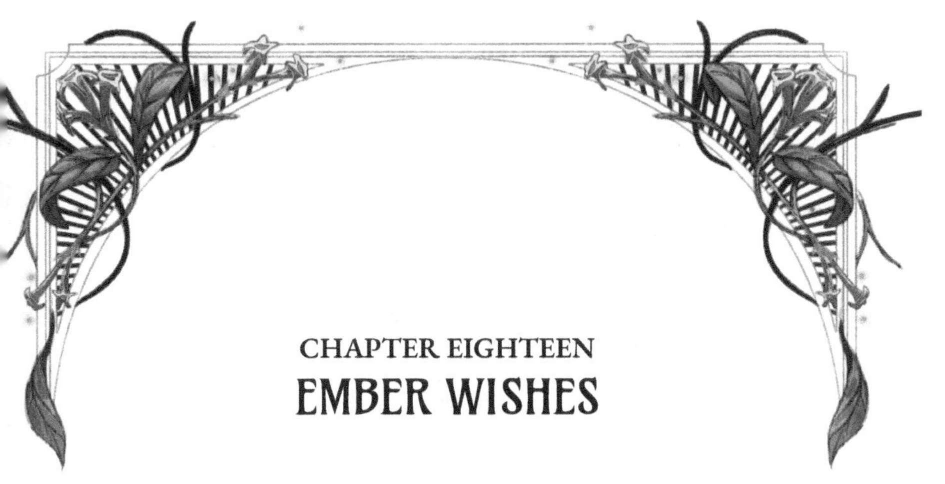

CHAPTER EIGHTEEN
EMBER WISHES

THE FIRST DAY OF SPRING BROUGHT WITH IT THE SWEET smell of nature bathed in the rosy hues of dawn. If Anaís were the poetic type, she would have entertained the notion that the peaceful awakening of spring reflected the promise of hope to come. She wasn't, but it was a welcome thought as she took in the view of the rolling hills and forested mountains from the safety of her bed.

Unlike every other innkeeper in town, the keeper of Tírn Ygra was true to her word—she did have a room. Although it wasn't as richly decorated as Ruaridh's inn or as well situated as An Comidh, it was filled with a warmth that could have only been imbued through the tender love of its caretaker. While decorations were sparse, the wood furnishings seemed to be made with stories as old as the trees from which they were crafted. Paintings of Nahonan landscapes hung on the wall in haphazard fashion. It reminded Anaís of a river—the muted blues, greens, and greys of the artwork trailing a meandering path across the textured cream walls.

She was still trying to figure out who the innkeeper reminded her of, but even after a good night's rest tucked into the coziest bed she'd ever had the privilege of sleeping in, her memories were nothing more than an annoying haze. Pulling back the covers, Anaís padded across the room to the wardrobe. Normally she wouldn't bother to unpack on an assignment, but the thought of spending multiple days rifling through her knapsack for the right clothing seemed like more effort than it was worth.

A honey-yellow dress stood out amongst the dark earthen tones of the clothes she'd picked for herself. She pulled the offending piece off the hanger and smiled at the feeling of the soft layers of chiffon against her skin. Golden thread was woven into the fabric to create intricate floral patterns, while glass beads added a touch of whimsy, casting flecks of morning light around the room. It was so very Simone and so very unlike anything Anaís would wear that it was almost laughable, though somehow that made it all the more perfect.

Anaís stepped into the dress and fastened the pearl buttons at the back, her smile growing wider as the dress swished around her legs when she spun in a circle. The glint of Simone's cosmetics tin perched on the vanity caught her attention, and she paused mid-spin. Should she? Simone would never know if she didn't use it, but curiosity and the pull of fate had her creeping toward the tin as if it were a wild animal waiting to attack.

Lowering herself onto the vanity seat, she opened the lid and peered at the contents inside. Rouges and creams and pigments stared back. A pot filled with a creamy crimson substance, which Simone had helpfully labeled as "cheek rouge," piqued her interest.

Anaís studied her reflection in the mirror. If she used a light hand, the rich color would complement her tawny skin tone nicely...

The sun had risen well above the horizon by the time Anaís closed the final pot of pigment. Cosmetic application wasn't as difficult as she'd feared, but choosing the right colors took time. As did blending. And then she had to tame her hair, but with the makeup and the dress a simple braid wouldn't do. Which was how her hair ended up in a woven crown braid, loose curls strategically pulled free to frame her features. She looked...different.

Simone would have been smug.

Giving herself one last once-over in the mirror, Anaís rose, tucked her feet into silk shoes, and made her way downstairs to attack the day—and search for breakfast.

SETTLING DEEPER INTO HER SEAT, Anaís turned her attention from her breakfast to the innkeeper—who she now affectionately knew as Mrs. Uí Mháille—as she enthusiastically answered her questions about the spring festival while making fruit tarts in the kitchen. Anaís didn't mind though, Mrs. Uí Mháille's good-natured mood was infectious. Seeing as she would need all her energy to make it through the day, she would take all the help she could get.

"In general, it's a bit quiet in these parts of town, but it will pick up as Fheile Earrach starts. You said you wanted to attend the opening celebration?"

Anaís nodded.

"The king's address begins at dusk," Mrs. Uí Mháille said as she transferred five tarts out of the oven, setting them on a rack to cool. "I would recommend arriving around three o'clock to wander some of the market stalls and to find a good spot. Make sure you have a full view of the lake."

Anaís swirled the tea in her mug, watching as errant flecks of tea leaves raced each other in the current. If the king was making an address, would the rest of the royal family be there? Would Eoghan be giving the address this year as rising king? Perhaps it would be best to avoid the "good spots," just in case.

Looking up, she asked, "What do the festivities consist of?"

"You'll have to go to find out." Mrs. Uí Mháille's soft countenance shifted into something slightly mischievous. Anaís hated surprises, but she couldn't help but smile in return. "And if my boy is anything like the man I've raised him to be," Mrs. Uí Mháille continued, her hands never stilling as she prepared the filling for her next batch of tarts, "he should be coming to visit any day now. I think you two would get along swimmingly. Oh, he could even show you around town! There are some lovely shops that only the locals know of. And you'll have to try the mince pies at Padraig's Pastries, it's an experience unlike anything you've ever tried. Unless you have mince pies in Freydlan?"

Anaís almost laughed at the distraught expression on the older woman's face. "No, we don't have mince pies. I'd like to try one though." As for her comments about her son... Anaís wasn't on the market to swim, as it were, but any information she could gather would make for less surprises. "What does your son do?"

"He's a..." Mrs. Uí Mháille's hands slowed, as if all her concentration was being spent on trying to decide how to compact the essence of her son into words. "Well, it's all a bit complicated for me if I'm honest. A lot of mathematics and trade. Sharp as a tack, that boy. He'll tell you more about it when he arrives."

There was something warm about her voice that sent a twinge of nostalgia through Anaís's heart. One that had her wishing she could bottle up the feeling, though whether it was to hold it close or toss it far away she wasn't sure. She settled on a nod and a simple "I would like that very much" instead.

Downing the last sip of her tea, Anaís set the empty mug next to her polished-off breakfast and asked, "You mentioned there are some shops in town only locals know about. What about in the city? I'd like to browse before going to the festival."

"Oh yes! Let's see, there's Nice Tea Meet Ya—they make the best tea blends. You must stop by Caughurn Street. All of the shops there are worth a visit. And you work with fabrics? Of course! You'll love House of Eli. They have a beautiful selection of fabrics. A bit pricy if I'm honest, but the quality!" Mrs. Uí Mháille dropped the whisk back into the bowl, sending a plume of flour into the air. "I'll call a carriage to take you into town."

Stars above, where did she find her energy? "No, that's all right, thank you!" Anaís called after the innkeeper before sliding out of her seat and following down the hallway. "I'd rather walk. It's a beautiful day."

"In those shoes?" Mrs. Uí Mháille called back, startling when she turned to find Anaís behind her. "My goodness, you're quiet, dear."

"I know quality materials when I see them. Trust me, these shoes will be fine."

IF HER LITTLE TOE HAD any say in the matter, Anaís really should have heeded Mrs. Uí Mháille's advice and taken a carriage. Though the blister was a token of success awarded by her first task of the day—she had carefully scouted the route she would take to the palace tomorrow evening. She wished she could forget it entirely and never walk that path again.

I don't need to walk it again today, Anaís reminded herself.

Repositioning the leather satchel on her shoulder, Anaís continued making her way along the shaded cobblestone path toward the festival. Simone had encouraged her to do something nice for herself, so she took Mrs. Uí Mháille's advice and browsed the shops in the city. It was the perfect distraction from the looming assassination of the man she had grown to care for, and from what would happen to her should she fail her mission. Eoghan was safe. If not for tomorrow, at least for today.

Folded inside her new bag was a swath of silk fabric for Simone as well. The raspberry-hued fabric was smooth to the touch and would hopefully be enough for a blouse and matching hair ribbon. A smile bloomed at the thought of presenting the gift to her sister. Simone had been right—this wasn't a holiday, but Anaís appreciated the reprieve nonetheless.

Rays of afternoon sunlight kissed her skin as she emerged from the shaded trail and into a sprawling garden. The alluring scent of roasted meats wrapped around her, mingling with the floral-perfumed air to create a strangely comforting aroma. Anaís hurried her pace, making her way through a short hedge maze and over a wooden bridge that spanned a babbling brook before stumbling upon the main area that housed the festival.

Couples danced in the courtyard, families meandered along flower-lined pathways, and errant groups of children chased bubbles floating in the air while others played spring-themed games in a meadow overlooking the lake. In the middle of the lake, observing the festivities from afar, stood the royal palace in all its glory. Golden shimmers of light danced along the crests of windswept waves, daring Anaís to ruin the tranquility of the magic surrounding her.

She blinked, and the water transformed into blood.

Warm and viscous, it dripped down her hands, staining her skin, staining her soul.

Balendin's blood. Eoghan's blood.

A child squealed with delight. Blood became water once more. Wiping shaking hands on her dress, Anaís straightened her spine and turned her attention toward the stands near the entrance, grounding herself in the sights and sounds and smells.

A vendor handed skewers of grilled lamb with garden vegetables to hungry customers. Two teenagers strolled down one of the aisles, passing a roasted potato topped with freshly churned butter and minced chives back and forth, giggling between bites.

Anaís approached an elderly gentleman selling what looked to be flaky dough pastries shaped as flowers. Signs on the table described their fillings—some with honeysuckle cream, others containing fresh berry jam. An assortment of tea cakes were displayed next to them.

"What would you recommend?" Anaís asked.

The man's eyes crinkled as he smiled up at her. "Well, I made the tea cakes—they're my wife's favorite. But she made the *pachimh*, which are my favorite. Personally, I'd recommend the cream-filled *pachimh* paired with a glass of *taebru*."

"*Taebru?*"

"Are you not from here, dear?" a middle-aged woman at the stand next to the man asked. Several carafes of jewel-toned drinks glistened atop her table. That must have been what he was talking about.

Anaís shook her head. "I'm from Freydlan."

"I thought I heard a bit of an accent! How lovely! I grew up in Freydlan before Da moved us out here for the weather." The *taebru* woman gestured to the gentleman selling tea cakes. "It's been our home ever since."

"It's too cold in that sun-forsaken kingdom." He shook his head disapprovingly, though a tinge of fondness shone through his expression. "Besides, the warmth of Nahonaugh makes it perfect for *taebru*. It's a traditional mixture of sweet and tangy fruit juices added to lightly fermented iced tea. Slightly fizzy. Very refreshing."

His daughter gave him a faux-unamused stare. "You need to stop overselling our wares."

"I'm not! It's a delicious pairing, and the young lady asked what I recommended."

"It sounds perfect," Anaís interjected. "I'll take both."

Day turned to dusk with a contented sigh, and under the shifting colors of the sunset the festival goers began to migrate toward the large open-air gloriette. Sun-bleached columns wrapped in flowering vines stretched to the sky, perfuming the air while providing shade for the royal family. Before she could single out individual faces, the crowd surged around her, pulling her deeper into its swirling mass. Stumbling, she followed the current until it deposited her wherever fate saw fit.

She wished she hadn't.

Guards lined the front of the gloriette, keeping the crowd a respectful distance away. Anaís fought the urge to shrink back. She was far enough from the front to blend in to the crowd pressed around her, and any undue movement could call attention to her area. Still, it was too close for comfort.

A hush fell over the people, and Anaís directed her attention toward the gloriette. King Ibhar stood on the balcony overlook, hand lifted high in a silent command for attention. Queen Siofra stood to his right. Anaís refused to look to his left.

The king's hand drifted to his side. Expectancy bubbled amongst the crowd. Seeming to sense this, he smiled, then spoke.

"Welcome, one and all, to the one hundred and sixth anniversary of Fheile Earrach. This festival represents more than the beginning of spring—the changing of seasons. It is a chance to celebrate renewal. The turning of soil, the planting of new seeds to nurture and grow while reaping the beauty that was planted before the harshness of winter tried to whither it away."

Anaís dared a peek at Eoghan. He stood with his head held high, yet she had the distinct impression that he was not looking down at his people. The set of his jaw and the softness in his eyes as he scanned the crowd told a story of determination. Defiance, almost. He was proud, not to be above them but to serve them.

"We celebrate Nahonaugh's prosperity through a new treaty with our neighbors to the East," King Ibhar continued. "One that will open new opportunities for all citizens, bringing in trade and allowing our talented artisans, merchants, and tradespeople to expand their influence."

As Eoghan's attention turned toward her section of the crowd, Anaís tucked her chin down and directed her gaze to the queen—she looked like she had swallowed something sour.

"We celebrate the turning of spring with renewed anticipation for the Turning of Kings as my son, your crown prince, prepares to ascend to the throne come autumn."

A deafening roar of applause burst from the crowd. Anaís startled, then forced herself to still. These were jubilant cries, not the vicious shouts of a riot. Regardless, she scanned the crowd to mark her exits.

King Ibhar lifted his hands again for silence, but an approving smile brightened his features. When the last of the applause died down, he continued his speech. "It has been my greatest honor to serve you as king. I welcome these next months with anticipation, knowing they will usher our kingdom into a bright and prosperous era."

King Ibhar finished as the last of the sun's light dipped below the horizon. Every head collectively turned toward the lake, waiting, watching in wondrous anticipation. Before Anaís could ask the woman next to her what was happening, a flare of light shot through the sky followed by a burst of stars.

Fireworks.

Thousands of glittering lights filled the night sky, embers of gold and red and purple coloring their heavenly canvas in mesmerizing patterns, reflecting onto the water below. Flowers of light bloomed. A water dragon swirled on clouds of blue fire. Somewhere in the distance, a child laughed with delight. But all Anaís could do was stand and stare at the fireworks, trying to ignore how her eyes darted to watch Eoghan's silhouette glow under the dazzling array of color after each burst of light. Trying to ignore the way he leaned against the railing, tipped his head up to the sky, and seemed to wish, as if each falling ember was a shooting star for him to claim as his own.

The last burst dissipated into the night, and hopeful expectancy rippled through the crowd. This was the end of an old beginning, the beginning of a new season. Tomorrow would mark the beginning of a new era.

Anaís swallowed the regret that threatened to choke her.

King Ibhar lifted his hands again. "Enjoy the festivities."

A low murmur surrounded her, growing into a joyful chatter as people dispersed in groups. The music from the orchestra swelled, then settled into a meandering waltz. With a final glance at Eoghan, Anaís turned and disappeared into the crowd, veering around the dance floor toward the far side of the festival where the gardens met the lake.

Lightning bugs floated lazily in the fresh breeze drifting off the water, their glow mixing with the silver starlight to illuminate her path as Anaís meandered past merchant tables. She should probably get back to the inn so she could rest for what was going to be a long day tomorrow. Still, it was nice to simply exist.

The music shifted to a lively reel, whoops rising through the crowd as more people came to the dance floor, going so far as to spill onto the pathways as they coalesced into groups. Resting upon a low stone wall, she watched while everyone seemed to move together to weave the intricate patterns of their traditional dance. One set blurred into another, the orchestra never tiring as more and more people joined the festivities.

Then a horrifying realization settled onto Anaís: her route out of the festival was completely blocked by the mass of spinning bodies. If she couldn't get through, she would have to wait, and if she had to wait only the stars knew when she would reach the inn. Fatigue would hasten the onset of her condition, which could hinder her mission tomorrow.

And if she failed her mission?

She sucked in a breath to calm her raging mind, but it caught in her throat before it could fill her lungs. She tried again. And again. And again. Taking in little sips of air as they came.

It wasn't enough.

This was why Simone's well-intended plan was a terrible idea. This was why Anaís worked in the shadows, why she worked on instinct alone. It was in that place of utmost focus where she could slip seamlessly into her role—a specialized weapon born to protect but forced to destroy.

This hope of being anything else? This was madness.

"May I have this dance?"

A voice came from next to her and she whipped around, hand going for the knife tucked in the back of her bodice when she caught sight of the man before her. The cacophony swirling about her collapsed into a pinprick of focus.

Eoghan Kavanaugh regarded her with coffee-brown eyes, his smile shifting into a look of concern as he took in her current state. "Anadali? Are you all right?"

The sound of his voice pulled her back to the present and she managed to take in a full breath of air. Anaís reveled in the feeling before replying with a quiet "Yes."

He raised his brow but didn't pry. Instead, he settled on the wall next to her, his shoulder lightly brushing her own.

"I thought my eyes were playing tricks on me when I saw you in the crowd." He glanced at her as if making sure she was real. "I'm glad they weren't."

"How did you know it was me?"

"I..." Eoghan paused, then shrugged, the corner of his mouth pulling into a contemplative frown. "Call it intuition."

Something about his words tugged at her heart, but she was still too shaken to properly parse the feeling out. "It was the dress, wasn't it?" Anaís said instead, rubbing the chiffon material between her fingers. "I was so frilly during my time in Nahonaugh you couldn't help but make the connection."

Eoghan barked out a laugh, though his expression sobered as he regarded her more intentionally. "You look lovely. I'm guessing if you're here like this you aren't on duty?"

"No," she said skeptically. "I'm not." Eoghan and his sense of duty too often led to interactions she wasn't sure how to categorize. It likely wasn't wise to experience one such interaction on the day before his—

Anaís shoved the thought down.

"Then if I may, I'd like to ask again." He stood and extended a hand. "Would you dance with me?"

Anaís looked at his hand, then back at the frenzy of skirts swishing, couples weaving around one another, women spinning away from their partner only to be returned right back where they belonged. It was enticing, yet terrifying.

Breathing out a sigh, she confessed, "If I'm honest, I'd simply like to cross."

Eoghan turned his attention to the crowd of dancers as if trying to map an ideal path through. "Unfortunately, I think this is one of those harrowing cases where if we cannot defeat them, we must join them."

The song ended, and in the beat of silence that stretched into the night, their gazes caught. She should simply muscle her way through the crowd and do away with him. She was Anadali Amadé. This was not her place; this was not her fate.

A lively jig brightened the silence of the night. The dancers swept into motion once more. Anaís's heart quickened at the thought of being swept into motion with Eoghan. She rose, grass tickling her calves as she closed the distance between them and slid her hand into his own. "Unfortunately, I believe you're correct."

He grinned, tipping his head toward the dance floor. "Shall we?"

Anaís studied the dizzying maelstrom of dancers. Her trepidation subsided as Eoghan's thumb brushed across her knuckles. He was the calm in the midst of the storm, her safety in the face of panic. She nodded, and before she could think twice about what she was about to do, Eoghan led her into the fray.

An overwhelming blur of colors swallowed her whole as the swell of the orchestra rose into the night sky. Fabric brushed against her skin, bodies bumped into her own. Only Eoghan's firm grip on her hand and waist kept her grounded as the flurry of dancers sucked them deeper and deeper into the unknown. Everything was too fast, too horrifically overwhelming for her to plan in the way she normally would. Not even training instincts could have prepared her for a moment such as this. Perhaps she should have accompanied Simone to more royal balls rather than stay with her Anadali. But what else was she to do? Abandon her duty for frivolities?

Suddenly, dancing didn't seem so frivolous anymore.

For the time being, she could only hold on tight to her general sense of direction and the instinctual desire to not be trampled as she trusted Eoghan to lead them safely across.

One minute, her dress was billowing around her as he twirled her across the dance floor; the next minute, they were stumbling across a grassy clearing, chests heaving as they broke free from the swirling crowd of bodies to emerge on the other side of the festival.

Eoghan let go of her slowly, his hair windswept, his eyes bright with joy. "A successful crossing, wouldn't you say?"

"It wasn't horrific," Anaís wheezed, trying to catch her breath. Her face hurt from smiling.

"Eoghan! There you are!" A familiar-looking man wove through the crowd. His attention caught on Anaís and his steps slowed. "Hello, who might you be?"

Eoghan stepped closer to Anaís. "Lochlan, you remember—"

"Toma," Anaís interrupted. "Toma Glaadris."

Eoghan's questioning gaze bore a hole into the side of her head, but she kept her focus on the man before her. She didn't mind Eoghan knowing who she was, but if no one else recognized her it was for the best.

"Lochlan Kavanaugh," he replied. "Royal guard, this fool's cousin"—he tipped his head at Eoghan—"and bearer of biscuits." Lochlan lightly shook a bag that Anaís hadn't noticed before.

"You got them!" Eoghan exclaimed, plucking the bag out of Lochlan's hand and peering inside.

"Got a swift kick to the shins for it, but I escaped otherwise un-scathed." He brushed an imaginary piece of dust off his jacket. "Go on, try one."

Eoghan took two biscuits from the bag, passing one to Anaís and keeping one for himself.

The biscuit was shaped like a rose, swirls of blush pink frosting adorning the top like dainty petals. She took a tentative bite, closing her eyes as the sweet, buttery crumb of the biscuit melted on her tongue, complimented by the subtle notes of vanilla essence and rosewater.

"Wait"—Anaís looked at Lochlan—"why would someone kick you?"

"He stole them," Eoghan said as he procured another biscuit.

Anaís sputtered.

Lochlan scoffed. "It's not stealing if *I* made them. My sister is selling them at the festival. Technically *she's* the thief, profiting from *my* labor. It's only—"

"Lochlan!" A young girl the spitting image of the man she hol-lered at came barreling toward them. "Get yer grubby paws—"

"Lovely meeting you!" Lochlan squeaked to Anaís. "See you later!" he yelled over his shoulder at Eoghan as he ran away.

"So, Toma, is it?" Eoghan's low voice sounded from behind her. Anaís turned slowly, relaxing as she met his teasing smile. "I would take offense that you revealed your name to my cousin first, yet I struggle to believe that your name is actually 'Toma'."

"Do you wish for me to grace you with my name, Your Highness?"

He paused, a small crease forming between his brows as he contemplated. Finally, he shook his head. "No, not unless you wish to give it. I do wish you would grace me with mine. How many times must I ask you to call me Eoghan?"

"It wouldn't be proper," Anaís said. In truth, it was the shield she carried to separate him from her. He had already broken down her defenses; this was the last piece of armor she had left.

"Neither is offering stolen contraband to a foreign warrior"—he held the bag of biscuits out—"yet here we are."

Foreign. *Enemy*, her mind supplied. It was best she remembered that. Shaking her head, Anaís backed away from him. "I need to leave."

His hand dropped to his side and he took a step forward. "May I escort you to—"

"No," Anaís bit out, guilt gnawing at her when he startled at her voice. "Thank you," she continued softly. "For the dance. And the biscuits, illegal though they may be."

Eoghan smiled, though it did little to mask the confusion written across his face. "It was my pleasure. Good night, Anadali."

Anaís simply nodded, then turned on her heel and left. Her throat stung. Her eyes watered. Tomorrow, Eoghan would die. Along with any future with him in it.

CHAPTER NINETEEN
SANDS OF TIME

ANAÍS CUPPED HER MUG OF TEA IN HER HANDS, SAVOR-ing the spicy yet sweet flavor of the Nahonan brew. In Dúndíor the teas were more delicate, containing a soft, floral quality about them. In the summer months they were served cold, usually with fresh berries added in to brighten the mild flavor. Here in the valley between mountains, it seemed as if everything was more intense—the colors, the landscape, the tea.

Her headaches.

She resisted the urge to rub her temples, not wanting to draw attention to herself from the young woman knitting in the chair by the fireplace. The curious once-over Anaís had received when she returned from the festival had been uncomfortable enough. Though, when she went upstairs to change into something less for-mal for dinner and saw the mess her hair had become paired with her bloodshot eyes from trying—unsuccessfully—not to cry, the judgment was merited.

Steam curled around her face as she took another sip, letting the hot liquid linger on her tongue as the tea worked to soothe the pounding in her skull. At least she wasn't losing feeling. She tried to distract herself by memorizing the ginger, cardamon, and black pepper notes so she could recreate it when she returned home. Perhaps there was a touch of chili powder as well.

The pitter-patter of little feet toddling down the stairs caught her attention as a young boy with freckles and a mop of unruly light-brown hair appeared, a pouch gripped in one fist and a notebook in the other. His dungarees were a size too big and puddled about his ankles with each step; it was a miracle he hadn't tripped his way down the stairs instead.

"Mama, I found it!" he shouted in Freydlensku as he jumped onto the landing. He looked up and caught sight of Anaís sitting on the sofa, his blue eyes widening at the sight of the strange woman who hadn't been there when he left. Scurrying to where his mother was by the fire, he edged around her chair and whispered. "How do you say hello in Nahraeg?"

"*Lé da'reagh*," she responded in kind, tousling his hair before returning to her knitting.

He nodded and turned toward Anaís. "*Lé da'reagh*," he greeted, his lilted accent making the word sound more like a question than a statement.

Anaís smiled at the boy and returned the greeting. "I can speak Freydlensku too, if it helps," she added in his native tongue.

The boy's eyes lit up. "Oh yes! That's all I know. Mama and Da can speak both. Da is from here, but this is my first time. Are you from Freydlan too? We were at the festival. Is that why you're here? I'm Aksel. What's your name?"

Anaís blinked as she took in all the information. His excitability was refreshing, but her tired mind was struggling to keep up. "I'm Toma," she replied.

Aksel dropped the pouch and notebook on the ground and plopped down beside them, his interest in them forgotten as he said, "I bet you have lots of good stories. Can you tell me one?"

Anaís looked to his mother, who shrugged with a tired smile. "Be my guest. Anything that will occupy him before dinner is a help to me."

"Hmm, let's see then," Anaís said, trying to bide her time as she waded through her sluggish thoughts.

Any real-life stories she told would probably terrify the poor child. The only tale she could think of was one Balendin used to tell her when she was young. Though now that she knew his tales held inklings of truth, she wasn't sure if even those could be considered age appropriate.

The logs crackled in the fireplace, punctuated by the occasional *clink* from the kitchen. The warming scent of ginger and cardamom wafted through the air, wrapping the inn with a homely aroma. Anaís breathed in deeply and allowed herself to become swept away by the simplicity of the moment. She wanted to feel at home, and that was what Balendin's stories were.

"Ah yes," Anaís said. "This one is a Tale of Old. May I borrow a piece of paper?"

Aksel quickly tore a sheet out of his notebook and placed it on the coffee table before rifling through his pouch and selecting a stick of charcoal. Anaís lowered herself onto the floor and began sketching out a crude map of Nythmaar as Balendin had once done for her. Aksel scooted to sit beside her. The chair creaked as his mother leaned forward to observe, her fingers fumbling over her knitting, then stilling altogether as Anaís began to speak.

"Long ago, before the four kingdoms rose up in the land of Nythmaar, many tribes were spread throughout the continent—all along the Eastern regions of Mir, up the river and over the mountains to the Northern land of Kópa, dotted along the Western coast, hidden away by the snowy peaks of the Nymyan Mountain range, and down, down, down the map into Tāpepe Takakou na Uul—the unknown jungles of Uul." She drew the defining landmarks as she spoke.

Aksel's eyes traced over the map with wonder. "And in the middle?"

Anaís smiled, it was the same question she asked Balendin as a child. "In the middle was a lake"—she drew the swirling waters surrounded by lush fjordland—"filled with water purified by the stone of the mountains as it bubbled up from the earth. It was called Takaniim, lifestream in the Old Language, gifted to the land by the Maker of old. These waters blessed the lands of Nythmaar, providing for her people and all the animals, both big and small, that lived on her shores."

"Like the little tirpokka birds that roost near the Fikjør Sea?" Aksel piped up hopefully. "Those are my favorites."

"Especially the tirpokka," Anaís reassured him.

Aksel settled contentedly against the sofa as she continued the story.

"Now the sœndjak from the realm below saw this and were filled with great jealousy, as they wanted the land for themselves with her people as their prize. Growing restless, they emerged from the eternal deep and struck out."

The fire popped and Aksel sucked in a breath. "Don't worry, I'm brave," he declared, though he scooted closer to Anaís.

"A great war consumed the lands, booming clashes of darkness and light exploding across the battlefield. Finding strength in unity, the tribes joined together to fight and with the help of the Maker, the sœndjak were sent back to the pits of darkness from which they came, unable to set foot on the land of Nythmaar."

"Good riddance," Aksel mumbled.

Anaís snorted a laugh. His mother shook her head with a fond smile.

Clearing her throat lightly, Anaís continued, "But, little by little, year by year, the people forgot the war. They forgot the One who helped them vanquish the darkness that once threatened their homes. The beautiful land that was gifted to all the tribes became nothing more than a remnant of their origins, a solemn reminder of all that should have been. And still, they forgot. Gods created from their own desire and design eroded the memory of their history and their true Maker.

"In time, clans joined and split, and cities were built on pride. To protect the sacred waters, the Maker hid Takaniim so it could never be misused by those who had gone astray, for it was a gift too great to be wielded by corruption."

Aksel leaned back and regarded Anaís with wide eyes. "How do we restore the lands?"

"Despite the betrayal, the Maker never left, working even to-day to counteract the evil that threatens to creep upon Nythmaar, though the people cannot see it, having been blinded by desire. But a time is coming when the people must rise up again and make a choice—to fight for the truth, or to be consumed by the darkness they let in. Though we do not know when or where or how, legend says that wonders more miraculous than you or I have ever seen will mark the start of a new era, but to secure them, the people must face the shadows lurking in the deep. A great war with much darkness must be fought, but in the end a brilliant, blinding light will shine through. Truth will be restored and an era of peace ushered in—not as when the sœndjak hid, for they will be abolished once and for all."

"How will we know when it's coming?" Aksel gasped. "I want to fight!"

"You don't need to worry about these things," Anaís reassured him. "It's simply a story. But your courage will take you far."

He scrunched his nose as he considered, and Anaís fought to stifle a laugh at the seriousness written on his young face. Seeming to come to a decision, he nodded once, then opened his notebook and began drawing with vigor. She glanced at his paper to see him sketching a lopsided stick figure holding a sword.

"*That* is a story buried deep in the sands of time. Where did you hear it?"

Rolling the charcoal between her fingers, Anaís looked up at Aksel's mother. Something about the contemplative look on her face gave Anaís pause. "My brother told it to me," she said slowly. "Long ago."

"Your brother was wise for ensuring the link to our peoples' past was kept alive. Wiser still for keeping it hidden in a children's tale."

Anaís frowned. "I don't understand."

"Not everyone believes it's 'simply' a story."

Before she could respond, a bell chimed, followed by a chipper "dinner is ready" from Mrs. Uí Mháille. Anaís followed Aksel and his mother, who belatedly introduced herself as Grethe, into the dining room to join Mrs. Uí Mháille and some of the other guests for dinner. An assortment of roasted meat, spiced stews, pan-fried vegetables, and flatbread was laid out across the wooden table and the smell made her mouth water. Jovial conversation filled the room, laughter punctuating the ends of phrases more often than not, particularly whenever Aksel tried to join in with the few words he knew in Nahraeg. Anaís contented herself with watching the scene unfold before her, occasionally providing new words for Aksel to learn when he pointed at different objects in the room. The combination of the meal and the atmosphere provided a warmth that filled her from the inside out.

The moon had nearly reached its zenith by the time Anaís made it back to her room. After spending the day exploring the city, she really needed a bath, and although dinner had provided some energy, all it had done was give her enough strength to prolong the inevitable. Her hands no longer felt like her own, and the telltale whispers of something much more than a headache were already swirling at the base of her skull. Washing up would have to wait.

She unceremoniously stripped off her dress and let it flutter to the floor before climbing under the covers, but as soon as she laid down the deep ache in her head mounted. A grumble left her lips as she rolled over, then shifted again to place another pillow underneath her head so she wouldn't be so horizontal. The feeling made her nauseous. Her condition always did this: it demanded rest, then resisted when she tried to comply. It took all and gave nothing.

One of the pillows met the floor with an unsatisfying plop and she rolled onto her stomach. Numbness tingled down her spine.

I am safe, she tried to remind herself. *In this inn, I am safe.*

Slowly, the numbness abated as tension melted out of her tired muscles. Anaís snuggled deeper into the mattress as the beginning of unconsciousness came to greet her. Blessed moments later, she drifted into a dreamless sleep.

CHAPTER TWENTY
MARROW & BONE

I T WASN'T DIFFICULT TO FIND SOMEONE WHO DIDN'T WANT to be found. Not when they hid from the world in hopes that their absence would draw the attention of the one they wanted.

The heir, the disappointment, the prodigal son. Cian was returning home.

Not home, he reminded himself. He had burned that prison long ago, the future it promised now a pile of ashes from which he built his new life. One where his mother was safe. One where he could be something other than the expectations set before him. Though if he was honest with himself, it was never about the expectations. It was the one who held them.

Now he was returning to a remnant of the past. The place that had started—and ended—it all. The place where, twelve years ago, his father had nearly ensnared Cian into his empire.

He exhaled a sigh, a plume of mist swirling around him as his warm breath intertwined with the cool mountain air. "I'm free," he whispered into existence. "I am free."

His proclamation did little to reassure his body, yet his legs obeyed the command of his will, carrying him deeper into the forest. For all he begged himself to forget—his training, his tracking, his obedience—they never left. A shame, really, that memories didn't only exist in the mind. They existed in *him*, wound so tightly into the fibers of his being that to undo one was to undo himself. That didn't mean he couldn't use them to keep those he loved safe.

Guilt pricked at the back of his mind—it was already the morning of the second day of the festival, and he had promised to spend the week with his mother. This was important, though. Her safety— the kingdom's safety—depended upon the outcome of this trip.

A bubble of defiance rose within him. He would not fear his past. He would not fear himself. He would not fear an uncertain future, because within the uncertainty lay possibility. And that possibility was his own to claim. It was his father's mistake in believing that fear only birthed more fear.

That would be his downfall.

Soft moss cushioned Cian's steps as he approached the fissure in the mountain. It was unremarkable, really. A dark rip in the rock that, despite its gaping presence, could easily be overlooked by man and beast alike. When darkness did not want to be seen, it did everything in its power to make it so. Breathing in one last lungful of fresh air, he steeled himself and entered the cave.

Voices trickled past him, dripping off the walls, trailing across his skin, each tendril of sound leaving a sickly residue in its wake. Cian suppressed a shudder and forced his hand to maintain contact with the tunnel wall, feeling his way blindly through the dark.

Step, by step, by step he inched his way forward. Treading lightly to avoid undue attention from the unnatural darkness twisting around him. Shuffling his feet to avoid being swallowed by a crevasse and sucked into the belly of the mountain. His hand dipped inside the wall, and a sucking dampness engulfed his fingers.

His stomach heaved. Bile burned his throat. Another step forward slid his hand free. Another step. Another step. Another step.

The scent of death trailed after him.

He really should have brought a light.

Cian wasn't sure if he had walked for minutes or hours—time and reality seemed to shift as separate entities. All he knew was that the texture of the stone tingled under his numb fingers. A bone-deep ache settled in his joints. Stale, frostbitten air clung to his lungs as if it too longed to be free of the mountain, waiting only to be released once he escaped from this ancient tomb. So long as it didn't become his tomb first.

Sunlight seared his eyes as he stumbled out of the mountain, blinding him with a pain that incinerated the icy bite of the dark. As he blinked rapidly, the scene before him dimmed into a quaint clearing. Budding leaves colored the once-bare tree branches, while small patches of snow clung to the earth beneath tall clusters of willowy grass. Odd. He didn't recall seeing snow clouds over the mountains earlier in the week.

Odder still was the log cabin standing proudly in the center of the clearing. A thing of eccentricities, it was stalky and lean and completely free of openings—save for the smoke-puffing chimney and the front door, which swung outward like a hand gesturing for him to go away.

That was new.

Emptiness backed by a winking light greeted him, followed closely by a stream of voices. The same whisperings he'd heard in the mountain. Were they the lifeline that guided him, or the hook that ensnared him? With his father, he could never be sure. Best to cut all strings and fend for himself. Wiping his hands on his trousers, Cian set his jaw, straightened his posture, and strode across the field and into the cabin.

His presence snuffed out the murmurs as soon as he crossed the threshold. A log popped in the fireplace. The door creaked as it swung shut, the soft click of the lock echoing like a death knell.

No one had touched it.

Like an infant learning to see, shapes began to coalesce before him as his eyes adjusted to the firelit darkness. A man leaned against a wooden post. Another three perched on mismatched chairs encircling a shoddy table. More still lounged about the room on plush furniture that looked to not have seen the light of day in over a century. They watched him silently, features hidden in the thick darkness that reigned in antithesis to the bubble of light produced by the fire. It was as if he had walked into the sitting room of death itself.

Movement in the recesses of the room caught his attention, a sick dread twisting his stomach. He turned his gaze away. Whatever hid there was a nightmare he did not need following into his dreams.

Mentally shaking himself, he dragged his attention to the present. "I'm here for Tadhg Ó Máille." His voice punctured the silence of the room.

A man enveloped in a wingback chair near the fireplace leaned forward, his deep blue eyes shining mirthlessly in the firelight. The same eyes Cian had inherited. "Who is he to you?"

"Father." Cian bobbed his head in acknowledgement.

Tadhg's expression remained unchanged as he leaned back into shadow, though now that Cian had seen his father, even the dark could not hide him. Wrinkles had softened the harsh planes of his face, but he looked otherwise the same as Cian remembered him to be. The same perpetual frown. The same straw-blond hair styled just so. The same reclined, yet dangerously alert tilt to his posture.

"Ah," Tadhg finally spoke once the silence had strained Cian's nerves to their limit. "The boy acknowledges the truth."

"I have questions."

"I might entertain answering them."

"What is your business with the Cross-Kingdom Seal?"

"The seal?" Tadhg's brows almost rose to his hairline. His father was mocking him. "Now why would you expect that to be me?"

"Enough of your—"

"Respect," Tadhg snapped, "will not be forgotten, *son*."

The blood froze in Cian's veins. He couldn't move. Couldn't breathe. The words in his mind struggled to find oxygen to whisper the truth. *I am free. I am free.* He inhaled a breath through choking lungs. *I am free.*

"What," Cian repeated, relieved the gravel in his voice sounded more menacing than terrified, "was your business? I saw the seal. You cannot deny your involvement."

His father's mouth drew into a contemplative frown before softening into something akin to pride. Cian instinctively relaxed. "I'm pleased with you, son. You've grown into a sharp young man. But as usual," Tadhg drawled, "you've focused on the wrong thing. Asking the wrong question."

Cian's throat bobbed as he tried to swallow.

"Think carefully," his father taunted. "Ask me a new question. Make it good."

Heart thundering in his chest, Cian glanced about the room at the men watching him expectantly. None of them flinched at the twisted shadows licking at their skin. In fact, the shadows seemed to emanate from them, wreathing them in a thick blanket of darkness. *The shadows are moving.*

Cian's heart stuttered to a stop.

These were the men—the creatures—who had been spying in the palace. Watching. Listening. Biding their time until time ran out. *They only stilled when the Anadali was near, as if waiting for something to happen.*

What had happened?

"The Anadali," Cian began. The men leaned forward. "She works for you. What is her involvement in this?"

Tadhg clapped slowly, each strike a bolt of lightning to Cian's chest. "Well done." He leaned forward, regarding Cian with something akin to curiosity. "Technically, she works for King Timun, but he and I have arranged a mutual agreement. Let's just say the Anadali will tip the scales for the good of Nahonaugh."

A floorboard creaked. Tadhg looked across the room at the man leaning against the post.

"You shouldn't tell him." The man's voice felt like steam on cold glass.

"Tell me what?" Cian interjected.

His father ignored him. "How else shall I see where his loyalties truly lie?"

The man shrugged languidly. "And when he exposes us?"

"He won't." Tadhg's glare pierced the man. Only his father was allowed to degrade Cian. Lift him up and beat him down. There was a certain poetry to the power of manipulation, and his father was a master at his craft. "He's my son," he continued. "He knows the consequences of misbehavior"—a sinister smile cracked his father's collected façade, one that Cian recognized all too well—"as should you."

Slowly, the man dipped his chin in acquiescence. A loud pop resounded from the fire in the hearth, nearly sending Cian jumping out of his skin. The floorboards creaked under his feet as he settled down, but the already erratic thumping of his heart had now been sent into a frenzy, fluttering to the tempo of the flickering flames.

I am free, Cian reminded himself. A bead of sweat snaked its way down his neck and under the collar of his shirt. It took everything within him to not reach up and wipe it away.

Cian looked at his father, at the firelight dancing across his skin, casting shadows over his features while alighting his eyes with a burning glow—eyes that were already watching him. Appraising. Calculating.

"My loyalty lies with the people," Cian finally said, his voice sounding much stronger than he felt. "You say this is for the good of Nahonaugh, I've spent my life working to serve those who live in this kingdom. It is my duty to know."

Tadhg let out a sharp laugh. "You've spent your life? Yes I'm sure you believe that, don't you. Tell me, who have you spent *your life* aiding?"

"I am Prince Eoghan's royal advisor," Cian spat, indignation burning out his fear. "This is not secret knowledge. I oversee merchant affairs concerning domestic and international trade, civil policies. We just devised a new treaty, one that will help the people and bring Nahonaugh out of isolation so she can begin to thrive again.

A treaty that *your* seal and *your* plans have infiltrated." Cian's voice rose. "Why? What is the meaning of this?"

"So that is all you are? A prized pet to help Eoghan?" Tadhg said, ignoring Cian's questions.

"*Prince* Eoghan."

"Hm yes I see." Tadhg leaned forward to steeple his fingers under his chin. "Tell me, how is the *prince's* condition?"

Cian blinked. He couldn't mean? No of course he didn't mean... he couldn't *know* of Eoghan's visions, no one did. He was bluffing. Pulling falsehoods out of thin air to derail Cian and coerce him into telling Tadhg secrets he didn't—

His father made a low whistle of disbelief. "Oh, how the giants fall. Who is it?" He raised his brow. "Who does he see in the dark?"

Cian bit the inside of his cheek until the tang of copper coated his tongue. Eoghan saw someone? Was there more than the vision he had mentioned?

A look of mock pity softened Tadhg's expression. "Did he not tell you? Does he not trust you?"

"Of course he trusts me." *Didn't he?*

"But not with this?"

"I don't trust you with this." Cian didn't, but even if he did trust his father, he couldn't have told him. Why hadn't Eoghan confided in him? They both had secrets, but this was important.

"How much damage can be done with a lie?" Tadhg asked. Cian glanced up. He hadn't even realized he had broken eye contact. "How much more in the absence of truth?"

Cian squeezed his eyes shut and took in a steadying breath. He would not allow Tadhg to manipulate his friendship with Eoghan. Tadhg was baiting him; this was all a distraction to what he came here for.

"You're ignoring my question." Cian opened his eyes, his turmoil calming into a silent, focused rage. "What is the purpose of the Anadali?"

"Not ignoring—guiding." Tadhg shrugged dismissively. "We have reason to suspect that Eoghan and the Anadali are connected by an ancient bond. One that is disadvantageous when it comes to ushering in a new era for the kingdoms at large. We have tried to sever it, but failed to do so permanently. Thankfully, the Anadali's methods are more...effective."

"Effective how?" Cian bit out.

Tadhg leaned forward. "Do you swear to secrecy?" He paused, gaze flicking to the shadowed corners of the room. "I will know if you betray me. Think carefully."

Cian nodded slowly. He could figure out how to reveal the truth when the time came. This information was too important. "On my life," he promised.

The look that glinted in his father's eyes told him those had been the wrong words at the right time. "Eoghan Kavanaugh dies tonight."

"No." Cian's mouth moved, but no sound came out. How could it, when all the air had been ripped from his lungs? He shook his head, backing up a few paces toward the door. This was not happening. He would not allow it. He took in a shaky inhale, the oxygen stirring the rage lit within him until it became a fire begging to be unleashed. "No. I would rather die."

"You'd die to remain silent and you'd die to tell. Sounds like a dead man walking to me."

"You cannot kill Eoghan." His words escaped in a harsh whisper.

"No, I suppose I can't," Tadhg conceded. Metal flashed in the firelight as he unsheathed a knife and began playing with the blade.

"But you and I both know of someone who can. However, I am now presented with a new problem. We can't just let you go, can we, gents?"

Murmurs of assent rose around him. Forms of darkness rippled in the shadowed corners of the room, pulled to light by the flickering of firelight that tentatively illuminated their features, somehow more corporeal yet less human than when he first laid eyes on them. While Cian was certain he couldn't see everyone, he felt them—the weight of their gazes drinking him in. It set every nerve in his body alight, flaying his flesh open wide for all to see and leaving him hanging in suspension to rot.

"There are consequences to misconduct," Tadhg spoke slowly, deliberately.

"You have no grounds to do this."

"I have grounds," he scoffed. "*You* lack context. This goes beyond a simple trade agreement. Perhaps in the future you will understand. Today, unfortunately, your time is short and I have none to spare for you."

"So be it," Cian leveled a cold glare at his father. "I have nothing left to say to you."

Turning on his heel, Cian strode toward the door. He never should have come, he should have trusted Eoghan with his findings instead. He was two paces from the exit when a blinding pain ripped through his arm. Tadhg's knife protruded from the doorframe. Cian's blood dripped from the blade, crimson and viscous and wet. The wound in his arm throbbed in response, each pulse a cry begging the blood to return to his veins. The world tilted. He blinked until it stopped moving.

"Cian."

Tipping his head back, he sucked in a lungful of air, trying to keep the tears at bay. Trying to keep the pain at bay. How deeply had the knife cut him?

"What," he said flatly.

"If you obey, I'll give you the antidote."

He kept his back to Tadhg. "For Eoghan?"

"For you."

Cian grit his teeth and reached for the doorknob. "I'm not the one dying."

"Aren't you?"

Slowly, he turned to face his father.

"Dead man walking." Tadhg shrugged. "Your wish was my command." Firelight glinted in his eyes as he leaned forward in his seat, a wicked grin spreading across his face. "Word of advice. Don't try to counteract the poison yourself."

If he wasn't outnumbered and about to pass out, Cian would have ripped the knife from the doorframe and flung it back at his father. He took a deep breath to steady himself.

"Run along to your mother's house." Tadhg made a shooing motion. "That's where you were supposed to be, wasn't it?"

Cian's hand spasmed, and he curled it into a fist. No, not anymore. He and Eoghan would figure this out. Together. No one was dying tonight.

Something must have slipped through his expression, because Tadhg added, "Or else she'll be joining you shortly in the afterlife."

No. It felt like all of his limbs had been frozen in place. Not his mother. His father couldn't.

He wouldn't.

He would.

This was the man who would willingly see the crown prince murdered. This was the man who would sabotage kingdoms to ensure his own whims remained unhindered. This was the man who would follow through on his threats with delight.

It was then that Cian felt it, a whisper of sensation that settled into the marrow of his bones before leaching out and infecting the blood that ran through his veins. His heart stuttered in his chest, as if it knew it was no longer pumping life through his body, but death.

"It's working already, isn't it?" Tadhg continued, as if Cian's pause had given him permission to speak. "I'll give you a few hours. If you haven't left the palace by nightfall—*without* the prince—your mother won't simply be cut with a poisoned blade."

Cian whirled around and stormed through the door, slamming it against the outside wall as he crossed the threshold.

"Shall we trail him?" someone asked.

"He will obey."

It was the last thing he heard when the door finally swung shut. He hated that his father was right.

Cian had intended to wrap his arm before entering the palace, but when he inspected the wound, there wasn't anything to speak of. Whatever they had coated the knife with had caused his skin to knit together again so quickly that the only indication anything had happened was the slice in his shirt sleeve and the blood enmeshed into the fabric. At least he had worn black. His predicament would have fascinated him if he didn't feel sick to his stomach. Was it the poison? Or was it the absolute terror he felt for his mother and Eoghan?

No, it would be all right. His steps faltered on the stairs and he leaned against the wall for support. He would get his things, wouldn't see Eoghan, would go visit his mother. Pushing off the wall, he trudged onward. It would be fine. They couldn't actually kill Eoghan, could they? Capture, maybe. Send away, maybe. But kill? Besides, Eoghan was strong—stronger than he let most people believe. And smart. He would not fall for poison, and it would take an army to bring that man down fighting. He could warn Eoghan. Subtly. But there were spies. Cian glanced at the shadows as he hurried down the hallway that led to the private wing of the palace.

No...he couldn't risk it. Eoghan would be all right. He was sure of it. But his mother? Tadhg *would* have her killed, of that Cian was certain. Eoghan would have to fight this on his own, but Ma? Cian wouldn't be able to live with himself if she died because of him. He was the only one standing between her and the wrath of his father.

So long as his heart beat inside his chest, his mother would live.

As Cian sped around the corner, he smacked face first into a wall. A human-shaped wall. Warm hands gripped his shoulders to stop him from falling.

"Cian?" Eoghan's voice cut through his panic. "Are you all right?"

"Yeah, fine." He pulled out of his friend's grasp. "I'll be going to visit Ma for the rest of Fheile Earrach."

"I thought you had already left?" Eoghan frowned, then shook his head as if dismissing the thought. "I must have gotten the days mixed up. Have a good time, yeah? You need it."

Cian tilted his head at Eoghan. There was something about his demeanor that seemed distracted, distant. "Are *you* okay?"

"I don't know. I feel..." Eoghan heaved a sigh. "I don't know. I'm going to train for a bit. It will pass."

"Have you had another vision?" Cian whispered. "A dream?"

When Eoghan didn't reply, Cian grasped his shoulders and gave him a brief shake. "Eoghan what's *wrong*?"

"Do you ever feel like you're standing at the edge of a cliff, teetering between chaos and serenity?"

"I...no." His hands fell to his sides. That wasn't what he was expecting at all.

"All logic and reason calls me to step away from the drop," Eoghan continued as if he hadn't heard Cian's response. "But I can't. I feel like I've already jumped, Cian, and I don't know why."

Their eyes met, and in that moment Cian's heart stopped. Eoghan looked broken. Haunted. Cian opened his mouth to say something, anything, but it was as if sound itself had fled from him. He couldn't risk it.

"Are *you* okay?" Eoghan asked.

This was the last time he would see his best friend, and yet Eoghan was making sure *he* was okay. Something wet trickled down Cian's cheek and he reached up, roughly wiping the tear away. "Yeah, I'm fine. Glad to see Ma is all."

Eoghan seemed to come back to himself with that. "Send Mina my love. And bring me back one of her pies."

"Come—" *get it yourself.* Cian choked back the rest of the words, recovering instead to say "here" before pulling Eoghan into a hug. "Take care of yourself." He patted Eoghan on the back and released him, the motion sending a fresh wave of pain up his arm.

"You too," Eoghan replied, and with a final wave goodbye he rounded the corner and disappeared.

CHAPTER TWENTY-ONE
SON OF THE KEEPER

NAÍS AWOKE TO THE GOLDEN GLOW OF THE EVENING sun filtering through her window curtains as they fluttered in the spring breeze. She stretched her arms over her head and yawned, but it turned into a stifled gasp when she glanced at the clock. Eighteen hours of uninterrupted sleep was unheard of, but she was grateful for it nonetheless. Rubbing the last of the sleep out of her eyes, Anaís pushed her covers back and sat up. Downstairs, the front door opened and closed, followed by the muffled sound of voices. Happy sounds, she realized. She smiled, though it slipped away at the thought of what needed to be done before she left for the evening.

Bathe, food, prepare.

In that order.

Her hair tumbled over her shoulder as she rifled through the closet in search of fresh clothes, but the stale smell of sweat and city pollution had her reaching for a ribbon to tie her hair back with instead. Anaís scrunched her nose. *Wash hair too.* She couldn't remember the last time she had, and there was no need to stay grimy when she had time to fix it. Besides, she could be smelled from a mile away. Just because she *was* death didn't mean she had to smell like it.

She took a linen dress off a hanger and pulled it on before grabbing a towel off the hook by the door. Hushed voices and the click of a door closing caught her attention as she set off in search of the washroom. Rounding a corner, she meandered down another hallway. A door to her left swung open. Cian stepped out.

Anaís froze. *Oh, this could be very good and very bad.*

Cian paused in front of the doorway, eyes narrowed at her. "Who are you?"

"I'm a guest at this inn, who are you?"

"I'm the son of the keeper of this inn," he replied, then frowned as his eyes trailed over her body. "I just arrived, yet you look familiar." He looked back into her eyes and Anaís felt her blood run cold at the glint of recognition she saw in his own. "Why?"

Distraction! Create a distraction! Countess Sigraith's flamboyant demeanor burst into her mind with every bit of drama as the woman herself. Anaís seized it and ran.

"That's not a very nice way to treat a lady," Anaís huffed, hugging her towel against her body as if to create a protective wall. "If you must know, I had a terrible ordeal at another inn in town, you see. He sold my room to someone else and threw me out just like that!" She waved her free arm for dramatic effect. "And then! Oh, I was so flustered I didn't know what to do, when all of a sudden I turned around and *smack*"—she clapped her hands together—"I ran straight into Mrs. Uí Mháille! The poor thing, I felt so terribly sorry! But can you imagine my luck when she said there was a vacant room at her inn? I couldn't believe it myself, if I'm honest. I made the trek out here and sure enough, there was a lovely little room waiting for me. I enjoyed some of the festivities in town just the other day, but I was so exhausted from everything that I retired early and must have slept all day today." She sighed and leaned against the wall as if the mere mention of the entire ordeal wearied her. "If you really do work here, could you be so kind as to point me in the direction of the washroom? I could use a freshen up."

Cian blinked a few times, as if his mind was trying to reconcile what his eyes were seeing and what his ears were hearing. "I, um... yes. Certainly. It's just down the hall. Second door to the left." He pointed awkwardly, wincing with the movement. "Is that all, miss?"

"Yes, thank you."

As Anaís made her way back toward the washroom she could hear him mumbling under his breath. "It can't be. No, that bumbling woman isn't... Miss!" he called.

Anaís poked her head around the corner. A clump of messy curls escaped from the ribbon keeping her hair back. She shoved the wayward strands behind her ear. "Yes?"

"I don't believe I caught your name, miss."

"Toma. Toma Glaadris."

He paused. "I'm Cian. Ó Máille. Pleasure to make your acquaintance."

"Likewise." She hesitated, then frowned when he showed no indication of ending their conversation. "Will that be all, Mr. Ó Máille?"

"If I may ask," he began, settling against the wall as he let his words linger in the air a beat too long. "What is your business here?"

"You're awfully nosy, Mr. Ó Máille," Anaís tittered brightly.

"Just Cian. Please." He paused to straighten the collar of his shirt, but his hand tremored and he dropped it to his side. Odd. He didn't seem to be afraid. Or injured. "Under normal circumstances it wouldn't be necessary," Cian continued. "But with so much activity in the city with the festival underway, one can never be too careful."

This wasn't good, though she didn't expect anything less from him. No wonder Eoghan held him in such high regard. At least, in terms of his job. Still, she needed to tread lightly. Glancing down the hallway, she stage-whispered, "Too careful of what, exactly?"

"Unsavory business."

Anaís pouted. "Well, now I'm less inclined to tell you because of that insinuation."

"I'm not insinuating anything. Please, Miss Glaadris, just answer the question."

"I make textiles."

He raised his brows. "A textile maker?"

"Yes, sir," she replied, smiling sweetly at him.

"From Freydlan?"

"Yes, sir."

"Visiting Nahonaugh during Fheile Earrach?"

"It's the opportune moment to combine business with pleasure, don't you think?"

Cian sagged a little deeper against the wall, as if this conversation was boring him. "What might your business need here?"

"The variations in regional climates between Freydlan and Nahonaugh promote diversity in natural fibers that can be used in the fabrication of textiles." Anaís shrugged. "Simply put, you have resources that we do not."

"Is that so?"

"Quite."

"I see." He licked his lips, the motion a strange blend of desperation and cunning. "How did a Freydlanian, a textile maker such as yourself, come to learn Nahraeg so proficiently?"

Anaís gave him a wry grin. Now he was pushing it, and she wanted nothing more than to shove right back. "If you're implying that my profession dictates my ability to learn, I think you'll find yourself sorely disappointed. Sir. If you must know, because I know you'll ask me anyways," she said haughtily, "Nahraeg seemed an advantageous language to learn. One of necessity, as it were, given the nature of my profession."

"Right. And *are you an Anadali from Dúndíor*?" he asked in her native tongue.

A jumble of words and emotions caught in her throat. *Deflect!* her mind shouted at her through the crippling fear. *Deflect, you fool!* Anaís tilted her head and grinned sheepishly at Cian, hoping it masked her terror as confusion. "I'm sorry, I don't understand?"

His shoulders slumped. "You've never been to Dúndíor?"

"I've never had a reason to, it's too far east." She waved her hand in the general direction. "Not an easy journey to make."

"Of course, my apologies."

"It's all right. Well, good evening, then." Anaís gave him a slight nod before slipping around the corner and disappearing into the washroom, not awaiting his response.

Turning the lock on the door, she tossed her towel onto the stool by the water basin. A silent sigh of relief rushed past her lips as she slumped against the wall, and then it hit her—Uí Mháille was the feminine form of Ó Máille.

Nahonan naming conventions would be the death of her.

She would need to be cautious when leaving the inn tonight, but at least she knew Cian wouldn't be at the palace. She didn't like him, but he was about as paranoid as she was, and she couldn't fault him for it. What she could fault him for, however, was not catching her. If this assassin business didn't work out, at least she could fall back on acting.

THE PROBLEM WITH BATHING WAS that it gave Anaís too much time alone with her thoughts. Thoughts that didn't leave her be when the last of the water drained from the washtub. They clung to her like a soapy residue, the bubbles of her past bursting open on her conscience in intervals as if to remind her again, and again, and again of her purpose. Who she must become on a night like tonight.

It was worse today. As if some part of her was begging her to remember her humanity. The memories came in flashes—how her skin had warmed beneath his touch as they danced together. The way his eyes had lit with joy.

Yet each flicker of hope reminded her of what would happen if she failed. The bite of her blade as it ripped into Balendin's skin. The emptiness in his eyes as life drained out of them. King Timun would not suffer failure. Especially not hers.

Though Anaís had seen little evidence in the city, Simone was right—something *was* coming. It was in the way her father had changed in the aftermath of the breach. In the way he had insisted upon a new era. He wanted her to bring them the future. She needed to be alive to stop it.

His Highness must *die.* Anaís couldn't bring herself to think his name.

She dressed numbly. Black linen pants that barely whispered when she moved caressed her skin. A tunic with reinforced stitching to protect from knife strikes settled on her shoulders. Anaís held her face covering in her hands—one that concealed the lower half of her face, and not her eyes.

A mask for diplomacy, a face covering for death. As if peace were blind and violence took without asking. Funny how two halves of the face could be shown, yet would be unrecognizable if anyone saw the whole. Or, maybe that was all anyone was—little shards of truth pieced together to form a mosaic, an illusion, able to be rearranged to suit their needs. Would she ever have the honor of knowing all the parts of someone? Though, even if they revealed their true pattern to her, could she say she fully knew someone if she refused to unveil herself too? Would she want to?

"No," pain told her.

"Yes," hope whispered back.

In the depths of her heart, she wanted to let go, to fall, and know that someone would catch her. She wanted to know that she was not alone in this vast expanse of a universe.

But that wish would never see the light of day. Who she was now kept her alive, protecting the hidden parts of herself that would shatter like glass if they were exposed to the cruelty of what the world had become. Of who she had become.

She had a duty to fulfill. A people to protect. An oath to uphold. All other hope was but a dream.

Pulling her face covering over her nose and mouth, Anaïs swung her cloak around her shoulders and disappeared out the window. Maybe when death took her, she would be free to hope. For now, death had a meeting with its next client, and she was the escort.

CHAPTER TWENTY-TWO
SILENT REVERIE

ANAÍS INHALED AND TRAPPED THE BREATH THERE, THE cool night air warming as it settled deep within her lungs. One heartbeat passed. Two. Soon it would be over.

A cloud of vapor erupted around her as she forced her breath outward, sending it into the darkness surrounding her. She hadn't had a chance to scout the bridge during her first trip, and now it lay before her in all its overengineered glory. As much as she enjoyed making quips about the engineers who constructed the bridge, she was grateful for the ostentatious design. There were handholds aplenty and various corners she could tuck herself into to rest—or hide—though she didn't need to do either. No one was guarding the underbelly of the bridge, and her eighteen-hour nap had chased away all inklings of fatigue that threatened to be her undoing.

Instead, she could focus on the rhythm of weaving between the beams and checking the stability of each segment before transferring her full weight onto the next. Even the cool metal that bit into her fingers drifted to the back of her mind as she traversed the expanse of the channel between the island and the mainland. The rumble of the water below felt far away. All that was left was her, the task at hand, and the moon lighting her way.

The side of the island appeared sooner than she had expected, and she braced her body between three crossing beams before leaning over the edge to map a route to climb up. To her dismay—and delight—the rock immediately surrounding the beams bolted into the cliff face was worn smooth, making it impossible to climb. Which meant, she hoped, that the engineers weren't as neglectful as they made the design appear to be—they anticipated the bridge to be a security threat and had prepared for it. While it made her job slightly more complicated, she had to admire the competency of those who stood in her way. Besides, it also made her job more fun. So long as she didn't slip.

She tilted her head back, eyes trailing the trusses to the top of the bridge. The beams were just close enough to reasonably climb, but it also meant she would arrive on the island at the mouth of the bridge. This would expose her to whoever was keeping guard and defeat the entire purpose of climbing under the bridge rather than simply walking across it. She would stick to her original plan; it would merely require a little more finesse. The engineers weren't expecting *her* to be the security threat. It did pose a problem for the way back, but a bit of climbing and swimming was as good an option as any. As for getting *there*...

Anaís studied where the cliff face transformed from smooth to rough before disentangling herself from the bridge and swinging around the final vertical truss, landing swiftly on the other side. Wind whipped at her hair, and she straightened her shoulders, though a cold ache settled in her hands as she gripped onto the bridge a little more tightly. Just because she *could* do this didn't mean her self-preservation instincts wanted her to.

A ten-foot expanse of beam lay between her and the smooth cliff, while a long drop she didn't care to think too deeply about gaped below. She swallowed and looked beyond the smooth stone toward the rugged face of the cliff where she was planning to jump. It was far, perhaps too...

She pushed the thought out of her head before it could form. The drop didn't matter, nor did the distance. She had done this before. She would make it.

Anaís uncurled her fingers from the truss and shook out her hands, flexing her fingers to get as much feeling as she could back into them. A quick pat to her belt confirmed her karambit was still tightly secured, as was her balisong. The blade in her boot wasn't going anywhere unless she wanted it to.

Then, before she could overthink, she ran down the beam and launched herself over the water churning below. Wind whipped around her, stinging her eyes and tearing at her clothes, but her trajectory remained true. A familiar weightlessness cradled her body as she reached the peak of her arc and certainty settled into her bones.

She would make it.

Her stomach fluttered as she began to fall, careening faster and faster toward the cliff as gravity and inertia beckoned her to her final destination. She twisted her body midair to brace for impact, keeping her eyes focused on the small crack she had been aiming for.

Numb pain tore through her shoulder. Rolling with the impact, Anaís slid along the sharp slope of the cliff before slamming her hand into the crevice.

A curse bubbled up her throat but she kept her lips clamped shut, breathing deeply through her nose to try and will the pain away. Anaís pressed her forehead against the cold stone.

"It's fine," she mumbled to the cliff. "I didn't need this arm anyway."

She waited a heartbeat, then slung her other hand into the crevice and repositioned her feet against the lip of the rock before extricating the hand that had broken her fall. Scratches littered her skin, blood seeped from a shallow cut in the palm of her hand, and her shoulder twinged suspiciously, but all in all it could have been worse.

A swirl of wind rushed down the cliff, and she looked up. Clouds partially obscured the moon, but enough light trickled through that she could make out the jagged edges of the rock above her.

Right. She still had to climb.

Sighing, Anaís flexed her fingers and began her ascent.

Contrary to popular belief, the window was one of the worst ways to break into a room when balancing on the side of a building. Tricky latches. The possibility of falling. Birds—the flying menaces. Stealth was an art, not a circus act.

Climbing over a ledge of the palace, Anaís jumped from the stone wall and rolled quietly to soften her landing on the balcony below. Glass-paned double doors greeted her as she rose. Slipping two pins from her belt, Anaís inserted them into the lock, gliding them up and down until the mechanism clicked. The Kavanaughs really needed to modernize their security.

Anaís slipped into the palace, locking the door behind her when it closed. The familiar glow of the moonlit hallway outside the library welcomed her; the column where she'd hidden mere weeks prior stretched to the ceiling like a beacon in the night. She trailed her fingers along the edges of the column's arrises as she passed by, a silent thank you for the shelter and the opportunity to plan her entrance.

Sticking to the shadows, Anaís crept up the stairs, pulling herself deeper into the recesses when a guard passed by, waiting patiently when one lingered, darting across hallways when the opportunity arose. Her ascent became a dance with the moon, weaving its silver threads of light with the shadows of its absence until a web of death followed in her wake.

Another set of stairs brought her to an unfamiliar hallway. Light splattered the ground in intervals. An uncomfortable tightness pulled at her chest, like an invisible thread winding itself around her heart.

Soft footsteps padded down the hallway—another guard. Anaís ducked into an alcove as she waited for them to pass. Unfamiliarity demanded logic, she reminded herself, rubbing her sternum to ease the tension. *I am Anadali Amadé. I will not die.* After a beat, she added, *I will not fail.*

Pressing herself deeper into the corner, Anaís analyzed the hallway. The guard, much to her dismay, lingered in front of the singular, ornately carved door, his profile cast in harsh shadow as he stood watch. Based on the schedule she'd noted during the talks, guards rotated every hour on the hour, which granted her a fifty-five-minute head start between killing the prince and escaping the palace grounds—more than enough time. Her fingers itched to draw her knife. She tapped them silently against her leg to dispel the energy instead. There was no reason for the guard to die tonight. Not when unconsciousness would suffice.

Anaís emerged from the shadows, stepping lightly as she moved. She prepared herself to strike. Three paces from him, the floor creaked.

The guard whirled around, unsheathing his sword in a slicing arc. Her body acted before her mind could catch up. She ducked, drew her knife, and lodged it deep in his chest, twisting and ripping it free before he could form a scream.

The guard slumped to the ground. He looked up at her, eyes wide and unblinking.

"Toma?" Lochlan rasped.

No no no no. Anaís's heart stopped beating. She reached her hand out, pulled it back against her chest, a sob caught in her throat as she dropped to her knees. The guard wasn't supposed to die. A *friend* wasn't supposed to die.

What of Eoghan? her heart asked.

Do not speak his name, her mind growled back.

Anaís sucked in a breath and placed a trembling hand on Lochlan's arm. "I'm sorry," she whispered.

A flicker of understanding softened his features. "Anadali," he mouthed instead. His eyes held no accusation. No resentment. Just simple understanding. Resignation. She was doing what was commanded of her, just as he was. Lochlan's eyes drifted closed. "Protect Eoghan." Sound shaped his words with the force of his last breath.

Then he was gone.

Anaís blinked. A tear carved a path down her cheek. "Be at peace, Lochlan." She placed her hand on his forehead, speaking softly despite the tightness in her throat. "May the stars guide you home." The blessing of Balendin's village. The blessing she had last spoken to the expanse of night sky along the Ulçok Sea after she buried her mentor.

Lochlan merited that honor.

Squeezing her eyes shut, Anaís forced the emotion away. She had a job to finish, and she could not, would not return home without doing as she was told.

Carefully stepping around Lochlan's body, Anaís made her way to the door. The tension in her chest grew sharper with each step until every breath became a battle. She leaned her head against the door. Forced air into her lungs. *You have five minutes,* she told herself. *Eoghan is not your friend.* The thread around her heart wound tighter. *He is not your friend*—Anaís squeezed her eyes shut—*he is your mission.*

Steeling herself, she pushed away from the door, twisted the knob, and slipped inside.

Moonlight filtered into the room through the open window, a gentle breeze fluttering the curtains. Eoghan was splayed on his stomach across the bed, his back rising and falling with the rhythm of his breath. He looked peaceful. Celestial, even, with the way the silver light dusted his dark skin in a hazy glow.

A plush rug cushioned Anaís's feet as she moved across the room like a wraith, avoiding the puddles of soft light as she neared his bed. Her hand curled around the hilt of her karambit. The curved blade slid free from its sheath with practiced ease. Anaís shifted her grip to strike. The pain in her chest gave an agonizing yank.

Breath rushed past Eoghan's lips in a sharp inhale. She stumbled backward into the shadows as his eyes fluttered open.

"Hello?" His voice was gravelly from sleep, but there was an unmistakable pull that sent a warmth through her veins and froze her where she stood. "I know you're in here."

No.

He rubbed the sleep from his eyes and pushed himself to sitting. "Are you here to take something?"

An electric hum filled her body as she pressed herself farther into the shadows. The pain in her chest settled into an achingly familiar throb—a soft tug guiding her to safety. To him.

It's not possible. It's not possible. She repeated the words in her mind like a lifeline. The comforter in her dreams wasn't a figment of her imagination or a stranger in the library. It was *him*.

She was supposed to kill *him*.

Eoghan pushed the blanket off himself, his linen pants sliding along his legs as he shifted to sit on the edge of the bed and looked into the darkness. At her.

No, not *at* her. Into the shadows where she hid. He could not see her, and yet...he could. A sadness filled his eyes. As if he knew this moment was coming, yet welcomed the inevitable with open arms. Welcomed her with open arms.

"Are you here to take my life?"

Something in the atmosphere of the room shifted with his words, as if the pain she kept buried deep within had burst forth, building in intensity until even the shadows bowed to its will. It left her exposed, stripped raw. Her soul ached to let him live.

Those were not her orders.

"Don't just stand there." His voice came out as a broken rasp, void of fear but filled with the same confusion and pain that sucked the air out of her lungs. "If you're going to kill me, do it with dignity."

Her vision flickered as Eoghan's room faded and she was left in the throne room with her blade buried in Balendin's flesh and her screams echoing off the walls.

With dignity, with dignity, with dignity.

Anaís's lungs filled with a sharp intake of breath, and when her eyes focused again, Eoghan was looking at her, his expression soft yet pained. His hands tightened around the bedsheets, chest shuddering with the weight of each breath as if her battle was his own.

Anaís shifted her grip around the hilt of her karambit. The once-familiar weight of the blade was unbalanced in her hand; it did not wish to complete the task. The string about her heart pulled tighter in a last bid for reason, smothering the life out of her if only to prevent her from severing the mystery that hung between them.

It does not matter, Anaís told fate. If he did not die tonight, the result would be the same. Only one would walk out of this alive, whether it be now or later.

She had to obey.

Anaís lunged out of the shadows, her blade poised to attack, a yell of fury locked away behind gritted teeth. Eoghan rose to meet her. The moment their bodies met, the night erupted into chaos.

Blade and fist struck through the air with deadly precision, each attack countered by a block equally as swift. She twisted her body, using his momentum to draw him closer and slam her knee into his stomach. Eoghan shoved against her, but she slipped under his arm. Brought her knife up and around into the opening he created. Pain tore across her temple as her blade pierced his chest. She stumbled backward at the impact. Stumbled again when his foot met her side. Air rushed from her lungs as she collided with the shelf behind her seconds later. Books *thunked* to the ground.

Gasping for air, Anaís slowly pushed herself up. Her vision swam, lungs burned, blood trailed down the side of her face. She blinked rapidly, bracing for another strike. None came.

Eoghan's head hung forward as he tried to calm his own breathing. A thick stream of blood ran down his chest. Her blade, coated in his blood, lay at his feet.

"Who sent you?" Fury laced his voice, but all she could feel was *him*.

Warmth enveloped her, burning brighter as pain lanced through her body, not from his touch, but from the thread around her heart that pulled tighter, pleading, begging them to stop.

"I won't—" The words caught in his throat, as if the thread had wound itself around his heart too. "I won't ask again."

Anaís was drowning and floating all at once and it hurt. She wanted it to stop. Whatever this was, it needed to stop.

It could only end with Eoghan's death.

Rushing forward, she slammed against him with all her strength. Momentum sent them careening into the bedpost. Eoghan bit out a curse. She vaguely registered the sting of his strike as she flipped her balisong open. The blade snapped into place. An opening appeared before her. She couldn't bring herself to drag the blade across his throat; a scream of frustration built in her own.

In her moment of hesitation, his hand wrapped around her neck, and suddenly she was traveling backward. A wall rammed into her back, her head braced from impact by the strength of his grasp. Eoghan's body pressed against her own, pinning her into place. Breath tickled her ear.

Breath.

She couldn't breathe.

Darkness licked at the edges of her vision.

She didn't need to see to shift her blade until the tip grazed the flesh between ribs that protected his lungs. Still, her hand would not push the blade in.

Eoghan startled at the sensation, and their eyes locked, his face mere inches from her own. Air rushed into her lungs as his grip relaxed, and her body sagged against his, kept upright by the pressure of his touch alone. The pained expression that hardened his features shifted to one that made her heart flutter in a way very different than the terror she'd felt not moments ago. In his eyes lay peace, sadness, disbelief.

Hope.

His hand slid off her neck onto shoulder, fingers gently curling into the fabric of her tunic.

"Who are you?" His question whispered across her skin like a prayer.

All at once the thread relaxed, and their souls sighed in tandem, the pain of separation long forgotten. Peace bloomed in its wake.

Tears clouded Anaís's vision as her dream of the lake swept over her, the presence that had chased away the nightmares trying to haunt her. She blinked again to see him drinking in every detail of her face, looking horrified by the violence he'd inflicted upon her yet stunned to silent reverie at the woman stood before him.

"Please," he repeated, "who are you?"

She released a shuddering breath. For the first time in a long time she felt clarity, yet it was tinged with a profound sadness.

"I'm sorry," she whispered. And she was. Sorry for Lochlan, sorry the world was as it was, sorry she was a coward and had not fought back until it was too late, sorry they would never know who they were to each other. They wouldn't have the chance. She would be dead.

Because she couldn't do it.

She couldn't kill the one whose presence kept her from

succumbing to darkness after Balendin's death. The one whose voice spoke life to her, who was forged to *be* Death.

Their arms brushed as she removed the balisong from his side. The blade clicked shut. His eyes remained focused on her own. Full of trust. Full of hope.

"I'm sorry," Anaís repeated.

Before Eoghan could formulate another question, she grabbed his shoulders and slammed her knee to his groin, shoving him away as he crumpled over. Anaís dove and tucked into a roll, snatching her karambit and using the momentum to sprint across the room and climb onto the window sill. A muffled groan rose where Eoghan lay, drawing her attention before she could escape into the night. He'd pushed himself to sitting, a question in his gaze, though she couldn't tell if it was her confusion or his own tugging at the mystery that lay between them.

Ducking her head, she slipped through the window and into the unknown.

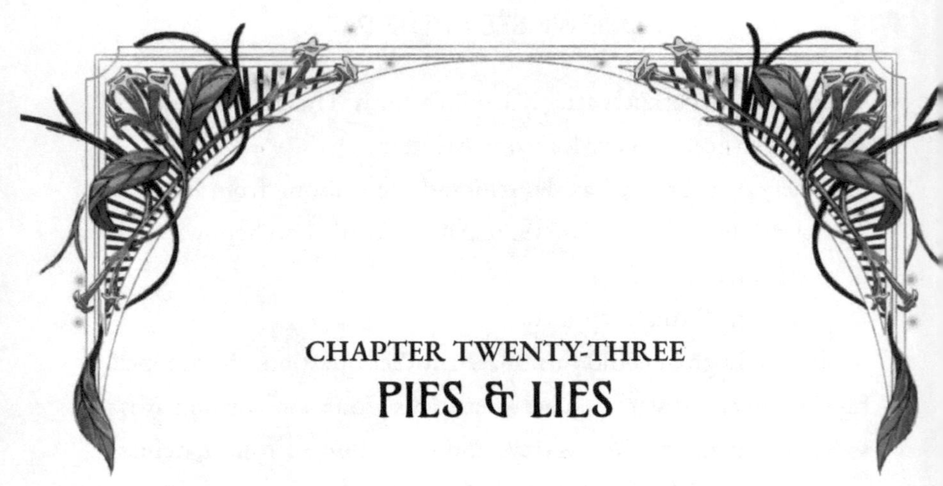

CHAPTER TWENTY-THREE
PIES & LIES

Anaís had spent an hour by a river near the inn scrubbing Eoghan's blood out of the finely woven fabric where his body had pressed against hers. Only five minutes were needed for the stain to come free and the water to run clear. Nothing she did could remove Lochlan's blood from her hands, Eoghan's blood from her chest.

Now, with the sun painting the morning gold, all Anaís had to show for her efforts were raw hands, a frayed tunic, and a weary soul.

Her hands ached as she gripped the banister and descended the stairs, squinting against the light reflecting on the polished wood.

"You've only just come back!" Mrs. Uí Mháille's distressed voice drifted up the stairs.

Anaís paused, her foot hovering over the next tread as she strained to listen.

"There's something I need to take care of at the palace." Cian's voice followed in the wake of his mother's. He must have just woken up; it was a pitch lower than normal and worn with disuse.

"It's the third day of Fheile Earrach. I can promise you there's nothing for you to work on today."

"Mother."

"Cian," Mrs. Uí Mháille warned, "Eoghan would want you to take time off."

Anaís's heart skipped a beat at the mention of his name. Carefully, she lowered her foot onto the tread it hovered over, and leaned against the wall for support as fragments of the night before tried to force their way into her mind. Her blade had not sunk deep enough to pierce anything vital. Nor should he bleed out, with proper attention.

He's all right. I'm all right.

The sound of Lochlan's pained breathing echoed in her ears. A sob caught in her throat, and she pressed her hand to her mouth as she slid down the wall.

He died because she mis-stepped. She should have seen the dip in the floor, should have moved faster. But as he'd swung, nothing could have overridden her instincts. Because in the face of attack, she was trained to do one thing and one thing alone—kill. Yet she couldn't kill the one she was meant to, and Lochlan had been caught as collateral.

No matter how hard Anaís tried, she could not bring herself to regret sparing Eoghan's life. Whatever had happened was neither feeling nor whim. He'd held the safety of her soul in his hands. To destroy him was to destroy herself, and she had chosen to destroy herself to spare him.

Perhaps she would not die when she returned home. She had made a tactical judgment call. If she explained that to her father...no. That was too risky. Simone. Simone would know what to do.

"Cian!" Mrs. Uí Mháille's shout brought her back to the present.

"I promise I won't be long," Cian countered. "And Eoghan asked me to bring him one of your pies. I'm sure that would brighten his day."

A chair scraped across the floor and something bumped into a wall. Frowning, Anaís adjusted the raspberry-pink fabric she had tied into a head scarf to cover the bruise blooming at her temple and crept down the steps to hear more clearly.

"Cian, what's gotten into you?" Mrs. Uí Mháille's concerned voice rose above the clatter.

"It's nothing I'm just...stressed." Cian's voice cracked at the end.

"Oh, my boy." The sound of fabric rustling filled the lull in conversation. Anaís could almost guarantee Mrs. Uí Mháille had her son wrapped in the tightest hug imaginable.

She didn't think it was possible, but her heart softened toward Cian. She didn't like him, not by a long shot—his air of infallibility came across as insufferable arrogance. But as she listened, witnessing him fall apart at the seams, she recognized in him a loyal humanity she had seen in few others.

She was glad for his sake that Eoghan was alive. His death would have destroyed Cian. Eoghan's life would destroy her, but that was a problem for when she arrived home.

"Come." Mrs. Uí Mháille's gentle command floated down the hallway. "You're whiter than a sheet. Have a nice breakfast, wake up a bit. I'll prepare Eoghan a pie you can take to him later—no, don't you look at me like that! Sit." A chair creaked as it accepted Cian's weight; Anaís couldn't help but smile.

She settled against the stairs as she waited. It was early enough in the morning that guests weren't likely to come down, but she also didn't want to risk standing up and causing the staircase to creak on the way back up. The clinking of dishes sounded from the kitchen, punctuated by Mrs. Uí Mháille's soft chatter that was too muffled to hear while she bustled about, making what was bound to be a feast fit for a king. The first sizzle of the griddle joined the kitchen symphony not long after, followed by a warm sweet smell that drifted up the stairs.

Anaís's stomach grumbled indignantly. *Not yet*, she chided. It would be rude to interrupt Cian's time with his mother.

It grumbled again, louder this time, and the clinking in the kitchen paused. Footsteps ambled down the hall, and Anaís stood abruptly, turning one way and then the other as she tried to decide whether she should risk dashing up the stairs or pretend to be casually walking down them. Mrs. Uí Mháille's head poked around the corner when Anaís was poised somewhere in between.

"Oh lovely! You're awake!" If Mrs. Uí Mháille had noticed her odd behavior, she didn't mention it. "I'm just making some breakfast. My son is already in the kitchen, you should come meet him."

"I...yes. That would be nice. Thank you."

"Oh dear, you're not a morning person, are you? That's all right, neither is Cian. You'll be in good company." Mrs. Uí Mháille waved her to follow, and Anaís complied. One did not simply say "no" to Cian's mother.

Cian tilted his head at Anaís as she trailed behind his mother into the kitchen. She gave him a brief smile and settled across from him at the small table in the corner of the kitchen, trying not to think of how Eoghan moved his head in the same way when he was trying to understand her. They really were like brothers.

Mrs. Uí Mháille set a steaming cup of spiced black tea in front of her before returning to her breakfast preparations.

"Thank you." Anaís blew on the hot liquid before taking a sip. "Is there anything I need to do before I check out this morning?"

"Why are you leaving on the third day of the festival?" Cian's voice had an edge to it, but it was more grating than unkind.

"Now don't be rude, Cian," Mrs. Uí Mháille scolded.

"It's all right," Anaís said. "I don't have the funds to stay longer. And I can't take too much time away from my shop. This was my treat to myself for having a good season last year."

Cian nodded as he lifted his tea to his lips, but abruptly set it down when his hand began to tremble. "And what do you make?"

He already asked her that the first day; he knew what she did. Either he forgot, which was unlikely, or this was still a test. He didn't believe her. Wise.

"Textiles," she replied.

Mrs. Uí Mháille set two plates stacked high with pancakes before each of them. A bowl of fresh berries followed. Then maple syrup. Then a platter of seared meats, hard and soft cheeses, and herb-infused oil.

"Mother," Cian croaked, looking up slowly at Mrs. Uí Mháille's beaming face. Her smile faltered when she saw the look on his own.

"Cian, please, you must eat. You hardly touched dinner last night. You'll fall ill if you don't keep your strength up. This isn't like you. Even when your fa—" She cut herself off abruptly.

Cian reached out and gave his mother's arm a gentle squeeze. "You're right, I'm sorry. It smells delicious."

He scooted his plate of pancakes closer to himself and spooned on a helping of berries, followed by a shaky drizzle of maple syrup. Anaís opened her mouth, to ask him what, she did not know, but closed it abruptly when he pushed the syrup in her direction. Misreading the look of confusion on her face, he said, "It's good, try some," before pointedly avoiding her gaze as he methodologically cut his breakfast into bite-sized pieces.

Shaking her head, she followed suit and tucked into her own breakfast. Her eyes widened as the first bite melted on her tongue. It was, without a doubt, the best thing she had ever eaten in her twenty-four years of life. Reaching over, she added another drizzle of syrup to her pancakes, not missing Cian's self-satisfied smirk as he mopped up syrup from his own plate.

The scraping of knives and clinking of forks made up for the absence of conversation. Mrs. Uí Mháille continued puttering about the kitchen as she prepared breakfast for the rest of the guests, humming softly while she moved about her tasks. Anaís settled deeper into her seat, taking a sip of her tea. This home felt warm, loving, peaceful. If her father executed her upon her return to Dúndíor, she was glad to have spent one of her last meals with this little family.

"Cian?" Mrs. Uí Mháille asked. "Would you be a dear and accompany Toma to the stables when she leaves?"

"Oh, that won't be necessary."

"I don't see why that's necessary."

Anaís and Cian spoke at the same time, meeting each other's gaze across the table with wide eyes.

Mrs. Uí Mháille made an indignant sound. Cian sputtered under the accusatory glare his mother directed at him. Anaís allowed her eyes to linger on Cian for the first time all morning. Only then did she note how horribly, horribly unwell he looked.

His hand trembled more violently than before as he raised his fork to his mouth. He hadn't eaten much of what his mother gave him, even though the food was absolutely divine. Cian chewed slowly, not as though he savored the flavor but as if he were afraid to swallow. He speared another bite with his fork and pushed it around absently on his plate.

"I would be happy to accompany you to the stables, Toma," he said without looking at her.

Anaís waited until Mrs. Uí Mháille's back was to them as she began washing up at the sink, allowing the sloshing water to mask their conversation.

"Are you okay?" she asked, leaning closer to ensure he alone could hear her.

"It's not your business."

"You look like you're about to topple over."

Cian spared her a glare. She returned it when he didn't look away, though it wasn't her eyes he was looking at. His gaze lingered on her neck where the high collar of her sweater had dipped lower with her movement. Bruises bloomed across her skin in the wake of Eoghan's touch.

She tugged her sweater higher and returned to her food.

"You look pretty rubbish yourself." Cian turned his eyes back to his plate, pushing a bite of pancake through maple syrup even though it was already saturated. "Have a rough night?"

"My blanket tangled around me and I fell out of bed," Anaís replied evenly.

"Peculiar."

"At least I don't play with my food."

He scowled, but put his fork down rather than try to eat any more breakfast.

❋ ❋ ❋

CIAN'S STEPS SHUFFLED ALONG THE dirt road as he and Toma followed the path toward the stables. Birds chirped overhead. Budding green trees dotted the landscape. Wildflowers bloomed along the rolling hills, swaying in the breeze.

And Cian walked next to a murderer. Or so he thought.

There was no proof, not *really*. She had acted sufficiently ignorant when he switched to Dúndían last night, her personality was that of a bubbly socialite, and his mother seemed fond of her. All arguments against his suspicions that Toma was the Anadali he met three weeks ago.

He glared at her from the corner of his eye—it was difficult to maintain civility with a suspected enemy when all he wanted to do was peel his skin off and perhaps vomit in a ditch.

If only the stars-cursed poison would allow him to think straight. Certainly then he would be able to deduce who this woman was.

"It's rude to stare," Toma commented.

Cian looked away. "You remind me of someone," he said before he could think better of it.

"Who?"

He shook his head and immediately regretted it. A wave of nausea slammed into him with the movement. Black spots danced in his vision. The sun overhead felt like a brand searing into his skin. Cian breathed in. Released it slowly.

Despite acquiescing to Tadhg's demands, there was still no antidote. Why had he expected, even for a moment, that his father would keep his word? And if Cian died, what would prevent Tadhg from slaughtering Ma?

He glanced at Toma again—at the bruises adorning her neck like fine jewelry. Strangulation. If she was telling the truth, if she was

Toma Glaadris, who had hurt her? And why? If that danger followed Toma to the inn...

"What really happened to your neck?" Cian rasped.

"I told you, I—"

"No!" he snapped, whirling at her.

Toma jumped back, knapsack slipping off her shoulder and *thunking* to the ground. "What is *wrong* with you?"

"I..." Cian ran a shaking hand through his hair. It was damp with sweat. *Get a hold of yourself.* "Sorry. I'm not mad at you. The past few days have been—" he cut himself off, eyes darting to the trees, to the shadows, anywhere one of Tadhg's men could hide. Dropping his voice to a whisper, he said, "Someone threatened my mother. I don't want trouble to find her. If someone hurt you, they could—"

Cian's heart seized in his chest. His knees buckled. Pain washed over him, only to recede as quickly as it came. Blinking, he looked up at Toma, who regarded him with a look of pure horror.

"Cian?" she asked softly, her voice muffled by the blood rushing in his ears.

He couldn't die before knowing whether Eoghan had survived the night. He couldn't die before warning his mother of Tadhg's plans, of the dangers awaiting them. Cian glanced back to the inn, then toward the stables down the road. Eoghan, Mother, die. In that order. Anything else was a waste of time.

Picking up her knapsack, Cian shoved to his feet and set off down the path, bowed beneath the weight of her luggage.

"Oy!" she called, jogging to catch up. "It wasn't..." she began, trailing off as she fell into step with him. "I promise your mother is safe. I'm just unreasonably clumsy." Toma adjusted the strap of her satchel across her chest.

Cian grunted, drained of the will to argue.

"Are you okay?" She repeated her question from breakfast.

Obviously not, if his wheezing was any indication. Besides, there was nothing to be done except carry onward. "If I told you no, would it make you feel better?"

"No."

"Then yes, I'm okay."

She raised her brow at him. "Cian."

"Toma," he countered, turning his head to meet her gaze. "Are *you* okay?"

"No."

He gave her a sad smile. "Then I think you know how I am faring."

Setting her knapsack down, he nodded to the stables before them. A young stable hand ran out to greet them, asking for identification before running off again to fetch Toma's horse.

"You remind me of someone I met not long ago," Cian said after a long pause. "She brought a lightness out of my friend that I had not seen in many years; she helped him find himself again. She was dangerous, but I trusted him. Tried to trust her."

Toma's throat bobbed as she swallowed. "And am I dangerous?"

"I don't know yet."

The clopping of hooves drew their attention back to the stable as Toma's horse obediently followed the stable hand. Giving her horse an affectionate pat, she slipped her foot into the stirrup and swung the other leg over, settling onto her mount.

"Have a safe trip back to Freydlan," Cian said, turning on his heel.

"Thank you!" she called after him. "Have a good time with your friend."

"We'll see," he mumbled back. Approaching the stable hand, he said, "Arrange a carriage for me, please." Cian dropped payment and then some into the boy's waiting hand. "I need to go to the palace. Urgently."

CHAPTER TWENTY-FOUR
PORTRAIT OF BLOOD

EOGHAN AWOKE TO THE CARESS OF A COOL BREEZE drifting through his window, carrying with it the smell of stone dampened by early morning dew. Pages of open books strewn across the floor fluttered in its wake. It was a sound too delicate to accompany the lingering nightmare clinging to the shadows of his room.

The intricate motifs on the ceiling blurred as he stared at them, unblinking. He wasn't sure how he fell back asleep last night, but apparently he had. Hesitantly, he turned his head toward the nightstand where a blood-soaked cloth and medical supplies lay. The wound carved into his chest needed proper medical attention, but he hadn't wanted anyone else to know.

Another gust blew through the window. Goosebumps erupted across his exposed skin; the pages of his books turned violently, but the cloth didn't move. The dried blood had frozen it in time. A portrait of last night, drawn in ink shed from his own body.

His head flopped lazily against the pillow as he forced himself to look away from the mess. The ceiling was safer. It had only witnessed the events of last night; it wasn't an active partaker. The floor had bruised him, the walls caged him, the windows mocked him. The one place he thought was safe was now a room filled with secrets upon secrets.

Unshed tears stung his eyes, the weight of last night sinking deeper into his chest. The frayed edge of the bandage scraped his fingers as he traced the outline of the cloth, trying to calm the anguish settling beneath his skin before it overflowed and carried him away with it. Each beat of his heart rocked his hand up and down, up and down. A lullaby for his aching soul. One that soothed him well enough to try to piece the fragments of his memories together.

He had been right—her name was *not* Toma, and she was not simply an Anadali.

Resignation washed over him, and he closed his eyes. Anaís Dí Sona. Firstborn of House Dí Sona. Anadali *Amadé*. She had deceived them all. That much had been clear when she nearly killed him. He couldn't tell if it was betrayal or rage humming in his veins, but his heart felt like it was twisted in knots and he couldn't find the beginning or end to begin unraveling it.

As governing bodies, he thought they had at least reached an agreement—one that went above attempted assassinations and perhaps, *perhaps*, settled on mildly good terms. Obviously, that had been a lie. Was that all that could be trusted anymore? The certainty of deceit and self-preservation?

Cool air filled his lungs as he tried to calm down, willing himself to look at the ceiling again as if, by memorizing the tangled web imprinted into the stucco, he would find his way out of the maze that was his heart. Because, while the politics frustrated him and the implications of an assassination attempt for his kingdom and eventual rule overwhelmed him, something else—a secret long buried deep inside—had slipped into the open, crossing from dream to reality.

And that terrified him, because it started and ended with Anaís.

A handbreadth to the right, and it would have been his heart that welcomed the sting of her blade. She had every intention of ending him where he stood. She could have ended him where he stood. She didn't. She *couldn't*. And no matter how scared he had been, he couldn't end her, either.

So consumed by pain from the thread joining them, it wasn't until the light had nearly gone out of her eyes that he'd realized a peculiarity. He had seen it, not in a dream, but tethered in reality: a glimmer of thread, woven emerald and gold and brown, binding her to him and him to her. Their lives were intertwined.

The thought should have incited terror. Why then, when recognition bloomed and the pain stopped, did he feel such peace?

Eoghan curled in on himself, the action sending a sharp pain rippling from his shoulder through his chest. A sob caught in his throat. He forced a breath around it.

It's fine. I'm fine.

The thought of bleeding out on his sheets formed in his mind. He pressed the heel of his hands against his eyes to rid himself of the image, but it only served to solidify the feeling. Sitting up, Eoghan tossed his sheets to the side, biting back a curse as the raw skin of his wound puckered with the movement. It really needed proper stitches and not his haphazard patch-up job of ointment and gauze. He stood, body shaking—the last vestiges of shock and adrenaline coursing through his veins as if preparing for Anaís to return and finish what she started. She wasn't here. He would have felt her.

Even now, he sensed a vague awareness tying them together. She was still alive, and an alarm had not been sounded, which meant she had not been caught leaving the palace. That thought brought him more comfort than he cared to admit.

Bracing against his nightstand, he waited until he was stable enough to move across his room to the wardrobe. He pulled on a navy-blue tunic and grey linen trousers. The shirt was nicer than what he normally would have chosen for breakfast, with silver embroidery woven into intricate patterns along the fabric. It was also one of the only shirts he owned that wouldn't incite agony to put on. Taking it off was a problem for another time. He fastened the ties by his neck with his good hand to ensure the bandage would remain covered, then lowered himself to the floor with a grunt to pull his shoes on. Somehow that task was the hardest of them all.

Mumbled whispers curled around the corner as Eoghan made his way to the dining room. People were always whispering here; in a place where worlds collided and idle talk ran rampant, how could they not? He didn't mind—it wasn't hostile, usually, simply the currency of the times. But there was something different in the timbre of their voices. Something darker. The lightness of morning gossip had been replaced by hushed truths soaked in fear. Creeping forward, Eoghan strained to listen.

"This wasn't a rogue drunk, this was a trained assassin."

He froze, hand braced against the wall. No one should have known. This was merely another morning—one in which he awoke to a hole punched into his chest and another in his heart. Two wounds he would take with him to the grave until he discovered why they afflicted him in the first place. But how did they know? Were they part of the plot? If so, even the most amateur of conspirators wouldn't be so stupid as to discuss an assassination in the place of execution.

"I don't know why anyone even considered it wasn't. If someone managed to get Lochlan..."

Eoghan's heart stopped beating in his chest, the rest of their words fading away. Or maybe it was beating too quickly. He couldn't quite tell. Was there a difference? Should he be worried that he couldn't tell? And why did it feel like he was suffocating?

Breathe. He wasn't breathing. Eoghan sucked in a gulp of air and tried to calm his racing heart. That's what it was, it was beating too quickly. In, hold—no don't hold. Breathe. Out. In, out. Lochlan was fine. The rumors could mean anything. Surely that was—

"Did you hear where they found the body?"

"Captain Riona mentioned the laundry chute? Such a strange place. They're not even sure where the murder happened, but wasn't Lochlan assigned to His Highness's wing last night?"

"If he was, none of the guards on rotation there saw anything unusual. Sullivan was sent to check on Prince Eoghan and said he was fine."

A chill crept through him. No one had checked on him. But Lochlan *had* been assigned to his wing last night, hadn't he? Though there was no blood outside his door. Eoghan looked at the bottoms of his shoes, as if he had walked through the puddle without noticing.

They were spotless.

"Clean hit too, straight to the chest. It's like there wasn't even a struggle."

"Does His Highness know?"

Eoghan tilted his head toward his chest in a daze. Clean hit. Her aim was true. Until it wasn't. She never missed. Why did she miss?

"No, but I would make yourself scarce when he finds out."

Eoghan leaned against the wall as his world collapsed around him. Lochlan was dead while he lived. Anaís would curse the day they met again.

*　*　*

EOGHAN PUSHED HIS BREAKFAST AROUND on his plate, ignoring the concerned look from his father. The dramatic tears from Queen Siofra. The less-than-subtle murmurs of conversation from courtiers and waitstaff alike as the breakfast room bustled with more activity than usual.

"Is there anything missing? Anything out of place?" someone asked. Eoghan didn't bother looking up to see who.

Me, he thought bitterly. *I am out of place.*

"It was a ruse; they wanted to shake us. They won't succeed."

"Do you think it was because of the treaty?"

Voices buzzed. Speculations cast. The weight of Lochlan's life buried under the intrigue of court drama and the excitement of an event that held little consequence to their detached lives. Eoghan let his head slump into his hands and tried to block them all out, wincing as the motion sent another wave of pain through his wound. He kept his eyes open. If he didn't, he would see her. That was a pain to be tackled alone.

The side door creaked open, a familiar figure drawing his attention. Cian met his gaze and blanched, as if looking at a ghost. Wasn't he supposed to be with his mother? Or was he coming back today?

Eoghan couldn't remember. It seemed his sole focus of existence had been compressed into the past five hours. Nothing before, nothing after. Just death and the absence it left in its wake.

Cian crossed the room slowly, coming to a stop a few paces away from where Eoghan sat. His face was the picture of utter desolation masked with relief.

Eoghan loved his cousin, truly, but if Cian had been the one who was taken... He forced himself to stop thinking. Instead, he stood, opened his arms, and embraced his best friend. Even the pain lacing his body and the numbness of his heart could not overcome the relief at seeing him safe.

"Was it her?" Cian whispered.

Eoghan released him. "Who?"

"You know who I mean."

Eoghan glanced around the room. "Not here," he muttered, sending a brief smile and nod to one of the nobility who gave him an odd look as he excused himself from the breakfast table.

"I don't care," Cian hissed, turning to face him fully. "Was it her?"

Eoghan glared at his friend, then grabbed his arm and all but dragged him out of the room, down a winding maze of hallways, and through the door to his study. He shut it firmly behind them and crossed his arms as he turned to face Cian, instantly regretting the action when blood began to weep from his cut. "Clarify."

"Pardon?"

"There was a murder in the palace. I need you to clarify your question. Was what *who*?"

"Was the Anadali the one who attempted to assassinate you?"

Eoghan raised his brow. "I don't follow."

"You're a terrible liar."

"I'm not lying." Eoghan wanted to slap himself. Why was he trying to protect the one who had almost slaughtered him in cold blood? Maybe he truly was mad. Maybe the comfort he felt wasn't the ally he thought he had found in the space between dreams and reality, but his life clinging to his bones, begging him to get away, reminding him of the sweetness of warmth, of feeling, of everything he wouldn't be if he were six feet under.

Yet he couldn't shake the feeling that when his gaze met hers and he stared into the depths of her soul, it was a reflection of his own. She was as one with him as he was with her. She was his guiding light in the darkness. Who was he to her?

"Why did your left arm shake when you opened the door?" Cian's question nudged away his thoughts.

"I'm cold."

"Stop. Lying." Cian gave him a halfhearted shove to the shoulder.

Pain flared in Eoghan's chest, and he bit back a curse, but as he glared at his friend, concern replaced any animosity he felt. Cian's skin was bone-white and damp with sweat, his breathing shallow. Something was very, very wrong.

"Cian, what's the matter?"

"Fine. I'll spell it out for you." Cian's voice was a raspy whisper, though it looked like he was trying to shout. "You look terrible. You won't stop fidgeting. You don't even seem surprised at the news of an assassination *attempt*."

"That's not what I meant. You're shaking."

"I'm fine. I'm...tired. Upset. Scared." A glassy sheen coated Cian's eyes. "It was her, wasn't it. I..."

Eoghan settled a hand on his shoulder, surprised at how warm it felt despite Cian's thin shirt and the chill that lingered in the air. "You don't need to be scared. We'll get to the bottom of this."

"There is no bottom," Cian breathed. "It's just dark." He swayed on his feet as unadulterated misery colored with pain twisted his features.

Eoghan steadied him with his other hand. Perhaps Cian was going into shock. "Come on," he nudged Cian toward the door. "You need rest."

"I'm fine." He tried to slip out of Eoghan's grip but slumped farther against him instead, chest heaving as if he had just spent two hours on the training field.

"I'm not asking," Eoghan grunted, wrapping his arm around Cian and guiding him out the door. Then, quietly, he added, "I lost Lochlan. I am not losing you too."

They arrived at Cian's chambers in silence. Eoghan guided him around the chairs by the fireplace, steadying him when his foot caught on the edge of the rug. By the time they arrived at the side of Cian's bed, Eoghan supported the majority of his weight.

"I don't need sleep," Cian rasped.

"If you don't decide when to rest, your body will do it for you."

Cian's hand shook as he gripped Eoghan's arm more tightly. "I told you, I am fine."

Eoghan leveled him with his best glare. "Cian Gallagher Ó Máille, I swear on my own grave that if you do not rest right now, I will tell your mother of your insolence, and there will be no continent too far, no mountain too high, no ocean too deep that will keep you from her wrath."

Cian immediately let go and tipped forward. Eoghan caught him before he could faceplant into the pillows and steadied him as he climbed the rest of the way in bed.

Eoghan removed Cian's shoes, then pulled the bed sheets up to his chin. An unreadable expression flashed across his face beneath the delusion of fever.

"I'll be back," Eoghan said before padding to the door. Peeking his head out, he waved over the first servant that stepped into the hallway. He spoke lowly as she approached. "I need you to fetch a healer."

She looked up at him with wide blue eyes.

"Quickly."

She curtsied and ran off, flaxen hair swishing across her back as she hurried down the hallway before disappearing around the corner. Eoghan narrowed his eyes after her, lips pressed thin. Giving his head a subtle shake, he shut the door and crossed the room, slumping into one of the plush armchairs.

Cian's chest rose and fell to an irregular rhythm. Quickly, then slowly. Deeply, then lightly. Sweat dampened the hair on his forehead.

"I called for a healer," Eoghan told him, "but if she doesn't come within ten minutes, I'll fetch one myself. She can give you something to counteract the fever."

Cian remained silent. Eoghan traced the embroidery on the fabric of the armchair, waiting for him to say something. Anything. Was this shock? Or had he fallen ill? How had he even left his mother's inn in such condition?

"Cian, what happened?" Eoghan finally asked.

"Please leave." Cian's voice was barely audible above the wet rasping in his chest.

Eoghan leaned forward. Surly he hadn't heard properly. "What?"

"Please leave."

He blinked. "Cian, I'm not leaving you while you're so ill. I need to make sure you're—"

"Leave." Cian bit out. "Now."

"Okay...okay." Eoghan stood slowly, hands held out as if calming a cornered animal. Lingering in front of the chair, he watched Cian's chest rise...and fall...rise and fall. He couldn't leave him alone like this.

"Go."

Eoghan turned on his heel and walked to the door, pausing at the threshold as he looked at his friend one last time. "If you need anything..." He trailed off.

Cian turned his head away.

A hollow sadness threatened to choke him where he stood. Instead, he left Cian's room, closing the door softly behind him.

Eoghan made it halfway to his room when his vision tunneled and the world tipped. Stumbling against a wall, he tilted his head down to see blood soaking through his tunic, dripping off the hem onto the floor by his feet. No wonder it hurt so much. He closed his eyes and slid down the wall, trying to will the lightheadedness away. Trying to will the past two hours of his life away.

Instead, like a man in a desert searching for an oasis, his mind focused on Anaís. Her body pressed against his own as their hearts beat in tandem. Her blade between his ribs, fingers digging into his skin as if preparing to drag him through it. The look in her eyes as they bored into his soul.

He loathed her for it. He loathed himself for it. Yet no matter how many times he replayed that moment in his mind, it ended the same. Every. Single. Time.

He would have let her do it. End him. Try as he might, he could not bring himself to hurt her. It seemed she felt the same.

Giving his head a light tap against the wall, his eyes opened to the panicked gaze of a servant bustling toward him. Right—he was delirious from blood loss. And he needed stitches.

"I accidentally cut myself while training, though I did not notice at the time." Eoghan spoke lightly, a difficult feat with how numb his lips felt. "It appears I'm in need of a healer. Fetch me one? Please?"

"Of course, Your Highness." The servant bowed while walking backward. "Right away."

"Ellis?"

He froze, then straightened with eyes wide, fidgeting with his uniform as he did so. "You know my name, Your Highness?"

"Of course." Eoghan made it a point to know all their names. At least, everyone he saw fairly regularly. "Ensure a healer has been sent to Lord Ó Máille's room first. He fell ill after breakfast."

Ellis bowed deeply. "Right away."

Eoghan tipped his head against the wall and closed his eyes once more, letting his mind take him back to the oasis until unconsciousness claimed him.

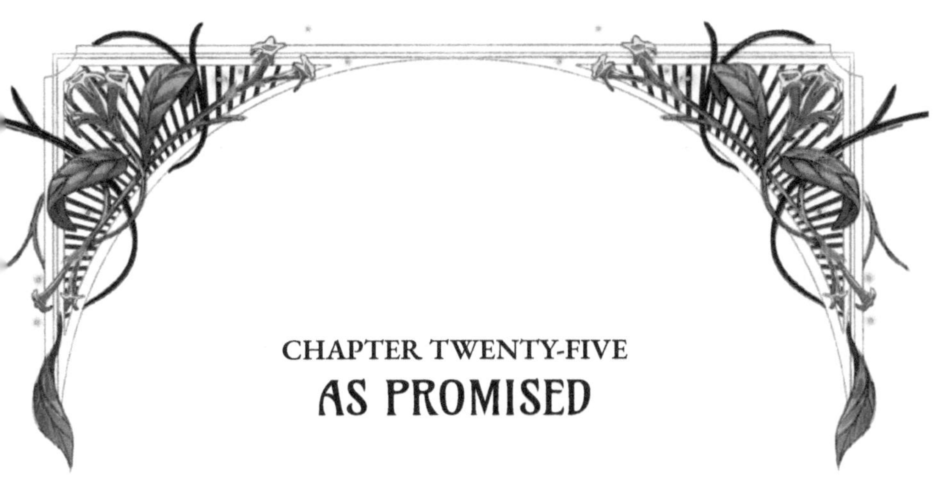

CHAPTER TWENTY-FIVE
AS PROMISED

HEAVY, SUFFOCATING SILENCE FELL OVER THE ROOM. Cian flung his arm wildly to yank the sheets off. They fluttered a handbreadth down his chest, settling at his sternum to continue rising and falling with each raspy inhale. Exhale. Repeat.

The blankets were not the problem.

No, it was the crushing sensation of guilt weighing on his chest. A night terror perched upon him, watching, waiting, taunting. Cian had left Eoghan to die, yet he lived. He should have been happy. Instead, he was consumed by an unending horror. Now Eoghan had left at his bidding, and the small boy within him who still cried when confronted with life's simple realities wanted him back.

How wretched the boy. How much worse was the man.

Because, at the heart of it, Cian had doomed himself for nothing. Risked his mother's life for nothing. The boy's misguided obedience of his father had poisoned the love of those who were truly family, be it blood or water that bound them. That poison had been made manifest by Tadhg's blade, and now Cian would pay the price. Maybe he deserved it.

It was the concerned look in Eoghan's eyes as he tucked him in that broke Cian. The simple, unconditional, love that man had for those he cared about. Cian didn't deserve *that*. Not after condemning his best friend to death.

Muffled footsteps hurried past his door, followed by the backwashed din of voices that trailed after them.

"...Highness...stable...asleep...tell the guards to..."

Cian forced himself to sit up, mind churning despite the ever-growing fever threatening to snuff out consciousness.

Had the Anadali really not been able to finish her job? Despite his muddled thoughts and sluggish reasoning, the truth had crept in like a thief in the night. It was her, of that he was certain. Indignation burned through the haze of his fever. How dare Eoghan's assassin protect him more thoroughly than Cian dared protect him, himself? How dare her failure do more good than Cian's success ever could have? That thought alone cut him to the core.

What had he done?

Thick black smoke writhed above his writing desk across the room without preamble, tendrils blooming and twisting like an unwanted blot of ink bleeding across fresh paper. It disappeared as quickly as it came, clearing to reveal a small glass vial with a note tied with twine around the lip. Cian blinked at it owlishly. Then, realization dawned.

Lunging across the bed, he tumbled over the edge as blankets tangled around his sweat-soaked skin. Dark spots danced across his vision, his knees buckled when he heaved himself up to stand, but desperation had already sunk its teeth into his flesh and drew him forward with an all-consuming need. He clawed at the ground, stone grating the tips of his fingers raw as he pulled himself across the floor. The desk shook when he bumped into it. Shook again when he grabbed it by the leg and rocked with all his weakened might.

The vial toppled onto his lap, and the note fluttered right way 'round to reveal a familiar scrawl he would rather forget.

"As promised," the paper read.

A relieved sob bubbled out of his throat as he tried pulling the cork stopper out. His fingers seized. The note ripped from the twine and drifted to the ground instead.

"No, no, *no!*" Cian pushed himself to his knees, leaning against the leg of the desk while using his good hand to pull open the drawer and feel around the contents within. It had to still be there. It had to. A thin rod of metal brushed against his skin and he yanked it free.

"Please work," he mumbled, shifting to brace the vial between his knees before jamming the letter opener into the cork. "Please work."

He twisted and pulled. The letter opener came free. The cork did not budge.

"No, work, dammit, *work!*" He stabbed the cork again, and again, and again, digging out small chunks with each strike.

A pungent smell poisoned the air of the room. Darkness consumed his vision. The letter opener slipped. A sharp pain bloomed in his knee. Cian's chest heaved, from pain or the stench of rotting death he could not tell. He did not care. The sound of the letter opener clattering to the floor disappeared to the back of his mind as he blindly brought the vial to his lips, tipped his head back, and drank.

He wished he hadn't.

Burning filled his veins, spreading further and further until every inch of his being was nothing but agony. He was no longer a man of flesh and blood. No, his blood had been replaced with oil and ignited, flaring into an unquenchable inferno. It was destroying him, destroying the poison. Unless he had simply poisoned himself again and driven the nail into his already closed coffin. Or perhaps he was already dead, and the past two days had been nothing but a sick joke.

But of course they weren't. They couldn't have been.

Because when the burning receded and his muscles relaxed as the last vestiges of poison left his system, reality came crashing back into him. He had left Eoghan to die, and he couldn't convince himself he wouldn't do it again. Somehow that realization hurt more than the poison or the antidote ever could.

A sharp rap on the door pulled him back to the present.

Wiping his forehead on his sleeve, Cian pulled himself to standing, surprised to find he didn't wobble.

"One moment!" he called, straightening his shirt and tossing the vial into the trash bin. Everything was normal. Everything was fine. Cian glanced at his reflection in the window and neatened his hair as much as the sweat-soaked strands reasonably allowed before plucking a book off his shelf and plopping himself into the plush armchair Eoghan had occupied not minutes before. "You may enter."

A healer and a meek-looking apprentice stepped into the room, the latter regarding him with wide eyes as she took in his appearance.

"His Highness said you were unwell, my lord. I am here to assist you," the former said.

Cian tucked a bookmark between the pages and shut it with a smile he hoped looked sincere. "Merely a simple case of food poisoning, I'm afraid. I'm feeling much better now though, thank you."

The healer regarded him curiously, then pulled a thermometer from her bag before crossing the room. "I was made to believe it was a more serious matter. May I take your temperature?"

Cian obediently opened his mouth, closing it again to secure the device under his tongue. He watched her watch the temperature rise, then stabilize—he assumed—when she squinted at the reading with pursed lips. She removed it from his mouth and wrapped it in a cloth before passing it to her apprentice.

"You are normal," she concluded.

"I'm glad to hear it." He felt anything but.

"Open."

"What?"

The healer met his eyes, her expression softening. "Your mouth," she clarified. I'm not finished with the exam. I'll need to check your throat for infection."

Cian nodded and complied. Waiting patiently as he was poked, prodded, and inspected for a disease the healer would not be able to find.

The healer blew out the candle she had used to check his pupil dilation—for what purpose, he wasn't sure—before riffling through her bag once more.

"I cannot find anything the matter with you, though I do not doubt that a case of severe food poisoning can leave as quickly as it came." She pulled out various packets of herbs as she spoke and began spooning precise measurements into a small drawstring bag. "I must ask that you add a teaspoon of this to your morning tea every day for the next week. It will help with hydration and any lingering queasiness." The healer passed the pouch to him and he accepted it with a nod. "Be sure to prioritize rest for the next few days," she continued. "Bread and light soups will be your friend."

"Thank you," Cian said with a lightness he did not feel. "Will that be all?"

The healer hesitated, the only sound filling the room was the rustle of fabric as her apprentice reorganized the herbs. "If I may, Lord Ó Máille?"

"You may." It came out as a question more than a statement. The boy wanted to listen. The man wanted to run.

"My colleague mentioned His Highness had been injured. Said he seemed a bit shaken up by it. If you feel well enough, might you keep him company? Sometimes friendship is the best medicine."

She might as well have flayed Cian's heart with a pocketknife. He simply nodded. The only sound that would have worked its way around the lump in his throat was one he wanted no one to hear.

"I'm sure he would appreciate it," she said with a relieved smile. "If your symptoms return, please don't hesitate to come to the medical wing."

The door clicked shut behind the healer and her apprentice.

Cian swallowed. There would be no going back after this.

CHAPTER TWENTY-SIX

A GOOD COLOR

IT WAS A WAKING NIGHTMARE ALL OVER AGAIN, A MEMORY from the past resurrected to haunt Anaís. Only, instead of taking on the hazy quality her memories normally did when she observed them through the veil of time, the scene before her unfolded in vivid color. Because this was not a memory. This was real. The throne room, the rigid posture of King Timun, the guards stationed in the recesses of their posts, Gio watching in horror as she stood before the king. All of it was real, and all it took were her four simple words.

Prince Eoghan is alive.

The ghost of her proclamation lay heavily in the silence of the room, embalming everyone within it in a suffocating embrace. Her words coated the floors, seeped into the walls, painted the room with the color of his life—the color of her treason. Air filled her lungs as her words returned to her, finding a home in her heart. She drew them closer, tucking them safely away as the spell broke and turmoil began simmering beneath the king's surface, drawing murmurs out of the guards, draining the color from Gio's already pale skin.

The king shifted slightly in his seat, composing himself. "Do you rescind your actions?"

"No." The word cracked like a whip in the silence.

The fabric of the king's cloak rustled. He stood, footsteps marking the passing seconds as he crossed the room. He stopped mere inches from her face. When he spoke, his voice was meant only for her. "Why?"

She pressed her lips together.

"Why would you betray me?" His shout ripped through the room.

Gio suppressed a flinch.

The guards stood straighter.

Anaís could not answer.

A low growl rumbled in the back of his throat as his glare seared into her. "You will learn." King Timun turned and stalked to his throne. "Get her out of my sight. Out! Captain Tadeo!"

Tadeo briskly crossed the room and stood at attention. "Yes, Your Majesty."

"Take her to the Butcher," he said, lowering himself onto the throne.

A static silence filled the room like the air before a lightning strike. The king picked a piece of imaginary dirt from his immaculate robes. Straightening the hem with a final brush, he turned his attention back to Anaís. Lines creased his forehead as he raised his brows, and his lips pulled into an emotionless frown while he appraised her. The expression was calculating, disconnected, as if he were considering a piece of meat at the market rather than his own daughter. Perhaps they were one and the same.

She lifted her head, playing into the role he saw her in. There was no remorse in his eyes. Only resolve. He would not regret his next words, only the actions she took to bring the punishment upon herself. Actions that she could not, would not rescind. Or regret.

"Tell the Butcher he has complete freedom," the king ordered Tadeo. "I leave her treatment at his discretion."

"Yes, Sir."

Tadeo grabbed her bicep and pulled her in the direction of her fate. Though they strode across the room in tandem, she had the strange feeling that she would not have been able to move without his guidance. Her body functioned as if everything were normal, yet her mind was somewhere far away. He could have gently nudged her off a cliff, and she would have kept walking until she met her end at the bottom.

She cautioned a glance at her guide. His lips were pressed into a thin line, his eyes sharp, focused directly in front of them. Tadeo pushed the door open and dragged her through. Her feet automatically stopped in response to his own movements, or lack thereof. The only break in their synchronicity was her flinch when he slammed the door shut.

A key grated in the lock, fingers dug into her arm, and then she was moving again. He was also looking at her now. Intently.

Anaís refused to meet his gaze. His hand tightened around her arm as he pulled her down another hallway, then another. They were going up, if the burning in her lungs was any indication. Or perhaps that was fear; these tunnels were built to inspire it. The long, winding labyrinth of possibilities, the dips and slants of the floor, the way the end appeared to never move closer or farther away no matter how desperately a captive dragged onward.

Illusions on illusions on illusions.

She knew this place like the back of her hand, but Tadeo could have told her they were walking on the ceiling and she would have believed him. Her arm jerked when Tadeo took a sharp turn to lead her up a set of stairs.

Anaís stumbled up them. She knew where this led.

Tadeo stopped, allowing her to right herself. Instead of dragging her onward, he turned, hands gripping her shoulders as his gaze bored into her. She was shaking. No, he was shaking. Not shaking her. He was...scared. The Captain of the King's Guard was scared.

"I know you are stubborn, but this is madness. What in the four kingdoms were you *thinking*?" he hissed.

She watched him watch her. The way his green eyes wandered her face as he looked for an answer, trying to uncover whatever it was she was hiding. He would not find what he was looking for. She wasn't hiding anything.

"Eoghan couldn't die." It came out as a broken whisper. She couldn't bring herself to care.

"Couldn't, as in he bested you in a fight? *You*, the greatest warrior in this kingdom. *You* who fights to the death. *You* his assassin, that he *let* live?" he asked incredulously. "Or you didn't *want* him to die?"

Something must have shifted in her expression because Tadeo recoiled from her as if she had burned him. "What is wrong with you?" His voice was quiet, yet the sound echoed off the stone walls and rattled against her skull.

She gave him a sad smile. "I do not know."

He opened his mouth, then closed it again, frowning.

"Fate will have it that this is not the end, Tadeo. If the king wanted me dead, he would have had Gio take my life in the throne room." Anaís shook her head. "No, this is simply a warning."

They both knew no one walked out of the Butcher alive.

Tadeo's gaze dropped to the floor as if his mind was trying to piece together the woman in front of him, and the specter of her physical form was too much a distraction. Or perhaps he was trying to figure out what he was going to tell Simone. *I took your sister to her demise.* At least Simone would have him for protection when she was gone.

"Will it work?" he finally asked.

"My father cannot break me more than he already has."

Tadeo nodded curtly. "Whatever reason you chose to let Eoghan live, hold on to that. Maybe it will help you pull through." He turned and continued up the stairs, not waiting for her to follow. "And you'd better not die," he added quietly, "or Simone will kill you herself."

"Tadeo?" Anaís whispered after him.

He looked over his shoulder.

"Tell her I'm sorry."

He gave her a sad smile. "You should tell her yourself."

The door creaked open to reveal a circular room bathed in light. The chamber was carved entirely of sandstone, lending warmth to what should have been a sterile chamber of death. A polished wooden table stood to the right of the door, stacked neatly with chains, metal pipes, little boxes filled with...

Anaís dragged her eyes away and immediately latched onto the mountain of a man approaching her and Tadeo. It was a miracle the Butcher didn't have to hunch as he stalked toward them, his movements silent despite his build. A scar ran across his face, more littered his tanned arms. She noted absently that he was wearing all black. Good to keep the bloodstains from showing. A hysterical laugh almost bubbled out her throat.

It burst before it could escape when rough hands ripped her from Tadeo's light grasp. Tadeo's hand lingered in the air while Anaís stumbled away, as if begging to take her back but not wanting to be taken himself.

The Butcher slowed, then placed her meticulously in the center of the room, straightening her uniform as he did so. His eyes trailed over her, though his gaze was distinctly different from the calculated way her father regarded her. This was a reverence that flowed with an undercurrent of excitement, like he was waiting for something to happen just by watching her. It made her insides twist and her skin crawl. She dropped her gaze and focused intently at the grate in the floor by her feet as she tried to calm her breathing. Panic would not help her survive.

She was not a fool. She was not a scared child. She was Anadali Amadé.

And she.

Would.

Not.

Die.

Her eyes tracked the man as he made his way back to Tadeo. He moved methodically, slowly; there was no denying his strength. Still, she'd fought bigger, and anything she needed was right there. Pipe to the head. Chain around the throat. Her fingers twitched involuntarily. She could make a break for it. Escape the palace. No one would know.

And where would that leave her? When the king found her gone, she would be hunted for the rest of her life. Simone would be left at the mercy of this mystery that infected the palace and threatened their kingdom—the information about Takaniim that King Timun had had Anaís steal in Nahonaugh, the century of inter-kingdom sabotage that Simone had uncovered what felt like a lifetime ago. Something was at the doorstep; Anaís could not leave it at that. And if Eoghan spoke of her actions to anyone in his palace, wrath would be wrought upon Dúndíor.

No. This was her mess. She would fight by surviving the punishment of her crimes. She *would* live to see another day—she had to—and she would be there for Simone as they uncovered this mystery together.

"Instructions?" The Butcher's low voice rumbled through the room like thunder.

Tadeo swallowed and pointedly avoided meeting Anaís's gaze. Had he seen the thoughts running through her mind? "At your discretion," he finally said.

The Butcher nodded in assent. Tadeo turned on his heel. Anaís's resolve melted away when the door closed behind him, and she was left at the mercy of the Butcher.

HER RIGHT EYE WAS SEALED shut. Her ribs, probably cracked, screamed under the pull of gravity. She couldn't feel her arms. She wished she couldn't feel her shoulders. Her toes scuffed the ground as she hung from the ceiling. When had her boots been removed? Her chin lolled against her chest, straining the muscles in her neck. It felt like she had been trampled by a herd of stampeding horses but, all things considered, it wasn't so bad.

She peeled her left eye open, the warm glow of the chamber assaulting her vision before fading to provide just enough light to see by. Her undershirt hung limply—the fabric at the back ripped open. Her trousers were in tatters. A shame, really. Those were nice trousers. Anaís tried moving her leg to assess the damage to the lower half of her body, only to find that her ankles had been loosely chained to the ground.

The chain holding her to the ceiling shifted, and an involuntary groan slipped from her lips as a fresh wave of pain rolled through her body. Her ribs were definitely broken. One pressed against her lungs. A spasm ran through her shoulder in protest of the new position, rattling the chains with the movement.

"Oh good, you are awake." The low voice of the Butcher reverberated through her bones. "Last trick. You are lucky, hmm? King said give you makeover." The hollow echo of a pipe rang out as he dropped it on the table amongst his other tools. "This is not so simple—like an art. First, I give you base layers. Bruising is a little slow but makes nice background. Restructure the ribs...beautiful. But now"—something pinged to the ground as he rifled through his tools—"we paint. I think red will be good color for you."

A chill crept down her spine at his words. She was a fool. A hopeless fool.

"I am curious to see...who will you be when the piece is finished."

Who are you? Eoghan's question, his words, his voice, came unbidden into her mind. In an instant, she was no longer chained to the ceiling deep in the bowels of the palace. Instead, she was ripped back to that night—his room filled her mind's eye, the tip of her blade pressed against his ribs, his hands secured tightly around her throat. But then the rage that contorted his features softened into confusion. His hands loosened against her skin as if he were repulsed by their violence. He looked at her, looked *into* her, and spoke— three simple words carried deep into her soul by a voice so smooth and rich and mellow.

In that moment, the realization of who he was had terrified her.

Now she clung to it like a lifeline.

A loud "Aha!" and the sound of metal rain tore her out of her memory, the silver glow of Eoghan's moonlit room shifting into the golden confines of the chamber.

Try as she might, she couldn't bring herself to regret her actions.

She fixed her gaze on the now grime-stained floor below her feet, blocking out the sound of the Butcher as he stalked toward her. Slowly. Anticipation rose with every beat of her quickening heart. As if that would hasten the inevitable, if only to grant her the mercy of embracing the aftermath sooner.

I am Anadali Amadé, she replied to Eoghan's question in her mind, her thoughts rising where silence had previously reigned.

The Butcher's footsteps stopped. Goosebumps erupted across her flesh in the wake of his breath, trailing hot and fast down her back as he observed his prey in agonizing detail. She could almost feel his presence reaching out to her, analyzing every micromovement, calculating where to strike. How to strike. His boot scraped the ground as he shifted his weight, the cat o'nine tails carving a path into the grime of the floor. The barbed metal knotted into the leather danced in anticipation against the stone, preparing to strike.

Breath left her lips in short bursts. Her heart thundered against her ribs in a bid to break free, roaring in her ears as it pumped life through her veins—a final battle cry to not stop beating.

I am Anadali Amadé, she began again, *and I will not die.*

A drop of sweat rolled down the bridge of her nose. A split second of silence filled the room as the whip pulled upward, suspending momentarily in the air when it reached the peak of its trajectory. In the quiet, she almost hoped that it had disappeared into thin air, that *she* would disappear into thin air—never again forced to taste the kiss of pain and the sweet sting of death. But time had only frozen itself into one horrific moment of anticipation and reprieve.

The whip fell.

Time shattered.

And all she knew was pain. White-hot, blinding pain as leather tore through skin and barbed metal bit into flesh, only to be ripped out again.

I will not die.

And again.

I will not...

And again.

I...

*   *   *

ANAÍS AWOKE TO A STRANGE noise. A low rumble from afar. A storm was coming. Or leaving. She couldn't tell if the thunder was approaching or moving away. She waited for a flash of lightning to count off the seconds between it and the ever-present roll of thunder. None ever came. *Odd.*

Perhaps if she could get up and analyze her surroundings, she could orient herself and find shelter. She just needed her arm to work. Why wouldn't it...

Her arm twitched and it felt like someone had struck a match and lit all the nerves in her body on fire. A scream caught in her throat. The low rumbling stopped. Her heart raced. The sound, she realized, was coming from her.

Her chest ached as she tried to calm her ragged breaths and focus on anything but the fire raging through her body. The ground was warm and cold, slippery and rough. She relaxed against it. The rain must have already come. But that wasn't right, was it? There was no thunder. There was no rain. No breeze. Copper. She smelled copper.

I think red will be a good color for you.

Slowly, carefully, she willed her fingers to move. Viscous liquid stuck to her skin, and gravel scraped against her fingertips. Dim light filled her vision as she forced an eye open, while disgusted awe settled like a rock in the pit of her stomach. Blood, her blood, was splattered against the walls, dotting the ground, coating her—a warm cocoon protecting her from the biting cold of the room. The Butcher was right, in a twisted sort of way. Red was a beautiful color. A contented sigh left her lips as she tried to press her cold skin farther against the floor. She was too tired to be angry.

Her eye drooped closed, and her mind settled on the last dream that made her feel safe—like she was floating and grounded all at once. A lake filled with wonder, sheltered by the embrace of the forest. A tether that drew her to safer shores.

Prince Eoghan is alive.

Did Simone know?

Panic spiked through her and focused her thoughts, doing little to overcome the pain but giving her the strength she needed to force herself to sit up. Then stand up. The shackles about her ankles fell away. Her hand slipped as she leaned against the bloodied wall. Darkness swarmed her vision. Her chest fluttered, small sips of air rushing past her lips.

She was not dead yet. There was still a chance. She could find Simone. Tell her.

Step after excruciating step, she forced her feet forward and stumbled out of the Butcher's domain. She had to find Simone.

CHAPTER TWENTY-SEVEN

TO SLIP THROUGH TIME

BLOOD LOSS HAD A STRANGE WAY OF ALTERING TIME. Slowing it down, speeding it up, then forcing it to disappear altogether before tipping the hourglass wrong side up and repeating the process all over again in a different time, a different place.

Hallways flickered into sprawling gardens. Wind burned her skin. Anaís slapped at her shoulder. If only skin were a coat, then she could take it off.

Someone screamed when she rounded a corner, then died.

Not dead.

Anaís's bare foot prodded the lump on the ground. Guard? Napping, maybe. She would rather like a nap. But that wasn't...

Time disappeared again.

A wooden door ran into her. Anaís stumbled backward, tottered forward, slumped against it. "Rude." She knocked her knuckles against it in retribution. Carved motifs bit into her skin in response. A fascinating door, then.

Leaning backward, Anaís tipped her head down and stared at the carvings, forcing her eye to focus as fatigue tried to slide it shut. "My apologies." She patted the door. "You are forgiven. I must hit you again, though."

She rapped on Simone's door, more forcefully this time. A confused "enter" drifted through the wood. The doorknob slipped beneath her hand. Grunting, she wiped it on her trousers and tried again. It was worse. The door shuddered as she kicked it with her toe.

"For heaven's sake!" Footsteps stomped nearer on the other side. "I said come"—the door whipped open—"in."

"Hello," Anaís meant to say. A moan came out instead. Her body sank through the new opening and came to an abrupt rest against the doorframe.

Simone stood frozen, staring at her wide-eyed, mouth dropped open in a little "o". Anaís shared the sentiment. She had talked to the door earlier, and it had understood well enough. She opened her mouth to try again. Sound caught in her throat, side burning as the doorframe pressed against her ribs. Ribs pressed against lungs that refused to inhale.

Panic flooded her body as darkness flooded her vision and time disappeared again.

Something soft pillowed her cheek. Something cold trailed down the other side of her face. The familiar pressure of bandages hugged her back, while a woolen rug tickled her bare stomach. It was an odd sensation—the contrast of a touch so gentle in a world filled with so much pain. Her eye fluttered open.

Darkness filled the room, pushed back by the warmth of a crackling fire and the lazy flicker of wall sconces. Simone sat on the floor, back propped against the wall, head resting on Tadeo's shoulder as she stared at Anaís with glassy eyes. Tadeo whispered something in Simone's ear. She nodded numbly.

"Simone?" Anaís's chest rumbled against the floor. At least she could make noise now.

Alertness came back to her sister's gaze. Simone lurched forward, appearing at Anaís's side swiftly despite the layers of fabric that made up her skirts. Tadeo sat up straighter. Anaís blinked. Time did not slip away.

"It's okay," Simone whispered, gently adjusting the damp cloth that cooled Anaís's forehead. "It's okay. I'm here. You're safe now."

Anaís let her eye drift closed as Simone ran her fingers lightly through her hair. Was she safe? Were either of them ever truly safe? Even if Anaís lived, even if she made a full recovery, what would become of her? Would the king let her return as Anadali Amadé? Eoghan had asked who she was, but who would she be without that title? Though it had strayed from its original meaning long ago, carrying her along with it. Now, her past and present mixed like two oceans colliding, roaring and volatile as she fought to distinguish the sky from the deep. If she remained suspended between them, she would drown.

The fire popped happily, pulling her out of her scattered thoughts and back into the present. She didn't mind. What use was thinking when up was down and down was up and time ticked to a tune of its own? Simone's fingers lingered in her hair before resuming their slow ministrations.

"Rumors have spread like wildfire. Tadeo said..." Simone's voice trailed off, and she swallowed thickly, as if she knew he'd spoken the truth but refused to believe it. Even when the truth was right in front of her. "Who did this to you?" she whispered.

"I brought this upon myself," Anaís whispered in kind, relieved she was able to form proper words this time.

"So it's true? The prince is not dead?"

A smile lifted Anaís's lips at the thought of him. "Eoghan is fine."

"How could you be so stupid?" Simone snapped.

Anaís flinched, her body locking as pain radiated through her. She breathed deeply, repeating the pattern until the fire consuming her nerves returned to a controlled burn.

"I'm sorry," Simone choked out, sliding her hand out of Anaís's hair and rocking back on her heels. "I didn't mean... I just... I know you didn't want to kill him, but you knew how Father would punish you. You *knew*!"

Anaís opened her eye. Simone's tear-streaked gaze remained transfixed on her back. "What is *wrong* with you?" Simone asked softly. "What aren't you telling me?"

"Everything is as it's meant to be. Even Eoghan." If Anaís couldn't think clearly for herself, she could at least reassure her sister.

"No, everything is not *as it's meant to be*!" Simone tossed her hands in the air in frustration. "Ten years ago, when Father commanded Balendin be executed, something changed. I thought you would come back to me, but it's just gotten worse. This year you started disappearing, and now you're bleeding out on my floor and you won't let me help you."

Anaís's heart stopped beating as tears welled in her eyes. Balendin's death was her burden to bear and hers alone. She wanted to remember her mentor, not her last act against him. How could she do that if anyone other than herself and her father knew? "How did you know that?" she managed to choke out.

"I—I never knew what Father was capable of, capable of making people do, but then I...yesterday I... Anaís, *you* did not kill Balen—"

"Don't say it," Anaís rasped. "Do not say it. I was there. I held the blade." A labored breath rattled her chest. "I don't want to remember, but I cannot forget."

"That's not something you had to bear by yourself," Simone said. "Why didn't you tell me? What aren't you telling me?"

"I can't do this anymore," Anaís whispered.

"I want to help you."

"I'm trying to protect you."

"From what?" Simone challenged.

"Everything. This mess, this kingdom, Father." Anaís swallowed, trying to force her mind to form thoughts that actually made sense. "Mother's death shattered him, and to hold onto her memory he held onto ruin. Martial law was created to sustain Dúndíor's people in times of hardship—not *foster* hardship—but it's consumed him. Without the impending threat of war, he would not have power as he knows it. Control as he knows it.

"You and I have always known we are just as trapped as everyone living in this kingdom. I didn't want to see my sister molded by cruelty," Anaís shifted to reach for Simone's hand, but stopped short when pain lanced through her arm. Simone scooted closer and linked her little finger with Anaís's. "You are such a light in this wretched place. Please forgive me for keeping you in the dark."

"I cannot fault you for trying to do what you think is right, but please"—Simone tightened her grip on Anaís's hand—"please, let me make my own decisions for myself. You forget, I am heir to the throne. Father taught me the art of politics, but the time I spent with you and Balendin reminded me of the gift of humanity. I am not so blind as you think."

Anaís blinked at Simone, her vision wavering. Why had she waited until she was on death's doorstep to see her sister clearly for the first time? Why had she thought hiding from the one person who knew her better than she knew herself would help anything?

"Will you tell me what's going on now?" Simone asked.

Fatigue slid Anaís's eye closed once more. "What part?"

"I thought the fact that you stumbled into my room half dead was prompting enough."

"It wasn't that bad," she mumbled against the pillow.

Simone brushed her thumb across the back of Anaís's hand. "You didn't see yourself." Her dress rustled as she shifted. "Tadeo, how long has it been? The healer said she would be back soon."

"I'll send for her. I'm not leaving the two of you alone."

Footsteps thumped across the room. The door latch clicked. Muffled voices drifted in. Moments later, Tadeo returned and sat on the floor next to Simone.

"Do you promise not to tell?" Anaís whispered. "Both of you?"

"I will take your secret with me to my grave," Simone vowed. "I won't let Balendin's fate fall on you next."

"Your secret is safe," Tadeo said. "I swear it."

Anaís sighed. There would be no going back after this. "I dream about him. We are...connected."

"Balendin?" asked Simone.

"Eoghan."

A heavy silence stretched between them until, finally, Simone asked, "How long has this been happening?"

"There was no beginning. Just a familiar comfort. A notion that I was not alone." Anaís's thoughts felt sluggish as she tried to string them together. "Then Balendin died. I couldn't see him—Eoghan. I did not know who he was. But we are bound. He is my lifeline in the dark."

"Why didn't you tell me about this?"

"How can I explain something I don't understand?"

Simone's earrings jingled as she shook her head. "Did you know, when we were first in Nahonaugh?"

"No." Anaís swallowed. "Perhaps there were signs, but I did not recognize them for what they were. How could I?" Anaís shifted. Her back felt wet. How nice would it be, to be in that sanctuary of dreams with him now? "It wasn't real," she added as an afterthought, "until the night I had to kill him."

Simone released a long breath. "It's okay. We'll figure this out together." She hesitated, then added, "I leave for Nahonaugh in a few days to finalize the peace treaty. I'll see what I can discover."

"No!" The sound tore from Anaís's throat. Simone was right—she was no longer a child, but this was insanity. "I'm coming with you!"

Muscles shook in her arms as she tried to push herself up. Simone kept her tethered to the ground with a gentle hand on her shoulder. "No, you need proper medical attention."

"I can do it!" Her voice broke from the strain in her body. "This was a warning, Sim. Why would the healers help?"

"No one," Simone's voice was low, dangerous, "gets to tell me what I can or cannot do for my sister. Anaís, look at me."

Her eye fluttered open.

"Let me protect you."

Each word was punctuated with an intensity Anaís had never heard from Simone. Rather than calming her, it sent a fresh wave of resolve rolling through her, pushing back the pain, the fatigue. "I just failed to assassinate the crown prince, and you are going to waltz back into enemy territory to continue talks of *peace* when neither king wants it?"

"Yes." There was a finality in Simone's tone that left no room for negotiation. "And you are going to let me help you. The Kavanaughs cannot accuse Dúndíor without formally declaring war. Which, in case you haven't noticed, they haven't done yet. You need to recover, and I need eyes here. I *will* get to the bottom of whatever is brewing."

"I will be with her, Anaís," Tadeo added, shifting closer to Simone. "I swear on my life I will keep her safe."

Anaís nodded. Her bandages puckered with the movement. A bubble of blood escaped, trickling down her side and carrying the last of her fight with it.

Simone gasped. "Tadeo, why has no one come yet?"

"How did you escape the Butcher's chamber?" Tadeo asked softly, yet there was an undercurrent of fear laced in his voice.

"I walked out," Anaís mumbled. "Door was unlocked."

Tadeo cursed, then jumped to his feet and strode across the room. "Keep the door locked," he said over his shoulder. "Answer *only* for me, do you understand?"

"What's happening?" Simone called after him.

"Nothing good. I'm bringing the healer myself, and then I'll find out."

"Be safe," Simone said as the door shut.

"Simone?" Anaís rasped. She wasn't sure what she wanted to say; why she had spoken at all. How did one go from coherent to jumbled in the blink of an eye? Time must have shifted again. The thread around her heart gave a subtle tug. Smoke filled her mind—not suffocating like in her nightmares, but smooth and musky. Snow-capped mountains...

"What is it?" Simone prompted.

"In Nahonaugh," her words slurred together, "follow the smoke. The one made of snow." Did snow make smoke? It sounded right. Felt right.

"Okay." A tinge of panic filled her sister's voice. "You hold on. Help is coming. Don't worry."

Anaís relaxed deeper into the rug. "Eoghan will tell you," she whispered. Then time disappeared again.

CHAPTER TWENTY-EIGHT
THE BULLSEYE

DEEP-GREEN HUES BLANKETED THE COUNTRYSIDE OF northern Nahonaugh like a patchwork quilt, stretching until it dropped off the horizon or ran into a mountain. After a week of traveling and visiting various villages throughout the region, Cian noted—with a realization that only boredom could bring—that these patches of civilization were the sole force powerful enough to interrupt the monochromatic scheme of nature. Though the color green still seemed adamant on taking over.

The village of Maulaidh was no different. Stacked-stone buildings functioned as both human abodes and trellises for climbing ivy. Tufts of hearty moss pressed their way through the cracks of cobbled streets. It was quaint in the way stubborn wilderness tended to be.

The hecklers, however, were anything but.

"It's the prince's royal advisor!" The faceless exclamation came from the crowd watching the small procession enter the village.

"Do you think he brings news of the assassination?"

"About damn time."

"I hope he stays for a while, he's quite handsome."

Cian blew out a frustrated breath. He hated gossip columnists. Sensationalized news of Lochlan's death and Eoghan's injury had spread like wildfire in the days following the Anadali's assassination attempt, inciting civil unrest in some of the smaller northern villages.

Investigators had not been able to link the event to Dúndíor, though they seemed to not have even considered the possibility. No thanks to the crown prince himself. Eoghan had remained mute on the point, claiming the perpetrator had fled after realizing he was awake. It had been dark, and Eoghan was unable to see their face. He had claimed that now more than ever, Nahonaugh needed an ally in Dúndíor.

Blatherskite.

When Eoghan tasked him with the duty of quelling the unrest, Cian had jumped at the chance to leave the palace behind. It wasn't the hubbub of the aftermath, the pockets of civil upheaval, or the fact that someone was dead that bothered him. After an assassination, such was the natural order of things.

No, Eoghan did not seem to trust Cian with the truth, and that cut deeper than he cared to admit. Perhaps Cian grudgingly tolerated gossip columnists. They were the reason he was able to leave, after all.

Fionn, a guard to his right, nudged his shoulder and nodded down the peasant-lined cobbled road. "The magistrate will see you first, but the square where you'll give your address is just beyond. The spies who surveyed the village prior to our arrival observed only half-hearted attempts at protests." He side-eyed a group of women huddled under the awning of a bakery, hiding their conversation behind fluttering fans. "Mostly middle-aged aunties with nothing better to do. The situation is less volatile than the newspapers claimed, but we must remain vigilant."

"My lord!" A ruddy-faced man pushed his way to the front of the crowd, sweat dripping from his brow. "My lord!" he panted, brandishing a letter.

The guards stiffened. Cian slowed his steps, strange familiarity blooming within him. Something was off, but...

"Keep walking," Fionn grunted softly as another two guards peeled away from the procession to subdue the man.

Cian narrowed his eyes. The sun shone overhead, yet a subtle haze of darkness cast a shadow over the messenger, curling up from his skin in delicate wisps of black smoke. His heart stuttered to a stop.

Tadhg had influence here.

"Stand down," Cian commanded, curiosity and dread drawing him toward the man until Fionn's grip on his shoulder stopped him.

The messenger looked from the guards—who had stilled their approach—to Cian. "My lord, I have a message of utmost importance."

"I'm sure." His hands itched to snatch the letter away. Apprehension kept them firmly at his sides.

"I am unable to return until I've delivered the letter." The messenger tugged nervously at his collar. "Master's orders."

Cian tipped his head for the guard closest—Tynan—to retrieve it. The messenger recoiled. "For your eyes only, I'm afraid."

Sighing, Cian closed the distance between them and accepted the sealed parchment. As soon as it passed from the messenger's hands, the man heaved a breath, and the darkness about him disappeared. Blinking, the man looked from the letter to his own hands to Cian, his ruddy skin now tinged with a sickly pallor.

"Ah yes. The letter. It's delivered now." He stumbled backward, then shuffled forward, hand outstretched. "I'll accept gratuity for my services."

Of course you would. Suppressing an eye roll, Cian dropped a few coins into the man's waiting hand. Tadhg probably didn't need to waste the effort to curse the poor man—he would have done the task of his own volition. Though, would *Cian* have accepted the letter without proof of Tadhg's influence?

Cian added three more coins to the man's pile.

"Pleasure doing business with you," the messenger stammered, then spun on his heel and ran. As the crowd swallowed the messenger, cacophony erupted around Cian.

"Will you accept all complaints?"

"Oy! I'm on the village council, shouldn't I be heard first?"

"The farmers deserve first say!"

A firm hand gripped Cian's arm, pulling him in the direction of the magistrate's hall. He tried to wrench away, only to realize it was one of his guards.

"Make way!" Fionn shouted, taking the lead.

"Formal address will be made in half an hour!" Tynan bellowed. "Go about your business."

Bodies and voices surged around Cian as the small procession pressed onward. Sweat dripped down his brow. His tunic stuck to his back. Yet none of the turmoil around him mattered, not when the maelstrom in his head made anything else seem like a calm summer morning. Cian clutched the letter more tightly in his grasp. This would not bode well for anyone.

* * *

THE SHEER CURTAINS FLUTTERED BEHIND Cian, a humid evening breeze sweeping across the balcony of his room at the inn. He was only on the second story—the top floor—yet with the stout architecture of the village it was the tallest livable building around. Only the watermills that flanked the river and powered the pumps to water the fields stood taller.

Leaning against the wrought-iron railing, Cian watched the villagers meander through their end-of-day rituals. Children played in the streets, freed from their daily obligations. Women brought washing inside while men readied community cookfires, allowing neighbors to prepare their meals outside rather than heat their homes in the already sweltering weather. There was a rhythm to it, this way of living, that he could feel as clearly as his own beating heart.

Even with the fiasco of his arrival and the tense atmosphere during his address at the square, he could have sworn he felt the same rhythm then, too. These people, as Fionn had said, weren't volatile. Curious? Yes. Concerned? Undoubtedly. News of the assassination and Cian's subsequent presence had introduced a stumbling point to the village's well-choreographed dance. It was a strangely refreshing reminder that life extended beyond the palace, beyond the capital.

If only that life hadn't followed him here.

Tadhg's letter sat on a side table adjacent to the balcony chair Cian had occupied earlier, one end of the envelope flapping in the breeze, the other end held in place by a half-finished glass of iced tea. Condensation dripped down the cup, ringing the parchment with an ever-growing splotch.

The letter remained unopened. Now that he had calmed from the initial shock, Cian was determined to keep it that way. He thought Tadhg's machinations and his own involvement in them had ended with the antidote. There was no going back to the life before Cian had condemned Eoghan to die, but he was also loath to discover what came next. Especially if that *next* brought him to Tadhg once again. If he didn't read the letter, it couldn't be real.

The sound of the door to his suite opening sent Cian jumping out of his skin. He spun around and frowned at the guard, who closed the door with the ease of someone walking into their own residence.

"If you're looking for your room, this isn't it," Cian deadpanned.

"Oh, no. I'm meant to be guarding you," Sullivan replied brightly. He was built like a rock—short and stocky with a cragged scar running up his neck. Though his fluffy, curly black hair and golden-brown skin almost made him look as jovial as he sounded. *Almost.*

Cian leaned against the railing, crossing his arms over his chest with a frown. "Then you can do so outside."

Sullivan raised his brows and tipped his chin toward the letter. "Did you not read it?"

"That's not your business."

"Tadhg's business *is* my business. At least where you're concerned."

Cian grit his teeth in frustration. Of course his father had managed to infiltrate his guards. "Maybe I didn't make myself clear." He pushed off the railing and strode across the room. Opening the door, he made a sweeping gesture toward the exit. "Out."

Sullivan sidestepped across the threshold, using the toe of his boot to prevent Cian from shutting the door in his face. "Read the letter, Ó Máille. I'm not getting fired because of you."

With a final glance toward the balcony, Sullivan removed his foot, Cian falling against the door as it slammed shut.

Stalking to the balcony, he ripped the letter open.

Follow Sullivan.

"Follow Sullivan," Cian mumbled sarcastically under his breath. "You're sending me on a stars-cursed goose chase is what you're doing." He crumpled the letter and shoved it in his pocket, downed the last of his tea, then trudged across the suite. The future was here whether he wanted it or not. Might as well see where this led.

The door swung open with more vigor than Cian intended.

Sullivan raised his brow expectantly.

"By all means, lead the way." Cian gestured vaguely down the hall. "Wouldn't want you fired on my behalf."

FROM THE VIEW ON HIS balcony, the village of Maulaidh had appeared to be arranged in neat little rows, like careful stitching on a well-loved sweater. From the ground, weaving between alleys and down cobbled streets, Cian felt as if he had entered a never-ending maze. The farther he followed his guide, the more ensnared he became.

Sullivan hopped over a low fence at the end of an alley between shops and stepped off the path, trudging through knee-height grass while whistling a peppy jig. The sound grated on Cian's already frayed nerves, as did a question whose answer eluded him over the past week.

"Who put Lochlan's body in the laundry chute?" Cian didn't expect the guard to know, but hopefully this would stop the whistling.

"That would have been a servant—someone Tadhg employed from Dúndíor, actually. Dastardly idea, that." Sullivan shook his head solemnly. "Dastardly, but a clever misdirection. I was the one who checked on His Highness after the commotion with Lochlan. Well, I didn't *actually* check, since he was supposed to be dead and that's a bit grim. Needless to say, when he walked out later that morning it came as a shock. But that problem's above my pay grade, so it didn't matter much to me."

"Huh," Cian intoned. The guard was more useful than he expected. "Do you know what Tadhg intends to do with that?"

"When Tadhg discovered that the prince had lived, he changed tactics." Sullivan paused to pick his way through a hedge, which opened to a well-worn lane on the other side. The sun dipped low on the horizon, stretching Cian's shadow like a bowstring drawn tight. Sullivan looked both ways before carrying on up the road. "The prince was more useful dead, but it's too much of an inconvenience to complete that process now. There are more crucial individuals who must be dealt with first. Which is where you come in."

Cian swallowed. He was to deal with someone? Or was he about to be dealt *with*?

"Ah, here we are." Sullivan opened a low wooden gate and escorted Cian along a meandering stone path that wrapped around the...house? he guessed.

The building was not stately enough to be a manor, nor was it quaint enough to be considered a cottage. Regardless of its size or lack thereof, it was beautiful. Flowering vines hugged the sun-faded brick residence. Leaf-laden branches swayed in the evening breeze, dancing over the pond where a family of ducks swam.

Rounding the house to the back garden, Cian was greeted by the familiar *thunk* of arrows hitting a straw target. Sullivan strode under a pergola that led to an open field where an archery range was set up, Cian following behind.

Tadhg released another arrow, frowning when it pierced the outer circumference of the target. Turning, he set the bow on a table. "About time. Sullivan, you're dismissed for the evening."

The guard bowed and strode toward the house, where servants bustled about with evening preparations.

"Do you still shoot?" Tadhg asked. At Cian's nod, he gestured to the bow. "Pick it up."

Cian crossed the distance, the tightness in his throat growing as he approached. The deep recurved limbs, the additional recurved tip. It was the bone composite bow his mother had given him on his twentieth birthday.

You're entering a new decade of life, she had said. *I thought this would be the perfect gift for my perfect boy.*

He was now one year shy of exiting that decade. If Cian could not avoid the future Tadhg had created for him, at least he could have a reminder of whom he was trying to protect.

Picking up the bow, Cian ran his hand along the smooth wood. The tightness in his throat hardened to a lump. Someone had broken into his room at the palace to obtain the bow. He felt violated.

"You're alive. You're welcome," Tadhg said.

Cian pressed his lips into a thin line. Logic and reason told him he could not charge blindly into this discussion. Not if he wanted to avoid a repeat of their first meeting. That, and he wasn't sure if he could speak without his voice breaking.

"My associates tried to convince me otherwise, but though I am the orchestrator of their plans, you are my son. You did not fail me, so I did not fail you. They've come to realize the value of this." Tadhg paused, his gaze boring into Cian's. "Do you?"

He nodded once.

"Good. How much did Sullivan tell you on the way here?" Tadhg asked.

Cian swallowed, trying to ease the ache in his throat. "Only that you've changed tactics and I'm to take care of something."

"That's a start." Tadhg procured a small drawstring bag from his pocket and tossed it to Cian. "I need you to handle this."

Easing the drawstrings open with one hand—bow gripped tightly in the other—Cian peered inside. Nestled against the suede fabric was an arrowhead, the tip of which was so dark it reminded him of a starless night sky.

Or the shadows the spies shrouded themselves in. The thought sent a shiver down his spine.

"It's a specially-made arrowhead, fused with the bone shard of an Uncreated," Tadhg said. "The shard breaks when it pierces its victim and... Let's just say you don't want to be around when an Uncreated is drawn to its unleashed shard." He gestured to the bag. "Put that away. I need to make sure your skills haven't gone soft."

Cian placed the bag into his pocket and accepted the quiver of arrows Tadhg passed him, slipping it over his head. He walked into position and looked down the range to where a row of targets stood seventy meters away.

"I'm assuming you want me to use the arrow on someone of importance," Cian said, stretching the muscles in his arms and loosening his shoulders to avoid looking at Tadhg.

"A princess," Tadhg said blandly. Cian stiffened, then looked over his shoulder. Tadhg merely shrugged, then flicked his hand as if to say "hurry up." "I'll give you your instructions later."

Sighing, Cian nocked an arrow, drew back, and released. It sank into the center of the target.

"What you do need to know now is that we are restoring the natural order of things. You've heard of Takaniim?"

Cian shook his head as he drew the next arrow. "No, I haven't."

"For as useless as the Anadali was at assassinating Eoghan, she was able to find some information about it in the library," Tadhg said.

Cian's hand tensed at the mention of Eoghan. He forced his grip to relax. Steadied his breathing. Aimed.

Tadhg carried on. "She uncovered less than my associates. Then again, they brought me excerpts of the book."

The arrow sank into the target. Cian drew another. Aimed. Released. *Thunk*.

"Takaniim was a sacred lake of sorts, hoarded by the one who created it. It was stolen from us, and its power along with it." Tadhg's voice lowered with impassioned fury. "The sœndjak have vowed to help us bring it back and ensure it remains under our jurisdiction. They have stipulations, of course. The world as we know it will come to an end"—he shrugged nonchalantly—"but so long as the sœndjak reign, *we* will rise victorious in this new era."

That did not sound good. But what was Cian to do? Walk away? As long as he knew what his father was planning, he could work to keep Mother safe. Maybe even keep Eoghan alive. "As long as who reigns?" Cian asked.

"Sœndjak." Tadhg said the word slowly, as if Cian were an idiot.

"I don't know what that means." He drew another arrow, wiping sweat from his forehead as he did. Even with the setting sun, the humidity was still terrible. He aimed. *Thunk*.

"You've met some of them already. The men at the cabin, for example. There are others of course. Shadow wraiths—in time, they may join your ranks—and Uncreated, as I mentioned before. Those are best left to me." Tadhg waved for Cian to stop when he drew another arrow. "Your grouping is fine. A little off center, but close enough."

Cian looked down range. The arrows were tightly clustered in the bullseye. One shaft had even been split by another arrow. He pressed his lips into a thin line. The grouping *was* centered.

"King Timun's daughter could not do her job, but you *did*—you kept your word," Tadhg said, drawing Cian's attention back to his father. "I want you to join us. You will be a necessary asset. Both as my son, and given your proficiency with the bow."

Cian looked from Tadhg to the arrows protruding from the target before sliding his hand into his pocket to feel the drawstring bag stored within. The arrow and its intended purpose sent unease crawling down his spine. But so did the memory of the poison. The threat to his mother. His fear for Eoghan, and the guilt that ate him alive.

"I don't have a choice, do I?" Cian whispered.

"No. But it's important to me that you feel like you do."

He nodded once. "Then I will join."

"No, you won't. I want you to sleep on it. Let me know tomorrow." Tadhg smiled, and the expression froze the blood in Cian's veins. "You will think about *why* you have no choice. Not because of me, but because of what *you* have done." Tadhg huffed a dry laugh. "What do you have to go back to, truly, after condemning your friend to die? After jeopardizing the safety of your own *mother*? You are not a liability to me. But to those around you?" He spread his arms wide. "This is why you have no choice. Not because I say so, but because you have made it so."

Before he could think, Cian drew an arrow and aimed at Tadhg's head. His chest heaved. His heart thundered in his ears. He wanted to scream. To unleash the entire quiver until the beast before him was nothing more than an empty husk of a man. Yet he couldn't bring himself to release the single arrow readied in his hand. Because Tadhg was right. Curse him, he was *right*.

"Your priorities are elsewhere now. It's time you accepted that." Tadhg turned and walked down the range, coming to a stop halfway between Cian and the target.

Tears blurred Cian's vision. His hand shook with bridled rage—at himself or his father, he wasn't sure.

"Hit the bullseye," Tadhg called back to him. "Don't hit me."

A sob clawed its way out of Cian's throat, choking him. He swallowed. Swallowed again. Adjusted his aim.

"I don't have all night," Tadhg goaded.

Cian squeezed his eyes shut and released the arrow. The familiar *thunk* sounded as it found its home in the target. Bile burned a trail up his throat. Dropping the bow, he spun on his heel and ran.

"I'll see you tomorrow!" Tadhg shouted after him. "And send your men back! You won't need them anymore."

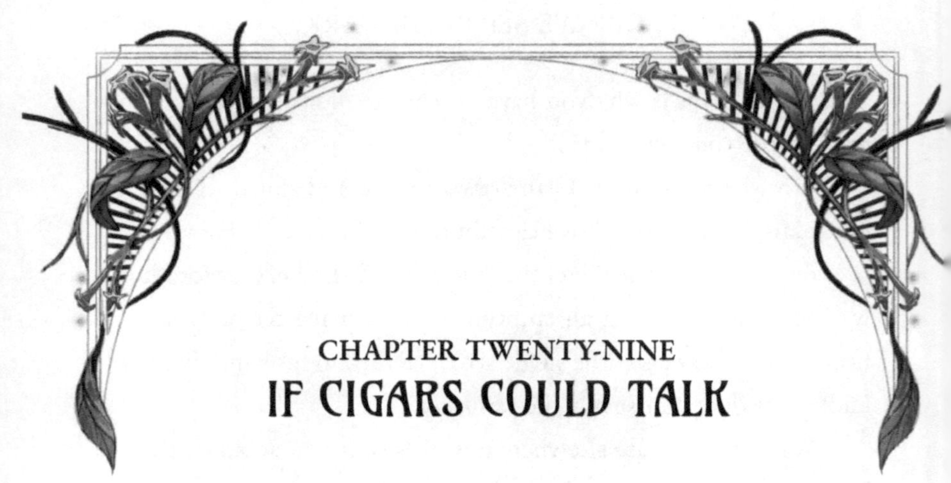

CHAPTER TWENTY-NINE
IF CIGARS COULD TALK

*F*ATHER!" EOGHAN CRIED, HIS SLIPPERED FEET SLIDING *across the stone floor as he raced to the king's side. "What's wrong? Where are you hurt?"*

"I'm fine, my boy." An amused chuckle intertwined with King Ibhar's words. "Merely bumped my foot."

Eoghan's small hand came to rest on his father's—the one that gripped his foot tightly. "Why are you holding it so?"

"Ah. It's a clever trick. If something hurts, one only needs to add a little pressure. It helps it not hurt so much."

Emotions built in Eoghan's chest until they squeezed his heart so tightly that he felt nothing at all. A week had passed since Lochlan's funeral, and people still gave him looks of pity as they walked by. Or of shame. He wasn't sure. How could he explain that if he felt less, he could have cried more?

Lochlan was his own flesh and blood. Now he was dead.

Anaís was his heart and soul. She had betrayed him.

His father was wrong. No tricks could dull the pain consuming him whole. A heart could not beat unless it was settled into the chest in which it belonged. But Lochlan was buried six feet under, and with each passing moment it felt like another part of his own heart was buried with him.

Today, Nahonaugh and Dúndíor would "solidify the peace treaty." He mocked the queen's voice in his head. No one had been able to connect the assassination attempt to Dúndíor, and for reasons unbeknownst to him, he had yet to reveal to anyone what had happened.

He didn't want peace. He wanted his cousin back.

Footsteps echoed down the hall, and his head shot up. His heart would have skipped a beat, if he still had one. Eoghan straightened his jacket and settled into place like a statue guarding the entrance of a tomb, watching as Princess Simone walked down the hallway toward him and the meeting room where they would finalize what began all those weeks ago. A guard trailed behind her—not an Anadali. A flare of anger surged in his veins, and he barely kept his hands from balling into fists. He had been looking forward to staring Anaís in the face and demanding answers, but she was a coward, leaving others to pick up her scraps.

His attention drifted back to the princess. She didn't appear angry or surprised to see him. She looked lost. Afraid, even.

Good. Eoghan was the walking dead. Let her be afraid.

She met his gaze and her steps faltered, but in the blink of an eye her shoulders drew back and her chin tilted up in a silent challenge. He inclined his head in return. *Challenge accepted.*

Stepping to the side, Eoghan gave the door a slight tug, allowing it to swing open on well-oiled hinges. "Your Highness. You did not bring your Anadali." It was a statement disguised as a question.

She tilted her head, scrutinizing him as if trying to peer into his soul. Too bad. There was only one person who could do that, and she wasn't here. The thought sent a knife into his chest. He shifted his stance, drawing himself up as he drew an iron shield around his heart.

"No." She smiled, but a flicker of uncertainty tainted its effect. "After the last meeting, she determined our hypervigilance was unfounded."

"One can never be too careful." An edge bit into his voice. "Sometimes threats like to hide in plain sight."

"What are you insinuating?"

"Nothing, nothing." He waved his hand nonchalantly as her guard took a step forward to intervene. "So your Anadali is doing well?"

She glared at him; any additional words locked behind the grim set of her lips.

Her guard placed a gentle hand on her lower back. "Your Highness?"

Princess Simone blinked once, then turned away, allowing her guard to usher her into the meeting room where the king, queen, and select members of the council were already seated.

Eoghan breathed in through his nose, then let a steady stream of air rush past his lips. It was all he could do to flush out the last of his emotions before sitting in a room for hours on end finalizing peace with a kingdom that wanted him dead. That had killed his cousin. That had betrayed his trust. If he didn't shout at or punch anyone by the end of the day, he would consider it a victory.

❋ ❋ ❋

PRESSURE BUILT IN EOGHAN'S SKULL as the meeting dragged on. Documents spread across the table, dressing the dark walnut surface in ink-scrawled cream sheets. Calming breaths only took him so far, and he was tired, so tired, of trying to maintain a cordial front in the presence of the council and the princess sitting across from him. For the good of his people, he would not let his anger taint the treaty they were signing. But the longer he sat there, the hotter it burned. The longer he suppressed it, the more of him it consumed.

Counselor Trijveson shifted a stack of documents over, pointing to a paragraph of text scrawled onto the parchment. "According to the terms we discussed here, there will be a restricted period of three months following the signing of the treaty. The royal family, diplomats, and individuals with appropriate travel documentation—which we will discuss next—shall be allowed to travel between Dúndíor and Nahonaugh by way of selected checkpoints here and here," he said, pointing at the map unrolled along the middle of the table.

Princess Simone leaned forward as she read, nodding slightly as her finger trailed beneath the text. "Yes, we agreed to this." Her eyes darted to look over Eoghan's shoulder before settling on the counselor and the quill he extended toward her.

"Then I'll have you sign here."

The sound of quill scratching paper etched into Eoghan's brain. Shapes blurred in the edge of his vision as Counselor Trijveson took the parchment from Princess Simone and passed it to him. The paper crinkled in Eoghan's hand. He took the quill and skimmed the document before scratching his own signature onto the parchment—the first part of the treaty sealed.

Eoghan glanced at the space that should have been occupied by Cian. Instead, his chair had been removed and the others shuffled around to fill the hole. They hadn't spoken much since Cian dismissed him almost a fortnight ago. Words had been exchanged as was expected of a working relationship between Crown Prince and royal advisor, but Cian's dismissive posture and indifferent glares were clear: stay away.

Then again, it wasn't as if Cian skipped this meeting to spite him. Small riots had broken out in some of the northern villages after news of Lochlan's death and his own injury had spread. And with the imminent enactment of the treaty, there would always be dissenters. For all his distance, Cian was still the only person Eoghan trusted to coordinate a peaceful transition amongst the people.

So why did he not trust Cian with the truth about Anaís?

Annoyance flared at the thought of her, and Eoghan rubbed his temples. Out. He needed to get out of this room. His foot bounced against the ground, each muffled thump pounding out a death march in his head.

"Your Highness?" someone across the table said. Eoghan waited for the princess to respond. Any words trapped behind his lips were better left unsaid.

A hand alighted on his shoulder. Eoghan let out a long breath through his nose. *Don't break. Do not break.*

"Eoghan, are you all right?"

He folded his hands in his lap and mustered every ounce of civility within him before meeting his father's eyes. "My apologies, I have a headache. May I have some water?"

His father gave him a strange look, but Eoghan averted his gaze before he could see the lie. One of the servants waiting in the corner of the room—one he recognized—darted forward with a glass of ice water balanced atop a serving tray. Ellis carefully set the water before him with a small bow before returning to his post.

"Thank you," Eoghan said, though Ellis was too far to hear it.

He took a sip, letting the cold water linger on his tongue before swallowing. Trying to ignore the covert glances cast his way as the meeting continued once again. Trying to ignore the frustration that now added fuel to his anger. He focused on Counselor Trijveson's words instead.

"Identification in the form of papers would be adequate, yes," the counselor said in response to a question Princess Simone had asked.

She nodded, eyes lingering behind Eoghan before catching his gaze.

He met her feigned cover-up briefly, but he wasn't about to humor her. When Cian looked over his shoulder, it was because something was hiding in the shadows. The only thing behind him was a fireplace. With a chandelier hung above the table and the afternoon sun filtering through the windows to illuminate the room, there was no place to hide. Pins and needles prickled the back of his neck in anticipation of someone watching him, but he couldn't risk turning around. Could he?

Another paper shuffled in front of him. He signed it without looking. It could have been his death warrant for all he knew. A small, humorless laugh escaped him, drawing the princess's attention. She met his eyes, then looked over his shoulder.

His foot bounced faster.

Hang it all.

Eoghan sat up and turned one way, then the other, pretending to stretch his back. A box of his father's Freydlandian cigars was perched behind him on the mantle, the tranquil snow-capped mountains and wisps of smoke decorating the container mocking his turmoil within. A subtle cast of fog swirled around the box.

Hang. It. All.

Another paper brushed in front of him. He signed it numbly. Hand lingering in the air, he waited for another paper to appear. Instead, someone began clapping. The gesture spread around the table, a polite tinkling sound that reminded Eoghan of a metal blade clattering across the floor. Memories flashed in his mind's eye with each strike. Moonlight drenching his room. A blade piercing his chest. Thread around his heart. The pain. The peace.

Her.

Eoghan's chair caught on the rug and clattered backward as he shot up. An echo of a mis-timed clap lingered in the air. Everyone in the room stared at him.

"Excuse me." He turned on his heel and strode from the room.

His father's voice drifted after him, but whatever had kept Eoghan's patience in check had fractured. He could not allow himself to shatter there.

Blood seeped from Eoghan's knuckles as he struck the punching bag in rapid succession.

He hated the princess. Hated the Anadali. Hated that Lochlan was dead. Hated how angry he was. Hated that he didn't know how to stop his anger from consuming him, for he no longer felt pain.

Because he was Anguish.

He was Pain.

His fist met the punching bag with a loud snap. Unshed tears blurred his vision as he stumbled forward to lean against the blood-slicked leather, chest heaving, hands throbbing. He should have wrapped them before coming to the training arena, but there were many things he should have done. Should have told Lochlan to stay at home for the festival, should have been there for Cian, should have known who the Anadali was.

Should have killed her when he had the chance.

But there was nothing he could have done to untangle his soul from hers, to stop his best friend from leaving, to prevent his cousin from dying. And so his life was a mockery of his heart, for it still beat but had no one to beat for.

"I can't do this anymore," he tried to yell into the night, but his voice was raw from pouring out his anger while he fought.

Now he didn't have any fight left to give.

Cool grass crumpled beneath him as he sank to his knees, his forehead pressed against the punching bag. It was the only thing keeping him from collapsing into a heap.

"Please," Eoghan whispered. "I can't."

A soft breeze rustled through the trees lining the training field, caressing his sweat-soaked skin with the likeness of an embrace. Eoghan inhaled, the calming scent of the forest rushing into his lungs. He exhaled, relaxing farther into the support of the bag. The breeze swelled again, carrying with it lake-cooled evening air.

Breath by breath, his fists uncurled, the tension eased from his muscles, the anger seeped out of his heart, as if something greater than himself was saying, *Breathe with me. Let go.*

He let his forehead slip from the bloodied leather and curled onto his side in the grass.

Let go.

Inhale. Exhale.

Let go.

He did.

Eoghan laid in the grass, breathing, allowing the breeze to carry away his anguish until the crickets sang their last tune and all that was left were the stars twinkling overhead. The pain was there, but he didn't feel as if he were drowning in it. His anger was there, but it no longer consumed him alive. He could breathe again, think again, he found himself again.

It was there that Eoghan decided he would do what he normally did, what he had always done: search for the truth himself. From his perspective, he only had part of the story. What was Anaís's story? And more importantly, what was The Story?

Eoghan pushed himself up, his muscles aching from staying curled on the ground for so long. He blinked, lifting his hand to rub the weariness from his eyes, but stopped himself before he could touch them. Dried blood crusted his hands, which he belatedly realized had transferred from the leather onto his chest and probably forehead too. He looked a mess. He felt a mess. But in a way he couldn't explain, he felt refreshed, too.

Picking up his tunic, Eoghan pressed it to his face instead, wiping off the dried sweat and blood as well as he could before pulling it on to cover the blood on his chest. That wasn't going anywhere without a bath. He shook his head and huffed out a laugh. For some reason, it felt like the right thing to do. Anyone who saw him would have thought him insane, but for the first time in a long time he felt the furthest thing from it. Grabbing a towel, he wiped down the bag as best he could before turning to head back inside.

Eoghan took one step and tripped over his feet. Fog had swelled around him, blanketing the training field in a soft cloud despite the warmth of the night. He tilted his head at it. The fog seemed to regard him with a sad tilt of its own. The gesture shouldn't have warmed his heart as much as it did.

"Not now, please." His voice rasped but held a certainty that fortified the hope growing within him. "I'm okay now."

Perhaps not entirely, but it was a start. That was all he could ask for after a fortnight of darkness. The fog settled as his words sank in, neither leaving nor drawing nearer, offering itself as a cocoon of safety for him.

"I promise I'll be all right," he reassured. Besides, that particular job was reserved for someone else.

Eoghan made his way across the training field back to the palace, the fog parting to swirl around his feet with each step, leaving dew-stained grass in its wake. That night, he dreamed of a serene forest dappled with sunlight and a kindred spirit who shared the secrets of his soul.

CHAPTER THIRTY
ANSWER ME, ANSWER YOU

THE FOLLOWING DAY ROLLED FORTH LIKE A COIN, ONE side carrying a promise, the other a threat. But as morning spun by and afternoon picked up the chase, Eoghan still couldn't make heads or tails of the strange feeling humming about him, as if he, too, was lingering on the edge of something substantial. It was reasonable enough, he supposed. Yesterday was...it was. Eoghan had no intention of backing down on his vow to uncover the truth, but that promise was a fragile thing that needed nurturing. *He* was a fragile thing that needed nurturing.

Today was not a gentle day for fragile things.

One moment, Eoghan was minding his own business as he made his way to the dining room for lunch. The next moment, there was a wall digging into his back, a death grip crushing his wrist, and the small but mighty form of Princess Simone glaring up at him with wrath in her eyes and vengeance in her stance.

"What did you do to my sister?" she hissed.

"I don't know what you're talking about." Eoghan suppressed a wince when he tried to pull his arm free, but her grip tightened like a vice.

Simone glanced about the hallway, perhaps realizing that they were, in fact, in a public space, before finally releasing his wrist. The bones in his arm protested the mistreatment as they shifted back into alignment.

"She was sent to *end* you, and she didn't." The force of her anger rumbled through her whisper. "Do you know what that cost her?"

"What is it to me?" Eoghan snapped, trying to catch his heart as it plummeted into his stomach. It could not handle breaking again.

"The king had her beaten inches from death for not killing you. So you will *answer* me when I ask you: why are you still alive?"

Eoghan leveled a glare at her, but she didn't back down. If anything, she shifted her weight to stand taller.

Why hadn't Anaís killed him? That was exactly what Eoghan wanted to know. Why hadn't he killed her? That was the question Simone should have been asking. Its answer—the one that had settled into his mind like an undeniable law of nature—changed everything.

Eoghan scrubbed a hand across his face and sighed. It was unlikely she would believe anything he said no matter if it were true or not, though if his promise to himself couldn't withstand a vengeful sibling, he would almost certainly lose his resolve when he came face to face with Anaís again. If they ever saw each other again.

He needed the truth; there would be no sweeping it aside simply because of a good night's sleep and a healthy dose of ignoring his problems. He owed that much to himself. To Lochlan's memory. And to Cian, if he returned home. Maybe the princess would have answers. She was Anaís's sister, after all. Lunch could wait.

Eoghan's attention rested on the dark circles under her eyes as he weighed how he wanted to begin. Unfortunately, the impossible often refused to be spoken of unless it was done so bluntly. "We had a connection—"

A sharp laugh cut him off. "Try again."

Eoghan suppressed an eye roll. "Will you let me finish?"

She pressed her lips into a thin line; he took that to mean "yes."

"I don't know why she didn't kill me."

"But you just said—"

"I know what I just said!" He had to restrain himself from gripping her shoulders and shaking patience into her. "I'm trying to explain. Please."

Simone nodded.

Footsteps sounded around the corner, dragging Eoghan back into the predicament of his current situation. They were in a public space. People liked to gossip. It didn't matter how or what or why, but if there was news it became currency, and these were secrets he would take to the grave.

Eoghan pushed away from the wall. "Walk with me," he said lowly.

The princess held her ground, glaring at him with disapproval as he listened. The footsteps stopped—someone was loitering. She opened her mouth to speak, but he shook his head swiftly and tapped his ear twice, praying she would understand the meaning.

Her jaw clicked shut. Nodding once, she fell into step with him as they walked down the hallway. "If you don't mind, I'd like to see the gardens before lunch. They looked lovely before, but now that spring has arrived it would be wonderful to see them in full bloom."

"Of course," he replied, catching on to her misdirection for the eavesdropper. "The gardener did exquisite work this year. There's a mixture of foliage—which you've already seen—as well as flowering bulbs staggered to bloom in succession as the season progresses. It's all color-coordinated to create a new, yet coherent, landscape that evolves through late summer."

She raised her brow at him. Obviously, he'd oversold his acting abilities, but he did enjoy gardening and sometimes the information simply fell out before he could stop it.

Rounding the corner, the sound of enthusiastic scrubbing drew their attention to the two young palace-keepers polishing the floor. An amused smile grew on Eoghan's lips. Alys and Carys were twin daughters of the head chef, known for their incredible lack of talent in the kitchen, their penchant for gathering "current news," and, despite their misgivings, their surprising tenacity for the work they *were* assigned to.

"Your dedication to the shine of the floors is astounding," Eoghan commented, though not unkindly, pausing to watch their work.

Both of the girls jumped, a chorus of "sorry, Highness" and "beggin' your pardon, Highness" filling the hallway.

"No, no, it's quite all right," he suppressed a laugh. "Don't be distracted on my account."

"Of course, Highness," they tittered.

He shook his head, gesturing for Simone to follow him once more as the girls set to work again. "Be sure to remember your lunch break," he added over his shoulder. "I overheard Macaulay say there was leftover pachimh."

Suppressed squeals and the sliding pitter-patter of slippers on well-polished hardwood sounded behind them, growing fainter by the second as the girls hurried to the kitchens.

He and Simone rounded another corner, bringing them to the

main staircase that led down to the foyer. They descended in lock-step, pausing briefly to greet one of the visiting courtiers before alighting on the landing.

"Why did you do that?" Simone asked lowly. "To the maids?"

"What? Talk with them?"

She shot him a glare.

This time Eoghan did laugh. "Would you rather they be afraid of me?" He tilted his head in question. "Does it make it harder for you to see me as the villain?"

A look of disbelief softened her features. "I never said. I didn't—" She cut herself off. "We're not talking about this here, remember?"

"Of course. The gardens are this way."

They continued on in silence, though it became less strained when they exited the palace and stepped into the warm embrace of the afternoon sun. Birds chirped happily, flitting between branches that swayed in time with the lazy breeze. Gravel crunched beneath their feet as they walked along the meandering pathway that led deeper into the garden. He hadn't been lying when he said the landscapist had done an excellent job this year. Bursts of vibrant pink, buttery yellow, and midnight blue colored the landscape and perfumed the air with a delicate sweetness. Simone paused to smell a low-hanging magnolia flower, her expression shifting into something contemplative as they continued their slow promenade.

She broke the silence between them when they reached a relatively secluded part of the rose gardens. "I can see why Anaís is fond of you," she confessed, more to herself than to him.

Eoghan blinked at her, unsure if he had heard properly. "I—what?"

"She mentioned *some things* about what I'm...mad at you for," Simone said, waving vaguely at his person. "And I meant what I said; I'm not leaving until I get answers from you too. But I don't think...I do think." An exasperated huff punctuated her frustration. "Everything about the past month has been royally messed up. And I mean that literally. But this? What she told me?" Simone slumped down on a stone bench, her skirts pooling around her. "I trust Anaís. She's the reason I'm even considering allowing you to live. But I need to know why she seems to think she can trust *you*."

Eoghan lowered himself onto the opposite side of the bench, all the words he wanted to say stuck in his throat. It was as if Simone had inadvertently slammed her hand on the rolling coin and stopped his world from spinning once and for all. Was he not alone in this?

"What did she mention?" The words came so quietly he wasn't sure she heard.

"What she told me in confidence will remain in confidence. I'm sorry." She turned to look at him. "Tell me what were you saying earlier? About the connection?"

He looked across the garden to avoid her gaze, but his eyes caught onto the column where he and Anaís had spoken amongst the roses all that time ago. It was his favorite spot, but after his almost-assassination he'd avoided it like the plague. Rather than the hurt he had been expecting, a warm fondness filled him. It was the place where he'd first felt that curious pull toward her—his own affections mixed with what he now recognized as inevitability.

"I felt her presence in my room before I awoke," he began softly. "I didn't know it was her. We fought." A dry laugh escaped him before he could stop it. "I still would have fought had I known it was her. I didn't want to die."

Eoghan stared at his hands in his lap. The hands that had gripped her neck and...he swallowed. The truth would not come if he refused to stop lying to himself. And the truth was, if he could go back, knowing what he knew now, he would not have fought at all. Though even in the heat of the fight, it seemed as if both of them held the same affliction—one could not truly hurt the other. It did little to change the pain they had inflicted.

"I almost killed her." The confession slipped from his lips and hovered in the air like a ghost. Waiting. Watching.

"Why?" Simone bit out. "Was it the goodness of your heart? 'Oh no, I can't have her death on my conscience. Better to let someone else do it.'"

He tugged on the neck of his tunic to reveal the beginnings of an angry scar beneath his clavicle. "I can assure you it wasn't the goodness of my heart."

Simone stared at the scar with wide eyes, her gaze lingering even after he covered the injury once again. He had the distinct impression that her world was crumbling before her eyes.

"Anaís really didn't want you dead, did she?" Simone asked.

"She didn't stab my heart, but I can guarantee you this didn't feel any better."

Simone shook her head absently, any anger she once seemed to harbor falling away with the movement. "Anaís is the one with intimate knowledge on how to kill a man. But from what she has told me that I've tried and failed to tune out...there are a lot of vital bits packed into that area. Arteries, nerves, the top of your lungs. It would have been an easy kill; second nature. But missing like that? It's intentional."

Eoghan released a long breath. "It makes sense."

"How so?"

"I physically could not harm her." He shrugged.

Her brows furrowed in confusion. "But you fought?"

"And then I realized who she was. Not her name or her title or where she was from. I recognized *her*. She's the one I—" Eoghan cut himself off. Simone may be Anaís's sister, but this was something he needed to discuss with Anaís. If they ever saw each other again. "You have your answer. Swear to me you will not speak to anyone of this."

"What is said in confidence will remain in confidence, I swear it. But Eoghan?" The intensity of her gaze sent a chill down his spine. "You need to talk to her about this."

Eoghan looked away, leaning back against the bench as her final words washed over him and the implications of their conversation sunk into his bones. He was no closer to what he wanted out of the truth, but the path to obtaining it rarely took him where he wanted to go. Simone was right. He needed to speak with Anaís, as much as the prospect terrified him.

For as honorably tight-lipped as Simone was regarding others, there was another matter that prickled at the back of his mind. The mantle had been empty when the meeting began, hadn't it? Of all the cigar boxes, there was no reason for *that* one to be there—not when it held the nitróg, the stone his father kept hidden away. Unless the fog had placed it there. But why?

It was probably nothing. Trivial. Once voiced, it would only draw attention to that which should not have attention drawn to it. Picking a leaf off a rose bush, Eoghan twirled it between his fingers. Should he? Shouldn't he?

"There is..." he trailed off. Shaking his head, he let the leaf flutter to the ground and turned to face Simone. "There is one other thing."

She matched his posture. "What is it?"

"What is your interest in Freydlanian cigars?"

Simone looked at him with wide doe eyes, obviously caught off guard by his question but not entirely naïve about what he was alluding to either. This strange solidarity was new, tentative at best. He did not want to push so hard that it broke, but he needed to know.

"During the signing. The box on the mantle behind me?" he prompted. Simone smoothed the skirts of her dress. "Either you find Freydlanian cigars to be extraordinarily interesting," Eoghan pressed, "or you know something you should not. Which is it?"

Simone narrowed her eyes at him. Eoghan held her gaze. He could almost see her weighing her options as micro-expressions flittered across her face, her resolve cracking the longer he remained silent. Her lips pressed together, then relaxed, as if she wanted to say something but was holding back.

"I'm not interested in smoking," she said carefully.

His own resolve cracked. Apparently, honesty did not merit honesty. Fine; two could play at this game. "Oh. All right. It's for the best then. Terrible habit."

Simone fidgeted with her skirt before clasping her hands in her lap to still them. "The box design was...unique. Snow-capped mountains to advertise what is little more than a stick of smoke and death."

Eoghan shrugged. "You didn't complain when my father enjoyed his cigar during the meetings."

"I'm not rude," she shot back.

"No, but you're dishonest."

The words left his mouth before he could stop them, but he couldn't bring himself to care. He was sick of reading between the lines. Sick of trying to uncover hidden agendas disguised in the folds of social eloquence. He expected it with court politics, but this was something else entirely. Simone's avoidance in the wake of his own vulnerable truth cut deeper than it should have. It seemed the only person who had ever deigned to speak plainly to him was Anaís, and she had tried to kill him.

Eoghan took in a fortifying breath before trying to speak with some semblance of tact. "I have answered your questions, however prying they might have been. So I will ask you again, and you will answer me. What is your interest in the cigars?"

Simone kept her gaze fixed on her hands. "Why do I feel like there is a right answer and a wrong answer?"

He shook his head sadly. "The only wrong answer you can give is a lie."

"Anaís." The name slipped quietly from her lips, but it hit Eoghan with the force of a wave against rocky cliffs. She looked up to meet his eyes, expression hardening. "What is in the box, Eoghan?"

"Cigars." He shrugged.

Simone shook her head. "Everyone knows a cigar box holds cigars. It must be something else"—she leaned forward—"because Anaís *wanted* me to ask you. She knew it would be there, she said you would tell me. That you would know what she meant."

Eoghan could not breathe. Could not think. How did Anaís know about the stone? More importantly, what tied them together such that she did?

"Eoghan!" Simone snapped. "The box."

"In the library, two hours after dinner, meet me there." He tried to swallow. It only served to make the tightness in his throat worse. "I think we have much to discuss."

"I do not see why we cannot discuss no—"

A crash and a shout sounded. Simone jumped in her seat. Eoghan shot to his feet, fists raised in preparation for attack.

"Unhand me, you fool!" An unfamiliar man's muffled voice drifted through the garden. "You know who I am. Her Highness has disappeared, do not hinder me!"

Eoghan lowered his fists and glanced over his shoulder at Simone. "Do you shirk your guards often?"

"I try to avoid the habit, but I doubted we could have had this conversation with an audience." She rose and tipped her chin in the direction of the scuffle. "Do you mind?"

"Stand down!" Eoghan shouted as he and Simone made their way down the path.

Rounding a bend, they came upon two guards stumbling away from each other. Captain Riona plucked a twig from her hair with a disgruntled sniff. Simone's guard rubbed his jaw, which had already begun to redden with a bruise.

Brushing past Eoghan, Simone accepted her guard's proffered arm. "Don't forget our meeting," she called to him, the pair carrying onward toward the palace.

"Wouldn't dream of it!" He glanced at Riona. "Is lunch still being served?"

"I'll have some brought to you." Riona saluted and hurried to her task before Eoghan could say anything more.

Lowering himself onto the garden wall, Eoghan tipped his face toward the sun and sighed. How was he supposed to explain a magic rock to Simone?

CHAPTER THIRTY-ONE
GREEN JUICE

STUPID.

The thought blossomed in Anaís's mind as she tried to open the eye that wasn't swollen shut. The room looked hazy in the early morning light—as if she were experiencing the world in the middle of a snowstorm. Silent. Buffered.

How could she have been so stupid as to let him live? It was impossible to have that sort of connection.

And yet she felt...something. She was sure he felt it too. Maybe he simply recognized her from their first encounter at the palace? No, he was too well trained to let his would-be assassin go.

And I'm too well trained to let my target live, she thought bitterly.

She tilted her head to look out the window, but caught sight of a glass filled with murky green liquid on the bedside table. It almost looked magical, her blurred vision and the sunlight filtering through the semi-opaque liquid causing it to glow. A note next to it piqued her curiosity, but the room tilted when she tried to lean toward the substance, and a searing pain in her back prevented her from moving any farther. She slumped against her pillows, defeated.

Cold seeped under her displaced bedsheets, and a shiver crawled up her spine. Her muscles seized against the pain. It only made her shiver harder. Maybe she should try to reach for the drink again. Medicine? She glanced back at the glowing liquid. Bits of herbs appeared and disappeared as shadows suspended in the draught. They were swirling, dancing in the light. Carried by the tune of an invisible current. It was mesmerizing. Dizzying. She wanted to vomit.

Later, she told herself. *I'll drink it later.*

Anaís closed her eye and let the pain in her body pull her into darkness once more.

<h1 style="text-align:center">CHAPTER THIRTY-TWO
HONOR BESTOWED</h1>

EOGHAN DRUMMED HIS FINGERS ON THE ARMREST OF his chair. He stood up. Sat down. Eyed the cigar box perched innocuously on the coffee table before him. Leaning forward, he rested his head in his hands and breathed deeply. Maybe this wouldn't go as poorly as he imagined. Simone did seem amenable to illogically logical happenings. At least, he thought they were logical. After everything he had been through, nothing seemed improbable anymore—least of all a magic rock.

A cool draft caressed his ankles and Eoghan shifted his hand to glare down at the fog. "Really? Right now?" he grumbled.

It billowed up as if impatient, then floated away to curl up on the hearth of the fireplace. The library door creaked open, and Eoghan stood as Simone swept inside, followed closely by her guard. Other than the one time Simone had escaped him, this guard in particular had been her shadow. Eoghan respected that. It didn't mean his respect extended to trust.

"Princess." Eoghan bowed his head in greeting when they reached the seating area. "Captain. Thank you for escorting Her Highness. You may station yourself just outside the door."

"With respect, Your Highness," the guard said cautiously. "I don't believe that would be a productive course of action."

Eoghan glanced between the two of them with a frown. "This is confidential information. I believe it is the only course of action."

The guard hesitated a moment before acquiescing with a nod. Looking down at Simone, who had looped her arm through his own, he said, "By your leave, my lady, I will be right outside."

"No, it's all right," Simone said brightly. Before Eoghan could protest, she turned to him and added, "I trust Captain Tadeo with my life. He was with me when Anaís told us about the assassination. He fetched aid when I could not leave her side. You can trust him."

Eoghan opened his mouth. Closed it. He wished to guard his vulnerability, but he would give it up if it meant finding answers. If it meant helping Anaís. While he did not necessarily trust the captain, he did trust Simone. "All right, you may stay," he said with a resigned sigh. "But you must swear to secrecy."

"I swear it. On pain of death."

"Wonderful, it's settled, then," Simone said, brushing past the two men and completely ignoring the fog as she sat in one of the chairs facing the coffee table. Leaning forward, she eyed the box with a mixture of curiosity and relief. "So that's it, then? The box? And whatever's inside?"

"Yes, it is." It should be, anyway. It was there when last he checked, unless the fog had meddled again.

Tadeo lowered himself onto the chair next to Simone, Eoghan following suit on the opposite side of the coffee table. Eoghan looked to the fog, then to the two sitting across from him. They couldn't seem to see it. Perhaps the fog had decided not to meddle after all.

Eoghan picked up the cigar box and slid it open. Simone sucked in an anticipatory breath. Tadeo leaned forward. Tipping the box, Eoghan caught the stone in the palm of his hand, relaxing when its familiar warmth flooded his body and pinpricks of celestial light began to glow. His father had neither seen the stone's light nor felt its warmth. Could others feel it too, or was Eoghan the odd man out?

"Oh! It's a rock!" Simone's tone wasn't mocking. Nor did she seem disappointed about being confronted with a rock. Her eyes were alight with the prospect of discovery.

"Indeed it is." He held it up between his thumb and forefinger, rotating it to show Simone and Tadeo the pinholes traversing the body of the stone. "This isn't a trick question, but what does it look like to you?"

"Besides a rock?" Tadeo asked dryly.

Simone gave his arm a light shove. "It's a lovely rock. Has a nice oval shape. Smooth with odd little holes. Looks to be igneous rock of the extrusive variety, but it's not as glassy as I would expect. In fact, it's rather dull."

"Igne...what?" Eoghan frowned. He looked to Tadeo, who shrugged.

"Igneous rocks are formed from lava. If the rock is extrusive, it cooled quickly above ground and its crystalline structure is quite small," Simone explained. At their baffled silence, she added, "What? Anaís liked rocks when she was younger, so she taught me about them."

"Yes but...there aren't any volcanoes on or near the continent," Tadeo said.

"Not now, but hundreds of years ago it was certainly a possibility." Simone shrugged. "Nythmaar is a continent, but compared to others we're small—technically an island. Given that smaller islands can move at the speed of some ships, who's to say that Nythmaar wouldn't, too? Though, we're likely much slower."

Eoghan leaned back in his chair, giving the rock a contemplative frown. *Where did you come from? Why are you here?* His father had said the stone originated during the era of Takaniim. Eoghan assumed that meant the stone had come from the lake itself, but perhaps not. Or maybe it had. He wasn't a geologist or an archeologist or...whatever one needed to be to uncover the secrets of ancient artifacts.

"Essentially," Simone continued, interrupting Eoghan's musings, "you've got yourself a very unique rock."

"It's called a nitróg," Eoghan supplied, feeling strangely pleased with the praise the stone had received thus far. It was nice to not be taken for a fool. "The name is derived from a combination of the words *ni'itrat* and *maróg*, essentially meaning 'guiding stone.'"

Tadeo snorted a laugh. "Are you sure it isn't because nitróg sounds like 'neat rock'?"

"I think it's cute," Simone said. "And guiding stone has such a perfect meaning—it led Anaís right to you!"

The stone was an addition to the many mysteries between himself and Anaís, but Eoghan suspected there was something more that drew them together. "Its purpose has been lost to time," he said instead, not wanting to dampen Simone's excitement. "It has been passed down the Kavanaugh bloodline for centuries. My father called it a gift of kings, but"—Eoghan shrugged—"perhaps only time will tell. Would you like to hold it?"

Simone extended her hand eagerly and gasped when it touched her skin. "It's so cold! Tadeo, feel!"

The captain's eyes widened when he did. "Ack!" He retracted his hand. "That would make an excellent ice compress in a pinch."

Eoghan settled against his chair, watching as the two observed the stone this way and that. Apparently the nitróg looked dull and felt cold, just as it had for his father. For some reason, that revelation didn't disappoint him. In fact, for the first time in a long time, Eoghan felt himself smiling. Maybe this wasn't a strange ordeal he had to shoulder alone, or a mystery he had to solve in secrecy.

Weeks ago, Cian said he had some ideas as to what was happening regarding the strange shadows. He had remained mute on the point ever since, which was odd, though Eoghan had yet to be forthcoming too—they both had some explaining to do. Come to think of it, Cian should have been back by now. He glanced around, stiffening when the fog perked up from its spot by the hearth. It drifted across the space between them to pool around Eoghan's feet, tickling his legs.

"Not you," he mumbled, though not unkindly. "Just...missing Cian."

The fog rose up. Before he could shoo it away, the room disappeared.

Wind whipped around Eoghan, pelting flecks of ice against his skin with stinging strikes. He stumbled away from the edge of the mountain and pressed his back against the jagged rock. "What have you done!" he shouted, but the storm howling around him consumed the sound.

Though the fog swirled madly against the wind, Eoghan recognized the subtle shift of its attention. He tilted his head, pressing himself between boulders in a sorry attempt to avoid being buffeted by the storm.

There, about thirty feet above, stood an abomination of darkness ripped from the deep. Hidden beneath the smoke-like shadows writhing about it, the creature looked human, yet *wrong*—as if an understanding of its true nature would break Eoghan's mind. The creature turned slowly, its gaze focused on the obscured horizon as if waiting for something.

Or someone.

Eoghan ducked into the fog, slamming his elbow against the mountain in his haste. His heart thundered in his chest. A moment later, the creature's lifeless gaze passed him by.

Releasing a shuddered breath, he slumped against the cold rock and caught sight of the haze of shifted realms. The power of the storm pressed around him, as it did the creature, yet he remained hidden from its sight. He wasn't sure if he found that comforting or terrifying.

"Is this what you wanted to show me earlier?" Eoghan whispered.

The fog nodded.

He knew the fog meant well, in its own strange way, but this was becoming too much. "Please refrain from taking me on excursions like this without asking first." He tipped his head back, letting it rest against the mountain. "Let's go back. I need to think. And see if I can meet with Anaís."

The cold rock beneath his head transformed into a plush wing-back chair. Eoghan sucked in a breath and leaned forward, the warmth of the library burning his wind-chapped skin.

"—it isn't meant to. What do you think, Eoghan?" Tadeo asked.

Simone furrowed her brow at him. "Are you all right?"

"Yes, I'm fine," Eoghan replied, trying to rub feeling back into his hands. "I, um, was just thinking—when you return to Dúndíor, Anaís will need to be updated on this information. Would you be amenable to…"

Stars above had the cold numbed his brain? Or was he simply tongue-tied at the prospect of finally meeting with her?

"Passing along the information?" Simone asked sweetly. "Giving her incentive to meet with you, as I suggested earlier?" Her smile was a bit too mischievous for Eoghan's liking. "It would be my honor."

CHAPTER THIRTY-THREE
CLOVER EYES

RIED GRASS CRUNCHED BENEATH CIAN'S FEET LIKE small bones snapping. The sound made his stomach lurch with each step.

Cian loved spring. He loved summer. He absolutely despised the transition between the two seasons.

The scorching heat gathered in the valley between the mountains like a hen brooding on her nest. When it seemed as if all that lived had succumbed to its suffocating death, the air would fill with water—imperceptibly at first—before gathering until it filled the lungs of every breathing thing and suffocated nature in a new way. Until, one day, the air was mercifully released from humidity's grasp and water poured from the heavens, flooding the landscape in torrential rain.

While the deeply-rooted trees of the forest and the plants harbored under their protection soaked up the rain and remained lush into the middle of summer, all that lived apart from their shelter drowned and was carried out to sea. Thankfully, summer was steadily approaching, and he would not have to suffer this in-between much longer.

There was, however, another more pressing in-between that seemed to stretch out like the doldrums of the Fikjør Sea. A tempest stirred on the horizon, but unlike the rains that came to consume Nahonaugh, Cian was coming for it.

The contents of his knapsack shifted uncomfortably as the slope in the path tipped downward to lead into Comidh below. He slipped his pack off one shoulder and slung it around him with a grunt, loosening the drawstring to procure the map Tadhg had given him earlier that morning. He had memorized the address hours ago, but apparently growing up in Lough Ygra and spending the majority of his life in the capital was not synonymous with knowing the ins and outs of a city.

A few weeks ago, he would have been offended at the notion. Today, he tried to welcome the prickle of excitement that came with the revelation of a new world opening.

DRY HEAT AND THE EERILY cool smell of molten metal assaulted his senses as he entered the smithy's workshop. The bell chimed overhead as the door to the front room shut behind him, though the droning rumble of the forge and the sharp strike of metal on metal from the back room drowned it out.

Contrary to the shady hovel he'd imagined, this space was surprisingly homely. A carved-oak display shelf filled with intricately shaped carafes, bowls, and cups stood proudly along one wall. Custom-made gardening tools hung in orderly lines on another, while finely crafted swords hung behind the front desk.

Cian's gaze dropped to the mountain of a man sitting hunched at the desk. A concentrated furrow knit the man's brows as he polished a set of knives, lost in the rhythm of the process. Cian tilted his head, observing him. Dirt-brown hair hung in curls over his forehead. Light-olive skin peeked through the oil stains on his arms. There was no way. And yet...

"Darach?" Cian asked.

The man looked up, round glasses sliding down his nose with the movement.

Stars above, what had Darach's parents fed him? He used to be scrawnier than a blade of wheat swaying in the breeze back in primary school. Perhaps it was from apprenticing as a blacksmith?

"Cian Ó Máille!" Darach's voice had outgrown the penny whistle timbre of youth. This was all too bizarre. "It's been too long! How are you? What can I help you with?"

The relief of recognition turned sour in Cian's stomach. There would be no hiding from his past or his present. But if his father had sent him here, there was no reason to hide. Tadhg had given him his instructions; this was what was best for the future. For the kingdom. For Eoghan. Perhaps Eoghan would not understand, but he would. In time.

Cian hoped.

"Too long indeed," he said lightly, rifling through his knapsack to retrieve the arrowhead. "I have a special order. Your father made this?"

Darach's expression darkened. "Who's asking?"

Seeing as Darach knew his surname and recognized the object in question, Cian thought it rather obvious. Still, he pulled out the letter and slid it across the smooth wooden tabletop. Darach snatched it before it could slide off. Confused satisfaction flitted across his features as he skimmed the paper. Then he stood, careful not to disturb the knives he was working on, and rounded the desk to touch a corner of the paper to a lit sconce on the wall.

At first, the paper simply existed while the flames licked it ragged. Then the fire blackened. Golden embers crept up the parchment, kissed Darach's fingers, and disappeared without so much as a curl of smoke.

"Huh," Cian intoned. After all he had witnessed from his father, he had expected something more sinister, but that had been...deceptively beautiful.

Darach nodded, satisfied. "Wait here."

A loud *clank* escaped from the back room as Darach slipped through the door. Cian glanced at it, then at the flame dancing in the sconce. Tearing a strip off a scrap of paper on the desk, he crept toward the sconce and hesitantly touched the parchment to the flame. Light flared in front of him as the paper caught fire.

The ribbon of embers fell to the ground as he dropped it, followed by a flurry of curses as he stomped on the flames before they could spread. The last flame died as the door reopened, revealing Darach and a man the spitting image of him twenty years his senior.

"You Tadhg's boy?" Darach's father asked.

Cian nodded, trying to keep the expression of curiosity gone awry off his face.

"I was wondering when I'd finally be able to meet you. Name's Murray." He held out his hand. "It's a pleasure."

"The pleasure's mine," Cian returned, grasping Murray's hand firmly in his own.

The blacksmith gave a decisive shake before gesturing to the arrowhead on the table. "How many more you need?"

"Two."

"That all?" Murray scoffed, though it was more amused than derisive.

Cian shrugged. "I don't miss."

"If you don't miss, why do you need spares?"

"They're not for me."

That earned him a laugh. "Two it is."

Murray strode to the table and picked up the arrowhead, rotating it slowly between his fingers as he inspected it. Hints of blue marine shifted under the dark pewter as it glinted in the light, while the bone shard embedded to form the tip seemed to consume all the light that struck it. A void as soulless as the being it came from.

Apprehension tried to rear its devious head. Cian tamped it down.

"Do you have the rest of the materials?" Murray asked.

"I started the process," Darach returned.

Murray passed the arrowhead to Darach and sent him to the workshop before turning to face Cian. "This will take about two weeks to complete. You picking them up?"

"Yes."

"Good. Anything else I can do for you before you go?"

Cian glanced at the door the arrowhead had disappeared through, then back at Murray. "No. Thank you."

"All right then. Tell your father I said hello."

The air outside the shop felt colder, ominous, as if holding its breath while watching Cian carry on to his next destination. "Go back to the palace," it urged him. But it was not time, not yet. He would return soon. Repercussions would only come if he did not see this through, and that was not a risk he was willing to take.

A cat twined between Cian's legs, nearly tripping him as he stepped into the apothecary. It meowed up at him, dodging his attempts to nudge the calico feline aside.

"That's Síle." A young girl with dark skin rounded a shelf, her curly hair held in two buns at the nape of her neck. Given her moss-green dress and cream apron with sprigs of herbs sticking out of the pockets, Cian guessed she was an apprentice at the shop. "She's blind in one eye, which is why she doesn't rightly care that you're poking her with your foot. She knows what she's owed, and that would be pats." The girl knelt, Síle deftly jumping onto her shoulders. "There, now you can reach her. Go on. Give 'er a pat."

"Uh, right." Cian hesitantly complied, tension seeping from his shoulders when Síle closed her eyes with a contented purr.

With the cat finally distracted, he took the opportunity to gather his bearings in the shop. Much like the smithy, the apothecary had a homely feel to it. The scent of rosemary and sage filled the space, though it wasn't overpowering thanks to a breeze drifting in through an open window. Drooping, flower-laden plants hung from the ceiling. Rows of shelves displayed everything from rare ointments and tinctures to everyday soaps. While the shop was empty save for himself and the apprentice, the muffled sounds of a woman humming and crates shifting came from the back room.

"Is there anything you're looking for in particular?" the girl chirped.

Startled, Cian dropped his hand. Síle gave a disgruntled meow. "I'm here for a special order."

"Wait here! I'll be right back." As she turned to leave, the cat leapt onto Cian, flopping herself over his shoulder with a rumbling purr. "Miss Máiréad! There's a gentleman here with a special order!"

The humming cut off for a shout—"Coming, dear!"—before picking up the tune once more.

Cian meandered down a random aisle with a sigh, petting the cat absentmindedly. It was one thing to see Darach, a childhood acquaintance from a time long past, working indirectly with Tadhg. But Darach was an adult now—he knew what kind of business he was involved in. This young girl? She was too pure, too innocent to be caught in a scheme such as this, even if she was simply trying to help him receive his order.

A pestering guilt clawed at his insides. What he had involved himself in *was* wrong.

But how could it be wrong when it was the only way he could make things right?

Turning down the next aisle, he came face to face with a jovial woman in her early thirties. Máiréad's brown hair was sun-kissed, skin tanned from a lifetime outdoors foraging for medicinal roots and plants. The basket she was holding hit the floor with a thud as the smile dropped from her face, though it shone through her voice when she called, "Bronagh, would you be a dear and finish organizing the back for me?"

"Sure!" The girl's voice sang through the shop, accompanied by the patter of her feet. "Síle, come!"

Síle's claws dug into Cian's skin as she leapt off his shoulder. Though reason told him it wasn't personal, the affront felt like an omen.

With a once-over that deemed him lacking, Máiréad scooped up her basket and brushed past Cian, waving for him to follow. "So he finally roped you into it, did he? Can't say I blame you. The pay's good."

She set the basket on the front desk and stepped around the counter, disappearing behind it when she crouched down. A moment later, a series of metallic clicks sounded, likely from a safe.

"You do have the second half of the payment, don't you?" Máiréad asked.

Cian stepped up to the till and dropped a satchel of coins onto the counter with a clinking thud. Rising, she placed a vial of clear liquid in front of him, delicately wiping her hands on her apron as if clearing herself of whatever Cian would do with the substance. That was his own burden to bear.

She stepped back, folding her arms across her chest. With a smile that didn't reach her eyes, she said, "Pleasure doing business, as always."

Cian picked up the vial, chills pebbling his skin at the sensation of the curved glass bottle against his fingers. He hadn't seen the vial, but he had felt it—his eyes blinded by delirium and pain. She had made the antidote. And likely the poison that nearly killed him.

He swallowed, shoving the vial deep into his coat pocket. "Do you know what Tadhg does?"

"I—no. I simply do as I'm told. Like I said, pay's good." Máiréad's cheeks flushed, with embarrassment or shame he couldn't tell. "But Cian, a word of advice—give Tadhg the vial, then leave. Get out while you still can."

No one left Tadhg's web. Not alive. Least of all his own son. Cian bowed his head with a derisive smile. "I'll keep that in mind." Giving the counter a pat, he turned on his heel. "Have a good day," he called over his shoulder.

As far as he was concerned, there was nowhere left to go but through.

* * *

CIAN WALKED THROUGH THE DOUBLE doors of the garden-level sitting room in the palace, an unwelcome yet familiar voice brightening the space as he stepped in. Princess Simone and Eoghan sat on a sofa at the far end of the room by the bay window, tea and miniature snacking cakes arranged on the coffee table in front of them. The former chattered animatedly, as if her sister hadn't attempted to murder Cian's best friend and upended his existence in the process. With the unrest in the villages and his errands that morning, he had forgotten about the princess's arrival. A minor oversight.

No matter; he could turn this into a favorable happenstance.

A woolen floral rug muffled his footfalls as he made his way toward the pair. A burst of laughter sounded, and a blond-haired man came into view when he leaned forward, comfortably occupying Cian's favorite seat.

Cian bristled. He had only been gone a week, yet he had been replaced. The thought was irrational, the feeling of betrayal even more so. The man was simply Simone's guard, and Cian had stripped himself of the title of Eoghan's friend the night he had left him to die.

A strained silence lingered in the air as Cian rounded the seating area and made himself known. "Princess Simone! What a pleasant surprise." The lie tasted bitter on his tongue. "Eoghan"—he dipped his head into a small bow—"you're looking well."

The princess smiled up at him, no animosity, no inkling of cunning visible in the curve of her lips or the softness in her eyes. Some people kept their intentions guarded in a box, but she wore hers openly in her expression. He would have reveled in the honesty from anyone else. But from her? It soured the guilt within him into a festering revulsion.

The vial in his coat pocket burned. He would break her; the risk was too great not to.

"Lord Ó Máille, lovely to see you again." The princess's voice brought him back to the present. "I don't believe you've met Captain Tadeo Constantin. He is my escort on this trip."

With green eyes the color of clover and wavy blond hair tied back with a short strip of leather, the captain was, for lack of a better word, a pretty boy. From the way the princess leaned toward him like a flower drawn to the sun, she thought so too. Though her attentions were likely not purely observational.

The captain stood to greet him. "It's a pleasure to make your acquaintance. I've heard much about you."

"Nothing too terrible, I hope?" Cian said it in jest, but a small part hidden deep within his heart was deathly serious. "Please, don't trouble yourself on my account." He gestured to the chair. "Have a seat."

The captain complied. Cian took the last remaining seat across from Eoghan, who had been silently dissecting his every move since he joined the conversation. Once upon a time, Cian could read his friend like an open book. Eoghan was still the same book, but in the past few weeks someone had transcribed him into a different language. Or Cian had forgotten how to read.

"What?" Cian huffed a laugh. "Do I have something on my face?"

Eoghan blinked, then seemed to come to. "No! No." He returned the laugh, but it held an undercurrent of confusion. "Most of your men returned yesterday, I was worried something had happened. I take it all is well in the villages?"

"The people are reassured. Morale is boosted. I do apologize for causing undue concern. I merely made a trip into town before returning."

"Of course. It's not an issue."

Movement caught Cian's eye, and he glanced at Simone.

"I don't mean to interrupt," she addressed both of them, "but I'll need to ensure my things have been properly packed if Captain Tadeo and I are to leave this afternoon."

"Of course," Eoghan repeated. "You will…"

"Yes." The princess's expression took on a mischievous edge as she rose. "I told you I would."

Eoghan gave her a reserved smile, though his shoulders drooped with obvious relief. It lasted a brief moment before he pushed himself to standing. "Right, well, let me know when you're ready and I'll see you off. In the meantime, Cian"—Eoghan turned to face him—"I'd like to hear your report about the villages."

"I'd be happy to give it." Standing, he followed the princess and the captain out of the sitting room. "Your study?"

"Cian?" Eoghan asked, lingering away from the others. He waited a few moments for the distance to grow before speaking quietly. "I apologize. Two weeks ago. I was…" He shook his head. "I'm sorry. I should have been more forthcoming; I should have been there for you—"

"It's not a problem," Cian interrupted, turning to leave before Eoghan could continue this particular conversation. Because there *was* a problem. Just not in the way Eoghan expected.

CHAPTER THIRTY-FOUR

BRUISES

A FEATHERLIGHT TOUCH TICKLED ANAÍS'S SUBCONscious. Then another touch, more forceful this time. Not in her head, but on her body. An ache bloomed from its epicenter, spreading outward until it snaked around her back and began to burn. Her arm twitched in response, a halfhearted reaction to shove the source of pain away, but something stopped it before it could begin.

The burning crawled up her neck. Her shoulders lurched, head lulling forward to follow the movement, swaying to death's lullaby as it rocked her into oblivion on suspended chains. A jolt of panic ran through her, the fragile in-between taking the form of a circular tomb of sandstone and light.

The Butcher stood behind her. Numbness licked her arms as she hung limply from the ceiling. Searing pain carved into her back as barbed leather tore at her flesh over and over and over again.

She had not had the strength to fight then. She would *find* the strength to fight now.

Her muscles screamed with fatigue as she swung wildly. Her back burned in a raging fire, but she would not stop. She refused to endure this any longer.

Hands clawed against her, struggling for purchase, pushing her down, down, down. Distant shouting filled her head, the muddled sounds growing louder and louder until her mind was forced to start piecing them together. Her name, she realized. Someone was shouting her name. Suddenly, as if she were being pulled out from water, sound came flooding in at full force, bright light filling her vision as her eyes opened.

What she saw brought more confusion than clarity.

A disheveled and horribly sleep-deprived Gio hovered over her as he pinned her down, while the blurry outline of a healer slumped against the wall gasped for air a few paces away.

"Anaís?"

She sucked in a ragged breath, transforming into a cough as pain shot through her ribs. Gio tentatively released her from his grasp, and she relaxed into the pillows beneath her. He muttered something under his breath, but she was too distracted to focus on his words. Everything hurt.

At Gio's beckoning, the healer slowly pushed off the wall and moved next to Anaís. She was short and stout, with dark-brown skin and the all-knowing gaze of a woman who had looked death in the face and sent it on its merry way.

"I'm going to tend to your bandages now. Mind that you don't thrash about like a fish out of water." The healer's words were stern, but relief softened her features. She placed a steadying hand under Anaís's head, the other on her shoulder, and gently helped her sit up. The bandages clung to her raw skin, and Anaís couldn't help the groan that escaped when the healer began removing them.

"You didn't pull any stitches. That's reassuring," the healer mumbled while looking over the damage done upon her waking.

Gio took a step back, gaze catching on Anaís's back before dropping to the floor. It did nothing to mask the sadness lingering in his eyes. As if they didn't want to believe what they saw.

"What happened?" Anaís croaked.

Gio bit his cheek. The healer answered for him. "You were beaten within an inch of your life, didn't take the medicine Simone left you, and caught an infection."

Infection. That explained a lot. The past, however long it had been between arriving at the palace and waking up here, explained a lot as to why she felt how she felt. Although in hindsight, everything should have hurt *more*.

"Why did you help?" Anaís rasped.

"When I became a healer, I swore an oath to serve those in need of my skills. Who needs those skills doesn't really matter, despite royal decrees. You aren't the only one concerned with protecting people." The healer paused to focus her attention on cleaning and spreading ointment on the cuts and gashes littering her back.

Anaís winced, partially at the pressure of the healer's hands on a particularly sensitive wound, but mostly because her words echoed what Simone had told her when she first came stumbling through the door.

"The king announced you were to keep your position as Anadali Amadé a few days ago," she continued, securing fresh bandages in place. "Your demotion and the decrees he had issued banning your aid were annulled. Besides, having *this* Anadali threatening my wellbeing if I didn't act immediately was motivation enough." She nodded in Gio's direction before mumbling, "As if I needed any to begin with." She retrieved a murky red concoction from the bedside table and held it in front of Anaís. "Drink this."

Anaís wrinkled her nose at the smell but swallowed it obediently.

The healer took the glass, satisfied. "It will be more comfortable for you to sleep on your left side for now. Two of your right ribs were fractured, but seem to be healing nicely. Though I imagine they'll be angry after your little stunt. I'll come check on you in a few hours."

She helped ease Anaís back down and tucked the blankets under her chin. If Anaís hadn't been so drained, she might have cried at the gentleness of the gesture.

The healer muttered something to Gio when she passed him on the way out, to which he replied with a curt nod. The door shut, and a heavy silence filled the space between them.

Gio still hadn't moved from his place by the window. He looked lost. Confused. Trapped in a maelstrom of thoughts that sucked him under, pushed him to the surface, dragged him back down again. Dark circles stood out starkly against his pale skin. His usually neat hair stuck out at odd angles, as if he had taken out his stress in the only way he knew how—on himself. He was only twenty, but appeared to have aged a decade in the span of a week.

"When Simone left, she warned me of what happened," he began. "I came to check on you after training and you..." He swallowed, eyes unfocused as if reliving those moments. "You weren't breathing. I needed to get you help."

"You went against direct orders of the king."

"To hell with the king!" Gio shouted, clarity flashing in his eyes for the first time since she had woken up.

Anaís looked at him in shock, but there was no regret written anywhere on his face. Only firm resolve. Gio always followed the king's orders to perfection, always sought to be the best he could be. She could lead him to the true ways of the Anadali—the ways Balendin had instilled in her—but she couldn't make him accept them. What had happened to get him to change his mind?

"You shouldn't say such things," Anaís warned.

"The king shouldn't try to kill the one I swore an oath to."

"You swore an oath to the king."

He recoiled as if she had slapped him. "The king may rule, but the oath I swore was to *you*."

"Do you know what I did?"

"It's not about what you did!"

"All of this is about what I did and what I failed to do!" she shouted. The sound grated at her throat, a deep ache burying itself in her lungs, in her ribs, but Gio needed to understand before he said something stupid in the presence of someone who *would* give repercussion to his words. "Do you understand the consequences of disobedience?"

Gio's eyes met hers, a potent mix of betrayal and ferocity swirling in their depths. "Yes."

"Then you should be thankful we're even having this conversation right now. The king showed mercy."

Gio shook his head and lowered himself onto the chair beside her bed. "The *king*," he spat, "has been deceitful in everything he has done. Everything I thought I was fighting for was nothing but lies. My father didn't cross the ocean to escape tyranny only to have me uphold it. I have dishonored him. I have dishonored your guidance. I was not following the way of the Anadali."

Any retort that had been waiting in her mind dissipated at his words. She nodded, but stopped short as a cut that snaked around her neck rubbed against the pillow.

"I apologize for my ignorance. And my pride." He sucked in a breath as he considered his next words. "If you will still have me, I would be honored to serve under you as Anadali."

Anaís's heart dropped at the uncertainty in his posture. "You *are* Anadali." She meant it in more ways than in title alone.

He shook his head. "I was a coward."

"A coward would not admit his faults and stand to amend them at the expense of treason."

"I have broken my oath to you."

He had also saved her life at the threat of his own. That alone was worth more than any vows he could have promised. "You do not have to make it again."

"Please," he whispered.

Anaís studied him. Gone was the assured confidence that he wore like armor. He appeared small. Desperate—not for a chance at acceptance, but for a chance to start over. To be the person he hoped he could have been had he not been led astray by the lies he believed. He didn't need to try again at who he was, for that man no longer existed. He needed to step into something new.

"Gio Toccileu, I hereby declare you Anadali Athaçla." *Second in command.*

His eyes widened in shock. "That's not what I—"

"I know. But I want to. You're a good man, Gio. Your father would be proud." He still didn't look convinced so she added, "Do not question my decision. I just might take it back."

He slumped back in his chair, a wave of unreadable emotions washing over his face. "Thank you." His voice cracked, and he cleared his throat. "I will not let you down."

"Have you heard any news from Simone?" Anaís asked, partially to distract herself from the emotion welling up within her, but mostly because she couldn't ignore the concern growing in the corner of her mind.

"No, not since she went to Nahonaugh with the captain. They should be back in a few days' time."

Anaís hummed in thought. Simone would be all right; she had to be. Tadeo would do anything to protect her, and no news was usually good news. At least, in the diplomatic sphere. She hoped. "And how much longer until I can assist with training?"

Gio raised his brow at her. "You cannot be serious right now."

"Do I appear to be in a joking mood?" she asked, matching his look. Though she had a feeling it was much less intimidating when she was cocooned in blankets.

"The healer said, and I quote—" He cleared his throat and mimicked her southern accent. "'You are not to leave this bed for two days. We shall reassess on the third. If and only if you are healing well *and* prove to me that you will follow my instructions, I will *consider* allowing you to walk—*gently*—around the room. Nothing more.'"

"You do that quite well."

"I spent part of my childhood in the south before coming to the city." The corner of his mouth pulled into a half smile at the memory. "But don't change the subject. Do you agree to her terms?"

Anaís breathed a long sigh. She didn't like it, but even with the draught the healer had given her, she still felt like death. "Yes."

"Thank the stars!" Gio lifted his hands to the sky dramatically, then let them fall back to his lap. "Respectfully, that woman is terrifying. I will not get on her bad side because of you."

❋　❋　❋

As DIFFICULT AS IT WAS, Anaís stuck to her promise. She stayed in bed for two days, with the exception of going to the toilet. If she was honest with herself, she relished the uninterrupted time to sleep and recover. It seemed the time did her mind just as much good as it did for her body, although she would have preferred different circumstances that led her to this predicament.

The healer, whom she now knew as Tippa, was finishing securing fresh bandages against her back. The ointment had most of the wounds already closing up, while stitches assisted the healing of deeper gashes—though even those wounds weren't as inflamed as before. Tippa smoothed the last bandage into place, stepping back to double check her handiwork before passing Anaís a clean tunic. She reached out to accept it but stopped short, a new wave of pain rolling over her as stitches pulled against still-healing skin.

Tippa quirked her brow in amusement when a flurry of choice words rolled off Anaís's tongue. "Maybe that is a bit ambitious, yes?"

"Point taken." Anaís tried to glare at the woman, but the stern motherly look she received in return was enough to soften her expression to a sheepish grin. "I promise I won't do anything too strenuous."

Tippa nodded. "Perhaps a wrap dress would be more accommodating. And discourage you from any fighting."

"I am a warrior. That would not be appropriate."

"Would you like to try putting the tunic on again?"

Anaís breathed out a sigh, her shoulders deflating with accepted defeat. "No."

"Then I will bring you a dress."

As soon as Anaís stepped outside, summer heat sank into her skin and drank her dry. If anything, the dress would prevent her from incinerating while she watched drills. The dusty blue cotton draped loosely around her body, while a leather cord secured it in place around her waist. At least she could still wear her boots, which brought more comfort than she cared to admit.

Several Anadali were already warming up by the time she made it to the training arena. A few men glanced her way as the door shut behind her, but their gaze was fleeting and filled more with lingering curiosity than judgment. Gio stood in a corner helping the bald recruit wrap his hands for combat training, and he waved her over when she caught his eye.

"You look rejuvenated." Gio grinned.

"It's the dress. Brings out the colors of my bruises."

He hummed in thought, his eyes lingering on the discoloration still visible on her cheekbone. "Best you not wear that accessory next time."

"Is it true? You defied the king and lived?" the bald recruit asked.

Anaís raised her brow at the recruit. "I made a judgment call. The king responded as he saw fit." The ambient chatter of the training room deadened, all eyes on her as she continued. "We are Anadali. We swore an oath to the crown, one that first and foremost protects the people. We lay our lives down so the young can grow old, and life can flourish, and the brutality of war is buried so deeply that neither beast nor man can dig it up from its grave. We do not defy." Her voice echoed through the room. "We are called to uphold a higher standard. To protect, even at the risk of ourselves. Do I make myself clear?"

The men saluted in unison. "Yes, Amadé."

"Good." She tipped her head toward the sparring ring. "Get to work."

Redirecting her attention to Gio, she asked, "You're working on blocking today?"

"I thought it would be easiest for you to observe. Less moving around on your part."

Anaís nodded, but her newfound resolve had given her a spark of energy that ignited an ember of defiance. She wanted to move around, stay standing, prove to herself and everyone else that she was strong. Capable.

Five minutes revealed that had been a very, very foolish idea. As much as she was loath to admit it, the bench was much more comfortable.

Settling back, she observed her men with a new sense of purpose. She would train the Anadali—all of them. Her father had tried to destroy the truth, the hope that had been instilled in her all those years ago. Too many people forgot that hope had teeth and truth wielded a sword. The heart of the Anadali would not die without a fight.

CHAPTER THIRTY-FIVE
UNHIDE TO SEEK

THE END OF THE WEEK CURLED INTO THE WEEKEND like a kitten ready for a nap. After nearly three months of traveling, espionage, almost dying, and committing herself to training all of the new recruits as Anadali, Anaís shared the sentiment. Still, it was nice to settle into a new yet familiar routine of devising training protocols and instructing drills.

Nicer still was passing along more responsibilities to Gio and watching him grow. Over the past two weeks, her once restless apprentice had found purpose in his new role. Though from her perspective, his role hadn't changed at all. The purpose he found was in himself—something he could carry with him regardless of what the future held.

Much to Anaís's amused dismay, Gio leveraged his rank as Athaçla to enforce Tippa's instructions for her healing process. Day by day, she regained her strength, moving from barking instructions while sitting, to administering corrections as she meandered past dueling recruits, to demonstrating basic technique against Gio—who had yet to disarm her, despite valiant efforts and the good-natured taunting from the rest of the men.

In a way, it seemed as if her men—both new recruits and seasoned Anadali alike—needed to see her in such a state. There was humanity in being human, a trait that had been stripped from her long ago. A trait she had only just received the opportunity to find again. She would not let it wound her pride that her almost-execution was what had given her the leverage she needed to thwart the king's plans in a way that extended beyond herself.

Still, she had her limits. The Anadali, whispering servants, and gossiping courtiers could make up whatever story made them feel better about the hurt she allowed them to see, be it one of bravery, foolishness, or some twisted tale of luck. She refused to let anyone, herself included, see the warring emotions that lingered just beneath the puckered scars and bruised skin. She had made her choices; that should have been enough.

Ensuring the curtains of her room were tightly drawn and her door securely shut, Anaís stripped off her tunic, wincing as stiff scabs and tender scars pulled with the movement. She grabbed the pot of ointment Tippa had left on her nightstand before moving to the washroom.

Perching herself on the countertop, Anaís twisted to see her back in the mirror and began mechanically applying the salve. The wound curving from her shoulder to the back of her neck stung when she rubbed with more force than necessary. She didn't care.

She was flesh and blood. Muscle and bone. She did not feel. It was easier not to. Because if she felt, she feared she would not be able to stop. So, with gritted teeth and the last ounce of determination she could muster, she carried on. Salve, rub, salve, rub, salve, rub.

Pounding echoed through her room, and she flinched, pressing against a particularly sensitive patch of skin.

"What?" Anaís snapped, partially because of the pain. Partially because she was without a shirt and did not want to be exposed—emotionally or otherwise.

"I'm home, can I come in?" Simone's voice drifted through the door.

Anaís rested her forehead against the mirror, her breath fogging the glass as she tried to calm down. "No."

The door handle jiggled. Something wiggled in the lock. Despite her washroom being hidden from the view of the main door, Anaís tensed. "Simone," she warned.

The door quickly opened and closed. The lock slid into place. The soft patter of Simone's footsteps approached.

"Simone! I'm not wearing a shirt!"

"Don't get your knickers in a bunch," Simone laughed, followed by the rustle of skirts as she plopped into a chair. "I'm staying right here."

"You could have waited outside," Anaís grumbled.

"You would have left me all alone in a hallway with nothing to do?" Simone asked with mock innocence. "While you're doing... whatever you're doing in there. What *are* you doing in there?"

"I did not miss this," Anaís mumbled to herself. Too loudly, it seemed.

"How could you miss it? You were unconscious. You're welcome, by the way. Gio told me you were an absolute idiot."

Anaís rolled her eyes, even though her sister could not see it. Scooping another dollop of ointment from the pot, she twisted around to apply it to her lower back, but Simone's presence had broken her mechanical focus. All she could see was mangled flesh and pain, so much pain, weaving beneath her scars and tying itself around her heart where memories of Eoghan hid. Her friend, her enemy, the compliment to her soul. He hadn't needed to destroy the walls she had built to protect herself—he was her walls. That *terrified* her. Tears prickled her eyes and she cursed herself for letting her guard down.

The sound of rustling skirts startled Anaís out of her thoughts, and she pulled a towel against her chest just as Simone poked her head into the washroom. "I'm shirtless!" Anaís yelped.

"You were taking too long." Simone paused, glancing at her back, at her trembling hand holding a glob of ointment, at the tear that had escaped and slid down Anaís's cheek. Wordlessly, Simone washed her hands, scooped the ointment off Anaís's fingers, and gently began applying it to her back. "Besides," Simone continued as if she hadn't just saved Anaís from herself, "I have news directly from His Highness Crown Prince soon-to-be-king Eoghan Kavanaugh."

Anaís inhaled sharply at his name. No, at the coolness of the ointment over a particularly painful scab when Simone happened to mention his name. No, because she needed to breathe—she was not allowed to feel.

Simone peeked around Anaís's shoulder and met her eyes in the mirror with a cheeky stare. "Oh? What's that?"

"Nothing," she muttered, looking away.

"You were right about him, you know?" Simone said gently. "He's a good man. He will be a good king."

Anaís said nothing.

"He mentioned something to me," Simone continued. "Not specifically, but I think it could be related to what you told me."

What you told me. What had she told Simone? Her memories before waking up to nearly pummeling Gio and Tippa were a haze at best. Why did she have the impression she had said something she should not have?

"Remind me... Remind me again what I told you." The words came out as a question rather than a request.

"About your dreams. Some sort of connection? You need to talk to him."

Like sun breaking through morning fog, the haze of time parted and the memories it revealed burned her. "Did you tell him?" She looked at her sister pleadingly through the mirror. "Simone, did you tell him? He can't know!"

Panic gripped her chest. Of course he knew. She had seen it, felt it. He knew of her shame, her cowardice, her hopes, her heart.

Simone stepped around Anaís and gently gripped her shoulders. "I told you I would take your secret with me to the grave. I meant it. But he has his own secrets—no, don't ask me, I don't know them. Both of you are too stubborn for your own good." She huffed a laugh. "In fact, you're likely the only person who could pry anything out of him."

Anaís shook her head vehemently. "It doesn't matter. I killed his cousin. I almost killed him."

"He wants to talk to you," Simone huffed.

"I don't want to talk to him."

"You can't keep hiding."

"I want to hide!" Anaís shouted. "That's all I'm good at. I hide and I destroy."

"Then what are you doing with the Anadali?" Simone snapped. "Gio told me you've given them a new purpose. A new hope. They're changing for the better because of *you*. Stop. Hiding."

Anaís's lower lip trembled. She couldn't do this. A tear slid down her cheek, then another, and another. Like a river breaking free of its dam, everything she had been holding back since she woke up released. Sobs wracked her body as she curled into herself. Simone shifted closer, then wrapped careful arms around Anaís, holding her together as she fell apart.

"I don't know what's wrong with me," Anaís finally managed to choke out. "I don't know who I am anymore."

"You are my sister. Loyal to a fault." Simone brushed a strand of hair off Anaís's forehead. "You have compassion for those around you, but you refuse to grant it to yourself. But I wish you would. I wish you could see yourself as I see you." She kissed the top of her head, then stepped back to meet Anaís's gaze. "You are not who Father forced you to be. You never were, not fully. You always fought back in your own way, but I see another change in you now. Whatever happened, his grip on you has broken. You *are* free; step into it."

Anaís took in a shuddering breath and nodded, wiping her nose on a corner of the towel covering her chest. She felt a mess, but she also felt...better. As if falling apart wasn't a fracturing, but a making of room for something new to grow.

"I don't know what is happening, or why this is happening," Simone continued. "But do you trust me when I say you ought to talk to Eoghan?"

"I trust you," Anaís said without hesitation.

"Will you do it?"

Anaís hummed noncommittally, and Simone heaved an exasperated sigh. "All right, I'll take that to mean yes. Come on," Simone said, disappearing back into Anaís's room. "Let's get you a shirt, and I'll tell you about what Eoghan showed me."

"Showed you what?" Anaís asked, rubbing her eyes as she slid off the counter and followed Simone. Grabbing her tunic off the back of a chair, Anaís slipped it over her head and settled onto the cocoon of blankets atop her bed.

Simone strode to her favorite chair by the fireplace, plopping into it with a contented sigh. "A nitróg," she replied.

"What?" Anaís asked, unsure she had heard properly. Her head throbbed with the beginnings of a tear-induced headache.

"A holey rock," Simone clarified, then rolled her eyes at Anaís's confused stare. "Not holy as in '*ahhh*'"—her surprisingly melodic note filled the air—"holey as in holes. Like the ones you stab into people."

Anaís blinked at her sister. "Did you just make a morbid joke?"

"I was trying to relate it to something you were familiar with." Simone shrugged innocently. "Anyway, the nitróg. As you can perhaps derive from its name—*ni'itrat*, to guide, and *maróg*, stone—it is, in essence, a guiding stone. To what and where and why, no one knows, but that's beside the point. The rock itself isn't all that important."

Anaís raised her brow. "So you've gathered useless information."

"No," Simone said with a huff, "I'm not finished yet. *You* are the reason the rock is important. The nitróg is a 'gift of kings,' or so Eoghan called it, passed down along his bloodline. But you knew where it would be."

"Simone," Anaís rubbed her temples. Her headache had sub-sided a bit, but this was bringing on a new one for an entirely differ-ent reason. "I know nothing of this rock. Besides, I was unconscious when you left. How could I have passed on information—that I did *not* know—to you?"

"You weren't unconscious the entire time; you were de-lusional. Or so I thought. But you saw the clue! The snow, the smoke. You knew."

"A coincidence."

"Eoghan would beg to differ."

Anaís felt herself deflate. She loved her sister, dearly, but this was ridiculous. Her dreams were an odd enough phenomenon. She didn't need connections and mysterious, ancient rocks to go along with it. No, what she needed was to train her Anadali. Maybe, *maybe* speak with Eoghan—unless his intention was to kill her, which she couldn't fault him for. And then what? Try to keep the kingdoms from destroying one another, she supposed.

Would life carry on as normal? Would her father want her to try to assassinate Eoghan again, or did he have other plans against Nahonaugh? He had officially reinstated her position as Anadali Amadé, yet hadn't so much as stepped into the same room as her since she had woken up. It was as if he was biding his time for something, but what?

"Tadeo can corroborate my account if you don't believe it," Simone said, hurt hardening her features.

Anaís winced. She hadn't meant to dismiss her sister's excitement or her ideas upon this discovery.

Simone was intelligent to a fault, but she was also a dreamer, content to keep her nose in a book for as long as she could. If anything seemed to have an interesting plot, Simone would go after it regardless of whether it was inked onto a page or unfolding before her very eyes.

"The captain saw it too?" Anaís asked.

Simone nodded. "Tadeo said it would have been improper for me to meet Eoghan alone without any guards present. Eoghan agreed to grant him entry once Tadeo swore on his life to secrecy and had my word to back him up."

Anaís's gaze lingered on Simone's face. On the determination in the set of her jaw. The vulnerability shining in her eyes. Weeks ago, Simone had confided in Anaís that something was afoot. She had been hesitant to believe her then. She would be a fool not to believe her now.

"Eoghan must have been desperate if he let a near stranger be privy to this secret relic of his," Anaís said.

Simone gave her a knowing smile. "We weren't privy to all of his secrets. Nor is he desperate for the reasons you might think."

"And why *is* he so desperate?"

The first dinner bell rang before Simone could answer. Reluctantly, she rose from her chair, golden skirts swishing around her as she made her way to the door. Her hand grasped the handle but she stilled, then looked over her shoulder at Anaís.

"Talk to him. Please?" Simone bit the inside of her cheek as if considering her next words. "You need each other. More than either of you realize."

"I'll think about it," Anaís promised, then tipped her chin toward the door. "I'll see you at dinner."

The door shut. Anaís stared at it, then allowed herself to flop backward, looking at the ceiling. Her wounds stung. The ointment sopped into her shirt. Another knock sounded at the door. Softer this time. Three raps, a pause, then another—the code she and Katka, her lady's maid, had devised years ago.

"You may enter, Katka," Anaís called, not moving from her position on her bed.

The door opened. Shut. Katka's footsteps whispered across the floor, stopping at the side of Anaís's bed.

Anaís turned her head. "You arrived early."

"I thought you would appreciate extra time to prepare for dinner, Your Highness."

Sighing, Anaís sat up. "Yes, I would appreciate that. Will my father be attending dinner tonight?"

"I am afraid not, Your Highness. Both the king and Captain Tadeo have departed for one of His Majesty's appointments."

Anaís's heart sank, though she wasn't sure why. A small part of her argued that it was because he was still her father, though it did nothing to excuse his actions. It was for the best, Anaís decided. She had the freedom to train the Anadali unhindered, and with the additional information Simone had confided in her...she needed unhindered time to think.

"It matters not," Anaís said. "You may choose what I wear tonight, Katka."

Katka's face brightened at the request. "Of course, Your Highness." She gave a slight bow, then glided enthusiastically across the room to Anaís's wardrobe. Her fingers danced across the fabric with reverence, hesitating as they alighted on a black gown. Katka looked over her shoulder. "Do you have a preference for color, Your Highness?"

"No, Katka," Anaís laughed. "You may choose."

Her lady in waiting smiled, then returned to her task, considering each dress with the utmost care before making her choice. Katka turned, holding a raspberry-hued gown draped with goldenrod silk that twisted around the waist and trailed up the bust. The silk gathered at the shoulder to flow down the arm in a wide sleeve, leaving the other arm free. A fine mesh made of looped silver and diamonds decorated the back, spanning from the slope of the shoulders down to the hips.

Simone had gifted Anaís the dress for her birthday last year. It was beautiful, but...

"I would rather not expose my wounds," Anaís said.

Katka shifted nervously on her feet. "If I may, Your Highness, but this will be more suitable than fabric. The mesh won't absorb the ointment and will allow your wounds to breathe, while the diamonds will reflect light, stealing attention from the skin it covers."

A contemplative smile grew on Anaís's lips. It seemed some of her practicality had finally rubbed off on Katka. "Very well," she said, sliding off the bed to stand so Katka could help her dress.

Her trousers came off first, followed by her tunic. Katka held the dress out, helping Anaís step in before maneuvering to the back to secure the mesh into place.

"I'm sorry," Katka whispered, her hands stilling briefly before continuing to work the clasps. This was the first time Anaís had allowed Katka to help her dress since that night, she realized.

"It's not your fault."

"I know, but it is horrible, the thing that happened."

Katka finished securing the mesh in silence before guiding Anaís to a small vanity to braid her hair. The cool metal of the mesh soothed the tender skin on Anaís's back as she moved, and the ointment didn't feel as horribly sticky as it would on cloth.

Anaís closed her eyes as Katka worked, allowing the gentle push and pull of Katka's meticulous hands to soothe away the last of her worries, if only for the time being.

"All will be made right," Anaís said, a quiet proclamation to herself. "One day, all will be made right."

"Then it will be so, Your Highness," Katka whispered in kind.

CHAPTER THIRTY-SIX

BADLANDS

Anaís pulled her cloak more tightly around her, making her way through the desert that stretched between the capital of Dúndíor and the small village of Qotiu to the north. Sand shifted beneath her boots, and her tunic pulled uncomfortably at her back, but the sensations quieted to white noise as she forged her own path under the light of the full moon. She had tried to sleep after dinner, but every time she closed her eyes, her mind returned to the discussion she'd had with Simone earlier that day.

You need each other. More than either of you realize.

Perhaps they did. But as the night deepened, her sleeplessness brought with it the stark realization that her initial reservations weren't the only reason she hesitated to see Eoghan again. The more she thought about their connection, about *him*, the more desolate Anaís felt. She thought she had finally found peace in the chaos, only to have it all ripped away. Eoghan protected her from her nightmares, but he couldn't protect her from herself. From her past.

Settled in the liminal space between wakefulness and dreams, it was memories of Balendin that had come to haunt her. How easily her blade had found its target, pierced his skin, taken his life. What a sick twist of fate it was to murder the brother she loved only to spare the man she should hate.

The thought had driven her from her bed and into the desert, yet even here it followed her like a ghost. Guilt twisted her stomach. Or was it bitterness? Regret? If she found it within herself to be defiant now, why couldn't have she done so back then? Why had she had to look Balendin in the eye, only to be the reason life left it? Shouldn't he have mattered more than whatever *this* was?

Eoghan. These dreams. This connection. It felt as if she was locked in a forbidden dance of fates intertwined, and apparently she was intent on following the music.

The whispering sands beneath her boots transformed into compacted, clay-rich soil, steadying her footing as she entered the badlands. Moonlight caressed the high interfluves around her, abandoning its purpose as a light source to play atop the banded terracotta and grey limestone formations. It didn't matter—the path she followed had been burned into muscle memory long ago. Simply another entanglement in the fated music she danced to.

Anaís kicked a rock in her path, a bitter smile curving her lips when a satisfactory *crack* emanated from the darkness that swallowed its trajectory. She couldn't decide if she wanted to forget Eoghan altogether or understand their connection. All she knew was she did not want to stop walking. And so she pressed on, deeper into the maze of carved ravines and eroded silt until interfluves collapsed into the earth and spiked spires of rock rose in their place, like spears shoved into the belly of a dying beast. Melancholy harmonics whistled around her as wind flowed between the formations.

There, hidden beneath nature's siren cry, was her name.

Anaís whirled around, goosebumps pebbling her skin as her heart thrummed in her chest. "Who's there?" she shouted into the night.

The groan of the wind was her only response. It danced around her, twirling her hair, rustling the fabric of her cloak, drifting away altogether before whipping around her with a howl.

"Show yourself!" Anaís demanded, slipping twin daggers out of her belt. Their familiar weight grounded her, easing her panic into a honed focus.

A shadow shifted to her left, and she twisted with the movement. Her muscles coiled, ready to strike. The wind sent dirt skittering across her boots. Anaís stared into the darkness, waiting, watching. She couldn't see it, but she knew—someone was watching her too.

The shadow shifted again, slowly, before moving forward and stepping onto the path. Moonlight trickled between the formations, bathing the figure in a ghostly light. A midnight-blue cloak engulfed their body, hood pulled low to obscure their eyes. Anaís flexed her fingers along the handle of her daggers, eyes flickering across the figure as she searched for a tell.

The figure seemed to track the movement, then relaxed their stance. "I am not looking for trouble." They spoke in a melodious accent. Female. It reminded Anaís of someone; she couldn't quite place who. The memory tickled at the back of her mind, but she brushed it away.

"State your purpose," Anaís ground out.

"I am Olia of Qotiu, and I am here to speak with you."

Her heart stopped as Olia reached up and drew her hood back, revealing the face of a woman twenty years Anaís's senior. Auburn hair shifted in the wind that had calmed to a light breeze. Her tanned skin almost glowed under the light of the moon.

In the silence that stretched between them, an owl hooted into the darkness, the sound accompanied by the flapping of wings. Somewhere behind a rock formation, dirt crunched under the cautious steps of a desert creature. Anaís couldn't focus her mind long enough to figure out what it was. She couldn't focus on anything through the force with which her memories screamed at her. If only she could grasp what they were trying to say.

"How did you know I would be here?" The words fell from Anaís's mouth before she registered she was even speaking.

Olia shrugged. "I knew you would come eventually."

"You don't even know who I am. Why would you expect me to come?" Anaís shifted her grip on her daggers. "Are you a spy?"

Olia seemed to shrink in on herself, lips tipping into a confused frown. "You do not remember me?"

Anaís shook her head.

"After what the king did to you, I am not surprised." Olia's words drifted across the space between them. "I helped Balendin train you for a time. You were very young."

"You knew Balendin?" Anaís demanded, though she knew it to be true. It was why Olia's accent was so familiar—one Anaís swore she would never forget. She couldn't even keep the memory of Balendin's voice alive.

"Yes, we grew up together in the same village."

Anaís swallowed, throat bobbing as if trying to dislodge the words stuck there. "You knew me?" she finally whispered.

Olia nodded.

"Prove it."

Olia tipped her chin toward Anaís. "Do you remember the day after your training session, the one where Balendin cut your brow?"

Anaís squeezed her daggers to prevent her hands from shaking. The tension would hinder her ability to attack, but she was too shaken to fight.

"Balendin and I agreed you would have trained as if nothing had happened and reopened the cut on your brow. Instead of working on swordplay like I had planned, I took you to the cliffs along the Ulçok Sea. They were my favorite place to go when I needed to breathe, and it seemed you needed space to do the same." Olia smiled as if lost in the memory. "You played upon the rocks for as long as you could, stopping just long enough to run back to me for another orange slice or a vanilla biscuit that the cook had made that morning. Those had always been your favorite. Balendin met us back at the palace that evening. Rather than going inside, he took us to the rooftop to stargaze. You identified your first constellation that night."

Look to the stars, they will show you the way.

The memory came as a whisper, silencing the raging thoughts in her mind. Herself, Balendin, and Olia lying on their backs on the palace rooftop, taking in the vastness of the galaxy. Three insignificant specks. Yet they existed—living, breathing, making their mark on the fabric of time, however small it may have been.

No mark, however small, seemed insignificant to her now.

"Anaís?" Olia spoke softly.

Something wet rolled down her cheek. Another rolling after it when she blinked. In fact, she couldn't see anything through the tears in her eyes. How had she gone from rarely crying to breaking down twice in a single day?

"Are you okay?" Olia asked.

Anaís let out a watery laugh, arms dropping to her sides. "No."

Moments had been stolen from her; now she was getting them back. Could they help her reconcile the pain of Balendin's memory with the hope of Eoghan's life? Balendin didn't die to spite her—he died to spare her so that she could live to carry on his legacy. Perhaps Simone was right. In her own way, she had never stopped fighting. She fought against the king, yes. But she was also fighting herself.

"I have some questions," Anaís said hesitantly. "Ones I think only you may know the answer to. May we talk?"

A soft smile grew on Olia's lips. "Of course," she said, gesturing to a low outcropping of rocks to sit upon.

Anaís looked from the rocks to Olia then back again before sighing and tucking her daggers back into place. It was true, she did remember the woman before her—as well as a child's hazy memory and the burial shroud of time would allow. Though it never hurt to be careful.

"I think we have already established I won't hurt you, no?" Olia said.

Anaís raised her brow.

"I taught you, remember? I know your expressions, and I know one of your first lessons was the art of wariness toward foes presenting themselves as friends."

Anaís smiled at that. "I fear I took that lesson a little too close to heart."

"Nonsense," Olia laughed. "Come, sit." She lowered herself onto a rock and pat the one beside her. "I will answer any questions you have."

"Why are you here?" Anaís asked, perching herself on the rock Olia gestured to.

"I told you, I knew you would return one day. And tonight?" Olia shrugged. "It felt like tonight."

Anaís frowned. "Yes, but what does that *mean*? You must realize, from my perspective that sounds insane."

"Have you not had stranger things happen to you?"

Yes. But Anaís wasn't about to voice that to a near stranger. At least not yet. Not until she knew Olia had answers.

"What did Balendin tell you of our myths and legends?" Olia asked.

"I didn't know they were myths and legends at the time. They were my bedtime stories, then anecdotes during orienteering expeditions." Anaís shrugged. "He told me of Takaniim, of the Final Battle, of Nāmi Attatikarou—the legend of the blue sun—among others. I learned they were proper myths and not fairy tales a few months ago."

Olia nodded, then smiled. "Yes, it does sound like Balendin to embellish sacred myth. There is one called *nanouk'tou*. It is less of a myth than it is an incredibly rare phenomenon. Though not unheard of, mind you. This is what brought Balendin and I together. It is what set us on our path to leave the village as warriors, to come to the city not knowing what we would find, but knowing we were drawn there. Then to the palace. It led us to you. The rest, you know most of it."

Anaís swallowed. "What is nanouk'tou specifically? What does it mean?"

"It is a reflection of souls. It bound Balendin and I together across space and time, it seemed. Our choices that followed were our own. Some may argue—call it "fate" or "destiny"—but to us it was a knowing. A conviction of what *must* be done, even if nothing made sense. Even if it hurt. Though I believe the hurt would have been much deeper had we never been drawn together at all."

Anaís shifted away, gaze falling on her hands curled into fists on her lap. Now Balendin was dead because of her. She felt sick. "I'm sorry," Anaís whispered. It didn't feel like enough.

A warm weight alighted on her shoulder and Anaís turned to face Olia. "Don't be. Balendin and I would have changed nothing."

"Yes, but why are you helping me if you know what I did? What my family did?"

"I am here because I *want* to be, both for the little girl I knew and the woman sitting beside me now. And for Balendin—he may be gone, but our work is not done." Olia turned to face her fully. "I think you already know this, but a person is not the reflection of the decisions of those who command them. You are not your father, that is simple to see. I believe in you; Balendin believed in you. You must know this—through the end he did not waver. There is destiny within you yet."

Anaís nodded; her voice would only betray her. Though the bitter ache of loss weighed on her chest, her heart fluttered behind its cage in a bid for freedom. She wanted to scream, to cry, to laugh— out of relief or desperation, she wasn't sure. But a crack was forming in her façade, one she couldn't patch up, and despite the burn from the light that trickled through and incinerated the shadows it touched, she wasn't sure she wanted to try.

So Anaís sat, allowing Olia's words to sink in, adding weight to what Simone had told her. There was no logic for her to cling to, not with the mystery of nanouk'tou, the sacrificial love Balendin had shown her, the trust Olia placed in her, or the strength Simone gave her. Logic, planning, calculation—somehow, none of it seemed to matter. The truth said she was here for a reason, loved for a reason, not alone for a reason. She had to believe that.

"I'm not a mind reader—this isn't some sort of magic," Olia continued, nudging Anaís's shoulder and adding courage to her train of thought. "So tell me, why are you here?"

Anaís let out a long breath, settling her weight onto her hands as she leaned back on the rock. Her eyes drifted closed as a sense of peace, of certainty filled her. It was time she stopped fighting. "How do you know—"

A rock ricocheted off a spire, and Anaís jolted forward, looking into the darkness. Olia tensed next to her, but began to relax the longer silence stretched.

"It is probably just a nuknuk," Olia whispered.

Anaís shook her head, squinting as she tried to make out shape in the shadows. Darkness billowed and twisted, like a shredded cloak fluttering in the wind. It coalesced around a form—man yet inhuman, physical yet immaterial. The creature should not have existed, yet it watched her with obsidian eyes not even moonlight dared touch.

"Were you followed?" Anaís breathed, her voice intertwining with the breeze.

"No," Olia whispered. "The village is a half day's walk from here."

Anaís swallowed, not daring to take her eyes off the creature hidden amongst the rock formations. How much of their conversation had it heard? "Do you see it?" she asked.

"No."

The blood froze in Anaís's veins. "Ten o'clock." Her lips barely moved. "Between the two formations."

A sharp intake of breath was the only confirmation Olia had seen it.

Cool metal settled into her hands as Anaís slid her daggers free. If the creature *was* corporeal, she could kill it, regardless of whether or not she knew what *it* was. The edge of the creature's mouth curved into a lopsided grin, its once-smooth skin splitting as it stretched until strips of deep-grey flesh seemed to peel from its skeleton. Blackened smoke and ichor oozed from the cracks. Anaís gagged. The creature disappeared.

A scream pierced through the night as Olia slammed to the ground. Anaís whirled, watching in horror while the creature dragged Olia through the dirt, the skin of its face unblemished as if nothing had happened.

Simone was wrong, Anaís thought numbly. *Conspiracies are the least of our problems.*

Another scream broke Anaís out of her trance. Her eyes locked with the creature's blackened stare. She didn't think—she charged. The creature dropped Olia, disappearing when Anaís sliced a dagger through where its chest had been. Momentum carried her forward, and she stumbled, catching herself against a rocky spire. Before she could right herself, a bony finger tapped her shoulder. Anaís threw her elbow back. A sickening crack sounded, followed by a grunt. She whirled around, only to be met with empty space between her and a wide-eyed Olia sat a few meters away. Olia's eyes grew wider when she looked up.

"Behind!"

Anaís scrambled forward as the creature slammed to the ground where she had stood moments before. Spinning, she raised her daggers again. The creature lurched forward, eyes glinting when Anaís jerked back. It was playing with her, she realized. *I could kill you*, it seemed to say. *But this is more fun.*

In the blink of an eye, the creature disappeared, then reappeared in front of her. Anaís stumbled back. Stumbled again when it shoved her. It made to shove her again, but Anaís twisted out of the way with a yell and ripped her dagger up its chest. Warm, viscous ichor spurted across her skin. The echo of the creature's scream hung in the air as it vanished again.

Anaís's chest heaved. Dirt shifted behind her, and she whirled, coming face to face with a trembling Olia.

"Back-to-back," Anaís rasped, pressing the clean dagger into Olia's hand.

The woman nodded. Anaís turned, dropping into a fighting stance as she stared into the night. Her heart thumped erratically. Five beats. Ten. She forced herself to inhale through her nose. Exhale through her mouth. Pushing fear of the unknown aside to allow the anticipation of battle to sharpen her focus.

Shadows writhed above a spire, knitting together to form the creature once more. Moonlight washed its unmarred form in silver light, making the creature look as if it was made from smoke rather than darkness itself. Even from such a distance, Anaís could tell it was watching her with a smug expression. She flexed her fingers against her dagger, but the creature simply bowed its head. Its body seemed to decompose before her eyes. It deformed into shadow, then disappeared.

A swathe of darkness passed in front of her, and she jolted, raising her dagger to attack, but it dissipated into the night with the creature. The arm that had once been covered in ichor was now clean.

A minute passed. Then another. Neither she nor Olia dared to move. Dared to breathe.

"Is it gone?" Olia broke the silence with a whisper.

"I think so," Anaís said, turning around to face her mentor. Scrapes covered her hands and the side of her face. Her dark blue cloak had bits of rock stuck to the fabric. "Are you all right?"

Olia nodded, passing the dagger back to Anaís. "I am fine. You?"

"Fine," Anaís replied absentmindedly as she tucked the daggers into their sheaths and turned in a slow circle to survey her surroundings. The creature had well and truly disappeared. The only sign of its appearance were the scuff marks in the dirt where Olia had been dragged and where Anaís had tried to fight.

"What was that?" Anaís asked, facing Olia once more.

Olia shook her head. "I do not know. I..." She trailed off, scrubbing a hand across her face. She stopped with a hiss when she brushed the scrapes on her cheek. "What were you going to ask me? Right before the creature came?"

"And tempt it to return?" Anaís laughed incredulously. "I think not."

Olia slumped to the ground, picking bits of gravel out of one of the deeper scrapes on her hand. Anaís frowned, then knelt before her, taking Olia's hand in her own to clean the wound.

"We either operate on the assumption that it wanted this information," Olia said, "or that it wanted to stop you from receiving whatever knowledge I have."

"And if it's both?"

"Then we can do nothing. I would like to give you answers, though. Perhaps they will remind you of something. Help us fight against whatever that creature was."

"I doubt it," Anaís mumbled, then sighed through her nose.

A book in the library of the Nahonan palace might have information. She wouldn't have access to it if she didn't talk to Eoghan, and she didn't want to talk to him until she knew what tied them together. Though the prospect of that was…daunting, given what Olia had described.

Anaís removed the last bit of gravel from Olia's hand. "You'll want to wash that when you get home," she said, then tore a strip of fabric from the hem of her cloak to loosely wrap the wound.

Olia nodded in thanks, but remained silent as if waiting for Anaís to fill the space between them.

Anaís scuffed the ground with her boot. "How do you know if you have this…nanouk'tou?" The word felt unfamiliar on her tongue. Unfamiliar, but right.

Olia smiled up at her. "What does it feel like for you?"

Anaís had thought her way through this so many times she no longer knew how to describe the sensation. It was like being torn apart and stitched together again. The warmth and comfort of being known, only tainted by betrayal, death, and a slow descent into insanity. Rationality could no longer distinguish what was real and what was fabricated by dreams. All she knew was that in her heart—whatever was happening—it *was* real. If she couldn't trust that, what else did she have?

"Confusing." It was all Anaís could think to say. The phantom sensation of the thread tethering her to Eoghan tugged gently at her heart. "And painful," she added. "Painful, but soft."

"Confusing and painfully soft," Olia replied.

Anaís made to object, but shut her mouth when she noticed Olia's knowing expression. That was an adept way to describe it, she supposed.

"Have you met them?" Olia asked. "You cannot change who your nanouk'tou is, nor can you get rid of what ties you together—the soul knows before the mind does. But it can be helpful if you have met them in person. Even in passing."

Anaís chewed on the inside of her cheek, embarrassment and shame rising within her. "I was sent to kill him."

Olia raised her brow. "And?"

"I couldn't do it."

Olia nodded slowly, then asked, "Did you want to?"

"Yes," Anaís whispered. "And no. I would have killed him if it had not stopped me. But it did, and I've never been so grateful for anything in my life." She let out an incredulous laugh. "I've never hated something so much in my life."

Olia released a breath and leaned forward, resting her elbows on her knees. "Nanouk'tou can be a confusing thing. Even more so when court politics try to meddle. Balendin and I didn't have that, and I still tried to thwart him at every turn for five years before relenting and seeing where it lead."

Anaís couldn't imagine anyone not wanting to work with Balendin, though her stubbornness against seeing Eoghan again put that into perspective. The plot of one of Simone's fantasy novels came unbidden to her mind, and Anaís winced at the thought. "It's not like soulmates, is it?" she asked.

"No," Olia scoffed, then composed herself. "This is destiny bringing you together for something bigger than yourself—two paths intertwined as you forge ahead, working in tandem as you bear the yoke of this journey together. For Balendin and I, that was teaching you all we knew. We didn't know why, but it was where our path brought us."

Anaís nodded, reflecting on the time she and Eoghan spent together, limited though it may have been. He did complement her—the calm to her storm, the eloquence to her analytical mind. Where they had not complemented one another was in battle. Though they were trained in different forms of combat, his deadly grace matched her own—both strong and swift in their own rights. Each an immovable force against the other. But if they were to fight as one? Heat bloomed across her cheeks at the thought of exploring that idea further.

Stars above, she *liked* him, didn't she?

"Did you fall in love?" The question escaped before Anaís could stop it. She pressed her hands to her cheeks to cool the burning, quickly dropping them when Olia gave her a strange look.

"It is hard to not care deeply for someone you get to know so intimately." Olia heaved a sigh. "Yes, we did. But love is not simply passion. Love is trust. Love is respect. Love is patient and kind and giving. It does not waver under pressure, it grows. It is a choice. Just as you have a choice to follow where nanouk'tou takes you. You don't have to like him or be friends with him, but do not be afraid of where it might lead. Do not be afraid of the one you journey with. Sometimes what we want the most and what we want the least can coincide in what we need."

"Simone wants me to talk to him," Anaís said. "I do want to talk to him, but..." In this case, it didn't matter what she wanted. She had almost killed him; she *had* succeeded in killing Lochlan. If she were in Eoghan's position, she would want her would-be assassin's body to be headless and bloated with the rot of death the next time she saw it. No, he would not *want* to talk to her.

He wants to talk to you, Simone's voice whispered in her mind.

"The most powerful things we can say are the words left unsaid." Anaís jumped at the sound of Olia's voice. She didn't realize she had spoken her musings aloud. "Take away the power of silence," Olia continued. "I encourage you to talk to him. I think you'll be surprised with what you find."

Perhaps not fighting did not mean giving up. It meant fighting for something greater than herself. A strange mixture of resolve and resignation settled in Anaís's core. "I will speak with him."

A satisfied smile curved Olia's lips. "Good. I will return to Qotiu. There are preparations I must make."

"Preparations for what?"

"I'm not sure yet, but I will send word when I know." Olia gave Anaís's arm a parting squeeze, then turned to leave. "Stay alert," she called over her shoulder.

"Wait!" Anaís unsheathed a dagger and held it out for Olia. "In case it returns. You shouldn't travel unarmed."

Olia shook her head, but accepted the dagger nonetheless. "I am not sure it would do much good—I'm humbled but not surprised to see that the apprentice has outranked the master. I *am* proud of you, Anaís. I know Balendin would be too."

Then Olia turned, disappearing into the shadows of the badlands as swiftly as she had come.

DAWN LIGHT CREATED A HAZY blur over the horizon, like evaporating dew on a warm morning. It was a mesmerizing sight, one Anaís wished she could appreciate without the blister forming on her right heel and the ache of healing wounds on her back. Each step toward the hannokry sent a throbbing pain through her foot, likely from wearing the wrong socks—she hadn't expected to walk as far as she did, nor had she expected to fight a corporeal ghost.

A shiver trailed down her spine. It was made of darkness itself, yet it fought her. The strike through its chest should have felled the beast, yet it had re-formed as if nothing had happened. And then it had left.

That was the part that confused her the most.

Anaís shook her head clear of the thoughts. She could worry about that later; for now, she needed to focus on the letter she was about to send.

The wooden door groaned against its hinges when she pushed it open. Dim light from the transitioning sky illuminated the edges of the room through windows cut into the domed ceiling above. Soft rustling greeted her as some hannok shifted to see what created the disturbance. Others, already awake with the break of dawn, drifted from rafter to rafter, their powerful wings spreading and snapping shut to maneuver around the space with precision.

Crossing the room, Anaís slipped into the hannok keeper's office and carefully sorted through the contents of his desk, selecting a sheet of parchment and a quill with an ink pot. Blank paper stared up at her, full of opportunity—missed and seized alike. Anaís stared back, sucked in a breath, and began working.

The quill slid into its stand with a satisfied clink. Anaís leaned back, looking at the letter she'd crafted with equal sentiment. She was no words-woman, but she had a feeling Eoghan would appreciate the effort. At least, she hoped he would. Anaís squinted at her handiwork, then signed it "Iladana Madéa." It was too simple a code, but she wasn't sure how else to tell Eoghan it was her. It looked enough like a name to avoid suspicion should her letter be intercepted, unlikely as it was.

Shrugging, Anaís tested the ink to make sure it was dry, then rolled it into a cylinder and tucked it into a wooden mailing tube, sealing the ends with wax. She returned the quill and ink pot to their rightful places, then slipped back into the hannokry and shut the door to the office behind her.

A soft golden glow filled the space, more hannok awake than asleep now that the sun had crested the horizon. Several watched her, heads cocked with curiosity and anticipation as they awaited her call. Anaís removed a sturdy leather glove from a hook on the wall, pulling it over her hand to cover just past her elbow. Scanning the rafters, she licked her lips, then gave three sharp trills and a low whistle that lilted at the end. A flurry of sound filled the air, hannok moving aside as the summoned raptor swooped from the rafters, talons stretched, wings pumping to alight gracefully on Anaís's outstretched arm.

With warm brown feathers that seemed to glitter like sand in the sunlight and talons that could shred skin more smoothly than a hot knife through butter, Simone's hannok was a beautiful creature. Keen grey eyes blinked at her, then Émi trilled and softly headbutted Anaís's arm.

Anaís ran a finger down the bird's neck, smoothing the feathers there. "I've missed you too. I have an errand for you."

Émi trilled two duplets and a triplet—the coordinates to the parliament building in Freydlan. Given the preparations with Counselor Trijveson as intermediary during the negotiations, it was where she was used to delivering letters.

"Not quite," Anaís smiled. This would be difficult, relaying both the location and Eoghan's status as the only person allowed to receive the letter. The technique took years to learn and more still to master, but the results were nearly foolproof. Nearly.

Wetting her lips again, Anaís sucked in a breath, then began her whistled song. Émi's stare seemed to pierce into her soul as she memorized the melody—the lilting highs and breathy lows weaving together as the song of coordinates took shape. The final note lingered in the air before dissipating into silence. Several hannok shifted nervously on their perch, as if relieved to have not been called to such a specific request. Émi simply blinked at Anaís, then relayed the song back to her with perfect precision.

Anaís clicked her tongue twice in confirmation, then raised her arm to send Émi on her way. The moment she disappeared through the window above, a new hannok took Émi's place on her arm, regarding Anaís with a disgruntled squint.

"Don't tell me that simple request ruffled your feathers," Anaís laughed.

Her own hannok—Eshari—puffed her chest and flared her wings, dichromatic feathers glinting brown and grey as she settled comfortably onto Anaís's arm.

"It would be too dangerous to send you," Anaís whispered. "The king already had you watched closely, but now? After what I've done?" she shook her head. "Émi has already delivered a message or two to Nahonaugh for the negotiations. Seeing her wouldn't be unexpected. Having her missing wouldn't be unexpected. But you?" Anaís ran a gentle finger down Eshari's back, smiling as the hannok tucked her beak to her chest to nap. "You're such a nuknuk! You only wanted attention, didn't you?"

Eshari cracked a grey eye open to glare at her.

"Come along then," Anaís sighed. "It has been too long since I've taken you out for drills."

Retrieving a kite and a small leather pouch filled with dried meat, Anaís opened the door and stepped out into the early morning sun, following the meandering trail that took her through the gardens that connected to the training field. There was a more direct route, but with the way Eshari settled deeper onto her arm and the tender warmth of the sun as it kissed the earth, Anaís wasn't inclined to rush what held the promise for a good day.

Cyprus trees swayed in the dry morning breeze, lavender and jasmine perfumed the air, and for the first time in a long time, Anaís found herself enjoying her home. It would never be lush and green like Nahonaugh, but there was something inspiring about nature's rugged beauty not only persevering, but thriving in this harsh climate. For years, she could only see herself within the desolation of her desert home. Now she felt a kinship with the hardiness of the life that grew in spite of it. Strange, how a change in perspective could so dramatically alter her perception.

The path carried Anaís along the eastern wing of the palace. Sun danced along the rippled glass of the windows as she passed by. From her periphery, a shadow shifted behind a glint of light. A chill erupted across her skin. Anaís stumbled to a stop. Eshari released a startled squawk.

The creature was back. In her home.

Anger melted away the iciness of fear, and she whirled on the figure, free hand reaching for her dagger. The creature cast a sideways glance at her, then stepped backward, melting into the shadows around it. Its absence revealed a scene that brought more confusion than clarity.

A blond-haired man sat across from King Timun. He was middle-aged, with a harshness about him that rivalled her father's own disposition. King Timun nodded at something the stranger said, then scrawled a note onto a sheet of parchment and slid it to the man.

Heart pounding in her ears, Anaís crept behind a cypress near the window, straining to catch what she could of their conversation. Perhaps it was a harmless meeting. Perhaps they couldn't see the creature in their midst.

The blond man looked up from the parchment. "You are aware of the repercussions?"

"I have a contingency plan in place." Her father shrugged. "From my perspective, there are no repercussions."

"Good, then it's settled. We're ready and stationed here"—paper rustled—"about a day's march southwest of the quarter point. I expect your warriors to arrive in short order?"

Anaís frowned. The quarter point? That was a region in the south where the borders of all four kingdoms came close to intersecting—one could walk in a circle from Kiivjachim to Freydlan to Nahonaugh to Dúndíor in about a day. What was their interest in that region? Unless...

"You can expect one company of warriors in four weeks' time," King Timun replied.

Unless he was planning to strike Nahonaugh from two fronts.

The blond scoffed. "One? That is not—"

"You requested my expertise, did you not?" King Timun interrupted. "I've seen what your shadow wraiths do. Trust my plans as I've trusted yours."

Anaís's blood ran cold. Her father knew of the creatures. The stranger *controlled* the creatures.

"You must hold to your end of the deal," the blond snapped.

King Timun laughed sharply. "Oh, you sorry sod, what do you think I've been doing these past ten years? No." His voice sobered. "I will send who I deem necessary, and they will arrive in four weeks. As for the Anadali, they are needed elsewhere. The Amadé has caused more trouble than she is worth."

"You're too soft when it comes to her."

A dangerous silence fell between the two men. Anaís shifted forward. When King Timun spoke again, his voice was steeped in anger. "Do not," King Timun whispered, "question my methods."

Anaís leaned back slowly. A twig snapped underfoot. She froze, Eshari shifting nervously on her arm.

A muffled curse came from inside the room, followed by the scraping of a chair. King Timun moved to the window, lips drawn together in a thin, emotionless line. Anaís shifted farther behind the tree, leaning against it for support as the king scanned the garden before drawing the curtains shut with a swift snap.

Eshari nudged her shoulder. Anaís straightened her spine. How deep were these secrets buried? Takaniim. The creature. The stranger. And now whatever the king was planning with them. She had four weeks to figure it out.

Composing herself, she turned on her heel. Fear would not solve her problems.

"Come along," Anaís whispered to Eshari. "We have work to do."

If the king did not have the gall to execute her properly, he deserved the annoyance of suffering her existence.

CHAPTER THIRTY-SEVEN

ALLEGIANCE OF PAWNS

EOGHAN SLUMPED AGAINST THE DESK IN HIS STUDY, forehead resting against the cool hardwood as he tried to let the tension seep out of him. It only made his headache worse.

A sigh escaped his lips, and he sat up, pushing his hands through his hair as he stared at the unfinished letter before him. Nearly two weeks had passed since Simone had left. Two weeks filled with paperwork, smoothing over the last of the unrest, and trying to figure out how to contact Anaís without breaking the peace treaty and sending their kingdoms into all-out war.

There were no rules preventing him from contacting his would-be assassin, but it seemed prudent to tread lightly. Politics had the habit of turning a light breeze into a hurricane, after all. Even so, what was he to say? His hearth was filled with burnt remnants of penned desperation, halfhearted threats, and a singular poem written during a bout of sleep-deprived delirium.

He crumpled the current letter he was working on, grumbling when ink smeared across his skin. At least his writing would be extra-illegible now. Eoghan leaned back in his chair, front legs tipping off the ground as he lined up his shot to the hearth. The paper flew through the air, a sharp tap against his window broke the quiet of the room, his chair slipped, Eoghan shrieked...

Cold flooring pressed against the back of Eoghan's skull, doing absolutely nothing to ease the throbbing in his head as he stared at the ceiling. Groaning, he rolled to his side, feet flopping unceremoniously onto the floor. He pushed himself up to ensure his discarded letter had made it into the fire—it had.

Another series of taps sounded at the window.

"What?" Eoghan snapped, turning around only to jump out of his skin at the sight of a *massive* bird of prey perched on the windowsill.

The hannok—it looked like a hannok—trilled lightly before tapping on the glass again. Eoghan stared, dumbfounded. The hannok stared back, had the audacity to deflate as if sighing in exasperation, then lifted a razor-sharp talon with a mailing tube tied around its ankle.

"Right. Of course. Right." Eoghan unlocked the window and swung it open, wincing when his wrist protested the movement. At least it—not his head—had caught the brunt of his fall.

The hannok whistled happily, powerful wings flaring as it landed deftly on his desk. It tilted its head at him, then gave an encouraging trill.

"All right," Eoghan said, tentatively reaching out to untie the tube from its ankle. "Please don't bite me."

Normally courier animals went directly to the parcel reception room. Why this one had chosen to come here directly was beyond him, but such creatures rarely misdelivered mail. Or so he was told.

Fetching a sharp letter opener from a drawer, Eoghan scored the hardened wax and eased the cap off the tube, allowing the parchment within to fall onto the desk. The hannok hopped backward, then eyed the scroll with interest. He unrolled it and stilled, drinking in the neatly inked sketch with equal parts need and confusion.

"Iladana Madéa," Eoghan said aloud, letting the name roll off his tongue. It felt familiar yet wrong, as if someone had used salt instead of sugar to bake his favorite cake. He squinted at the letters, trying to separate them out until they made some semblance of sense. "Iladana," he said again, slowly this time, letting each syllable linger as if he could discover the meaning by taste alone. Tilting his head at the parchment, Eoghan blinked, then laughed as realization hit him—a backward scramble.

Iladana Madéa. Anadali Amadé.

He ran his thumb absently across the parchment's textured surface, scanning the drawing with new perspective until the meaning etched itself into his mind.

"This is real," he whispered to himself. "We're meeting. In one week."

Eoghan bowed his head as a wave of emotion washed over him. Hope rising, trepidation sinking, and an unidentifiable feeling twisting deep within his heart as the two clashed. He pressed the heel of his palm to his sternum in an attempt to ease the pressure.

The hannok trilled softly, then hopped forward and gave his arm a gentle nudge with its head.

"If I send you back with a reply, will you take it directly to her?" Eoghan asked, dropping his hand back to the desk. It seemed ridiculous to talk to a hannok, but with the way it watched him with keen grey eyes, he couldn't help but feel as if the raptor *knew* it was in the process of shaping history.

45°25'S 167°43'E
Seven days from receipt. Sunrise.

Hadana Madea

"You know what? It's fine I—" Eoghan gripped the edge of the desk, then released it as he came to a decision. "No, I'll be vague," he muttered, tearing a strip off the parchment Anaís had sent him.

"Confirmed," he wrote, then looked up at the hannok with a frown. "Is that too ominous?"

The hannok huffed and stuck its talon out.

"No, you're right. I'm overthinking this." Eoghan tucked the note into the mailing tube and slid the cap on. Crossing the room, he rotated the tube over the flames in the hearth, allowing the heat to melt the wax and seal the tube shut. He removed it from the fire and blew on it before returning to the hannok's side. "You're sure you will take it to her?"

The hannok bobbed its head solemnly.

"All right." Eoghan tied the tube around its ankle, then backed away as the hannok spread its wings and shot out the window. He watched the raptor soar off and disappear behind the mountains, then whispered to himself, "What am I doing?"

Nature grew claws this far east. Rather than dense forests of evergreens that surrounded Eoghan's home, the flora bordering Dúndíor was an odd mix of spiny desert trees and sturdy oaks. Tussock grass and the occasional cluster of flowering shrubs softened the jagged hills that poked out at intervals like teeth, but nothing could camouflage the craggy gorge that dropped to the river below.

That was where Eoghan found himself just as the sun began to illuminate the desert sky in a veil of dusty rose and violet—traversing down the steep slope of a cliff face toward the maw of the roaring waterfall below. If he slipped, he would die. Even if he made it to the base of the waterfall, he still had to figure out how to cross the river—and hopefully not slip and die—before making his way into the shelter of the cave by the river. A fine place to meet, so long as it didn't fill with water. Which would drown him. And then he would die.

A long sigh rushed past his lips as he inched down the rope he had secured to a boulder above, slowly making his way toward his destination. A wrap braced the ligaments in his wrist—which he had merely sprained, not broken—though it certainly wasn't happy about the climb.

Finally reaching solid ground, Eoghan shook out his arms before picking his way along the lower riverbank. Rock walls towered above him and cast the gorge into darkness despite the steadily lightening sky, inviting the chill of night to overstay its welcome. The cave itself rested across the wide expanse of river which, now that Eoghan was closer, looked more like a restless lake than anything else. Mesmerizing as it was, the river's girth also meant there was no way for him to cross and remain dry. Sighing, he positioned himself so the current would do most of the work, waded into the water, and swam toward his fate.

The meeting place was less of a cave than an overhang sheltering an outcropping of boulders jutting out of the river. Disgruntled and dripping wet, Eoghan sat himself on a boulder smoothed by erosion and time. While the water wasn't very choppy near the alcove, the river upstream raged, spurred on by the roar of the falls loud enough to drown out a conversation to any passersby. Not that he suspected there would be many of those.

He could see now why Anaís wanted to meet here. It was open yet secluded, neutral territory for the both of them. While he was sure she wasn't one for poetic symbolism, there was a peace amidst the chaos. A foreshadowing of what was to come, or so he hoped.

He was tired of the murkiness of his own thoughts, swirling round and round as they stirred what was once clear resolve into a hazy pool of doubt and uncertainty. He could not piece her together—not as the woman he met at the palace what felt like lifetimes ago. Not as the assassin who came for him in the dark of night. No, what eluded his grasp was *her*—the woman behind the title. The woman who plagued his dreams, whose eyes had pierced his soul when they met his for the first time. He'd thought he understood her motives. The day he'd received her letter, he thought he was ready for the truth.

Now he wasn't so sure.

Eoghan ran his fingers gently along the scar that she had carved into his skin. "This entire situation is a mess," he mumbled.

Rustling pulled him out of his thoughts, and he looked in the direction of the sound, giving Anaís a brief nod when she broke through the underbrush and started making her way up the river to where he sat. At least she had the foresight to descend the proper side of the gorge to avoid a swim in the river.

Eoghan turned back around and tried to steady his nerves. *This meeting is going to change everything.* He took in a breath of the fresh morning air and held it before slowly letting it out again. *It has to.*

A yelp and a splash had him whipping around, the momentum almost throwing him off the boulder.

"Anaís?" Eoghan whispered, pressing a hand against the rock to steady himself. The only indication that anyone had been there were concentric ripples marring the flow of the water. Frowning, he rose slowly and crept forward. "Anadali, are you there?"

Nervous anticipation hung in the air as he scanned for any signs of life. A bird chirped, then fluttered away with a squawk when a hand shot out of the water and slapped against the boulder, looking for purchase. Anaís's head popped up shortly after. She pulled her body onto dry land and rolled over, limbs splayed.

So much for avoiding the river.

The concerned frown on Eoghan's face softened into a look of amusement. "Have a good swim?" he asked in Dúndían. It felt right, given it was the first language they'd used when they met...and given what had happened the last time they'd spoken in Nahraeg.

"That is a lot deeper than it looks." She scowled, chest heaving as she tried to catch her breath. "You will speak nothing of this."

"You went down so fast I didn't see anything to speak of."

Anaís propped herself up on her elbow, using her free hand to push her drenched hair off her face. "Anadali Amadé, bested by a slippery rock."

"A formidable adversary, I'm sure."

"You'd better take this secret with you to the grave."

"Oh, I'll cherish this memory for the rest of my days." Eoghan reached his hand out for her to take.

Anaís sent him another glare, but he could see her trying to fight off a smile.

In a moment of weakness, Eoghan allowed himself to study her. Her lips held the same thoughtful curve as the woman he knew. Her words carried the same fiery wit that warmed him from the inside out. The tantalizing mix of golds and browns and greens in her eyes still held the secrets of his soul. Yet there was something about her posture—a defiant confidence he had never noticed before, tied down by a burden he could not name.

She was the same, yet she had changed. He was the same, yet he had changed. Could those altered pieces find reconciliation, or were they too damaged to ever fit again? There was only one way to find out.

"Come on." He wiggled his fingers at her. "We have much to discuss."

Her hand clasped his forearm, and an electric pulse flooded his body, chasing away the lingering chill of his river-soaked skin. He jerked back, surprised, hauling her up with a force that sent her careening into his chest.

"Sorry," Eoghan breathed, gripping her shoulder to steady her. He wanted to take a step back, put distance between them, but he couldn't bring himself to move. She was so close. Too close. Not close enough.

"Thank you, Your Highness." Her breath tickled his skin.

Eoghan released her, forcing himself to step away, trying to smile lightly as if his reality had not been fundamentally altered in the span of a heartbeat. "How many times do I have to ask you to call me Eoghan?"

"Perhaps once more, Your Highness."

Anaís dropped her gaze and brushed past Eoghan, a flurry of sparks tickling his arm with the contact. Making her way to the edge of the boulder, Anaís lowered herself to where he had been sitting before she had fallen into the water. His eyes lingered on her as she laid her cloak and boots out to dry before opening her knapsack to check the contents. Her soaked shirt clung to her back while she moved, emphasizing the graceful strength hidden beneath.

Eoghan sucked in a breath and looked away. *Focus, Eoghan*, he chided. His buried feelings for her didn't matter. Not until he knew—

"Are you coming?" Anaís asked, glancing over her shoulder.

Eoghan grunted in reply, focusing instead on his feet as he crossed the water-slick boulder and sat next to Anaís.

A damp but legible map was spread out before her, notes scrawled across it in what he now recognized as her handwriting. She glanced at him again before staring intently at the map. A heavy silence hung between them, though it did little to weigh down the anxiety rising within him. What was he supposed to say? *From the moment I laid eyes on you, I knew you would be the death of me, but I didn't think you would take it quite so literally.*

The elusive thread that tied them together gave a subtle tug, winding tighter as Anaís seemed to fortify her walls in the silence. He wanted to reach out and unravel her until there was nothing separating them. He craved her candor, the easy way with which they had been able to speak before that night. He did not want the stifling heaviness of whatever *this* was.

"Thank you for meeting with me," Anaís said, startling Eoghan out of his thoughts.

He replied with the first thing that came to mind. "Princess Simone did suggest we talk."

She sighed and tipped her head back to the sky as if begging for patience. "Of course she did."

"Don't worry, she didn't mention anything too incriminating. Besides, security has gone up since you tried to assassinate me." He clamped his mouth shut, glancing at Anaís. That was too bold, but he was too on edge to filter his thoughts as he normally would. Her expression remained impassive, the neutrality of it only serving to intensify the sting in his heart. Perhaps he had misinterpreted the princess's vague hints. Maybe coming away with his life was a fluke and the connection he thought they had was simply a one-sided figment of his imagination.

Anaís nodded, the movement shaking free a hint of emotion—anguish. "That is understandable." She rolled a stick of charcoal between her fingers as if gathering her thoughts. "Simone and I have come to the conclusion that there are forces at work—ones we have not been able to identify, but have enough evidence to suggest that they are manipulating foreign and domestic policies. A recent excursion has enlightened me to some new developments that I believe to be pertinent to the safety of both our kingdoms. Which is why I wanted to speak with you. To determine our next steps. Among other things..."

She trailed off, biting the inside of her cheek.

Eoghan stared over the water, allowing her self-inflicted silence to linger uncomfortably. He hadn't mentioned any of his suspicions to Simone regarding the curious incidents both himself and Cian had experienced, but he had a feeling that what Anaís was alluding to was similar in nature. If not an extension of it. Shadows that moved, fog that could enter different realms. It must be spreading, but why?

"What exactly were you enlightened of?" Eoghan asked. "If our kingdoms are in danger as you suggest, I need to know what we're facing."

"I fought a corporeal ghost in the badlands of Qotiu."

At least her candor had not completely disappeared. Eoghan raised his brow as if to say "Elaborate, please."

Anaís glanced at him. "It's exactly as it sounds. A shadow appeared like a blot of ink in water, but rather than dissipating it formed this...*creature*. It attacked. I fought it."

Now that was a new development. Cian had never mentioned any of the shadows anthropomorphizing. Though he did say they watched. And there was that...thing...the fog had shown him on the mountainside. "Did you kill it?"

"I ripped my blade up its chest, and the creature knit itself together again. So, no. I don't think it *can* be killed."

Though the morning sun now spilled rays of warmth into the gorge where they sat, a chill crept down Eoghan's spine. He pressed his hand against the scar she had given him.

"Long ago," Anaís said, her voice barely rising above the rumble of the waterfall, "when Nythmaar was a continent defined not by borders, but by the tribes of her peoples, a lake by the name of Takaniim blessed the lands with life-giving water. According to legend, it disappeared, taking with it the fate of Nythmaar itself. Tribes fell, empires rose, and a new era was born. The era we live in today. Prior to leaving for the diplomatic negotiations, my father gave me a task—find any information I could gather regarding the waters of Takaniim, record it, and bring it to him."

"All of that information is restricted." Eoghan frowned, then inhaled sharply as realization dawned on him. "That was you!"

Anaís turned her head with a force that sent her braid whipping around her with a wet *snap*, wide eyes meeting his own. "How did you know someone was there?" she demanded, though her question held a curious lilt of anticipation.

"Would you believe me if I said I felt compelled to be there?"

"I don't know." Anaís held his gaze as if searching for something before glancing away. "Hours after fighting the creature, I witnessed my father and a foreign man discussing what sounded like troop movements. The creature was present. I can only conclude that all of this is interconnected—his request for Takaniim, the appearance of the creature, whatever he is planning." She hesitated, before adding in a whisper, "You."

The severity of her implications stilled Eoghan's heart. "Troop movements where?" he asked cautiously.

"Southwest of the quarter point. They didn't discuss their plans outright. At first I thought they might march on Nahonaugh, but now I'm not so sure. Just before the first negotiations, my father as good as told me he didn't want war against Nahonaugh but was striving for something bigger." Anaís shook her head, looking nearly as lost as Eoghan felt. "In three weeks' time, he's sending a company of warriors to add to the stranger's ranks." She ran her fingers along a ridge on the boulder before adding, "The stranger also commands the creatures. Shadow wraiths, I think they're called."

Eoghan leaned back on his hands, watching the water rush by. How he wished it would sweep away these problems too. "We prepare for battle, then."

"Given the relationship between our kingdoms, you should already be prepared." Anaís gave him a sidelong glance. "But none of that matters if we try to fight something that does not die. That's my first order of business—find out exactly what King Timun is planning and how to stop him."

Nahonaugh *was* prepared for war, though it felt childish to argue the point. She was right: there was no sense in sending men to fight a lost battle. Eoghan tipped his chin at the map. "I assume you're going out there. You'll need backup."

"I'll bring a select few of my Anadali with me."

"I'm coming."

"You're a civilian." She glared at him. "I'm not bringing you into what could become an active war zone."

"I've been sucked into different realms, trailed by sentient fog, stalked by shadow creatures, and almost killed because my death apparently supports King Timun's plans that may or may not involve the destruction of my kingdom." He glared back at her. "I. Am. Coming."

Anaís pressed her lips together but gave a curt nod. "Can you fight?"

"You tell me." Eoghan retorted.

The thread between them gave a soft tug. Anaís sucked in a breath. Eoghan stilled. But then she shifted, pulling the map toward her, and the sensation left as quickly as it came. Surely he hadn't imagined it. Had he?

Anaís cleared her throat, drawing his attention back to her. "As for these unkillable creatures and Takaniim, the tracker you shackled me with during the negotiations gave me some ideas. As did a lesson Balendin once taught me." She smoothed out the crinkles in the map and sketched a spiderweb of lines along the parchment. "Ni'ika is an ancient star cluster that forms the keel of a ship. It was said that when Toutahi aligned with Atti, mariners saw it as a time for favorable sailing because it was a sign for still waters. This is the closest allusion to the idea of Takaniim—it was known for its placid waters, said to reflect the heavens themselves. These two stars will align again in about three weeks' time, intersecting here, over Tāpepe Takakou na Uul on the outskirts of the quarter point." She circled the location and sat back, gesturing for Eoghan to look at the map.

The Unknown Jungles of Uul. He leaned forward, eyes tracing across the stars overlaying the topographical expanse of the Kingdom of Kiivjachim.

"Warriors converging at the quarter point in three weeks," Eoghan said softly. "This alignment in three weeks." He glanced at her, then at the map. "We try to learn their plans, figure out how to kill these creatures, devise a counterattack..." he trailed off. "I can almost guarantee you there is no coincidence in this timing."

"I'm counting on it." She smiled grimly. "Whatever we find won't be pleasant, but I would expect nothing less from the enemy we're facing. King Timun may have his plans, but these are creatures of myth—they'll have their own. Systematically scouting the region during the stars' alignment should give us a heading, as well as additional time to prepare before the warriors arrive—though I suspect they will be the least of our worries. It's the creatures and what they want with Takaniim that I'm concerned about."

Anaís rolled the charcoal stick between her fingers, considering. Finally, she said, "I propose we start here, on the Dúndían side of the border, in two weeks." She shifted to mark the map, and the sleeve of her shirt slipped off her shoulder, revealing puckered skin that curved up her back, tapering to a thin scar around the side of her neck.

Eoghan's breath caught in his throat; everything else she said drowned out by an onslaught of memories.

What did you do to my sister? Princess Simone's voice howled in his mind. *Do you know what that cost her?*

He never stopped to think about what the consequences were for her. He had assumed his attempted assassination was a sick joke—a way for some unseen power to taunt him with the harsh reality that his life could be over in an instant. Or not. All someone had to do was give the order.

Eoghan hadn't paused to consider that maybe the order *had* been given to end his life, but someone else came between the decree and the punishment to stop it. No, someone else had taken that punishment *for* him, and she was sitting right next to him.

Perhaps they were never enemies. Perhaps they were simply pawns on opposing sides of a chessboard. Both of them used to further the goals of those above them at their own expense. Both used in a game of strategy that should never have been theirs to play. But in a twist of fate the pawns refused to comply, and now the future hung in the balance.

These plans could wait. This clashing of forces between myth and men could wait, for all he cared. What was the point of setting out to defeat a myth when it felt like fate itself was adamant on breaking him first? He had *promised* himself he would discover the truth, promised himself that when he spoke with Anaís, he would find clarity. He *saw* the tether that night. Felt the tug today. Yet here he was, ignoring the very thing that bonded his soul to another.

Who else would take the place of the one who was meant to die? Who else would be his light when darkness seemed to chase him in the day? He could not move forward, could not work with her, could not do anything until he *knew*.

"Can I ask you something?"

"Sure." Anaís continued drawing on the map as she waited for him to speak.

He took a breath, releasing it slowly through his nose. "Why didn't you kill me?"

Her hand hesitated. "I don't know what you're talking about."

"Anaís," Eoghan said bluntly. Before he could lose courage, he asked in his native tongue, "Please, I need to know."

Because he needed to know everything. Why wasn't he dead? Who was she? Was he not alone?

Her eyes widened ever so slightly as an emotion only his very soul could understand flickered in their depths before she tore her gaze away and looked out over the roaring water.

His mind was reeling, but all he could focus on was the pounding of his heart and the words that drowned out all other thought, singing with the rhythm of each pulse that thrummed in his veins. *I'm not alone, I'm not alone, I'm not alone.*

He turned to face the river in a daze and closed his eyes. Water rushed around them. Wind rustled the trees. Slowly, slowly, the beating of his heart calmed. *I'm not alone... She feels it too...*

Just as he lost hope in hearing a response, she whispered, "You wouldn't understand."

His eyes opened to the coursing water rushing by, bringing with it a sense of clarity. "I fear I may be one of the few who can," he replied in kind. "So please, I need to know. Why am I here?"

Rock scraped beneath Anaís as she shifted to tuck her knees against her chest, like a shield to protect her from what she was about to say.

"When I was young, I killed the Anadali who raised me."

Eoghan's gaze darted to her, but she was still. Staring out over the water. Unseeing. She shook her head, as if trying to chase the memory away. Her fingers curled tighter into the fabric of her trousers, but she remained quiet. Eoghan wasn't sure if he wanted to scream at her or hug her. He settled on a simple question. "Why?"

"The king made me do it... *Had* me do it." She sucked in a breath and released it slowly. "I was fourteen. Balendin couldn't protect the queen, but I was the one who couldn't protect the border. I was the reason Balendin had to protect my mother against anyone at all."

His brows rose. Border...the breach of the treaty. She must have been the one who took down the soldiers. He thought it was just a scuffle, but...why were there Nahonan soldiers at the border at all?

"It was a punishment and a promotion," she continued. "The day I killed Balendin was the day I died. I drowned in it, the blood I shed. And the king, my father, he reformed us—the Anadali. I was too scared to fight back. Too tired."

Eoghan wanted her to stop talking. It was too much for him to process, but he had asked her for the truth and she had lived it.

Stars above, she had lived a nightmare while he'd basked in a gilded cage of ignorance.

"After Balendin's death, Simone and this...comfort. This protector I had in my dreams was all that kept me from succumbing to that darkness." Fabric shifted over the rocks as Anaís turned to face him, the green and gold of her eyes arresting his attention. "It's you. I couldn't kill the man who protected me. I couldn't kill you."

A breath caught in Eoghan's chest as she returned her gaze to the water below. He probably should be saying something, anything, but his thoughts were a hurricane roaring louder than the waterfall that echoed off the steep cliffs surrounding them.

"I'm sorry," she continued, but her voice sounded far away. "About Lochlan. I waited for the guard to leave, I didn't know it was him, but...my cowardice destroyed too many lives that night."

That pulled him out of his thoughts. "Your cowardice?"

"I should have pushed back against my father. Every action has a consequence, but the ones I did and did not take led to a price much higher than I thought I would have to pay. I wanted peace. I caused ruin."

Eoghan shook his head. "You're as bad as Cian, you know. With your guilt. It's hard to fight against someone who is supposed to love you and does everything but." He studied her as the morning sunlight cast gentle shadows over her features and illuminated the frizz of her dried curls in a halo of gold. "I see you."

She turned to look at him, her eyes piercing his own. "What?"

"The colors of your eyes," he said in Nahraeg. "They're the same color as this thread. I used to only see it at night, in dreams. I called the one on the other side my kindred soul." He smiled softly. How little he had known at the time. How little he still knew. "It wasn't until we tried to kill each other that I saw it in a space beyond dreams, connecting me to you. I've had premonitions—visions. The morning you and Simone arrived, I was drawn into a different realm. I thought I was going insane." He let out a breath, a feeling of peace washing over him as he carried on. "It is why I need you to know that I do not blame you for all that happened. To me. To Lochlan. And although I feel a great many things that I have yet to untangle, whatever this is has been my lifeline."

Something shifted in the air between them. The roar of the waterfall was not so angry. The chaotic churn of the rushing river settled into an assured current. The waves lapping the secluded boulder seemed to hush.

"Before I sent you the letter, I went to the badlands bordering Balendin's old village." Anaís's voice intertwined with the peace of the gorge. "An old friend told me about nanouk'tou, a reflection of souls. This is what we have. I'm not sure why...no one knows why the connection happens, if at all. Maybe we needed each other. Maybe it's something bigger than we can comprehend. But she said it does not go away."

Eoghan nodded once as he processed this new information. "So, we are traumatized but not alone."

"I guess so?"

His lips quirked into a smile. "That's not so bad, is it?"

"It's nice to be understood." She uncurled her legs and stretched out on the boulder, mirroring Eoghan's posture. "I...never thought I would have that."

"I know the feeling."

She looked at him. Really looked at him. And smiled. Shy at first, but then it bloomed into something full and unashamed. Her eyes were rimmed red with what he realized were unshed tears. But stars above, the joy that lit up her features and soothed the lingering hurt in that moment? He had never seen something so pure in his life.

Her expression softened, brow scrunching slightly as if she was considering something. "I think I know of a way to request leave without drawing suspicion from my father. I'll finalize the details and send word directly by hannok. Can you be prepared to meet here in two weeks?" She marked a spot on the map, then wrote out the coordinates. It looked to be at the southern edge of Dúndíor that bordered both Nahonaugh and Kiivjachim, about fifty miles northeast of the quarter point.

He memorized the location, then nodded. "Of course."

"So." She stood and brushed the dirt off her trousers. "Where do we go from here?"

Eoghan blinked, warm affection blooming in his chest. Her personality reminded him of a hummingbird. Not flighty and delicate, but sharp and precise, jumping from topic to topic in a way only she could understand, but he was determined to follow regardless. How could he not? She was mesmerizing. Anaís tilted her head at him as if waiting for an answer. Right. A question needed a response.

He pushed himself off the ground, trying to refocus on their conversation—or what was left of it. "In what context?"

A red flush colored her cheeks, and she looked away. "All of them," she said, tugging her boots back on and gathering up her cloak and knapsack.

He huffed out a laugh. If he was being honest with himself, today hadn't gone at all like he expected it to. It wasn't better, it wasn't worse. It was simply different. It was strange, he realized, having someone he trusted so completely. The one who was sent to take his life was now the one he trusted with it.

A flicker of uncertainty quelled some of the hope written on her features. Eoghan opened his mouth to reply, but shut it when she spoke. "Allies?"

Her hand hovered outstretched between the two of them, an open invitation to seal this new relationship, but the notion didn't sit right with him. The pain of all she had survived—the atrocities she had the courage to reveal to him and those kept hidden in her past—had buried deep beneath her flesh and weighed heavily in her bones. He alone could not fix that, but they were brought together for a reason. They could be strong together. He owed it to her, and to himself, to hold nothing back. She had all of him already, in a manner of speaking. He wouldn't let anything prevent her from having that in the land of the waking. Stars knew he needed her too.

"Anaís?" he spoke softly.

"Hm?"

Eoghan placed his hand in her outstretched one, his heart sinking as the space between her brows furrowed in confusion, her unfocused gaze locked on their clasped hands. He traced the skin along the back of her hand with his thumb, drawing her attention to the present. To him.

"You know things about me that I have never told anyone," he began. "You know things about me that I do not know myself, and that should terrify me, but it doesn't. Because I know you. I know your soul and you know mine. I trust you as I trust no one else."

Anaís smiled sadly. "I'm afraid I don't have a good record of extending or receiving trust."

"My trust is mine to give, and I give it to you. I only hope, one day, you find you can extend your trust to me."

There it was, the glimmer of hope. Clawing through doubts

and uncertainties. Burning brighter as the truth of his words settled around her.

"I think we are very much beyond allies," Eoghan whispered.

"Yes, I think so too."

His eyes drifted to their clasped hands, then trailed up, lingering on the scar that curved around her neck, following the curve of her slightly parted lips, finally coming to a rest when her gaze captured his own. "Can I hug you?"

"Please," she breathed.

He tugged her gently toward him, wrapping his arms around her as she settled her head against his chest and slipped her arms around his waist. Warmth traveled through him, between them, chasing away lingering tension, ridding his mind of the heaviness that had once clouded it and replaced it with an inexplicable sensation of peace. Of purpose. She sighed against him, the last bit of uncertainty melting out of her body as she melted into him, as if she didn't want to let go. Neither did he.

"I should probably get back to Simone and tell her the plan." Anaís's voice rumbled against his chest before she pulled back just enough to look up at him. Green and gold flakes highlighted the rich brown of her eyes, a forest he wanted to wander into and never leave. Perhaps he had escaped her blade, but this woman would be the death of him one way or another.

He nodded but made no move to let go. "Travel safely."

"I will," Anaís smiled at him. "I'll see you in two weeks. Then we'll be one step closer to finding out what is going on."

The light brush of his fingers along the curve of her waist sent a shock through his system when she stepped away. Eoghan swallowed thickly, grateful his voice remained mostly steady as he replied, "See you in two weeks."

RED DROWNING

FOR THE FIRST TIME SINCE SUMMER BEGAN, THE WEATHER chose not to resemble a moist armpit. Instead, the afternoon air carried the delicate scent of jasmine on lightly humid currents. Not dry. Not soul sucking. Just...nice. The perfect atmosphere for some light research at a cozy sitting area situated in the dappled shade of the gardens.

Eoghan sipped his tea—iced black, lightly sweetened—while he leafed through the pages of *Pre-Nythmaarian Geography*, stopping when he came to an aside about the region of Uul—the location of present-era Kiivjachim. The librarian had been less than happy with his request to not only read, but check out two restricted tomes from the library. However, holding the title of Crown Prince had its benefits, and he wasn't above leveraging them when necessary. With mellow blue skies and the pleasant warmth of tempered sunlight, reading outside was absolutely necessary.

Placing a paperweight on the page to prevent the breeze from stealing his place, Eoghan reached across the table and pulled *Encyclopædia of Time* closer to him, flipping through the pages to cross-reference the approximate period outlined in *Pre-Nythmaarian Geography*. He wasn't expecting much, but somewhere in the pages of these books he hoped to find an aside on the origins of Tāpepe Takakou na Uul. Or, better yet, the nitróg—the guiding stone. Perhaps it would be of use to their expedition. The little rock had caused him enough strife as it was; he might as well see if it could prove its worth. Even a hint as to what he and Anaís were facing would be invaluable.

Eoghan turned the page and paused, squinting suspiciously at the text as he read.

Following the gathering of seminomadic tribes in western Nythmaar and the near-subsequent coalition of High Chiefs, the first known attempted establishment of distinct borderlands—led by Hytak Frijlen (namesake of present-era Freydlan)—took place in 57DT.

That was a long sentence if he had ever seen one. Unfortunately, that was not the only thing odd about this page. Why was he already in the year 57DT? Placing his tea on the table, Eoghan returned to the previous page and skimmed the bottom paragraph.

87DT: One of the bloodiest periods recorded in a first-person written account, the fortieth decade of Ikktaku Tumaalihu heralded the micro-age of what is now known as the Red Drowning—alluding to the engorgement of lungs with blood until bursting. Regarded by the general populace as a supernatural disease, official records suggest the selected massacre of citizens refusing worship of Tumaalihu as divine—

Eoghan shut his eyes and sucked in a breath, trying to burn the text he had just read out of his mind. Unfortunately, forgotten history rarely did anyone any good. Even if it wasn't the history he was searching for. No, the history he needed was gone—literally. Thirty years had been removed. The short, ragged edges of torn pages poked from the binding like a petulant child sticking out its tongue, mocking him.

Rubbing his temples, Eoghan let out a frustrated groan. There was nothing in these books on Tāpepe Takakou na Uul other than it being a sizable jungle—poorly mapped yet well explored. Which was ridiculous. The nitróg had yet to be mentioned at all. And now this.

"I hate research," he grumbled.

"Now that's not true."

Eoghan jumped, knee slamming into the table and sending his iced tea toppling over the edge. Glass shattered.

Cian grimaced. "Sorry."

"It's fine." Eoghan gripped his knee, trying to ignore the embarrassment of being caught off guard twice in one week. "The past few days have turned me into a jumping ninny. Apparently."

Cian nodded at the books as he sat opposite Eoghan. "What are you looking at?"

"Nothing. Just. Trying to figure some things out."

"What kinds of things? I might be able to help." There was a curious note to Cian's voice, one Eoghan didn't quite know what to make of. Perhaps it was the sound of reconciliation?

Eoghan shrugged, then pushed the books toward Cian. "I'm trying to find some information about Kiivjachim. It might be related to what you and I discussed a while ago—back when the Anadali and Princess Simone first came for the peace treaty."

"There was a plethora of things we discussed that week," Cian laughed, though it didn't reach his eyes. "Let's see...your unbecoming fraternization with the enemy—"

"That was neither unbecoming, nor with an enemy," Eoghan retorted, perhaps with more bite than necessary. He sighed and ran his hand through his hair. "Sorry."

Cian leaned forward, hands planted on the table. "No, you're right," he said evenly. "It was much worse than that."

Eoghan blinked. "What?"

"Nothing," Cian said, glancing at the books laid before him. He tapped his finger twice against the small map of Uul that Eoghan had been studying in *Pre-Nythmaarian Geography*. "Uul is a curious place. Not as curious as what lies there now." He waved his hand languidly and turned the page. "It's said that those who enter are never seen again."

Eoghan pressed his lips into a thin line, trying to ignore the spike of hurt that dug itself into his chest. "That can't be true. Kiivjachim is more of a territory than a kingdom, but the wilderness of Tāpepe Takakou na Uul is relatively well explored."

Cian raised his brow but didn't offer any additional information, contenting himself to leafing through the pages in the book instead. "Interesting," he muttered, lingering on a sketch of the Nymyan Mountains before Freydlan had claimed their snowy peaks as her own.

"Cian?" Eoghan asked.

He ignored him, turning a section of pages over in one chunk to take them farther back in time. Cian traced his finger along the map of a place Eoghan didn't recognize. "Very interesting."

"Cian." Eoghan repeated.

"Shh." He turned the page, tilting his head as he read the text.

The spike dug deeper, prodding at a fleshy corner of Eoghan's heart. One he never thought he would have to protect. His patience snapped. "Cian!"

Cian frowned but kept his eyes focused on the text, using his finger to set the pace as he read. "You will not do what is necessary. I will do what I must. You asked me to, remember? *A while ago.*"

Eoghan reached across the table and slammed the book shut, trapping Cian's hand between the pages. "Listen to me," Eoghan spoke lowly. "There is no time for whatever wedge has been between our friendship. The shadows are back, and they're no longer shadows. They can take corporeal form. They can fight, Cian. One tried to attack Anaís. She butchered it, and it *would not die*. You've seen them in Nahonaugh, but it's spreading. They are going to tear this kingdom apart."

Cian dragged his gaze up from the book and met Eoghan's stare with eyes that had been drained of hope and replaced with heavy resignation. Eoghan couldn't swallow the tightness in his throat. *Come back*, he willed. *Cian, what happened? Come back.*

Cian slowly pulled his hand out of the book. The cover thumped closed under the weight of Eoghan's hand. "You're on a first-name basis now?"

"Yes," Eoghan whispered.

"Fascinating. I saw this coming, and yet here I am, surprised. I suppose I shouldn't be. She couldn't do her job properly." Cian tapped his finger against the scar on Eoghan's chest. "And you couldn't do your job properly. A perfect match."

Eoghan felt like he was trapped in a lake that had frozen over. "What did you say?"

"All of this goes much deeper than you realize. Months ago, I told you I had an idea of how to fix the problem. I fixed it."

"Cian?" Eoghan couldn't think, couldn't breathe. "What have you done?"

For a brief moment, Cian looked conflicted. Torn. Then, resolve settled over his features as he stood, rounding the table to place a hand on Eoghan's shoulder.

"I wanted to warn you then, but I could not. So I'm warning you now. Stay out of this." Cian heaved a sigh. "I'm sorry. I'm doing this for you. I hope you can understand."

Eoghan didn't want to understand. He wanted his friend back. He wanted...

She couldn't do her job properly. That was the reason he was alive. *I wanted to warn you then. I wanted to* warn *you...*

"You knew." Eoghan's voice cracked under the weight of understanding. Rising, he stumbled away from Cian, vaguely registering the sound of the chair clattering to the ground and the crunch of glass beneath his shoes. No, all that mattered was that Cian knew. The night Eoghan was supposed to die, he *knew.* "Cian what did you do?"

"I haven't *done* anything." Cian shrugged. "Not yet. I have some errands to see to. Hopefully that will give you some time to reconsider. We can talk afterward."

"Reconsider what?" the words rumbled low in Eoghan's throat. A dare. A threat. A mask to his pain. What was Cian playing at? He wanted Eoghan to stay out of it, but who else knew of what they were facing...*Anaïs.* Eoghan tensed as if preparing to fight, a surge of protectiveness washing over him. Yes, Anaïs could take care of herself, but she would have to do so only *after* whatever came for her fought its way through him first. "If you so much as lay a finger on her—"

Cian laughed dryly. "Do you think I could win in hand-to-hand combat against her? No, you need not worry." He turned and began making his way toward the palace. "Think on it," Cian called over his shoulder, then disappeared around the bend.

Eoghan stood, dumbfounded. And then he ran. His feet pounded against the path, kicking up gravel as he sprinted toward the bend. He had let Cian walk away once, and that decision nearly destroyed everything. He would not make that mistake again. Eoghan rounded the bend, coming to a skidding stop.

Cian was gone.

CHAPTER THIRTY-NINE

LEGEND OF THE BLUE SUN

O*NCE UPON A TIME ON THE EVE OF A BLUE DAWN, fate woke up.* Thus began the tale of Nāmi Attati-karou—the Legend of the Blue Sun. When Anaís was a child, the idea of the sun burning any color other than its own was both delectably marvelous and tantalizingly horrific. Now, with the rising sun warming her back and the dappled shade of Tāpepe Takakou na Uul licking the sandy earth on the Dúndían side of the border, she thought she understood.

Blue was not a color, it was a feeling—the elated swoop in her stomach when she leapt from building to building under a twilit sky, the unending numbness of degradation as she lay motionless facing the Ulçok Sea, the navy of Eoghan's tunic when they first met and their story began—though in reality, it had begun long ago. Calm and storm, hope and ruin. A thousand shades wrapped into one word: blue.

Today, blue was possibility—hope for a new future, danger lurking in the unknown, courage to claim it regardless. It was on this blue dawn that everything would change, because fate was finally waking up.

The shifting of the small group of Anadali recruits behind Anaís melded with the rustling of tree leaves as they set up a temporary camp. Today would mark their tenth day of hiking—the halfway point as measured by her men, the beginning as measured by her own standard.

Following her meeting with Eoghan at the gorge, Anaís had demanded a meeting with King Timun and bartered leave with a select group of her recruits on what she described as an orienteering mission. It would push the men to their limits and prepare them for the trials she would set before them upon their return to the capital—trials that would grant them the title of Anadali should they succeed. In reality, it was the only way she could think of to leave the palace for an extended period of time unquestioned.

She hadn't expected the king to grant her request, though it was not without his own. Gio was to remain behind while Tadeo—the captain of the King's Guard—would accompany her in his place. The king did not trust her—wise. Frustrating, yes. But wise. Though perhaps not as much as the king had hoped. Simone did trust Tadeo, after all.

Regardless of her clandestine intentions for the mission and the setbacks encountered, her men had impressed her. With their tenacity, resourcefulness, and grit during the expedition mixed with their improvements in combat, Anaís no longer dreaded the thought of bringing them into her ranks as she once had. That was something the king had not accounted for, and she *would* use that to her advantage upon their return.

Footsteps sounded behind Anaís, and she turned as the bald recruit approached. His name was Daza, but he had been nameless for so long she had a feeling "bald recruit" wouldn't leave her mind anytime soon.

"Breakfast is ready, Amadé," he said, bringing his fist to his chest in a salute. His other hand precariously gripped a steaming mug of tea and three strips of jerky.

At this point, finding a comfortable spot on the ground and mustering the will to eat something before falling asleep were about as intensive as breakfast preparations would get.

"Thank you." Anaís accepted the food and tea. "Before you rest, can you send Captain Tadeo over?"

Daza saluted again and sauntered off.

Taking a sip of tea, Anaís watched with amusement as he poked Tadeo on the shoulder, jerked his chin in her general direction, flopped on the ground, and promptly fell asleep. She wished she could do the same—sleep, or at least rest—but there was work to do yet. She stifled a yawn as Tadeo approached.

"You summoned me?" he grumbled, but a glint of amusement sneaked its way into his voice.

"Come," Anaís said, walking to the outskirts of camp and away from prying ears. "I'm putting you in command until I get back."

"From where?"

"Scouting ahead." Anaís tilted her head toward the forest, trying to ignore the way a fledgling headache pressed against her skull with the motion. "I'll be gone for two hours, at most."

"Who else is coming with you?"

"No one. I'm going alone."

Tadeo raised his brow. "I'll tell Etrit he's in command. I'm coming with you."

"You're staying here."

"What would Simone have me do if she knew you were going into uncharted, potentially hostile territory alone?" he hissed. "Mistakes happen when you're tired—no, don't you *dare* tell me otherwise. We're all exhausted, but for some reason you're insistent on hiding it. Simone almost lost you once; I'm not letting her lose you again."

"Tadeo," Anaís whispered, but her voice was sharp. "I'm going *alone*. I have—" She cut herself off. Could she risk telling him? Simone trusted him; that had to be enough. But did she trust him?

Tadeo spoke before she could decide. "The king doesn't trust you, but he does trust me, if that's any indication of my abilities in misdirection." Glancing toward the Anadali, he lowered his voice. "You need to tell at least one person the truth of why we're on this expedition. I'm not here to keep an eye on you. I'm here as an ally."

Anaís didn't think it was in his nature to spy, but with an admission like that? "You're telling me that you're a liar at best and a traitor at worst?"

"No, I'm telling you..." Tadeo pinched his lips together into a frown, as if he was about to reveal something he wished he didn't need to. Shifting closer, he whispered the last thing Anaís expected to hear. "Simone is my wife."

She gaped, but snapped her mouth shut at the defensive look Tadeo directed at her.

"We married last year. Only the officiant and Simone's seamstress know." He softened as he spoke. "I only stayed on the King's Guard to be close to her. It just so happened that I was good at my job and was promoted to captain in the process. She and I... We..." Tadeo shook his head. "When I first started courting her, we both knew the arrangement wasn't proper. If the king found out, he would have either stripped me of rank or executed me, depending on his mood. But—"

"She loves you," Anaís said. "And you love her. You don't have to explain this to me. I may be inexperienced at the art of romantic relations, but I'm not blind. You hide it well, don't worry," she added before the look of dread on Tadeo's face could cross over into full-blown panic. "But I'm also her sister. I know when she's smitten."

"Then please trust me when I say I can keep this secret safe as well. Where are you going, really? Was this an orienteering mission, or is there more?" Tadeo rubbed the scruff on his jaw, frowning in thought. "Simone has been dropping hints but won't explain further."

"No." Anaís let out a sigh. Having Tadeo as an ally wasn't a terrible idea. "This isn't simply an orienteering mission." Peering into the trees, she added, "I'll explain more later, but I do need to go now."

"All right. I trust your judgment," Tadeo conceded. "But if you're gone a minute longer than two hours, I'm leading a team to extract you myself."

"I'm meeting with Eoghan." The soft confession bloomed between them before she could stop herself.

"Inexperienced at the art of romantic relations indeed," Tadeo said with a smirk. "How long has this been going on? Three months? Four?" Anaís glared at him, but he carried on, undeterred. "Tell you what, I'll give you two hours and *five* minutes."

"It's not like that," Anaís grumbled, though it didn't hold the weight she wanted it to. Sighing, she added, "I trust you can handle the men until I get back?"

His playful expression shifted into one of duty. "Of course."

"Good."

Drawing herself up, Anaís strode back to the haggard crew of men slumped in various states of leisure on the ground. She didn't know what awaited them in the forest, but for the next while she could give them a break.

"Captain Tadeo is in command until I return," Anaís barked. One of the men groaned. She leveled him with a stern yet amused glare. "Rivalry between Anadali and the King's Guard is not permitted because you are not yet Anadali. You will have that honor once we return home and you have proven yourselves worthy. Do I make myself clear?"

"Yes, Amadé," the men said in unison.

"Good. Rest up. We leave in six hours."

THANKFULLY, THE LOCATION SHE HAD given Eoghan was a short thirty-minute hike around the edge of the forest. Every time she dipped farther into the trees than she needed to, trepidation crawled up her spine. Gnarled branches twined together like ancient runes, while leaves rustled warnings to one another in the breeze. The forest was an entity that was and always would be. Time was simply passing through.

Rounding the thick stump of a towering tree, Anaís paused before entering the clearing, leaning against the cool bark while she watched Eoghan. He sat on a tree stump; elbows propped against his thighs, head resting thoughtfully against his hands as he stared into the forest away from her. There was something melancholy yet determined about his expression, but that didn't stop the wind from dancing around him, tugging playfully at his dark hair and rustling his clothes—a goldenrod-yellow tunic with silver embroidery and loose cream linen trousers that locked impeccable, despite what had likely been a long hike to this location. Though if the knapsack plopped unceremoniously on the ground next to him had anything to say on the matter, it most certainly was.

Her heart gave a funny *stutter-thump* when he turned and looked at her, a smile that rivaled the sun brightening his features.

Like a fool, she smiled back.

"You made it safely," Eoghan said, standing and making his way across the clearing to meet her in the middle.

She extended her hand to clasp his in greeting. "So did you."

He eyed her hand, then raised his brow. "Really?" the look seemed to say.

Anaís wiggled her fingers at him in jest. "Come on, we have much to discuss."

"Ah, my apologies." Eoghan gently took her hand, pulling her toward him to envelop her in a hug. "What would you like to discuss?" His voice rumbled pleasantly against her chest, melting away her tension from the past ten days.

He smelled of cedar and black tea and the wilderness between Nahonaugh and Dúndíor—earthy and free. She had wondered where they stood after their meeting at the gorge. Not allies, not friends, but...*something*. If safety was what that something looked like—felt like—then she didn't mind at all.

"Nothing much." Anaís leaned back to meet his gaze. "Just the fate of our kingdoms."

A slow smile spread across his lips. "Is that all? After going through all the trouble to leave the palace, I had expected something more daring from a clandestine meeting with the Anadali Amadé."

"Come on," she laughed, stepping out of his embrace toward the tree stump. His hand trailed down her arm, pinky finger catching her own as they walked together. She shifted her hand until their fingers intertwined. From the corner of her eye, she caught the tail end of a contented smirk lifting Eoghan's lips.

"I brought a map to go over the plan, but we'll have to scout separately," Anaís said as they lowered themselves onto the ground, regrettably letting go of his hand so she could rummage through her knapsack. "You can keep this one." She handed him the map in question.

"Why separately?"

"I have a team of Anadali recruits with me. I told the king I was taking them on an orienteering mission. And...I think I'm being watched."

Anaís couldn't explain it. She had no real proof, what with the way the king seemed to ignore her until she demanded his presence. Though it wasn't necessarily him she was worried about. It was the threat of the creature that terrified her more than she cared to admit. She had yet to see it again, but her mind warned her that every dark corner held the possibility of something more lurking within. The creaks in the night became a warning siren of the inevitable. The prickling on the back of her neck that happened when someone was watching hummed in a near-constant reminder of what *could* be watching. Now that she had seen part of the truth, she couldn't un-see it. Nothing had happened yet, but something would. The silence had long overstayed its welcome, and it had a habit of departing with a scream.

Eoghan furrowed his brow at the worry that must have been written on her face. "That's why I think it would be prudent to scout together."

"Are you scared?" She nudged his shoulder playfully, but the gesture felt flat, even to her.

"Yes," he whispered. Eoghan held her gaze for a heartbeat before turning his attention back to the forest, the same melancholy look there and gone in an instant. His shoulder pressed against her as he sucked in a breath, then released it slowly.

Something deep within her ached. "What happened?" she demanded softly.

He blinked at her as if weighing the importance of his thoughts. Then slowly, carefully, Eoghan said, "That night, when you came to assassinate me..." He trailed off, then breathed a resigned sigh. "Who gave you the order?"

"My father."

Eoghan's throat bobbed as he swallowed. "Who else knew?"

"Simone," Anaís admitted. "But when she signed the treaty, she knew why I could not hurt you. She wants peace."

"I know. She's somewhat of a very demanding friend now," he said with a sad yet fond smile. It faded when he added, "Anyone else?"

"No. Why?"

"Something happened to Cian. That night... He knew I was meant to die." Eoghan huffed a humorless laugh. "He must have had a good reason to not say anything then, but a week ago..." His gaze turned distant, as if trying to find where it all went wrong.

Anaís wrapped her arms around Eoghan, and he sank into her embrace, seeming to find strength as he rested his head against hers.

"He left." The words were quiet, and something about the proclamation made her think Eoghan meant it in more ways than presence alone. "I fear for what he may have involved himself in."

"We will find him," Anaís whispered. "We will help him. No one is too lost to be found." It was something she wished she had known long ago. Now that she did, it was the lifeline she clung to—not the words, but those who extended them. Simone, Olia, Eoghan.

She and Cian may not see eye to eye, but she wasn't about to withhold the same gift of redemption that was given to her freely.

Eoghan nodded, the movement tickling her hair. "Thank you," he mumbled, then huffed a dry laugh as he sat up and scrubbed a hand down his face. "Sorry."

"What if I told you I cried twice in one day recently?"

"Then I'd say I should like to find the person who made you cry and give them a stern talking-to."

"Go on then," Anaís laughed, gesturing to herself. When he regarded her with furrowed brows but remained quiet, she continued softly, "We are traumatized but not alone, remember? Nanouk'tou. We're in this together. I'd like to see where this goes."

His gaze lingered on hers before he dipped his head with a nod. "So do I."

Perhaps, as she did, he meant it in more ways than one.

Eoghan nudged the forgotten map with his foot. "I know we discussed scouting locations at our last meeting, but I did bring something that might help us in our search." Reaching into his pocket, he produced a small, smooth stone with pinpricks traversing its body. "It's called a nitróg—a guiding stone."

Anaís's eyes widened in realization. "Simone told me about this. She said it's what I foresaw?"

Eoghan nodded, turning it over in the palm of his hand. "It doesn't do anything really, but I've noticed it feels different to different people. I'm curious how it feels to you."

Anaís looked from Eoghan to the rock. It was unassuming in the way most important things tended to be. Yet it held a strange beauty.

Flecks of silver and purple and blue caught the dappled light of the forest as he turned it absentmindedly. Holding out her hand, Anaís caught the rock when Eoghan dropped it onto her waiting palm. A liquid warmth pooled beneath her skin, traveling up her arm and through her body.

"It's warm," she marveled, holding the rock up for closer inspection. "And beautiful. Look"—she nudged Eoghan's side—"there are new colors. Rose and lilac and—"

Eoghan gasped and Anaís looked up, stiffening at the sight of fog pooling around them. It twined between the trees, blooming and shifting as if it was the breath of the forest itself.

"What is it?" Anaís whispered.

He looked at her with wide eyes. "You can see it too?" At her nod, his expression softened with relief. "In all honesty, I'm not sure what it is. It's been a frequent companion these past few months. Took me to a different realm on our first meeting, actually."

Anaís scooted closer to Eoghan, away from the fog that had been inching toward her almost curiously.

"It's harmless for the most part," Eoghan laughed, but did not move away. Narrowing his eyes at the fog he added, "No funny business."

To Anaís's utter shock, the fog seemed to shrug in reply.

"This is the first time the fog has shown itself to anyone else. And the first time the nitróg has responded in such a way," Eoghan mused. "Normally when I hand it to someone, it goes cold and dark. Still not much of a guiding stone, but it's interesting."

"Have you tried it in the dark yet?" Anaís asked. "Maybe the flecks of color provide light?"

Eoghan frowned pensively. "There's a thought. May I try something?"

With Anaís's hum of affirmation, he reached to take the rock from her hand. As soon as his skin touched the nitróg, the fog twirled around them, curling around Anaís's palm and weaving between Eoghan's fingers before seeping into the stone.

Neither moved. Neither breathed. Then, with a sigh that seemed to come from the trees themselves, the fog billowed up and through the pinholes of the stone, weaving into a map as it settled in the clearing before them.

"Is that what you expected to happen?" Anaís whispered, afraid that if she talked any louder it might disturb whatever *had* happened.

Eoghan looked from the fog map, to Anaís, to where his hand now rested atop hers—the rock held between them. "No, I can't say this was on my list of possibilities. But, um, I think I know why it's called a guiding stone now."

Anaís laughed. "Thank you for that astute observation." Leaning forward, she picked up the parchment map and spread it out on the forest floor. "Do you think the fog map will stay if we release the nitróg? I'd like both hands to make annotations."

Giving the fog a stern look, Eoghan slowly removed his hand, taking the rock with him and tucking it back into his pocket. The fog wavered, then steadied. "I'm not sure how long it will last, but it should hold for now."

Anaís rose and walked around the fog map, comparing it to her hand drawn one. "They are different," she remarked, updating the sketch of her map. "But both maps are obviously variants of Kiivja-chim and Tāpepe Takakou na Uul."

"I did read that Kiivjachim was well explored but not well mapped," Eoghan said. He had stood and was now staring intently at a part of the map that seemed unable to decide what form it wanted to take. "This may be why."

Frowning, Anaís made note of the vague spot on her map. "It will take a few days to get to, but I think this should be our ultimate destination. I don't like how the fog is behaving here. No offense," she added quickly when the fog seemed to bristle at her assessment. Turning to Eoghan, she said, "Given the shadow creatures and sentient fog—*nice* fog—we should probably go where unnatural things are afoot. And it's near the quarter point." Heaving a sigh, she dropped the map to her side. "I don't like this at all."

"Which is why I'd rather we scout together," Eoghan said. Anaís sucked in a breath to argue, but released it when he added, "However I understand the need for discretion."

"Thank you," she said softly. Returning to the tree stump, Anaís sat on the ground and began updating the other map she brought. Eoghan settled next to her, watching as she drew. "My recruits and I can take the larger area—it will be safer for us to go deeper in as a group. You can take this region. I'll debrief my men, then meet you here at midnight." She made a mark on the map, but then her hand stilled. If there were creatures in the forest, her larger group should keep their attention away from Eoghan and onto her. He should be safe. But at night?

Eoghan's hand brushed lightly against hers. "What is it?"

"I think I can trust my men. I just need to make sure." She looked up at him, and something about the tender resolve in his expression solidified her own. "I don't want you camping in the forest alone.

You'll stay with us." It was a risk she would have to take. By tonight, they'd already be in too deep anyway.

"I can agree to that." Eoghan accepted the proffered map, startling when a heaving *woosh* sounded. In an instant, the fog map had dispersed, settling back into its playful dance with the tree branches around them. He folded the map absentmindedly before tucking it into his pocket. "We should probably try to figure out nanouk'tou at some point as well. I can't imagine that it's only related to this." He tipped his head toward the fog, though when he turned to face her, he looked nervous. Bashful, even. Finally, he asked, "Do you still feel the...thread?"

Anaís looked at him, lips parted in surprise. "You felt that too?"

He nodded.

"Now that I think about it, I haven't felt it since the gorge. It's as if once I saw you and you saw me, it—"

"Stopped trying to strangle you for being an idiot?" Eoghan rubbed the back of his neck sheepishly. "Er, well, me. I was an idiot."

Anaís barked a laugh. "In that case, it thought we were both idiots. Sometimes it was simply a tug in the right direction. Other times...I'm almost convinced it would have gone so far as to kill us both that night, had we not stopped."

"And now? What do you feel?" Eoghan asked.

Anaís bit the inside of her lip while she thought. Despite leading a team of recruits, hiking through the wilderness had given her a long time to sort through her emotions about Eoghan, about all of this. Sitting next to him now, it was as if the missing pieces had fallen into place and her once daunting world was illuminated with brilliant clarity. But how did she explain *that*?

"Does it ever seem odd to you that there are two types of darkness?" Anaís found herself saying. "One is a beast of claws that bite, and teeth that gnash, and a gaping hunger that consumes the life out of all it touches. A void where dead things rot and souls wither but cannot truly die."

A shuddering breath escaped Eoghan's lips. "And the other?"

"It is a cocoon. The soft caress of mist on a winter morning. A haven to quench swirling thoughts. The shade of an oasis tucked in the heart of the desert. It is a place that is safe, secure, untouchable by fear."

Anaís swallowed, rubbing at the dust smudged on the leather of her boots. It frightened her how easily the next words wanted to roll off her tongue, and how little fear she truly felt at the prospect of Eoghan knowing her heart. "You are my safe haven that shelters me from the void. I have always known that. But now that I know it's *you*? My soul is at peace. It has a safe place to rest; it knows where to rest."

Unshed tears clung to Eoghan's dark lashes, glinting in the sun when he looked up and tried to blink them away. Dirt crunched as he shifted, and Anaís missed the feeling of his shoulder pressed against hers. But then he draped his arm across her shoulders, pulling her against his side. Her head found a home on his chest, eyes fluttering closed when he rested his head atop her own.

"It's not often that I'm left speechless," Eoghan whispered. He traced lazy patterns along her arm, each touch leaving a trail of electricity in its wake. The fog cooled her exposed skin, settling around her like nature's blanket, while the steady thrum of Eoghan's heart became her own soft lullaby.

"It feels too simple to say," he continued. "But the only reason I can see through the darkest night is because you are the light that guides me." Her head rose and fell to the breath of his sigh. "I keep trying to define nanouk'tou, to find words that encompass all that I feel, because I feel a lot. But perhaps, for me, it is the kind of thing that is better left untouched by my own devices. Something that is allowed to bloom and grow. I meant what I said—I'd like to see where this goes. All of it."

Anaís draped her arm across his stomach in response. She was too tired for anything else. Ten days of hiking had left her physically drained, but ten days of fitful sleep for fear of what lurked in the shadows had left her with a weariness that seeped into her bones. She hadn't realized what a toll it had taken until she had someone to share the burden with.

"When are you expected back?" Eoghan asked.

Tadeo's two-hour threat surfaced from the recesses of her memory. "Soon," she mumbled.

"When are you starting the expedition?"

"A few hours." Anaís winced, headache mounting as her mind sluggishly began cataloging all the preparations she would need to make before then.

"They can wait. You need to rest."

She shook her head, but made no move to get up. She wouldn't have been able to even if she wanted.

"I'll watch over you." Eoghan brushed his thumb across her brow, as if his touch alone could chase away her headache. Yet in that moment, perhaps he was the only one who could. "Try to get some sleep."

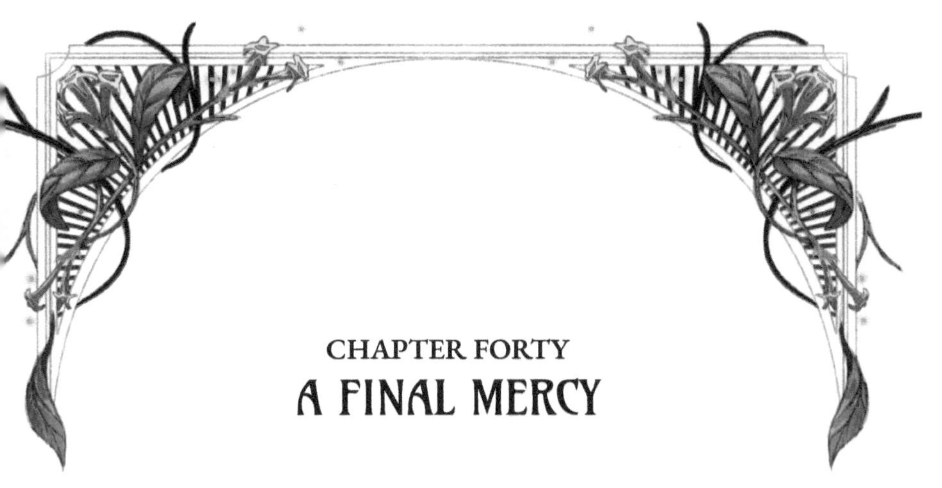

CHAPTER FORTY
A FINAL MERCY

NAÍS ARRIVED BACK AT CAMP THREE HOURS LATER than intended. At some point during her nap, she vaguely registered Eoghan's grip tightening, the brush of his chin against her hair as if shaking his head no, the low rumble of his voice and the familiar whisper of another's response.

Though Tadeo had sent her a knowing look upon her return, he didn't ask. Anaís didn't tell.

Now, they walked in tense silence—not from words unspoken, but from the forest that swallowed them whole. Trees towered overhead, gnarled branches choking out the sun that had illuminated the desert sky. The little light that did manage to fall through the canopy dripped like blood onto the forest floor. A tree to her left boasted a gouged scar in its trunk, as if a beast from legend had torn into it.

Lightning, she told herself with a shudder. *It was most likely caused by lightning.*

With each step, Anaís tried to remind herself that she wasn't walking away from her blue dawn, but toward it. Glancing over her shoulder, Anaís studied the trees, familiarizing herself with the look of the forest should they get turned around. Twisted branches watched her retreating form, waving a solemn goodbye as they shifted in the breeze.

Blue dawn, she reminded herself. Steeling her resolve, she turned back around and signaled a change of formation to Tadeo, who marched with her at the head of the procession of Anadali. Dried leaves crunched beneath boots as she and Tadeo stepped to the side of the path to allow the recruits to march between them. Daza and Etrit fell into position at the front, followed by Qamar and Liuz, then Paio and Bazán. Anaís and Tadeo shifted to the rear, shoulders brushing as they silently fell into line.

And so the hours passed—defined only by the cycle of formations. Daza and Etrit navigated, making annotations on the map. Qamar and Liuz scouted ahead. Paio and Bazán marked their path onto the trees with chalk. Anaís and Tadeo stalked forward with weapons drawn, ready to protect the group from unseen threats. Cycle. Repeat. Cycle. Repeat. Until all Anaís knew was the march as they trekked ever further into the unknown.

The map crinkled in Anaís's hands as she shifted it, trying to catch the light so she could see what she was writing. Given their current position, they were a few hours from the end of the route she had planned, and still no closer to finding answers. She only hoped Eoghan had better luck with his section of forest, otherwise they would have to make a new plan when she met him at midnight. But sundown was fast approaching, and her group still needed to finish scouting and march to camp.

Glancing up with a frown, Anaís caught sight of a fern nestled into the crook of the roots of a thick-stumped tree. Familiar. The map hung forgotten at her side as she continued to march, observing her surroundings with hannok-like scrutiny. Ten paces later, a tree scarred by lightning passed by on her left. Too familiar.

Air rushed between her teeth in a lilted whistle. *Halt.*

The men stood at attention, though their stance held an under-current of trepidation that mirrored her own.

"Bazán. Scout ahead. Check for markings on the trees. Don't leave my sight," Anaís said, scanning the forest around her. "Liuz. Backtrack. Same orders." She drew her gaze from the trees to look both Anadali in the eyes. They saluted, then turned and jogged into the distance.

Daza shifted his grip on the hilt of his sword. "What is it?"

"I'm not sure." Anaís glanced at Bazán, then Liuz, making sure they didn't scout too far. "But this part of the forest feels too familiar."

The soft thump of boots drew her attention forward. "Nothing," Bazán said. "Trees are clear."

Liuz materialized beside him. "Trees are marked as we left them."

Anaís rolled her lips together as she considered. The vague region from the fog map was still a distance away. It couldn't have shifted, could it? She shook her head and positioned herself at the front. There wasn't time to question when they were already committed. "Fall in."

The men did. The procession carried onward. They made it twenty paces when a crack shot through the air, echoing off the trees as if passing along whispered warnings.

Danger pain fear death trapped trapped trapped...

The Anadali froze. Tadeo stopped breathing. The back of Anaís's neck prickled.

"Defense," she murmured, turning slowly to peer into the depths of the forest while her men fell into formation beside her, creating a loose circle back-to-back with their packs discarded in the middle.

"Anaís?" Tadeo breathed.

She grunted in acknowledgement, keeping her attention fixed beyond the darkness. There was something in there. She could see it, if only her eyes—

"Anaís!" Tadeo hissed urgently.

Her head whipped toward him. She took in his wide eyes, his pallid complexion hidden beneath the dirt and grime, then followed his gaze. An inky mist stirred in the distance, tendrils flicking out and snapping back like tongues of shadow. The ink coalesced, and from its depths rose the creature.

Their eyes locked. Anticipation drew tight as a bowstring as they observed each other. Anaís rested her hand on the hilt of her blade, fingers flexing in challenge. *Try me again*, she wanted to say. *I dare you*.

The creature tilted its head with curiosity, as if confirming who it saw. The satisfaction in its eyes spread into a skin-splitting smile. And then it disappeared.

The forest held its breath. Moments dragged by. Tension coiled in her muscles like a spring, winding tighter and tighter until a singular question drifted into her mind and threatened to break her:

In sending Eoghan alone, had she sent him to his death?

No! Her mind screamed. *I would know.* Whether or not it was true she did not care, but in that moment she *had* to believe it. Her men needed her to focus. Her kingdom needed her to focus. Eoghan needed her to focus—because he was still out there and she would do everything in her power to protect him. To protect her people. Anaís tucked Eoghan's safety in the back of her mind, letting it provide strength for the task at hand. The creature would come back, and she would be ready.

Stillness reigned over the forest.

One of her men breathed the softest sigh of relief. "That was—"

The air whistled as an arrow shot from the trees. Reacting on instinct alone, Anaís grabbed it just before it pierced Tadeo's skull. A soft whimper sounded in the back of his throat.

Her patience snapped. Whoever had shot that arrow would pay.

"Show yourselves!" Anaís shouted into the darkness, dropping the arrow to her feet.

The darkness complied. Men materialized from the depths of the forest, the crunching of leaves mingling with the soft hiss of blades scraping against leather sheath as swords were drawn. Some wielded axes. Others gripped short spears or bows.

And then appeared a man, twirling the shaft of an arrow between his fingers as he prowled forward; ginger hair impeccably coiffed, blue eyes impossibly cold.

"Hello, Anaís," Cian said.

Her jaw dropped. "What are you—"

"I was hoping to find you here. Well. There." He gestured with his head in the direction they were heading. "But I'm on a tight schedule, and my patience is waning."

He left, Eoghan's words echoed in her mind. Anaís understood now what he had meant.

"You don't have to do this," she found herself saying instead. It didn't matter that her Anadali would overhear; she had promised Eoghan that she would help. "He misses you, Cian. You're his friend—whatever you've done, whatever you knew, he knows you wouldn't betray his trust. I don't know what you've fallen into, but trust me when I say you can stop. Act of your own accord. I did." The words spilled out of her, desperate, imploring. "You don't have to do this. There is something more out there; we need to fight together. Not against each other."

"I know." He gave her an amused smile. One tinged with sadness and coated in resignation. "And yes, I do." His eyes flashed upward. "Wear her down, please."

Anaís watched in disbelief as Cian nocked an arrow, aimed at one of her men behind her, and let it fly.

Battle erupted around her. She made it two steps before something rammed into her from behind. Gnarled roots and jagged stones bit into her as she rolled across the forest floor, coming to an abrupt stop at the base of a tree. Dazed, she stood and unsheathed her sword. A bony hand wrenched it from her grasp, a stinging pain trailing across her skin as the edge of the blade skimmed across her forearm. The fabric of her uniform tightened around her neck. The creature lifted her off the ground, then settled her on her feet away from the tree. It brushed her shoulders off. Took a step back. And watched her expectantly, her own weapon at the ready in its grip.

Anaís glared at her short sword, grasped inexorably in the creature's hand. It had a wicked blade, and of the five she owned, it was her favorite. She wanted it back. Somehow, that thought helped silence the terror of fighting an enemy she could not defeat.

Not yet, she reminded herself, rolling out her shoulder before unsheathing twin daggers. *Let's see how well you can regenerate without a head.*

She lunged forward, feigning high before ducking beneath the creature's counterattack and sweeping its legs out from underneath it. Instead of falling, the creature disappeared in a cloud of smoke. Her sword clattered to the dirt. The creature reappeared in front of her and landed a swift kick to her ribs before she could grab it. Anaís rolled with the blow, using the momentum to bring her feet beneath her to strike again.

Her world became a pinprick of focus. All she knew was the creature and the song of her blades as they tore through the air. Yet no matter how precise her attack, the creature met each strike as if it knew how she was going to move before her blade fell.

Frustration rose within her. Balendin had drilled into her the importance of keeping a level head, but something about this fight made her want to act irrationally. Balendin had never fought one of these things. She had to try.

Anaís dove into the creature's next blow, gritting her teeth at the sting of its strike. It swung again. As its fist slammed into the side of her face, she dropped a dagger and grabbed its arm. Twisting beneath it, Anaís put her back against the creature's stomach and flipped it over her shoulder. Then she dropped to a knee and plunged her dagger deep into its eye.

The creature let out a bloodcurdling shriek. It clawed at her arm, nails biting into her skin as she threw her weight behind the blade. Bone cracked. The creature disappeared in a swath of smoke.

Anaís fell forward, chest heaving as her dagger sank into the forest floor. Sweat dripped down her face, dirt coated her body, and blood slicked her arms and stuck her uniform to her skin. She just needed one moment. One forsaken moment to breathe and find the strength to help her men.

Her gaze snapped up. Battle raged around her. Liuz and Qamar were nowhere to be seen. Tadeo fought in the center of three men, blades clashing with unbridled fury. One man fell; another replaced him. Anaís pushed herself up, yanking her dagger out of the earth as she started toward Tadeo, only to stop moments later when something yanked her backward.

No.

She stumbled over a root. A dagger hissed through the empty space where her head used to be. The creature appeared before her, eyes glinting before attacking with renewed vigor. *Wear her down,* Cian had said. She dodged back as the creature tried to swipe the blade up her chest. Either it had decided the game was too easy—Anaís blocked another attack, the blow stinging her arm as she tried to force the creature back—or it was tired of playing games. She danced back again before lunging in with her own attack, but her movements felt languid, her strikes imprecise.

Air rushed from her lungs as she slammed into the ground. The creature wrenched her head back. A knee dug between her shoulder blades, pinning her down. The cold bite of a blade pressed against her neck. Tiny sips of air fought to fill her lungs as darkness licked at the edge of her vision. Then the creature jerked her head to the side and traced the tip of the blade along the curve of her throat before ramming the dagger into the earth next to her head. With a wicked smile, the creature disappeared in a swath of ink.

Her cheek pressed against the dirt as she lay there, heart thundering against her chest. Breath by painstaking breath, the darkness receded. She vaguely registered someone shouting her name, then gentle hands rolled her over and Tadeo's worry-lined face filled her vision. An arrow flew past his head, and he flinched with a curse before hauling them both behind the safety of a tree.

Gnarled roots rose around them, giving the illusion of safety. She forced herself to sit up, then peer through a gap in the roots. Bodies littered the forest floor, leaves slick with the blood of both friend and foe. Though the Anadali had skill, they lacked numbers—only Daza and Etrit remained standing. Barely. And Tadeo...Anaís turned to study him. Someone needed to get word back to the palace, and she would not make Simone a widow. There were some battles where retreat was inevitable, while others... This one... Anaís swallowed. They wanted *something* with her, and the creature had not yet returned. It was now or never.

"You need to leave," Anaís whispered. "Eoghan and I planned to meet ten minutes, directly northeast of the next camp at midnight. Tell him of this place, of what happened."

"Anaís, I—"

"Then return to Dúndíor. Inform Simone. Inform Gio. Prepare for this darkness to spread and find out how to stop it. Do not trust the king."

"Anaís—"

She gripped his shoulders. "Do *not* trust him. Do you understand me? I don't know what is happening, but this ambush was planned. Was it my father, I don't know. But whatever is happening—the enemy knew. We cannot give them another advantage."

"I swore an oath to Simone to protect you, I will *not* break that."

"You swore an oath to me before we left," Anaís bit out, hoping the gruffness hid the waver in her voice. "As your commander, I am *ordering* you to leave. Are you going to disobey a direct command?"

He glared at her. "No."

"Go." She tipped her head toward the trees away from the battle. "I'll provide a distraction."

He looked to his weapons, then into the trees. When he returned his gaze to her, his expression was pained.

"Don't you dare go soft on me, Tadeo Constantin." She gave him a rough push toward safety. "Go."

He complied. Reluctantly at first, but then a resigned purpose settled over his posture.

It was time to end this.

Anaís rose, stumbling against the tree trunk as a wave of dizziness slammed into her. Resting her head against the bark, she closed her eyes and breathed deeply. Her lungs still burned. Her bones ached. Her face hurt. Dried blood crusted her forearms from where the creature had clawed at her, tugging and cracking with each movement to create a new channel for fresh blood to trickle down. Daza and Etrit needed help—if they were still alive—and Tadeo was her last hope. The enemy would not search for him while she still lived, so she would give him the only thing she had left: time.

Opening her eyes, she reached to draw her daggers but was met with empty sheaths. Her hands curled to fists. Kulimaçar, then. That would have to do. Her lips rose into a small smile. How far she had come since she had last battled Balendin.

Anaís darted around the tree, leaping over fallen men and weaving around obstacles as she ran toward the fray. Daza and Etrit held their ground in a small clearing as they fought back-to-back, using the forest and fallen men around them as a natural filter for the handful of enemies who tried to reach them. Anaís picked up a rock and hurled it, the projectile hitting its target with a satisfying crack. The man screamed. Two warriors glanced in her direction, confusion twisting their faces before recognition dawned, and the confusion morphed into rage. They made to meet her charge, then stopped abruptly. It did not matter what their tactics were—she would not, could not waver.

Pain tore through her shoulder. A scream ripped from her throat as her vision went black. The world tipped; Anaís blinked. Dirt bit into her knees. One hand stung from catching her fall, the other curled protectively against her chest.

"Stand up," she whispered to herself. "Stand. Up."

Anaís tipped her head down to collect herself. She wished she hadn't. An arrow protruded through her shoulder, a warm patch of blood blooming around the shaft like a flower waking to a new dawn. *A blue dawn.* The thought tickled the back of her mind. A strangled laugh rose in her throat. Sitting back on her heels, Anaís raised a shaking hand to the shaft. It wasn't supposed to be there. If she took it out, all would be made right. Then she could help Daza and Etrit and find Eoghan and...and she would never see him again.

Her chest heaved with each breath as panic rose within her. It felt as if she was being torn apart from inside out, but she could not stop it. She was going to die, and she would never see Eoghan again.

Calm! some rational part of her mind shouted. *Calm down and stand up. Your men need you.*

She had not survived everything she had been through to die like this. Not on her knees, while she still had air in her lungs. Anaís took in a slow breath. Then another. She carefully shifted her weight, bringing one leg under her to stand up. A firm grip landed on her shoulder, pain forcing her back down.

"I would not do that if I were you," Cian drawled from behind her.

His hand slid up her neck, cupping under her jaw to lift her head. Daza and Etrit were on their knees, arms wrenched behind their backs. A blade dug against Daza's throat. Etrit's head lulled against his chest, the hair that fell across his forehead dripping with blood. The warrior restraining him pressed a hand against his neck, lips drawn in a concentrated frown. Finally, he looked up and shrugged. "Must have hit harder than I thought."

Etrit's body flopped unceremoniously to the ground as the warrior let him go, wiping bloodstained hands on his trousers and taking a step back.

"Let go of me," Anaís growled. She wanted to scream. To punch something. To—

Cian gave her jaw a light squeeze before releasing her. "As you wish."

Anaís swayed and slumped forward to lean on her good hand. Leaves crunched beneath Cian's boots as he walked around her, coming to a stop as his body blocked Daza from sight. He crouched, eyes locked on the arrowhead he had shot through her.

Cian's hand rose. Lingered. Then he ran a gloved finger along the shaft of the arrow, tracing a bloody path along the wood until it came to rest on the arrowhead itself. He tapped it twice with a frown, then removed his hand and regarded the blood coating his fingertip before wiping it on her uniform.

"This is an unfortunate way to meet."

Anaís tried to glare at him but couldn't choose which Cian to look at. Everything was blurred. Doubled. "What." The word slurred around her numb lips. "Do you want."

"Where is the nitróg?" Cian asked.

She furrowed her brow at the word. Eoghan's rock? "What?"

"The funny-looking rock," he clarified. "Like a small wheel of cheese with holes poked into it. Where is it?"

"I don't know." Her tongue refused to move.

She hadn't lost that much blood, had she? Anaís glanced down. Her eyes drooped closed.

Cian pat her cheek. "Eyes up. I have a few more questions before the poison fully sets in."

A jolt of panic cleared her mind of the pain that fought to numb it.

"Why do you seek Takaniim?" Cian asked.

"A lakeside holiday," Anaís retorted with passable enunciation.

"Charming. Why did you drag Eoghan into this?"

A fresh wave of pain dug into her heart at the mention of his name. She wished he was here with her. She wished he was far away, safe from the forces that sought to tear them apart.

At her silence, Cian gave her a hollow smile and said, "A better question would be this: if two objects are tied together, what is more important—the removal of one object or the cutting of the string that binds them? The response is simple. In the end, they are one and the same. It did not matter if it was you or him. The string is severed either way."

Tears clouded Anaís's vision. Was that all fate was, then? Something that went beyond time and space to bring her and Eoghan together, only to tear them apart?

Cian heaved a sigh, then looked over his shoulder. "Nathair, bind and gag the survivor. He's coming with us."

A scuffle sounded, followed by a shout and a crunch. Something broke in Anaís at the sound. Using the last of her energy, she launched herself at Cian. He grabbed her shoulders and eased her back down, frowning at her as if remembering something he would rather forget.

"I told Eoghan I wouldn't lay a finger on you." His gaze lingered on his hands resting on her shoulders. "Said nothing about arrows though." The weight of his hands lifted. "It was coated in a poison to slow your heart rate. To stop you from dying too quickly. For your sake, I hope you do." He grasped the shaft. "This is my final mercy for him."

Without warning, Cian snapped the shaft, reached behind her, and pulled the arrow out of her body. Unconsciousness welcomed Anaís before she hit the ground.

CHAPTER FORTY-ONE
YOUR HIGHNESS

WHEN EOGHAN WAS SEVEN, HE RAN AWAY FROM home. Not in the permanent sort of way—though he had certainly considered it a time or two—but in the sort of way that allowed one to forget who one was for a time. He had wandered through the sleeping city, peering into the windows of unlit shops and creating tales of "what if" along the way.

What if he had been born a baker's boy? *What if* he apprenticed as a leatherworker and learned to make the finest vests the kingdom had ever seen? *What if* he gave up princedom and chose to pursue glassblowing instead? He could fill the kingdom with glistening baubles and ornaments that danced in the wind, and use his gift to brighten the day of every man, woman, and child—if only for a moment. *What if, what if, what if?*

A yell and a thump had broken Eoghan free from his game, pulling him back to the darkened street with a bone-jarring yank and the chilling realization that he no longer recognized where he was. It sounded again—angry and vicious and wild. Then it stopped. As he strained to decipher the silence that reigned, he heard it. Voices. Not menacing, but kind.

Tiptoeing with the stealth of an uncoordinated kitten, Eoghan had made his way toward the sound. Perhaps someone needed saving. He certainly needed saving—or directions. Light spilled through a shop window as he rounded the corner, painting the sign in a golden hue. *Finnegan's Fight Club*. He peered through the window, a shy smile lifting his lips.

He no longer had to ask the question *what if*.

The bell had chimed over his head when the door swung open, chimed again as the heavy hinges slammed it shut. Fighters froze. A burly man muttered a word Eoghan had been warned never to use. For what did one do when the bastard prince of a kingdom asked in his small boyish voice, "Can you teach me?"

As the years trickled by, Eoghan ran away when he could. Or ran *toward*, rather, for he was no longer trying to forget who he was, but remember the boy he had become that night. That was the version he liked best of himself—brave and free.

The men at the fight club had taught him properly, with the gruff softness of fighters passing their art on to a younger generation. It was there that Eoghan had learned the tenants: courtesy, integrity, perseverance, self-control, indomitable spirit—he liked that one best—Sir. One always ended with a "Sir." It was there that he had won his first fight, fair and square. It was there that he had first experienced true pain—a broken arm when his opponent happened to miss the mat when he took Eoghan down. He had wished on every star that it would be the worst pain he ever felt.

Twenty years later, he had been stabbed by the woman who now held his heart.

Today, Eoghan was dying.

Skin did not split. Blood did not drip. But as he collapsed to the ground—one hand fisted in the dirt, the other pressed against his shoulder as if to staunch the invisible wound that consumed him—he could have sworn that each heaving breath he took would be his last.

A blink of an eye left him in a clearing littered with corpses. Another blink took them away. No matter how hard he squeezed his eyes shut, Eoghan could not unsee the prone form of a woman whose soul complimented his own.

It wasn't real. He tried to force a breath past seizing lungs. It had looked so real. A yank pulled him back to the present—the thread wound urgently around his heart. *Get up!* it pleaded. *Get up and run!*

For the second time in his life, Eoghan ran toward.

The forest seemed to clear a path for him as he sprinted through the trees. Gnarled roots slid beneath a layer of dirt. Wind coaxed low-hanging branches upward at the last moment. Yet no matter how hard he pushed himself, each footfall taunted him with the same rhythmic words. *She's. Gone. She's. Gone. She's—*

"Stop!" The shout tore from Eoghan as he skidded to a halt, slipping farther than expected. Pain lanced through his chest, and he doubled over, gasping for breath.

"It wasn't real," he heaved. "It wasn't real, Anaís is fine, it wasn't..."

Blood, so much blood, glistened beneath his boots. The soil drank it in until it could drink no more, leaving the top layer engorged and mottled and sickly. Bright splotches of crimson-slicked leaves dotted the ground. Corpses...

Eoghan stumbled back.

Trees surrounded him, tucking him safely into a clearing in the forest. The *same* clearing. *No. No no nono…*

He scanned his surroundings, heart hammering in his chest as if it wanted to break free and find Anaís itself. But she could not be here, because if she was, it meant she was dead. And if she was dead, he would have no one to blame but himself. Damn the king and the Anadali with her, he should have insisted they stay together.

The thread gave his heart another tug. His head whipped to the left. And there lay Anaís.

She looked like a goddess of old, with her dark hair splayed around her like a halo. A celestial who had destroyed the enemies of the forest. Now she had simply laid down to slumber, waiting until the next enemy threatened her lands. Waiting to protect those under her care once again.

Eoghan walked toward her as if in a trance. He did not feel the sting of the ground when he fell to his knees beside her, or the dampness that seeped through his trousers as he lifted a shaking hand to feel for a pulse. His hand froze before he could touch her. His heart seized.

There was a hole pierced clean through her shoulder. Blood darkened the fabric of her uniform, adhering it to her body like a second skin. A lump formed in his throat. He could not lose her. Not like this.

"I'm sorry," he tried to say, but all that came out was a broken sound ripped from somewhere deep within his soul. Eoghan curled into himself as another sob tore free. He pressed a hand over his mouth and took in a shaky breath. "I'm sorry," he finally managed to choke out. "I'm sorry I'm sorry I'm sorry."

It was all he could think to say.

Gently, carefully, he brushed a strand of hair off her face. The ghost of a smile curved Anaís's lips as his fingers lingered on her skin, but it couldn't have been. This was all a horrific nightmare from which he would never truly wake.

"Eoghan?" His name sounded like a prayer carried on the wind, yet he heard it clearly.

Now he was delusional. Delusional, but desperate. Never once had she called him by his name. It was always Your Highness, said with respect. Your Highness, said in jest. Your Highness, said breathlessly on that day by the waterfall. The day he realized he never wanted to let go.

"Anaís?" he asked.

"This looks a lot worse than it feels... Feels a lot worse than it looks." Her eyes fluttered open, brow scrunching in pain as she tried to focus on his face before slipping shut again. "I forget which way round it goes," she mumbled.

"It's okay." A laugh bubbled free. Nothing else mattered. She was alive. "Don't speak. I've got you."

"I am Anadali Amadé. I am not weak." Her words were whisper-soft, yet filled with conviction. "I will not die."

"No. No you won't." He would do everything in his power to make sure of it.

Sitting back on his heels, Eoghan removed his knapsack and pulled out a linen blanket. He tore one strip, then another, then another, each rip of the fabric fraying his nerves. But puncture wounds *needed* to be staunched. His stomach heaved.

Eoghan drew in a deep breath. Released it.

"I'm going to pack your shoulder," he said, unsheathing a knife from his belt and cutting away the uniform surrounding her wound.

Anaís grimaced but nodded. With a final breath to steady his shaking hands, he shoved the strips of fabric into her shoulder.

She jerked back with a shout.

"Sorry." Eoghan threw a knee onto her to hold her down, packing more fabric deeper into the wound. "I know, I'm sorry. Just breathe. I'm sorry." He was babbling now, but it was all he could do to distract himself from the slickness of her blood against his skin and the sound of her screams. Until finally, blessedly, there wasn't any space left to fill.

Keeping one hand planted firmly on her wound, he wrapped the final strip of blanket tightly around her shoulder. His hands fell to his sides. A sob tried to force its way out of his throat. Eoghan swallowed it back down, steeling his resolve as he eased off her—he had to stay level-headed.

"It's over," he whispered, wiping his bloodstained hands on his trousers.

Sweat beaded along Anaís's forehead, her breathing ragged. Pulling the last of his tattered blanket over, Eoghan gently dabbed the sweat off her skin.

"We're going to get help now." He set the blanket aside and cradled the back of her head. "I'm going to lift you."

Slowly, carefully, he sat Anaís up, then shifted to ease her into his arms. It did not matter that they were at least three days' hike from the nearest village—that Eoghan knew of. She would live. She had to live.

"Eoghan?" Her voice froze him in place.

"Yes, my love?" The endearment slipped out before he could stop it. But with the way Anaís's face softened, smoothing away the pain furrowing her brow, he wanted to say it again.

"Will you stay with me?" she asked.

"Of course. I'll stay with you all the way to—"

"No." Her eyes opened to meet his, and for the first time since he had known her, Eoghan saw fear within them. "I don't..." Anaís inhaled sharply. "I'm falling asleep. Please stay."

Her words cut into Eoghan with a finality that threatened to bleed him dry, but he swallowed his anguish. For her, he would be strong.

"Okay." Eoghan nodded once. Sucking in a breath to steady himself, he asked, "Do you want to sit up or do you want to lay down?"

She tipped her head until her forehead came to rest against his own. Her eyes drifted shut. "I want you."

Eoghan blinked, trying and failing to keep his tears from falling. Trying and failing to keep himself from falling apart. But her three simple words had cracked him open.

"Then I am yours," he said softly.

Shifting to put his back against a tree, Eoghan carefully settled Anaís onto his lap, resting her head on his chest.

"It's okay." He wiped away a tear running down her cheek. "I'm here. I'm not leaving you." He wasn't going anywhere.

Her nose brushed against his tunic as she relaxed against him. Though her lips moved, no sound followed. "Thank you," she seemed to say.

Eoghan didn't reply, couldn't reply. So instead, he stayed there, tracing meandering patterns along the edge of her hair until her face softened.

Her breathing evened. Slowed.

Eoghan pressed a kiss to her forehead. "I love you," he whispered against her skin.

The silence of the forest was his only reply.

EPILOGUE
THE HUNT

THE AIR WAS THICK WITH THE SOUR TASTE OF SMOKE and inevitability. Despite the balmy summer breeze drifting through the evening air, Cian felt numb. Extra-corporeal. A crackle of sparks drifted heavenward from a fire across the campsite, rimming two familiar shadowed figures in a haze of light.

Swallowing, Cian tightened his grip on the chain around the captive's neck and glanced where he had left his men. The sound of their laughter filled the clearing, amplified as if the forest behind them refused to take in the sound, spitting it toward Cian instead.

So, it disapproved of his actions. That made two of them. Unfortunately, he couldn't please everyone. Not the boy inside screaming at him to fix this mess. Not the man he had become who'd set out to destroy Anaís. Cian was an in-between.

That somehow made it worse.

Giving the chain a tug, Cian stalked across the field toward the hill where his father's command tent stood. It would not do to be late. It would not do to give an unsatisfactory report. But he was an hour behind schedule and had failed his mission. Fate was in the balance, and like an insolent child, Cian had gone and hidden the scales. Whatever happened now would be his fault.

The murmur of voices rose as he approached the firepit. The man who had questioned Cian's loyalty on the eve of Eoghan's would-be assassination frowned at him from across the flames. It had been over a month, and Cian was only just beginning to understand the hierarchy of the sœndjak. This being before him was more man than beast—a slave to its superiors, a death wish to humanity. The fallen abomination Anaís had fought was a shadow wraith. Damned as living death, or so the legends claimed. But truth was infallible, and legends were not. Cian had his suspicions. Then came the creatures of the deep—the Uncreated—who bore many names, though no title could encompass an eternity of horrors.

Each creature was more powerful than the last, more terrifying than the last.

"Report," the man commanded from across the firepit.

A jolt of panic shot through Cian's veins, but he tamped it down as he continued past, dragging the captive along. In the blink of an eye, the man stood before him blocking the path.

"I said *report*," the man snapped.

Cian glared at him. "I don't report to you."

Tension shrouded them like a wet rag, snuffing out the oxygen and making the air too thick to breathe. But if there was one thing Cian had learned, it was that he would rather be shot with a cursed arrow than yield.

The man spat on Cian's boots before stepping to the side and gesturing him forward with an exaggerated bow. Cian grunted in response as he walked by, heart hammering in his chest despite the confidence he wore like armor. If he wanted to survive any of this, there was no room for weakness.

Arriving at the base of the hill, Cian pulled the captive to a halt. "What's your name, Anadali?"

"Daza," the captive replied curtly.

Cian turned to face him. "I need you alive for what will happen next. When we are in there, don't say a word. Do you understand me?"

Daza glared, jaw locked in insolence. The dried blood crusted on his face cracked with the movement.

Cian wrapped his hand around the chain, yanking him forward. "Do you *understand*?" he repeated lowly.

Rage flashed across Daza's face, his voice eerily quiet when he said, "You will pay for what you did in the forest."

"Yes," Cian growled, "or no. I need an answer."

The muffled sounds of the camp filled the silence that stretched between them. Cian let it linger. Let it build. Let it weigh on Daza until the gravity of his situation broke him. Cian needed him to comply if any part of this plan was to work.

Moves and countermoves, Eoghan would say. Eoghan would also hate him for what he had done, but it was too late to undo the past. The day Cian abandoned Eoghan and left Nahonaugh, the darkness trying to drown him had almost succeeded. And tonight? Cian shoved the memories away, drawing his attention to the present. There was no going back, and the path he followed now was a treacherous balance. Especially if he wanted to escape this place alive.

Daza finally averted his gaze, the fight that once fueled him tempered by the weariness of a man who had lost everything. "Fine," he conceded.

Cian nodded, then loosened his hold on the chain, guiding Daza forward once more. The command tent greeted them once they crested the hill, and before he could overthink it, Cian pushed through the entrance to face his father.

Candlelight illuminated the tent, flickering as eddies of disturbed air drew the flame into their currents. A patchwork of sheepskin rugs covered the ground, the foundation atop which a large table stood. Maps spread across the surface—some of various Nahonan villages, though many depicted the desolate passes of the Nymyan Mountains that bordered Freydlan. With the eternal snow and ever-changing landscape carved by avalanches and glacial erosion, he wasn't sure why anyone bothered to record it. Unless that was where his father thought Takaniim hid. Cian craned his neck to better see one of the maps.

"You're late," Tadhg observed, shifting a stack of parchment atop the map Cian was trying to read. Rounding the table, he leaned against it and folded his arms across his chest. "The mission?"

"Completed," Cian said. A half-truth.

Tadhg grunted in reply, attention shifting to Daza. His eyes roved across the shackles binding his hands and the chain wrapped around his neck. He tipped his chin at the captive. "What are you planning with this one?"

"If everyone dies, how will the rumors start?" A sardonic smile twisted Cian's lips. "This one can be convinced of some very good lies, I think."

Tadhg raised his brow, considering. "He won't break easily."

Daza stiffened. Cian kept his eyes trained on his father as he replied, "I'm counting on it."

"Do what you must, then." Tadhg shrugged, the movement freezing as an oppressive heaviness filled the room.

The candlelight seemed to shudder when the feeling spread, as if an unseen force was reaching for something. Or *someone*. Two wicks snuffed out. The temperature plummeted. As quickly as it came, the feeling retreated, leaving a lingering scar in its absence.

Cian fixed his gaze on the ground, trying to steel himself for what came next. He breathed in. *Do not look upon the creatures of the deep.* He breathed out. From the corner of his eye, a dark mass appeared.

Tadhg bowed. "What news?"

"A delay in the forest," a voice steeped in malice intoned. "It would not let me in. Curious, don't you think?"

"That's not possible," Tadhg breathed.

"Perhaps," the Uncreated mused. "Would you like to know what I found when I arrived?"

Fear constricted Cian's throat. From the corner of his eye, Tadhg shifted uncomfortably.

"She was gone." The threat in the statement was palpable.

"Gone, *dead*, or gone..." Tadhg trailed off. A cursed sort of hope blossomed in Cian's chest, followed quickly by rising confusion.

"Her body was not there. No tracks. No trace. Simply..." *Gone.* The word lingered, left unsaid. "The archer?" A chill wrapped around Cian, biting into his skin when its formless gaze turned to him. "You shot her?"

Cian's tongue stuck to the roof of his mouth as he tried to swallow. "Clean through," he finally managed.

"With my arrowhead?"

"Yes." His heart slammed against his ribcage. Death was the only way to sever nanouk'tou, but the arrowhead had not shattered when it pierced her. Had not released the curse that would have guided the creatures of the deep—along with their wrath—to end her. Cian was still not sure if the unbroken arrowhead happened by his own doing or something else entirely.

"That," the Uncreated said, "is what is not possible." The chill around Cian receded as Daza stiffened. "You witnessed this act?"

Daza nodded, the chain around his neck shifting with the movement.

"You watched while she breathed her last, and her soul slipped from this realm into the next?"

"No," Daza whispered.

"Speak, archer."

Cian let out a shaking breath. Curse or no, the creatures of the deep were still likely to find and kill her. He had removed the arrow to quicken her death. Spare her that pain. It *was* a mercy. Apparently Anaís was too stubborn to accept even that. If she had escaped—if she was alive—he would have to adjust his plans. Infuriating woman.

"She would have succumbed to her wounds within the hour," Cian said truthfully. "The men were tired—"

His head snapped to the side, the tang of copper filling his mouth. Cian could already feel the hand-shaped welt blooming across his face. He sniffed once, composing himself, before looking at Tadhg with a blank expression.

"Not dead enough!" Tadhg shoved a chair, the sheepskin rugs softening the thud as it toppled to the ground. It only seemed to amplify his fury.

"No, this was not the work of the boy. It appears we have a different problem." The Uncreated heaved a sigh. "Send your messenger—Katka, was it?—back to Dúndíor and ready your best men. Tonight, they hunt."

AUTHOR NOTE

There are many notes I could make, but the one I want to leave you with is the answer to this question: why 45°25'S 167°43'E?

If you looked it up, you may have found that it's the coordinates to Te Anau, New Zealand. I lived in New Zealand for a few years (Ōtautahi Christchurch, to be exact), and it's a country that holds a special place in my heart.

I went on my first solo trip across the South Island and ended up on a bus to Piopiotahi Milford Sound. It was exceptionally wet, as the weather tends to be on the West Coast, but exploring nature from the edge of Te Anau to the heart of the sound was nothing short of life changing.

In te reo Māori, Te Ana-au (from which the name Te Anau is derived) means *cave of swirling water*. Given the nature of the meeting place, it felt like it was meant to be. While all of the locations in this book are entirely fictitious, there are nods to places that have had a lasting impact on me. These coordinates are one of them.

ACKNOWLEDGEMENTS

When I was a kid, I thought acknowledgement sections were silly. *The author did all the work, who else is there to thank?* I thought. Oh little Robin, you young grasshopper. How wrong you were.

For starters, I'd like to thank my mom. In a roundabout way, she dared me to write this book. In a deliberate way, she supported me through the highs and lows of actually writing said book. Thank you dad for listening to all of my unhinged plot and thematic ideas, even though half the time you had no clue what was going on. And my sister, Bryna, for being a kickass beta reader and absolute legend at roasting me when I wanted it least but needed it most.

A massive thank you to Brigitte Cromey and Amanda Auler for alpha reading my Very Messy first draft, providing a listening ear, and helping me navigate the world of publishing. This book would not be what it is today without your insight and support.

To my beta reading team Elisabeth W, Bryna R (yes, you again), Paige G, and Laurel Burgess, thank you for your feedback and enthusiasm. You helped me polish the plot in ways I didn't think were possible, yet here the book stands in its shiny glory.

To Jenni Sauer for our yap-n-write sessions (or our straight up yapping sessions). I'm not sure I would have been able to finish this book without you. Or if I had, it would have been a very lonely road.

To Claire Banschbach for providing feedback and encouragement on my first three chapters, and Selina Gonzalez for helping this Very Confused newbie author with the ins and outs of independent publishing.

To my editors: Addison Horner for helping this book become the best version of itself, and Brigitte Cromey for polishing the grammar and punctuation so it shines.

To the artists who helped bring my vision to life: Kei-Ella Loewe for the incredible cover, Virginia Allyn for the beautiful map, and Seeking Stars Studio for the lovely illustration in chapter thirty-seven. I'm still in awe that I get to call this stunning book my own.

To my formatter, Greg Rupel, at Enchanted Ink Publishing. Thank you transforming my book into its final book form.

To all the friends I met on Instagram—from those who were there when I first started posting random language learning things back in 2016 to those I've met on bookstagram. Your kindness and friendship mean more than you know.

To my friends at church, especially Brian B, Sarah B, Bettina A, Claire J, and Allison M. Thank you for your friendship and for being there through the highs and the lows of the past three years.

Last, but certainly not least, to God, without whom I wouldn't have been able to write this book. Thank You for entrusting my hands and my mind with this beautiful story, and for helping me bring this book to life every step of the way.

ABOUT THE AUTHOR

Often mistaken for an elf due to her height, Robin is actually two hobbits in a trench coat. She has degrees in mechanical engineering, biomedical engineering, and biology (the last of which was an accident). When not writing or engineering, you can find her hiking, Irish dancing, reading, or trying a new hobby. She likely lives in the US, but Scotland and New Zealand aren't out of the question. Keep up-to-date with her work here:

WWW.ROBINRAKKEBY.COM

Instagram: aspoonfuloflanguage